WHERE
the
FOREST
MEETS
the
STARS

WHERE
the
FOREST
MEETS
the
STARS

GLENDY VANDERAH

LAKE UNION
PUBLISHING

Published by Lake Union Publishing, Seattle

www.apub.com

Amazon, the Amazon logo, and Lake Union Publishing are trademarks of Amazon.com, Inc., or its affiliates.

ISBN-13: 9781542040068 (hardcover)
ISBN-10: 154204006X (hardcover)
ISBN-13: 9781503904910 (paperback)
ISBN-10: 1503904911 (paperback)

Cover design by Shasti O'Leary Soudant

Printed in the United States of America

First edition

For Cailley, William, and Grant
and for Scott

1

The girl could be a changeling. She was almost invisible, her pale face, hoodie, and pants fading into the twilit woods behind her. Her feet were bare. She stood motionless, one arm hugged around a hickory trunk, and she didn't move when the car crunched to the end of the gravel driveway and stopped a few yards away.

As she shut down the car, Jo looked away from the girl and gathered binoculars, backpack, and data sheets from the passenger seat. Maybe the kid would return to her fairy realm if she wasn't watching.

But the girl was still there when Jo stepped out of the car. "I see you," Jo told the shadow on the hickory.

"I know," the girl said.

Jo's hiking boots scattered chips of dry mud up the concrete walkway. "Do you need something?"

The girl didn't answer.

"Why are you on my property?"

"I was trying to pet your puppy, but he wouldn't let me."

"He's not my dog."

"Whose is he?"

"No one's." She opened the door to the screened porch. "You should go home while you still have some light." She flicked on the outside bug bulb and unlocked the door to the house. After she turned on a lamp, she returned to the wooden door and locked it. The girl was only around nine years old, but she could still be up to something.

In fifteen minutes, Jo was showered and dressed in a T-shirt, sweat-pants, and sandals. She turned on the kitchen lights, drawing a silent batter of insects to the black windows. While she readied grilling sup-plies, she idly thought of the girl under the hickory tree. She'd be too afraid of the dark woods to stick around. She'd have gone home.

Jo brought a marinated chicken breast and three vegetable skew-ers out to a fire pit in a patch of weedy lawn that separated the yellow clapboard house from a few acres of moonlit grassland. The forties-era rental house known as Kinney Cottage was perched on a hill facing the woods, its rear side open to a small prairie that was regularly burned by the owner to keep back the encroaching forest. Jo lit a fire in her stone circle and set the cooking rack over it. As she laid chicken and skewers over the flames, she tensed when a dark shape rounded the corner of the house. The girl. She stopped just yards from the fire, watching Jo place the last of the skewers on the grill. "Don't you have a stove?" she asked.

"I do."

"Why do you cook outside?"

Jo sat in one of four ragged lawn chairs. "Because I like to."

"It smells good."

If she was there to mooch food, she'd be disappointed by the empty cupboards of a field biologist with little time for grocery shopping. She spoke with the rural drawl of a local, and her bare feet were evidence that she'd come from a neighboring property. She could damn well go home for dinner.

The girl edged closer, the fire coloring her apple cheeks and blond-ish hair, but not her eyes, still changeling black holes in her face.

"Don't you think it's about time you went home?" Jo said.

She came nearer. "I don't have a home on Earth. I came from there." She pointed toward the sky.

"From where?"

"Ursa Major."

"The constellation?"

The girl nodded. "I'm from the Pinwheel Galaxy. It's by the big bear's tail."

Jo didn't know anything about galaxies, but the name sounded like something a kid would invent. "I've never heard of the Pinwheel Galaxy," Jo said.

"It's what your people call it, but we call it something else."

Jo could see her eyes now. The intelligent glint in her gaze was oddly shrewd for her baby face, and Jo took that as a sign that she knew it was all in fun. "If you're an alien, why do you look human?"

"I'm only using this girl's body."

"Tell her to go home while you're in there, will you?"

"She can't. She was dead when I took her body. If she went home, her parents would get scared."

It was a zombie thing. Jo had heard of those games. But the girl had come to the wrong house if she was looking for someone to play Alien Zombie with her. Jo had never been good with kids and make-believe games, even when she was as young as the girl herself. Jo's parents, both scientists, often said her double dose of analytical genes had made her that way. They used to joke about how she'd come out of the womb, with an intent frown on her face, as if she were formulating hypotheses about where she was and who all the people in the delivery room were.

The alien in a human body watched Jo flip the chicken breast.

"You'd better get home for dinner," Jo said. "Your parents will be worried."

"I told you, I don't have—"

3

"Do you need to call someone?" Jo pulled her phone from her pants pocket.

"Who would I call?"

"How about I call? Tell me your number."

"How can I have a number when I came out of the stars?"

"What about the girl whose body you took? What's her number?"

"I don't know anything about her, not even her name."

Whatever she was up to, Jo was too tired for it. She'd been awake since four in the morning, slogging through field and forest in high heat and humidity for more than thirteen hours. That had been her routine almost every day for weeks, and the few hours she spent at the cottage each night were important wind-down time. "If you don't go, I'll call the police," she said, trying to sound stern.

"What will *police* do?" She said it as if she'd never heard the word.

"They'll haul your butt home."

The girl crossed her arms over her skinny body. "What will they do when I tell them I have no home?"

"They'll take you to the police station and find your parents or whoever you live with."

"What will they do when they call those people and find out their daughter is dead?"

Jo didn't have to feign anger this time. "You know, it's no joke to be alone in the world. You should go home to whoever cares about you."

The girl tightened her arms across her chest but said nothing.

The kid needed a jolt of reality. "If you really have no family, the police will put you in a foster home."

"What's that?"

"You live with complete strangers, and sometimes they're mean, so you'd better go home before I call the cops."

The girl didn't move.

"I'm serious."

The half-grown dog that had begged for food at Jo's fire for the past few nights skulked into the outer circle of firelight. The girl sat on her haunches and held her hand out, cajoling him in a high voice to let her pet him.

"He won't come closer," Jo said. "He's wild. He was probably born in the woods."

"Where's his mother?"

"Who knows?" Jo set down her phone and turned the skewers. "Is there some reason you're afraid to go home?"

"Why won't you believe I'm from the stars?"

The stubborn-ass kid didn't know when to quit. "You know no one will believe you're an alien."

The girl walked to the edge of the prairie, held her face and arms up to the starry sky, and chanted some kind of gibberish that was supposed to sound like an alien language. Her words flowed like a foreign tongue she knew well, and when she finished, she smugly turned to Jo, hands on hips.

"I hope you were asking your alien people to take you back," Jo said.

"It was a salutation."

"*Salutation*—good word."

The girl returned to the firelight. "I can't go back yet. I have to stay on Earth until I've seen five miracles. It's part of our training when we get to a certain age—kind of like school."

"You'll be here awhile. Water hasn't been turned into wine for a couple of millennia."

"I don't mean Bible kind of miracles."

"What kind of miracles?"

"Anything," the girl said. "You're a miracle, and that dog is. This is a whole new world for me."

"Good, you have two already."

"No, I'll save them for really good stuff."

5

"Gee, thanks."

The girl sat in a lawn chair near Jo. The grilling chicken breast oozed greasy marinade into the fire, smoking the night air with a delectable scent. The kid stared at it, her hunger real, nothing imaginary about it. Maybe her family couldn't afford food. Jo was surprised she hadn't thought of that right away.

"How about I give you something to eat before you go home?" she said. "Do you like turkey burgers?"

"How could I know what a turkey burger tastes like?"

"Do you want one or not?"

"I want one. I'm supposed to try new things while I'm here."

Jo put the chicken breast on the cooler side of the fire before going inside to gather a frozen burger, condiments, and a bun. She remembered the last cheese slice in the refrigerator and added it to the girl's dinner. The kid probably needed it more than she did.

Jo returned to the yard, laid the patty over the fire, and put the rest on the empty chair beside her. "I hope you like cheese on your burger."

"I've heard about cheese," the girl said. "They say it's good."

"Who says it's good?"

"The ones who've already been here. We learn a little about Earth before we come."

"What's your planet called?"

"It's hard to say in your language—sort of like *Hetrayeh*. Do you have any marshmallows?"

"The Hetrayens taught you about marshmallows?"

"They said kids put them on a stick and melt them over a fire. They said it's really good."

Jo finally had an excuse to open the marshmallows she'd purchased on a whim when she first moved to the cottage. She figured she might as well use them before they went stale. She got the marshmallows from the kitchen cupboard and dropped the bag into the alien's lap. "You have to eat dinner before you open them."

The alien found a stick and sat in her chair, marshmallows sheltered in her lap, her dark eyes fixed on the cooking burger. Jo toasted the bun and placed a skewer of browned potatoes, broccoli, and mushrooms next to the cheeseburger on a plate. She brought out two drinks. "Do you like apple cider?"

The girl took the glass and sipped. "It's really good!"

"Good enough to be a miracle?"

"No," the alien said, but she downed more than half the glass in seconds.

The girl was almost done with her burger by the time Jo took a bite. "When did you last eat?" she asked.

"On my planet," the alien said around a cheek bulged with food.

"When was that?"

She swallowed. "Last night."

Jo put down her fork. "You haven't eaten for a whole day?"

The girl popped a potato cube into her mouth. "I didn't want to eat until now. I was kind of sick—from the trip to Earth and changing bodies and all that."

"Then why are you eating like you're starved?"

The girl broke the last piece of her burger and tossed half to the begging puppy, probably to prove she wasn't starving. The dog gulped it down as fast as the girl had. When the alien offered the last morsel in her hand, the puppy slunk forward, nabbed it from her fingers, and retreated as it ate. "Did you see that?" the girl said. "He took it from my hand."

"I saw." What Jo also saw was a kid who might be in real trouble. "Are those pajamas you're wearing?"

The girl glanced down at her thin pants. "I guess that's what humans call them."

Jo sliced another piece of meat off her chicken breast. "What's your name?"

The girl was on her knees, trying to creep closer to the puppy. "I don't have an Earth name."

"What's your alien name?"

"Hard to say . . ."

"Just tell me."

"It's kind of like *Earpood-na-ahsroo.*"

"Ear poo . . . ?"

"No, Earpoo*d*-na-ahsroo."

"Okay, Earpood, I want you to tell me the truth about why you're here."

She gave up on the timid dog and stood. "Can I open the marshmallows?"

"Eat the broccoli first."

She looked at the plate she'd left on her chair. "That green stuff?"

"Yeah."

"We don't eat green stuff on my planet."

"You said you're supposed to try new things."

The girl pushed the three broccoli florets in her mouth in quick succession. While she chewed at the lumps in her cheeks, she ripped open the marshmallow bag.

"How old are you?" Jo asked.

The girl swallowed the last of the broccoli with effort. "My age wouldn't make sense to a human."

"How old is the body you took?"

She poked a marshmallow onto the end of her stick. "I don't know."

"I'm seriously going to have to call the police," Jo said.

"Why?"

"You know why. You're what, nine . . . ten? You can't be out alone at night. Someone's not treating you right."

"If you call the police, I'll just run away."

"Why? They can help you."

"I don't want to live with mean strangers."

"I was joking when I said that. I'm sure they'll find nice people."

The girl smashed a third marshmallow onto her stick. "Do you think Little Bear would like marshmallows?"

"Who's Little Bear?"

"I've named the puppy that—for Ursa Minor, the constellation next to mine. Don't you think he looks like a baby bear?"

"Don't feed him marshmallows. Sugar isn't what he needs." Jo pulled the last pieces of meat off her chicken breast and tossed them to the dog, too distracted to finish her food. As the meat disappeared into the mutt's gullet, she gave him the remaining vegetables from her two skewers.

"You're nice," the girl said.

"I'm stupid. I'll never get rid of him now."

"Whoa!" The girl brought flaming marshmallows to her face and blew at the fire.

"Let it cool off first," Jo said.

She didn't wait, stretching the hot white goo to her mouth. The marshmallows vanished in short order, and the girl roasted another batch as Jo carried supplies into the kitchen. While she quickly washed dishes, she decided on a new strategy. Bad Cop clearly wasn't working. She'd have to gain the girl's trust to get anything out of her.

She found the girl seated cross-legged on the ground, Little Bear happily licking melted marshmallow off her hand. "I'd never have believed that dog would eat from a human hand," she said.

"Even though it's a human hand, he knows I'm from Hetrayeh."

"How does that help?"

"We have special powers. We can make good things happen."

Poor kid. Wishful thinking about her grim circumstances, no doubt. "Can I use your stick?"

"For marshmallows?"

"No, to beat you off my property."

The girl smiled, a deep dimple indenting her left cheek. Jo punctured two marshmallows with the stick and hovered them over the fire. The girl returned to her lawn chair, the wild dog lying at her feet as if she'd miraculously tamed it. When the marshmallows were perfectly brown on all sides and sufficiently cooled, Jo ate them straight off the stick.

"I didn't know grown-ups ate marshmallows," the girl said.

"It's a secret earthling children don't know."

"What's your name?" the girl asked.

"Joanna Teale. But most people call me Jo."

"Do you live here all alone?"

"Just for the summer. I'm renting the house."

"Why?"

"If you live down this road—which I'm sure you do—you know why."

"I don't live down the road. Tell me."

Jo resisted an urge to contest the lie, remembering she was the Good Cop. "This house and seventy acres around it are owned by a science professor named Dr. Kinney. He lets professors use it for teaching and graduate students use it while they're doing their research."

"Why doesn't he want to live in it?"

Jo rested the marshmallow stick against the fire-pit rocks. "He bought it when he was in his forties. He and his wife used it as a vacation house, and he did aquatic insect research down in the creek, but they stopped coming here six years ago."

"Why?"

"They're in their seventies, and his wife has to be near a hospital because of a medical condition. Now they use the house as a source of income, but they only rent it to scientists."

"You're a scientist?"

"Yes, but still a graduate student."

"What does that mean?"

"It means I'm done with the first four years of college, and now I take classes, work as a teaching assistant, and do research so I can get a PhD."

"What's a PhD?"

"A doctorate degree. Once I have that, I can get a job as a professor at a university."

The girl licked her dirty, dog-drooled fingers and scrubbed them on the blackened marshmallow stuck to her cheek. "A professor is a teacher, right?"

"Yes, and most people in my field also do research."

"What research?"

Relentless curiosity. She'd make a great scientist. "My field is bird ecology and conservation."

"What do you do, exactly?"

"Enough questions, Ear poo . . ."

"Earpoo*d*!"

"It's time for you to go home. I get up early, so I need to go to sleep." Jo turned on the spigot and pulled the hose to the fire.

"Do you have to put it out?"

"Smokey Bear says I do." The fire hissed and steamed as the water conquered it.

"That's sad," the girl said.

"What is?"

"That wet ash smell." Her face looked bluish in the fluorescent kitchen light filtering through the window, as if she'd become a change-ling again.

Jo turned the squeaky spigot handle to off. "How about you tell me the truth about why you're out here?"

"I did tell you," the girl said.

"Come on. I'm going inside, and I don't feel right about leaving you out here."

"I'll be okay."

"You'll go home?"

"Let's go, Little Bear," the girl said, and the dog, improbably, obeyed.

Jo watched the alien changeling and her mongrel walk away, their fade into the dark forest as sad as the wet ash smell.

2

The alarm woke Jo at four, her normal time on the days she traveled long distances to her study sites. In the light of a small lamp, she dressed in a T-shirt, button-down shirt, cargo field pants, and boots. Not until she turned on the fluorescent stove light did she remember the girl. Hard to believe when she'd thought of little else during her restless first half hour in bed. She looked out the back door at the empty chairs circled around the fire pit. She flipped on the front porch light and stepped into the screened room. No sign of the girl. She'd probably gone home.

While her oatmeal cooked, Jo made a tuna sandwich and packed it alongside her trail mix and water. She was out the door twenty minutes later and at her site by dawn. While the morning air was still cool, she searched for indigo bunting nests along Church Road, the least shaded of her nine study sites. A few hours later, she moved on to the Jory Farm site, and after that, to Cave Hollow Road.

She quit at five, earlier than usual. Insomnia had become routine in the last two years, since her mother's diagnosis and recent death, but for some reason her anxiety had been especially bad for three nights running. She wanted to be in bed by nine at the latest to catch up on sleep.

Though she'd stopped at a farm stand first, she arrived at Turkey Creek Road early enough that Egg Man, a young bearded guy, was still seated under his blue canopy at the road's intersection with the county highway. During her infrequent days off work—mostly because of rain—Jo had noticed he kept a regular schedule, selling eggs on Monday evenings and Thursday mornings.

Egg Man nodded his head in greeting as Jo rounded the bend. She waved and wished she needed eggs to give him business, but she still had at least four in the refrigerator.

Turkey Creek Road was the five-mile gravel road that dead-ended at the creek and Kinney property. Driving it took a while, even in an SUV. After the first mile, it got narrow, snaky, potholed, and washboarded, and toward the end it was precariously steep in a few places where the creek washed it out in heavy rains. Jo's return trip on the road was her favorite part of the day. She never knew what the next bend might bring—a turkey, a family of bobwhite quail, or even a bobcat. At its end, the road brought her to a pretty view of the clear, rocky creek and a left turn that led to her quaint cottage on the hill.

But it wasn't wildlife she saw staring back at her from the cottage walkway when she turned onto the Kinney property lane. It was the Ursa Major alien and her Ursa Minor dog. The girl was wearing the same clothes as the previous night, her feet still bare. Jo parked and jumped out of the car without removing her gear. "Why are you still here?"

"I told you," the girl said, "I'm visiting from—"

"You've got to go home!"

"I will! I promise I will when I've seen five miracles."

Jo took her phone from her pants pocket. "I'm sorry . . . I have to call the police."

"If you do, I'll run. I'll find another house."

"You can't do that! There are weird people out there. Bad people . . ."

The girl crossed her arms over her chest. "Then don't call."

Good advice. She shouldn't do it in front of her. Jo put the phone away. "Are you hungry?"

"Kind of," the girl said.

She probably hadn't eaten since her meal at the fire. "Do you like eggs?"

"I heard scrambled eggs taste good."

"There's a guy who sells eggs down the road. I'll go get some."

The girl watched Jo walk back to her car. "If you're lying and bring the police, I'll run."

The desperation in the girl's eyes put Jo on edge. She spun the car around and turned onto Turkey Creek Road. About a mile from the cottage, she stopped at a hill where she was more likely to have a connection and dialed information to get the sheriff's nonemergency number. After three unsuccessful attempts, she laid the phone in the console. She had a better idea.

She arrived at the outer road just in time. Egg Man had taken down his canopy and **Fresh Eggs** sign, but he hadn't put away the table or three unsold cartons of eggs perched on his chair. Jo pulled her car into the roadside weeds and grabbed her wallet. She waited behind Egg Man while he leaned over the table to fold its legs. She'd never seen his whole body because he'd been seated behind the table when she bought eggs. He was about six feet tall and muscular from daily hard work, the kind of proportional strength Jo preferred to weight-lifting bulges.

He turned around, smiling and making more eye contact than usual. "Sudden urge for an omelet?" he said, noting the wallet in her hand.

"I wish," she said, "but I don't have cheese. I'll have to settle for scrambled."

"Yeah, it's not really an omelet without cheese."

She'd bought eggs from him three times in the five weeks since she'd arrived, and he'd never spoken as many words to her. Usually his side of the transaction was a nod, a calloused hand taking her money, and *Thank you, ma'am* when she said he could keep the change. Egg Man was a mystery to her. She'd assumed a guy who sold eggs on the side of the road would be a bit slow, but his eyes, the only feature that stood out in his heavily bearded face, were as sharp as shattered blue glass. And he was young, probably around her age, and she didn't get why a smart guy that age would be selling eggs in the middle of nowhere.

Egg Man dropped the folded table into the grass and faced her. "A dozen or a half?"

Jo didn't detect any hint of the drawl common in most Southern Illinoisans' speech. "A dozen," she said, handing him a five from her wallet.

He took a carton off the chair and exchanged it for the bill.

"Keep it," she said.

"Thank you, ma'am," he said, stuffing the money into his rear pocket. He picked up the table and carried it to his old white pickup.

Jo followed. "Can I ask you something?"

He rested the table in the open bed of his truck and turned to her. "You can."

"I have a problem . . ."

His eyes lit, more with curiosity than concern.

"You live on this road, don't you?"

"I do," he said. "Property right next to Kinney's, as a matter of fact."

"Oh, I didn't know."

"What's the problem, neighbor?"

"I assume you know the people who live on this road—you probably sell them eggs?"

He nodded.

"A girl showed up on my property last night. Have you heard of any kids missing from home?"

"I haven't."

"She's around nine years old, slim, long dark-blonde hair, big brown eyes . . . pretty face, interesting, kind of oval with a dimple on one cheek when she smiles. Does she sound familiar?"

"No."

"She has to be from around here. Her feet are bare, and she's wearing pajama bottoms."

"Tell her to go home."

"I did, but she won't. I think she might be afraid to go home. She hadn't eaten for a whole day."

"Maybe you'd better call the police."

"She says she'll run away if I do. She told me this wild story about being from another planet and borrowing a dead girl's body."

Egg Man lifted his brows.

"Yeah, pretty crazy. But I don't think she is. She's smart . . ."

"Lots of crazy people are smart."

"But she acts like she knows exactly what she's doing."

His blue-glass eyes sharpened. "Why can't a person with a mental condition know exactly what she's doing?"

"That's sort of the point I'm making."

"Which is what?"

"What if she's smart enough to know what she's doing?"

"Meaning?"

"She knows going home isn't safe."

"She's only nine. She has to go home." He opened the passenger door and set the two remaining egg cartons on the floor.

"So I call the police, and when the kid sees them coming, she runs, and who knows what happens to her?"

"Do it on the sly."

"How? She'll run into the woods before they even get out of the car."

He had no advice.

"Damn it, I don't want to do this!"

He studied her sympathetically, his arm draped over the top of the open truck door. "You look like you put in a long day."

She glanced down at her muddy clothing and boots. "Yeah, and it's getting longer than I'm up for."

"How about I come over and see if I know the girl?"

"Would you?"

"Can't promise it'll help."

Jo held out the dozen eggs. "Bring these when you come. I'll tell her you ran out and had to go home to get more. Otherwise, you might scare her off."

"This little girl has you in a state."

She did, come to think of it. What the hell was going on with her?

He put the eggs on the passenger-seat floor with the others. "What do you study?"

She hadn't expected Egg Man to ask. She blanked for a few seconds.

"Last summer there were a bunch of fish students at Kinney's," he said. "Summer before, it was dragonflies and trees."

"I study birds," Jo said.

"What kind?"

"I'm looking at nesting success in indigo buntings."

"Plenty of those around here."

She was surprised he knew the name of the bird. Many people couldn't name one beyond cardinal, and even those were often called redbirds.

"I saw you out walking a few times," he said. "Did you put up those pieces of orange surveyor tape?"

"I did. Turkey Creek Road is one of my study sites." She didn't tell him the flags marked nests. If local kids found out, they might mess with them and spoil her results. She watched him fold the stadium chair. "Are you, by chance, missing a dog?" she asked.

"I don't keep dogs, just a couple of barn cats. Why do you ask?"

"A starving puppy is my other problem."

"When it rains, it pours."

"I guess so," Jo said, returning to her car. She didn't see girl or dog when she pulled into the cottage driveway. She unloaded her field gear and the fruit and muffins she'd bought at the farm stand. The girl was hiding, or maybe she'd sensed trouble and split.

As Jo put away her purchases, three soft knocks tapped the kitchen door. Jo opened the door and looked down at the girl through the tattered screen.

"Are you going to make the eggs now?" the girl asked.

"The guy ran out," Jo said. "He's bringing some."

"How can he bring some if he ran out?"

"He's going home to get more. He lives on the property next to this one. Over there."

The girl looked west where Jo pointed.

"Want a blueberry muffin?"

"Yes!"

Jo plopped a muffin in her dirty hand.

"Thanks," the girl said before burying her mouth in it.

The food brought the dog from around the corner of the house, but the girl was too hungry to share. She'd already finished the muffin when Egg Man's white pickup rumbled down the gravel driveway half a minute later. Jo took the muffin paper from the girl's hand and tossed it onto the cold ashes in the fire pit. "Let's get those eggs," she said, beckoning the girl around the side of the house.

"Oh no!" the girl said.

"What?"

"Little Bear ate the muffin paper."

"I'm sure he's eaten worse. Come on."

They met Egg Man at his pickup. As he handed the carton of eggs to Jo, he sized up the bedraggled girl from filthy bare feet to greasy hair. She looked much worse than she had the night before. "You live around here?" Egg Man asked the girl.

"She told you to ask me that," the girl said. "That's the real reason you brought the eggs. You weren't really out."

"A whippersnapper," Egg Man said.

"What's that?" the girl said.

"It means you've gotten too big for your britches. And speaking of britches, what are you doing going around in pajamas?"

The waif looked down at her lavender star-spangled pants. "The girl was wearing these when she died."

"What girl?"

"The human whose body I took. Didn't Jo tell you?"

"Who's Jo?"

"I am," Jo said.

Egg Man held out his hand. "Nice to meet you, Jo. I'm Gabriel Nash."

"Joanna Teale." She squeezed his warm, coarse hand, very aware that she hadn't touched a young man in two years. She held on a little longer than she should, or maybe he did.

"And what's your name, zombie girl?" he said, offering his hand to the girl.

The girl backed away, afraid he'd try to grab her. "I'm not a zombie. I'm visiting from Hetrayeh."

"Where's that?" he asked.

"It's a planet in the Pinwheel Galaxy."

"Pinwheel? Really?"

"You've heard of it?"

"I've seen it."

The girl looked askance at him. "No you haven't."

"I have. With a telescope."

Something about what he'd said made the girl all beamish. "It's pretty, isn't it?"

"It's one of my favorites."

It must be a real galaxy. At least the girl hadn't lied about everything.

Egg Man leaned against the front of his pickup, hands tucked into his jeans pockets. "Why'd you come to Earth?"

"It's school for us. I'm like what Jo is—a graduate student."

"Interesting. How long do you plan to stay?"

"Till I've seen enough."

"Enough what?"

"Enough to understand humans. When I've seen five miracles, I go back."

"Five *miracles*?" he said. "That'll take forever."

"By miracles I only mean things that amaze me. When I've seen those five things, I'll go back and tell the stories to my people. It's like getting a PhD and becoming a professor."

"You'll be an expert on humans?"

"Just on the little bit of your world I've seen. Like Jo will be an expert on bird ecology but not other kinds of science."

"Wow," he said, looking at Jo.

"Smart little alien, isn't she?" Jo held the dozen eggs out to the girl. "Would you put these in the refrigerator for me?"

"You'll let me in your house?"

"Yes."

"Only because you want to talk to him about me."

"Put the eggs away."

"Don't say anything mean."

"Go on." The girl ran for the front door. "Walk," Jo called, "or your scrambled eggs will be on the sidewalk." She turned back to Egg Man. "What do you think?"

"I've never seen her before. I'm pretty sure she doesn't live on our road."

"She has to be from somewhere close. Her feet would be a mess if she'd walked far."

"Maybe she lost her shoes since she got here . . . dipped her feet in a stream and forgot where she put them." He got off the pickup and rubbed his hand on his beard. "Her accent sounds like she's from around here—but all that stuff about graduate students and professors . . ."

"She got that from me."

"Obviously, but she looks too young to put it all together as well as she does."

"I know, that's what I was trying to tell—"

The girl burst out the porch door at a run, bare feet slapping the cracked concrete. "What are you saying?" she asked breathlessly.

"We were saying it's about time you went home," he said. "Do you need a ride? I can take you in my truck."

"You're going to drive me across the stars to my planet?"

"You're too smart to think we'll believe you're an alien," he said, "and you know a girl your age can't be out on her own. Tell us the truth."

"I am!"

"Then Jo has no choice but to call the police."

"Toh-id ina eroo-oy!" the girl said.

"Toad in a *what?*" he said.

The girl burst into her alien language, speaking as fluently as she had the night before, but this time the speech was spoken as an invective at Egg Man, with much arm and hand gesturing.

"What was that?" he asked when she'd finished.

"I was telling you in my language that you should be nice to a graduate student who came all the way across the stars to see you. I'll never get to be a professor if you don't let me stay."

"You know you can't stay here."

"Are you getting your PhD?" the girl asked.

He looked at her strangely.

"If you are, you'd know it's wrong not to let me get mine," the girl said.

He walked to his truck and opened the door.

"Wait . . . ," Jo said.

He closed the door. "You're on your own with this," he said out the window.

"What if she'd shown up on your doorstep?"

"She didn't." He pulled out of the driveway fast, scattering gravel.

"What the hell? Henhouse on fire?" Jo said.

"What fire?" the girl said.

"Never mind."

Clearly, something had pissed him off. Maybe he was insecure about Jo's level of education. He'd changed when the girl asked if he was getting a PhD.

"I saw pie in the kitchen. Can I have a piece?"

Jo stared at the empty road as the rumble of Egg Man's truck faded. Why couldn't the people of his community take care of their own? Why would it be left to her, the outsider who didn't know their ways, their unspoken rules?

"Can I?" the girl said.

Jo turned to her, trying not to look nervous. "Yes, you can have pie. But first you should eat something substantial." And before that, Jo somehow had to call the sheriff without the girl knowing.

"Are scrambled eggs substantial?"

"They are," Jo said, "but I want you to clean up before you eat. You have to take a shower."

"Can't I eat first?"

"I've told you the rules. Take them or leave them."

The girl followed Jo into the house like a hungry puppy.

3

After her own quick shower, Jo sent the girl into the bathroom with a clean towel. She shut the door, listened for the water, and hurried outside with her phone when she was certain the girl was bathing.

The forest was gray, the same shade of twilight that had delivered the changeling to the cottage the night before. Jo walked down the driveway, swiping her fingers at mosquitoes, and beads of sweat mixed with water dripping out of her hair. Little Bear skulked nearby, following her every move like a spy for the alien child.

Connecting to the internet and finding the nonemergency sheriff's number took more than seven minutes. When the sheriff's operator answered, Jo rushed through the call, afraid the girl would come outside and hear her. She told the woman she needed a deputy to pick up a girl who might be homeless. She gave her address and a few directions to get there. The woman asked questions, but Jo only had time to say that she was very worried about the girl and she wanted someone to come out immediately. She hid the phone in her pocket and rushed back to the house.

Just in time. The girl was in the living room wrapped in a towel, long hair dripping down her thin shoulders. Her dark eyes studied Jo's. "Where were you?" she said.

"I heard something out there," Jo said, "but it was only the dog." She walked closer to the child, hoping that what she saw were smears of mud the girl had failed to wash away. The marks weren't dirt. She had purple contusions on her throat and left upper arm, and her right thigh was scraped and bruised. The high neck of her hoodie had covered the bruise on her throat. Her left arm appeared marked by fingers, as if someone had gripped her hard. "How did you get those bruises?"

The girl backed away. "Where are my clothes?"

"Who hurt you?"

"I don't know what happened. Those were on the dead girl's body. Maybe she got hit by a car or something."

"Is this why you're afraid to go home? Someone hurts you?"

The girl glowered. "I thought you were nice, but I guess you aren't."

"Why am I not nice?"

"Because you won't believe me."

Jo was relieved. She'd been afraid the girl knew she'd called the sheriff. And good thing she had. The situation definitely required police. Jo hoped they would take the call seriously and come quickly, but in the meantime she had to keep the girl occupied.

"Let's get you dressed and make those eggs," she said.

Jo couldn't let her wear the same filthy clothes. The girl didn't mind putting on one of Jo's T-shirts and leggings rolled to the calves. She helped Jo in the kitchen, even washed some of the dishes before they ate. Jo tried to get her to talk about where she was from while they cooked and ate, but she kept to her outlandish story. Despite the "green stuff," a few baby spinach leaves, the girl scarfed down three scrambled eggs. She followed the eggs with a big slice of apple pie, after which she said her stomach hurt.

Once they finished cleaning, the girl pleaded for Little Bear to be fed, and Jo let her give the dog leftover beans, rice, and chicken that had been in the refrigerator too long. They put the food on a plate on the concrete slab behind the house, and the dog ate it even faster than its alien guardian had eaten. "I'll wash the dish," the girl said.

"Leave it out there. Let's talk in the living room." She didn't want the girl anywhere near a door when the sheriff arrived.

"Talk about what?" the girl said.

"Sit down with me." She led the girl to the shabby blue couch. She hoped the girl would confess what had driven her into the forest before the deputy arrived, while she still had some trust in someone. "I'd like to know your name," she said.

"I told you," the girl said.

"Please tell me your real name."

The girl put her head on a pillow and curled up like a poked caterpillar.

"There are people who can help you with whatever's going on."

"I'm not talking about this anymore. I'm tired of you not believing me."

"You have to talk about it."

The girl pulled a lock of her damp hair across her nose. "I like the smell of your shampoo."

"Don't change the subject."

"There is no subject."

"You can't hide from it forever."

"I never said anything was forever. After five miracles, I'll be gone."

"Damn it, you're stubborn." More like terrified. What had happened to the poor kid?

"Can I sleep here?"

The little alien didn't look well. Her hollow cheeks were pallid, and plum half moons beneath her lower lashes enlarged the size of her fawnlike eyes. Jo's mother's eyes had looked like that before she died, but without eyelashes and with a sheen of morphine. "Yes, you can sleep here," she said. She unfolded a blanket over the girl and tucked it around her thin body.

"Are you going to sleep?"

"I'll read a little, but I'm too tired to get far in my book."

The girl rolled onto her back. "What do you do all day that makes you tired?"

"I look for bird nests."

"Really?"

"Yep."

"That's weird."

"Not for a bird biologist."

"That's what's weird. I heard most Earth ladies are waitresses and teachers and jobs like that."

"I guess I don't fall in the category of 'most Earth ladies.'"

"Can I look for nests with you? It sounds fun."

"It is, but right now you have to sleep." Jo rose and walked to the nearest bedroom of two.

The girl sat up. "Where are you going?"

"To get my book. I'll sit with you while I read." She entered the dark bedroom, grabbed her old copy of *Slaughterhouse-Five*, and brought it into the living room. She sat at the end of the couch next to the girl's feet.

"What is that book?" the girl asked.

"It's called *Slaughterhouse-Five*. It has aliens in it."

The girl made a skeptical face.

"Really. They're called the Tralfamadorians. Do the Hetrayens know them?"

"Are you joking me?"

"I'm—"

A pounding fist banged the outer screen door. The deputy had arrived. He or she had probably knocked once and Jo hadn't heard. She'd had the noisy window air conditioner turned on high to hide the sound of the approaching squad car.

Glendy Vanderah

The child had frozen like a cornered deer, her wild eyes fixed on the front door. "Who is that?"

Jo put her hand on the girl's arm. "Don't be afraid. I want you to know I really care about what hap—"

"You called the police?"

"I did, but—"

The girl sprang to her feet, throwing the blanket over Jo's arms to ensnare her. She speared Jo with a glare of wounded condemnation, and in the next seconds, a blur of girl streaked into the kitchen. The rear door was unbolted and the screen door thudded shut behind her.

Jo pulled off the blanket and laid it over the warm niche where the child had been. She wouldn't have used force on the girl. No one had any right to expect that of her.

The fist pounded again. Jo went onto the porch and faced a uniformed man through the screen door. "Thanks for coming," she said. "I'm Joanna Teale."

"Did you call about a girl . . . a 'homeless' girl, you said?" the man said with a local drawl.

"I did. Come in." She led the deputy onto the porch. He looked toward the open wooden door, his face sallow in the glow of the bug bulb. "Is she in the house?"

"Come inside," Jo said.

The deputy followed her into the living room, closing the door behind him to keep in the air-conditioning. Jo faced the man. His nameplate said he was K. DEAN. He was in his midthirties, balding, a little pudgy, and his plain, round moon of a face was eclipsed by a deep scar that ran from his left jaw up his cheek. With the casualness of habit, the man dropped his gaze to Jo's chest. Certain he'd find nothing as riveting as his scar there, Jo waited for his eyes to return to hers. Two seconds, maybe less. "The girl ran away when you knocked," she said.

He nodded, peering around the house.

"Do you know of any missing kids or AMBER Alerts around here?" she asked.

"I don't," he said.

"There aren't any missing children?"

"There are always missing children."

"From around here?"

"Not that I know of."

She expected him to ask questions, but he was still looking around as if evaluating a crime scene. "She showed up yesterday. She's around nine years old."

He turned his attention to her. "What made you think she's homeless?"

"She had on pajama bottoms . . ."

"I think those pants are what kids call a 'fashion statement,'" he said.

"And she was hungry and dirty. She wasn't wearing shoes."

His slight smile didn't move his scar. "Sounds like me at age nine."

"She has bruises."

Finally, he looked concerned. "On her face?"

"On her neck, leg, and arm."

Suspicion tinged his green eyes. "How did you see them if she had on pajamas?"

"I let her shower here."

His eyes narrowed even more.

"Like I said, she was dirty. And I had to keep her busy while I waited for you to arrive. I gave her dinner, too."

The way he was looking at her, as if she'd done something wrong, was infuriating.

"I still don't see how you came up with her being homeless," he said.

"By homeless, I meant she's afraid to go home."

"So . . . she isn't homeless."

"I don't know what she is!" Jo said. "She has bruises. Someone is hurting her. Isn't that all that matters?"

"Did she say someone hurts her?"

The girl's alien story would muddle the already exasperating situation. "She wouldn't tell me how she got the bruises. She wouldn't tell me anything, not even her name."

"You asked?"

"Yes, I asked."

He nodded.

"Do you want a description of her?"

"All right." He didn't take out a notebook, only nodded more as Jo described the girl.

"Will you look for her—in the morning when it gets light?"

"If she ran, she doesn't want to be found."

"So what? She needs help."

His contemplation of her seemed judgmental. "What kind of help do you think she needs?"

"Obviously she needs to be removed from whoever hurts her."

"Send her to a foster home?" he said.

"If necessary."

He mused for a moment, stroking his fingertips on his scar as if it itched. "I'm gonna tell you something," he said, "and you might take it wrong, but I'll say it anyway. One of my friends in middle school was taken from his mother because she drank and pretty much let him run as wild as he wanted. He was put with people who took foster kids for the state money—which happens more than you'd think—and he ended up a lot worse off than if he'd been with his mama. The foster father hit him, and the mother verbally abused him. My friend died from an overdose when he was fifteen."

"What are you saying . . . you think she should be left in an abusive home?"

"Now, I didn't say that, did I?"

"You implied it."

"What I *implied* was, don't pull that girl outta the pan and drop her into the fire. Those bruises might be from climbing a fence or falling out of a tree, and if you turn her in, she'll probably say that even if it isn't true. Kids are smarter than we think. They know how to survive the shit that's dealt them better than some welfare worker who never spent a day in one of those kids' shoes."

Were those the unspoken rules Jo had sought? Or were they only the opinions of one bitter man who'd lost a boyhood friend?

"I guess this means you won't look for her?" Jo said.

"What would you have us do, get the dogs out after her?"

She showed the deputy to the door.

4

Jo took a flashlight out the back door and looked for the girl. A front that was expected to bring rain the next day had moved in, its clouds conquering the moon and stars. Jo already smelled a hint of rain in the warm humid air. But she found no trace of the girl.

The rain arrived a few hours later, a hard patter on the cottage that woke Jo out of a deep sleep. She thought of the girl, possibly alone in the dark woods in the rain, and she wished she hadn't called the sheriff. She looked at her phone. 2:17 a.m. Just a few hours into her mother's birthday. She would have been fifty-one.

She went to the bathroom, more for distraction than for need. As she washed, she leaned toward the sink mirror, assessing the healthy glow of her skin and sun-lightened streaks in her hair. Her face was thinner and her hair still wasn't long enough to pull back, but she almost looked like herself again.

Almost. The hazel eyes in the mirror mocked her. But who was reflected there, the old Jo or the new *almost* Jo? She gripped the sink and bowed her head, staring into the dark tunnel of the drain. Maybe this was how it would be from now on, two versions of herself living inside one body. Jo looked up at the woman in the mirror as she flicked the switch, purging her with darkness.

The storm continued all morning, and she couldn't work in the rain. She slept past her usual waking time, until about an hour past dawn. After she dressed, drank her coffee, and ate cereal, she gathered the laundry, a rain-day ritual. The alien child's clothes were draped over the laundry basket. Jo stuffed them into the duffel bag along with her dirty clothing, towels, and a bottle of detergent.

She packed a courier bag with her laptop and enough raw data for an hour's worth of data entry. As she locked the front door behind her, something moved in her peripheral vision. The old afghan she kept on the wicker porch couch was stretched over a long lump the exact dimensions of the alien. She was pulling the blanket over her head, trying to hide.

Jo tried to transform the intensity of her relief into anger. But she couldn't. "I guess you haven't figured out how to hide your human body yet," she said to the lump.

The edge of the afghan came down from the girl's pale face. "I haven't," she said.

"What are Hetrayen bodies like?"

The girl considered for a few seconds. "We look like starlight. It's not exactly a *body*."

Creative answer. Jo pondered what to do. If she called the sheriff, the girl would run again. The only possibility would be to lock her in a room until the deputy arrived. Jo wasn't up for that, and even if she were, the house didn't have any rooms that couldn't be opened from the inside.

The girl intuited Jo's thoughts. "I'm leaving now. I only came back because I couldn't see to go nowhere last night."

Though the girl tried to hide it, Jo saw a shadow of the distress she had experienced when she ran from the house. With clouds covering the moon and stars, she wouldn't have been able to see her hand if she held it in front of her face. She had stayed near the cottage lights.

The girl sat up and pushed the blanket aside. "Usually I sleep in that old shed back there, but rain was dripping on me."

"That's where you went the night you came to my fire?"

She nodded. "There's a bed out there. I share it with Little Bear."

When Jo had moved into the cottage, the one full-size mattress that was left in the house over winter had been ruined by nesting mice. Many biology students would have used the urine-tainted bed anyway, but Jo wasn't quite that tolerant. She'd dragged the smelly, chewed mattress out to the shed and used some of her research money to buy a cut-rate queen mattress.

"You shouldn't go in that shed," Jo said. "It looks like it's going to fall down any day."

"I know. There's big holes in the roof. And now our bed is all wet." She'd said the last tragically, as though the foul mattress had been all the security she had in the world.

"Are you hungry?" Jo asked.

The girl eyed her suspiciously.

"How about some pancakes?"

"I bet you're tricking me again," she said.

"I'm not. I'm on my way out, and I don't want to leave you here hungry."

The girl mournfully stared into the rainy forest, considering what to do. *Don't pull that girl outta the pan and drop her into the fire,* the deputy had said. Were those really her only options? Jo had a sudden urge to bundle the child into her arms and hold her. "I have syrup," she said.

The girl looked up at her. "I heard syrup on pancakes is good."

"I can't believe you remembered to pretend you've never had it."

"Were you trying to trick me?"

"I wasn't." Jo returned the key to the lock and opened it. "Come on, then."

After the girl stuffed herself with pancakes and orange juice, she begged Jo to let Little Bear come in from the rain and eat a pancake on the porch. Jo relented on the condition that the mutt and his fleas didn't enter the house. Wearing Jo's raincoat, the girl went to the shed with a pancake to lure the dog. The hungry dog slunk onto the porch to get the food, but only when Jo retreated into the house. "If he pees or poops out there, you have to clean it up," Jo said.

"I will. Can I give him a bowl of water?"

"Sure. I'm going to the Laundromat now."

"Why isn't there a wash machine here?"

"I guess Kinney doesn't want to waste his money on one when this place is only rented for a few months of the year."

"Is that why there's no TV?"

"Probably."

"You could bring your own."

"There's no cable or internet," Jo said.

"Why not?"

"Kinney is from a generation of biologists who believe you work, eat, and sleep when you're immersed in the natural world."

"How long will you be at the Laundromat?"

"A few hours." She'd been trying to decide whether to lock the girl out of the house while she was gone. Instead, she put her binoculars in her bag with her laptop. Those and her wallet were the only two items she owned that were worth stealing.

"Don't turn on the stove while I'm gone," she said.

"You're going to let me stay inside?"

"I am—for now. We're going to talk about what to do when I get back, okay?"

She didn't answer.

"Don't mess with that desk while I'm gone," Jo said.

The girl looked at the desk piled with books, journals, and papers. "What is all that?"

"It's my science stuff. Stay out of it."

She followed Jo onto the screened porch. Little Bear was curled in a tight ball on the rug, his wary gaze on Jo as she walked to the screen door.

"Remember, don't let the dog in the house," Jo said.

"I know."

Jo put up her hood and bustled through the steady rain to the driveway. The girl watched her load the car and get in, her small body ghostly and distorted through the translucence of the rain-soaked porch screens.

During the forty-minute drive to the small town of Vienna—pronounced *Vī-enna* by locals—the rain reduced to a drizzle, though the sky was dark with a threat of more. Downtown Vienna looked like places she'd seen in old movies, and something about that was oddly comforting. As she cruised the mostly empty streets, two old-timers seated under a store awning lifted their hands at her, and she returned the greeting. She passed the sheriff's station on her way to the Laundromat.

She sat in her usual blue plastic chair facing the window while her laundry churned in two washers. She brought up Tabby's face on her phone contacts, a photo of her wearing striped cat ears, a plastic goldfish dangling like a cigarette from her lips. Tabby had been Jo's closest friend since sophomore year of undergrad when they were lab partners, and she'd also stayed at the University of Illinois for her graduate work. She'd gotten into the veterinary school, a very good program, but she often questioned why she hadn't switched to a school with better surrounding scenery than corn and soybean fields.

"Hey, Jojo," Tabby answered on the third ring. "How's Dawg Town?"

A town named Vienna in rural Illinois was hilarious to her, and she was certain it must be more about dawgs, Vienna-brand hot dogs, than the capital of Austria.

"How'd you know I'm in Vienna?" Jo said.

"I only ever hear from you when you're doing laundry. I also know it's raining down there because you'd wear the same disgusting clothes until they fell apart rather than do laundry on a nice day when you could be working."

"I didn't realize I was so predictable," Jo said.

"You are. Which means you're working your ass off even though your doctors told you to take it easy."

"I took it easy for two whole years. I need to work."

"Those two years weren't easy, Jo," Tabby said in a quiet voice.

Jo stared out the misty Laundromat window at a puddle in a crater of broken asphalt, its surface dimpled with rain. "Today is my mom's birthday," she said.

"Is it?" Tabby said. "You okay?"

"Yeah."

"Liar."

She was. She'd called Tabby to ask her advice about the girl but had instead blurted out the bit about her mother's birthday.

"Pick up your water," Tabby said.

"Why?"

"We're doing a toast."

Jo lifted her battered blue water bottle, predictably situated next to her.

"Ready?" Tabby said.

"Ready," Jo said.

"Happy birthday to Eleanor Teale, the flower whisperer who made everyone and everything around her bloom. Her light is still with us, growing love across the universe."

Jo raised her bottle to the gray sky and drank. "Thanks," she said, wiping fingers on her lower lashes. "That was a good toast."

"El was one of the coolest people I ever met," Tabby said. "Not to mention my surrogate mom."

"She loved you," Jo said.

"I know. Shit . . . now you're making me cry, and I was trying to help you feel better."

"You did," Jo said. "But guess who's coming to visit today?"

"Don't tell me . . ."

"Yeah, Tanner."

"I wish I was there so I could kick his ass!"

"He deserves no such attention."

"Why would he fucking dare come there?"

"I doubt he wanted to. He and two other grad students are at a workshop with my advisor in Chattanooga. They're going to break their drive back to campus at Kinney Cottage and stay overnight."

"You have enough room for four more people in that house?"

"Not beds, but most biologists will sleep anywhere."

"Put Tanner in the woods. On an anthill."

Where would Jo put the girl? During the drive from the cottage, she'd come up with only one possible solution. But if that didn't work . . .

"Are you there?" Tabby said.

"I'm here," Jo said. "This weird thing happened two nights ago . . ."

"What?"

"A girl showed up at the house, and she wouldn't leave."

"How old is she?"

"She won't say. I think she's around nine or ten."

"Jesus, Jo. Just tell her to go home."

"I tried that, obviously. But then I saw bruises."

"Child-abuse kind of bruises?"

"I think so."

"You have to call the cops!"

"I did. But when the deputy got there, she ran away."

"The poor kid!"

Before Jo could say the girl had come back, the call-waiting tone sounded in her ear. She looked at the screen. Shaw Daniels, her advisor, was calling. "I have to go. Shaw is calling."

"Okay, bye," Tabby said. "And call me sometime when it isn't raining, damn it."

"I will." Jo hung up, then accepted the incoming call. "I was just going to text you."

"I'm surprised I got you," Shaw said. "Between study sites?"

"It's raining. I'm in the Laundromat."

"Good, you're taking a break."

Would any of them ever let her be the person she was before her diagnosis? She suspected Shaw was mostly stopping in to assess her health. He'd tried to make her hire a field assistant while she recovered, and he'd opposed her living in the Kinney house alone.

"Are you still up for a visit tonight?" Shaw asked.

"Of course. What's your ETA?"

"We'll get on the road after the last session, at around three o'clock. We should be there by seven thirty—eight at the latest. If you can wait, we'll take you out for dinner."

"Do you mind if we eat in? I was going to grill burgers. But I may have to make them inside if the rain keeps up."

"Are you sure you want to go to all that trouble?"

"It's no trouble at all," Jo said.

"If you insist," he said. "See you soon."

After stops at the grocery store and farm stand, Jo returned to the cottage in the early afternoon. The girl was gone. Jo hoped she had gone home. But when she imagined the brutality the girl might be facing, she regretted wishing for it. She scanned the house, noting the girl hadn't stolen anything. The only item out of place was a textbook, *Ornithology*, taken off the desk and left on the couch.

Jo pushed the girl out of her thoughts. She had a lot to do before her visitors arrived. After she straightened the house, she began preparing pies for dessert, one peach and one strawberry-rhubarb, made with fruit she'd bought at the farm stand. Normally she wouldn't spend her precious field time so frivolously, but the rain was still coming down and she wanted the dinner to be nice for Shaw—if not for Tanner Bruce. Tanner, also one of Shaw's PhD students, had been only one year ahead of her when she entered graduate school, but now he was three years ahead and nearly finished. Shortly before Jo left school to care for her dying mother, she'd slept with Tanner. Three times. But the only contact she'd had with him since she left was his signature on a sympathy card from Shaw and his graduate students.

Jo's hands perfunctorily rolled out a circle of pie dough while her mind traveled to the last day she'd spent with Tanner. The July night was hot, too warm to sleep in the tent, and they'd stripped and made love in a deep pool of a stream near their campsite. The memory would have been one of the best of her life if Tanner Bruce weren't in it.

"Who are the pies for?"

Jo's attention snapped back to her hands. The girl had slipped into the house without a sound, her hair and Jo's oversize clothing damp with rain.

"Where were you?" Jo asked.

"In the woods."

"Doing what?"

"I thought you'd have that policeman with you again."

Jo laid a smooth round of floury dough in one of the new pie pans. "I've decided you and I should work this out on our own. Do you think we can do that?"

"Okay," she said.

"Tell me where you live and why you won't go back. I'll help you with whatever is going on."

"I told you all that already. Can I have some pie when they're ready?"

"They're for later, for my guests."

"Who's coming?"

"The professor who oversees my project and three graduate students."

"Are they ornithologists?"

"They are. How do you know that word?"

"From your *Ornithology* book. I read the preface and first two chapters," she said, pronouncing the word *pre-fāce*.

"You actually read it?"

"I skipped the parts someone from Hetrayeh wouldn't understand, but not that much. I liked the chapter about bird diversity and how their beaks match what they eat and their feet match where they live. I never really thought about that before."

"You're an advanced reader."

"I use the dead girl's brain to do things, and she was smart."

Jo wiped her floury hands on a dish towel. "Go wash and I'll let you pinch the edges of the piecrusts."

The alien ran for the sink. When she finished washing, Jo said, "I need a better name to call you than Earpood. Can you think of a regular name?"

The girl put her chin in her hand and pretended to think. "What about *Ursa* . . . because I'm from the place you call Ursa Major?"

"I like the name Ursa."

"You can call me that."

"No last name?"

"Major."

"That makes sense. Have you ever made piecrust, Ursa?"

"We don't make pies on Hetrayeh."

"Let me show you."

Ursa mastered piecrusts as quickly as she grasped college-level reading, and while the pies baked, scenting the kitchen with their sweetness, she helped Jo make potato salad. They used Jo's mother's recipe—the only potato salad worth eating, in Jo's opinion. Next they prepared ground beef to make burgers the way Jo's mother had, with Worcestershire, bread crumbs, and spices. Jo hadn't cooked so elaborately for herself since she'd lived at the cottage. She liked the idea of

making her mother's recipes on her birthday—a way of honoring her—
and the food preparation helped distract her from the mounting tension
of seeing Tanner again. Even the girl wasn't enough of a diversion.

When Ursa put away the butter, she surveyed the beer cooling in
the refrigerator. "Are the ornithologists alcoholics?"

"Why would you think that?" Jo said.

"That's a lot of beer."

"It's for four people."

"You won't drink any?"

"I might have one."

"You don't like to get drunk?"

"I don't." Jo saw mistrust in the alien's eyes. "Have you had bad
experiences with people who drink a lot?"

"How could I have? I just got here."

5

After they ate sandwiches and the pies were set out to cool, Jo sent Ursa to change back into her own clean clothes. When Ursa came out of the bedroom and saw Jo working on her laptop, she sat on the couch and read more of the *Ornithology* text.

Jo turned her screen so Ursa couldn't see her use her phone to get on the internet. When she got a connection, she googled *Ursa missing girl* but found nothing. Though the sheriff's deputy knew of no missing children in the area, she tried *missing child Illinois*, which brought her to the National Center for Missing and Exploited Children website and a depressingly long list of missing Illinois children. Many of them were probably dead, their bones concealed in graves that would never be found. Some of the photographs were of kids who had been missing since as far back as 1960, and a few were computer reconstructions of dead children who'd never been identified. One nearly made Jo cry. It was a photograph of a pair of shoes—all that was recovered of a teenager's remains.

Jo used the same website to look at photographs of children in nearby Kentucky, and also in the bordering states of Missouri, Iowa, Wisconsin, and Indiana. Ursa Major wasn't on the lists, though she'd been away from home for at least two nights. Jo set down the phone. "How's *Ornithology* going?"

"I don't like systematics that much," Ursa said.

"It's not my thing either." She took her car keys off the desk. "The rain has stopped. I'm going to drive down the road to monitor a few nests. Want to come with me?"

"Yes!" She sprang off the couch and slipped on Jo's oversize flip-flops. "How do you monitor a nest?"

"I look at it and see how it's doing."

"That's how you get a PhD?"

"There's a lot more to it than that. I record the fate of every nest I find, and from that data I can calculate the nesting success of indigo buntings in each of my study sites."

"What do you mean by *fate*?"

"Fate is what happens after the nest is built. I monitor how many eggs are laid, how many hatch, and how many baby birds fledge from the nest. *Fledge* means they fly away from the nest. But sometimes the parents abandon the nest before the female lays eggs, or the eggs are eaten by a predator. And sometimes the eggs hatch, but the babies are eaten by a predator before they fledge."

"Why don't you stop the predator from eating the babies?"

"I can't stop it from happening, and even if I could, saving individual baby birds isn't the purpose of my study. The research is meant to help us understand how to conserve bird populations on a bigger scale."

"What is the predator?"

"Snakes, crows, blue jays, and raccoons are the main ones in my study sites." Jo slung her field bag over her shoulder. "Let's go before the weather turns again. I don't like to scare birds off their nests when it's raining."

"Because the eggs can't get wet?"

"I don't want eggs or babies to get wet and cold. Research should have as little impact on nesting success as possible."

When they left the cottage, Little Bear trotted over from the shed. He was much tamer, letting Ursa pet his head. "Stay here," she told the dog. "Do you understand? I'll be back soon."

Ursa didn't like that she had to sit in the back seat and use the seat belt. Someone had been letting her sit up front unbuckled. Jo explained why the seat belt was necessary and how the front airbag could kill children if it opened.

"If the airbag kills kids, why do they put it in the car?" Ursa asked.

"Because people who make cars expect kids to ride in the back seat where it's safest."

"What if a truck hits the back of the car where the kid is sitting?"

"Are you going to follow my rules or not?"

She clambered into the back seat and put on a seat belt.

The dog ran after the car as they left the Kinney driveway. "Jo, stop! Stop!" Ursa pleaded. "He's following us!"

"How will stopping help?"

Ursa leaned out the back-seat window and watched the dog vanish with a bend in the road. "He can't keep up!"

"I don't want him to. He can't come to my study site. Bringing a predator would freak out my birds."

"Jo! He's still coming!"

"Stop hanging out the window. This road is narrow, and you're going to get whacked by a tree branch."

Ursa stared miserably at the passenger-side mirror.

"He knows this road. This is where he was born," Jo said.

"Maybe he wasn't. He could have jumped out of a car."

"More like he was dumped out of a car by someone who didn't want him."

"Will you go back for him?"

"No."

"You're mean."

"Yep."

"Is that where Gabriel Nash lives?" Ursa asked, pointing at the rutted dirt lane and **No Trespassing** sign.

"I think it is," Jo said.

"Maybe Little Bear will go there."

"Egg Man probably wouldn't like that. He has chickens and cats."

"Why do you call him Egg Man when his name is Gabriel?"

"Because buying eggs is how I know him."

"I thought he was nice."

"I never said he wasn't."

Jo drove to the farthest nest to make sure the dog didn't catch up, turning around at the western end of the road and stopping at the first piece of flagging tape. She took out the data from the folder marked TURKEY CREEK ROAD and showed the page to Ursa. "This is called a nest log. I have one for every nest I find, and each one gets a number. This one is TC10, which means it's the tenth nest I've found in my Turkey Creek Road study site. At the top of the log, I record information about where and when I found the nest, and on these lines underneath I record what I see each time I monitor it. The nest had two eggs in it the day I found it and four the next time. The last time I visited, it still had four, and I noted that I flushed the female off the nest."

"Will the babies be hatched yet?"

"It's too early. The female incubates for around twelve days."

"*Incubates* means she keeps them warm?"

"That's right. Let's see how she's doing." They left the car, and Jo showed Ursa how she marked instructions on a piece of orange flagging that would direct her to the nest. "INBU is the code for indigo bunting, the main bird I study, and this is the date I found it. The other numbers and letters say the nest is four meters to the south-southwest, and it's about a meter and a half off the ground."

"Where? I want to see it!"

"You will. Follow me." As they pushed through wet roadside weeds, the buntings remained silent. Not a good sign. They should be chirping alarm notes. Jo's suspicions were verified when she saw the wrecked nest.

"What happened to it?" Ursa said.

"You have to figure that out, like a detective who looks at clues to solve a crime. Sometimes inexperienced birds build a weak nest that falls down. If the nest wasn't constructed well, rainy weather like we had today could have made it fall."

"Is that what happened?"

"From the clues I see, I don't think so."

"What are the clues?"

"First of all, I remember this nest was sturdy. Second, I see no eggs on the ground. Third, the parents are completely gone from the territory, which means this probably happened before the rain hit. And the biggest clue is how much the nest is torn apart. I'm guessing a raccoon pulled it down. If a snake or crow had gotten the eggs, there probably wouldn't be that much damage."

"The raccoon ate the eggs?"

"Whatever tore up the nest ate the eggs. On some nests I set up cameras so I know for sure what predator did it."

"Why didn't you have a camera for this one?"

"I can't put cameras on them all. Cameras are expensive. Let's go to the next nest."

"Will they all be eaten by that stupid raccoon?" Ursa asked as they walked back to the car.

"I doubt it. But my hypothesis is that buntings will have lower nesting success in human-made edges, along roads or crop fields, than they do in natural edges, like next to a stream or where a big tree has fallen. Have you ever heard the word *hypothesis*?"

"Yes, but people from Hetrayeh use a different word." She crawled into the back seat. "I had a hypothesis about you today."

"Did you? What was it?"

"If you didn't bring the police back again, you never would."

She'd articulated a hypothesis with remarkable competence. And with too damn much confidence. Jo twisted around to look at her.

"What does that mean? You think your hypothesis is proven and you're staying with me?"

"Just until the five miracles."

"We both know that can't happen. You have to go home tonight. Shaw—my advisor—will be here in a few hours, and I'll be in trouble if he finds out you've been living on the Kinney property for two days."

"Don't tell him."

"How am I supposed to explain a girl sleeping at my house?"

"I'll sleep somewhere else."

"You will. *At home.* That's why we're out here. You'll show me where you live, and I'll bring you to the door. I'll tell whoever takes care of you that I'm going to check on you every day. And I will check on you. I promise I will."

The girl's brown eyes swamped with tears. "You lied? You didn't really want to show me your bird nests?"

"I did. But afterward you have to go home. My advisor will—"

"Go ahead, take me to every house, and the people will say they don't know me!"

"You have to go home!"

"I promise I'll go home when I see the miracles. I promise!"

"Ursa . . ."

"You're the only nice person I know! Please!" She sobbed, her face almost purple.

Jo opened the rear door, unbuckled the girl's seat belt, and held the child in her arms, the first time a head pressed against her bony chest. But the girl didn't notice what was missing. She tightened her grip on Jo and cried harder.

"I'm sorry," Jo said, "I really am, but you must see I'm in an impossible situation. I could get in trouble for letting you stay with me."

Ursa pulled out of her arms and dragged the back of her hand across her runny nose. "Can we see another nest? Please?"

"There are four more, and you can see them all. But afterward you have to go home."

She wouldn't agree. Most obstinate child in the universe. Jo drove on. Other than a flush in her cheeks, the girl had completely recovered from her cry by the time Jo parked at the next orange flag. "I hope the raccoon didn't get the eggs," Ursa said.

"It should be babies. They would have hatched within the last day."

Ursa jumped out and read the text on the flag tied to a sycamore sapling. "It's an indigo bunting nest that's seven meters northeast and one meter off the ground."

"Good. Now we'll find northeast with my compass." Jo showed her how to use the compass and sent her in the correct direction. As Ursa approached the nest, the parent birds began to call in alarm. "Do you hear those loud, abrupt chirps? That's what indigo buntings do when you get too close to their nest." The agitated male balanced on a milkweed plant, his sapphire feathers lit by a setting sun that had finally emerged from fleeing rain clouds. "The male is right there in front of you. Do you see him?"

"He's blue!" Ursa said. "He's all different colors of blue!"

Her excitement was intense and real. But if she was from that road or any other nearby road, she would have seen that bird before. Buntings were common on Southern Illinois roadsides.

"I see the nest!" Ursa said. "Can I look inside?"

"Go ahead."

Ursa parted belly-high weeds and peered into the nest. "Oh my god!" she said. "Oh my god!"

"They hatched?"

"Yes! They're really little and pink! They're opening their beaks at me!"

"They're hungry. Their parents had trouble finding insects for them in the rain today." Jo looked at the four newly hatched buntings. "We have to leave them alone. Do you hear how upset the parents are?"

Ursa couldn't take her eyes off the tiny birds. "This is a miracle! This is it, the first miracle!"

"Haven't you ever seen baby birds in a nest?"

"How could I have? I'm from a planet that doesn't have baby birds and nests."

"Let's go," Jo said. "Their parents need to feed them while there's still light."

When they got to the car, Jo asked, "Was that really the first indigo bunting you've seen?"

"It was. It's the prettiest bird I've seen on Earth so far."

They checked the next nest, which had four eggs. After that was a white-eyed vireo nest. Vireos weren't Jo's target species, but she took data on any nest she found. The nest was still active with three vireo nestlings and one cowbird nestling, and on the way back to the car Jo told Ursa about brown-headed cowbirds and how they laid their eggs in the nests of other birds, called "hosts," that raised them.

"Why don't cowbirds want to take care of their own babies?" Ursa asked.

"By laying their eggs in the nests of other birds, they can make lots more babies because other birds do all the work. In nature, the winner is the one that produces the most young."

"Are the vireos mad about raising the cowbird babies?"

"They don't know they're raising cowbirds. They get tricked into doing it. And often the host's babies don't get enough food because cowbird nestlings are bigger, grow faster, and cry louder for food. Sometimes the host species' nestlings die."

"Will the vireo babies die?"

"They looked okay. Their parents are doing a good job of keeping everyone fed."

Ursa stalled getting in the car to look at the last nest. She stopped to look at flowers, asked Jo about a beetle, and pretended to be fascinated by a rock she found in the weeds. Ursa remained preoccupied with the rock in her hand while they drove to the last nest, passing Egg Man's lane on the way. They left the car, but before Ursa had time to read the flagging tape, a white Suburban with a university plate drove around the bend. From behind the wheel, white-haired Dr. Shaw Daniels waved at Jo. He parked behind her car and ducked his lanky body out the door. "Working at this late hour?"

"It isn't late," Jo said. "It's only six o'clock. I didn't expect you until closer to eight."

"The last session was canceled because of food poisoning."

"You're kidding?"

He shook his head. "It was something people ate at the reception the night before."

Jo looked through the open driver's side door at Tanner, seated in the back of the Suburban with Carly Aquino. The guilt in his returned gaze was obvious, as was his attempt to hide it behind a smarmy smile. What had Jo ever liked about him other than his pretty face? She looked away from him, at Leah Fisher in the front passenger seat. "Did any of you get sick?"

"We're all okay," Leah said.

"Fortunately, we didn't stay at the reception for long," Shaw said, "because we had dinner with John Townsend and two of his students." He kept glancing at Ursa. "And who is this?" he asked.

"Ursa lives around here. I was showing her how I monitor nests."

"Nice to meet you, Ursa," he said. "I'm Shaw. What do you have there?"

"It's a rock with pink crystals in it," Ursa said.

"Cool," Shaw said, his gaze falling to the flip-flops that dwarfed the girl's feet.

"She was barefoot," Jo said. "I loaned her those so she wouldn't hurt her feet. Are you hungry?"

"Very," Shaw said. "All we had for lunch was a few chips in the car."

"Good. Go up to the house and have a beer while I check this last nest."

"Did I hear the word *beer*?" Tanner called from inside the car.

"You did," Jo said. "Lots of it. The door to the house is unlocked."

As Shaw drove away, Jo hiked toward the bunting nest, her worries about Ursa momentarily erased by Tanner's apparent guilt. An awkward conversation was at hand, and considering what a coward Tanner was, he'd prolong the tension for as long as possible.

Fierce barks sounded down the road. Jo had never heard the half-grown dog bark like that, but it had to be him. "Damn it, the dog is going at them," she said.

"He won't hurt them," Ursa said.

"How do you know? He's defending the Kinney house like he lives there. I should never have let you bring him onto the porch."

"I'll teach him not to bark."

"You'll take him off the property . . . when you leave."

The barking hadn't stopped. Jo hurried in the direction of the last nest.

"Shaw is nice," Ursa said behind her.

"He is, but that doesn't mean he won't make you go home."

"I don't have a home here!"

Jo stopped walking and faced her. "Don't even think about telling him you're from another planet. Don't tell any of them that. Do you understand?"

6

Lightning glimmered in distant southern clouds. "I hope that's heat lightning," Jo said. "I don't want to miss another day in the field."

"It's good for you to take a break," Shaw said.

Her illness again. All four had asked her how she was feeling. And Carly and Leah had suggested she get a field assistant to help her. They wouldn't even let her put the burgers on the grill. *Sit down, Joanna. We'll cook dinner while you rest.*

"I'd better close my car windows just in case," Jo said, walking away from the fire.

"I'm going in for another beer. Anyone want one?" Tanner said behind her.

"No thanks," Shaw said.

"I'm good," Carly said.

"This is my last," Leah said.

Ursa was catching fireflies and putting them in a jar Jo had given her. When she saw Jo leave the group circled around the fire, she followed at a distance. Jo had let her eat dinner with them and listen to their conversation around the fire, but soon Jo would have to make her leave. Already she had evaded questions about why the girl was hanging around the cottage, and fifteen minutes earlier, Shaw had said, "Isn't it about time that little girl went home?"

Jo sat in the dark car in the driveway, pressed the ignition button, and closed the windows she'd left open in her hurry to rescue her visitors from Little Bear's assault. The dog had instantly calmed after Jo and Ursa arrived, but she'd had to explain that he was a stray that wouldn't leave. "Probably you fed him, which means you're stuck with him," Shaw had said critically.

If he only knew.

"Nice ride." Tanner's voice came out of the darkness.

He'd had at least six beers, enough to lubricate him for the speech Jo had expected all night. She locked the car as Tanner's handsome face emerged from shadows cast by the porch lights. "I know," Jo said. "It's the first newish car I've ever owned. But I'd truthfully feel better having my old Chevy down here. These gravel roads are beating the crap out of it."

Tanner put his hand on the shiny red hood of the Honda SUV. "It was your mom's?"

"She insisted I take it, and my brother didn't want it."

"I caught another lightning bug, Jo. I have four now," Ursa called from under the hickory tree.

"But you have to let them go soon," Jo said.

"I will," she said.

"Cute kid," Tanner said. "Won't her parents be worried she's out so late?"

"I think the home situation is a little questionable," Jo said.

"That sucks."

"Yeah."

"Jo . . ."

She crossed her arms over her chest and waited. Tanner stepped closer, his features obscured by a tree shadow, and his faceless proximity made the humid darkness feel like a church confessional.

"I'm sorry I didn't go up to Chicago to see you," he said. "But I thought . . ."

"What?"

"I thought you wouldn't want me to see you like that."

"Like what?"

"You know . . . sick. No hair and all that." When she didn't respond, he twisted his neck from side to side to crack it, his standard nervous gesture. "Was I wrong . . . ?"

"You were right. I didn't want to see anyone." If she'd learned one thing in the last two years, it was that life could be hard enough without adding petty resentments.

He took a swig of beer to wash away the last of his sin. "Did you want one?" he asked, holding the beer out. "Should I get you one?"

"No thanks."

He took another long drink from the bottle. "You look great, by the way."

"Great for a cancer survivor?"

"Just great."

"Thanks."

"Are you going to do reconstruction when you're feeling better?"

"I am feeling better."

"But probably you have to wait awhile . . . ?"

Jo took her arms off her chest. "This is how I want it. Now that I've experienced the chest freedom a guy has, I'll never go back."

He half smiled, assuming her humor came from bitterness. "I can see why you would want that after everything that happened. But at least your mom was diagnosed in time to save you." He tilted his head to one side to crack his neck. "I mean . . ."

"I know what you mean, and you're right. She even said it herself. No one gets a mammogram at age twenty-four. If she hadn't gotten sick and found out she carries the mutation, my cancer might not have been found until it was too late."

"I hope you don't mind that I know, but I heard you made them take out everything."

"They didn't take out everything. I kept my uterus. I'm pretty sure they left in most of my brain, too."

He didn't smile this time. "Maybe you should have waited to make that decision."

He was probably expressing opinions exchanged between professors and graduate students during the two years she'd been away. "My mom's mother and sister died of ovarian cancer before age forty-five," she said. "I wasn't going to sit around waiting for that time bomb to explode."

"Didn't you save the eggs or anything?"

"Why, so I can pass this misery on to a daughter?"

"I see your point. But what about the hormones?"

"What about them?"

"Doesn't having no ovaries make you go into menopause?"

He'd definitely been discussing her medical decisions. He'd probably never uttered the word *menopause* before she'd been diagnosed. "I'm on hormone replacement therapy," Jo said.

"Does that make you feel normal?"

She supposed kicking him in the nuts wouldn't appear very normal. Instead, she said, "Yeah, I feel great."

He nodded, tipped the bottle to his lips, and drained it. "You know that actress"—he tried to remember the woman's name, but his brain cells were too pickled—"she had one of those mutations, too, and she had everything taken out. She had reconstruction, and they say she has really nice . . . you know . . ."

"She has really nice tits because she's rich enough to make her body any way she wants it. And she never had cancer. She could save her nipples and any skin and tissue that wasn't at risk."

He got brave enough to look at her chest. "But don't you think someday you'll—"

"No! Get over it! If I'm happy with what I look like, you should be happy with it. Do you get that, Tanner? Is it even possible for you to see me as a whole person anymore?"

"Shit . . . Jo, I'm sorry . . ."

"Go back to Carly. And you two can quit pretending you aren't together to spare me the grief. There isn't any." She walked away into a numbing black cloud of cricket and katydid noise. It was like going under anesthesia, the darkness driving deeper and deeper the farther she walked. When she came out, she was standing next to the creek. She'd been crying.

"Jo?"

She turned around. In the shadowed moonlight, the girl looked like a changeling again, her pale face marked with the veins of forest branches.

"Are you okay?" she asked.

"Of course," Jo said.

"I think you're lying."

The sound of Little Bear lapping water from the creek filled the space between them.

"Ursa, you have to—"

"I know. I'm going," she said.

"You're going home?"

She unscrewed the lid of the jar and held the glass in the air. Her fireflies discovered their freedom one by one, an expanding constellation in the dark forest. She put the lid back and gave the jar to Jo. "Come on, Little Bear," she said.

Jo watched girl and dog walk up the slope toward the road. "Where are you going?"

"I'm going where you want me to go," she said.

7

Jo worked an exhausting fifteen hours in the Shawnee Forest the next day, as much to purge Tanner Bruce from her mind as to make up for lost time after the rainy day. Maybe she also did it to prove she wasn't sick. She monitored and searched for nests in all of her "natural edge" study sites, the most difficult to work in because they had to be far from human disturbances, and once she reached them, she often had to wade through riparian thickets of catbrier and stinging nettle.

The sun had dropped behind the treetops when she, and the variety of creatures that had attached to her, climbed into the Honda. Exercise and the green world had rejuvenated her, as they always did. Tanner and his loutish opinions were still with her but ignorable, like a malfunctioning idiot light on a car dashboard.

But she couldn't clear the little alien from her thoughts. From the moment she awoke, Jo had chastised herself for not seeing the girl to her door, though she doubted the girl had gone home. When Ursa walked away she'd said, *I'm going where you want me to go.* The more Jo tried to interpret what that meant, the more ominous it sounded. Yet she'd just stood there and watched the girl disappear into the night.

She turned onto Turkey Creek Road, certain the girl would be at Kinney Cottage waiting for her. Then she would wish the girl *had* disappeared. In the last bit of gray twilight, she pulled up the gravel driveway. She looked at the hickory in the front yard. No girl. No dog.

She dropped her gear on the screened porch and walked to the fire pit. "Ursa?" she called. The only reply was the *peent!* of a nighthawk foraging over the field behind the house.

A car was coming. No one drove that far down the road unless they were lost. A **No Outlet** sign at the start of the road prevented most people from mistaking the road for another. Jo strode out front as Egg Man's white pickup, barely recognizable in the late twilight gloom, rounded the corner. His tires crunched to a stop behind her car, and he turned off the motor. Whatever he had come to say would take some time.

Jo walked out to meet him as he stood out of the truck.

"I heard you come down the road," he said. "I've been waiting for you."

She kept distance between them. "What's up?"

He stepped closer. "I think you know what. You've dumped the alien on me."

"I didn't tell her to go to your house!"

"Why didn't you take her to the police?"

"Did you?"

He walked nearer, close enough that she scented strong cooking aromas. Whatever he'd had for dinner smelled good enough to make her hungry.

"You should get this light fixed," he said, looking up at the utility pole.

"It went out two weeks ago, and I decided I like it better dark."

"It's not better when some hooligans decide a dark house is an easier target than a lighted one."

Hooligans. Who used words like that anymore?

He rubbed his hand back and forth over one bearded cheek. "This girl is a real piece of work. You know what she's doing right now?"

"Reading *War and Peace*?"

"Then you know."

"Know what?"

"How weirdly smart she is."

"I told you that the day we talked about her."

"Yeah, but now I've seen it up close. My mother thinks she's really bright, too."

"Your mother?"

"I take care of her. She's sick."

"I'm sorry," she said, echoing what so many people had said to her. He nodded.

"Did the alien tell you her name?" Jo asked.

"She calls herself Ursa Major because that's where she's from."

"Same name she gave me. I'm thinking Ursa might be her real name."

"So do I," he said. "I looked all over the internet for a missing girl called Ursa."

Jo moved closer to him. "Did you see that Missing and Exploited Children website?"

"I did," he said.

"Did you see the picture of the shoes?"

"You saw that, too? How can that be? How is it no one misses that dead boy?"

"Sounds like you've been going through the same process I did," she said.

"At least five times I nearly called the sheriff's office. But I decided to talk to you first."

"I have no advice," she said. "Unless you're willing to lock her in a room."

"What's that supposed to mean?"

"Exactly what I said. I called the sheriff the night you and I talked. She didn't tell you about that?"

"No. What happened?"

"She ran away, like she said she would. The deputy never even saw her."

"Damn," he said. "I had a feeling that would happen if I called. What did the deputy say? Did he know of any missing kids?"

"He didn't. He acted like I was wasting his time. He didn't say he'd try to find her—even when I told him about the bruises."

His body visibly tensed. "She has bruises?"

"On her neck, arm, and leg. They're covered by her clothes."

"Jesus. Do the bruises look like they're from abuse?"

"There are finger marks in one of them."

"Did you tell the cop that?"

"I made it clear I was certain someone had hurt her. But the guy is biased against kids being taken out of their homes. He told me a story about his friend in middle school. The kid was put with abusive foster parents, and he ended up killing himself."

"He told you not to turn her in?"

"Not exactly. But he said people often take foster kids for the money. He said even if Ursa's bruises were from abuse, she would lie about how she got them. He said a foster home might be as bad as where she came from, and she would know that."

"What kind of screwed-up advice is that for a cop to give?"

"Is it?"

"You agree with him?"

"I don't know," she said. "I haven't had time to think since I talked to the guy. I had visitors yesterday . . ."

"Ursa told me."

"You know what I figured out yesterday? I don't think she's from around here."

"Strange that you say that . . . ," he said.

"Why?"

"I had the same thought today. When I showed her newborn kittens, she went nuts. She said they were a miracle. She'd obviously never seen small kittens, and country kids see lots of them."

"She had another miracle?"

"Only three to go, she says."

"Her first miracle was baby birds."

"She told me," he said.

"Like you said, a country kid would have seen baby birds at least once by her age. I think she's from a city and maybe got dumped out of a car."

"She talks like she's from around here."

"Maybe Saint Louis," Jo said.

"They don't have that much country twang over there."

"Paducah?"

"I searched every southern state that might produce that accent, even as far as Florida," he said. "She isn't listed as missing."

"If her caretakers dumped her out of a car, they obviously won't report her missing."

"Maybe she ran away," he said. "She's too smart for whatever idiots would do this to her. I never told you what she's working on."

"What?"

"She saw some books about Shakespeare on our shelves and asked if I liked him. When I told her I love Shakespeare . . ."

Jo lost his next few words while she absorbed that Egg Man loved Shakespeare.

". . . she was going to name the six kittens after people in Shakespeare's plays. She asked to use my computer to read about Shakespeare's characters so she could decide which names to use. That's what she's doing right now, studying the plays."

"She did this with me, sort of plugged in to my interest in birds—even read some of my *Ornithology* textbook. I think she does it to make people attach to her."

"Maybe that's how she survives her screwed-up family."

"They obviously aren't attached."

"No shit."

Jo leaned against the front of his truck and pressed her hand to her forehead.

"Are you okay?" he said.

"I'm too tired to deal with this right now."

"You look like you need to sit down."

She stepped away from his truck. "I put in a fifteen-hour day. What I need is a shower, dinner, and sleep."

"First, would you talk to her?"

"About what?"

He crossed his arms over his chest. "I have a confession. Ursa and I came over to look for you twice tonight."

"Why?"

"She's worried. She says you have cancer."

"God damn it! Let's just broadcast it from every cell phone tower."

He uncrossed his arms. "I didn't know that was possible."

"I don't think it is, but the graduate students and my advisor have been thorough enough."

"Are you in remission?"

"I guess that's what they call it."

"Would you let Ursa see you're okay and maybe tell her that? She's afraid you're going to die."

"We're all going to die."

"Let's do a nine-year-old version."

"Yeah. I have to talk to her anyway. I felt bad about sending her away last night."

"You had to. She said you were going to get in trouble with your advisor."

"Is there any detail of my life you two didn't discuss?"

"We never got into your choice of undergarments."

Undergarments. His mother must be influencing his vocabulary.

"I'll drive you over in my truck," he said.

"I'm a mess."

"So's my truck."

She knew nothing about Egg Man—a.k.a. Gabriel Nash—other than that a guy who loved Shakespeare should be too educated to sell eggs on a country road. She remembered his sudden display of anger after Ursa asked him if he was getting a PhD. And Jo had seen no evidence of his alleged mother. Maybe he'd killed Ursa and he was using her as bait to lure Jo into the same trap. For the hundredth time that day, Jo berated herself for letting a nine-year-old go off into the woods alone.

He saw her hesitation. "Follow me in your car, if you prefer."

"I think I will."

"You're smart to be cautious," he said.

"What does that mean?"

He considered how to answer. "If I wanted to hurt you, I've had plenty of opportunities since you've lived here."

"So have I, if I wanted to hurt you," she said, because he had no right to see a woman living alone in the woods as an invitation for violence.

He smiled slightly, a hint of white teeth in the darkness. "Usually more than one person rents the house. Why is it only you this summer?"

"It's just the way it worked out," she said.

The truth was, a graduate student who studied hill-prairie insects had planned to live in the Kinney house that summer—until he heard he would be sharing it with Jo. He used his research money to rent another house, claiming he wanted to be nearer to his study sites. But Jo suspected he didn't want to live in close confines with a woman who wasn't exactly a woman anymore. More than a few of the male graduate students had been awkward around her since she'd returned, especially the ones who used to flirt with her. Her psychologist had warned her of such reactions from men, but the injury of it couldn't be alleviated by any number of therapy sessions. Dealing with the pain was a day-by-day ordeal. Nature and her research were some of her only respites.

"That's too bad," Egg Man said. "Must be kind of lonely."

"It's not," she said. "I prefer to live alone when I'm doing research. Having people around is distracting."

He opened his truck door. "I guess that was a hint. Follow me over."

8

The furrowed lane that led onto Egg Man's property hadn't been graveled for years, and only the width of his truck kept the forest from conquering it. Jo took the road slowly, the Honda rocking and squeaking as its tires dipped into deep troughs. She heard loud woofs before Little Bear's eyes appeared, glowing in the headlights. He continued barking, running between the truck and SUV as the press of dark forest opened into a yard lit by a utility light.

Egg Man sprang from his truck and tried to shush the dog.

"I see you've inherited Little Bear as well as Big Bear," Jo said, stepping from her car.

"I told Ursa he can't stay on my property."

"Good luck with that."

"I know," he said. "I let her feed him."

"I'm seeing a pattern here."

"I had to. I didn't want him to have a hungry belly around my chickens and piglets."

"You have pigs?"

"Haven't you smelled them?"

"I wouldn't know the smell of a pig from a horse."

"Like most city folk."

City folk pricked her ears again. "Do you eat your pigs?" she asked.

"Actually, I read Shakespeare to them." He smiled at her. "Yes, I eat them. We live off the land as much as possible. I hate going into grocery stores."

"Problematic aversion."

"You have no idea," he said, but she didn't get his meaning.

He glanced at the lit windows of the cabin. "The story with Ursa is that she lives around here, but her parents have issues. That's what my mother thinks, but she's still not keen on her being here."

"Didn't Ursa tell her the alien story?"

"Yeah, but that only made my mother feel more sorry for her. She says Ursa is creating a fantasy to escape her reality."

"Which is true."

"No, it isn't," he said. "Ursa doesn't believe that crap."

"Then why does she stick to it?"

"Because she's smart."

"How is it smart to pretend she's an alien?"

"I don't know. I'm too stupid to figure it out yet."

Ursa bounded out the front door, ran across the porch, and jumped over the three steps as if she'd been doing it for years. "He found you!" She wrapped her arms around Jo's middle and laid her head on her belly. "I missed you, Jo! And guess what? I saw another miracle!"

"I heard—kittens," Jo said.

"Can she go see them?" she asked Gabe.

"We won't disturb them at night, and Jo needs to eat." He said to Jo, "We have plenty of leftovers from dinner."

"Oh . . . thanks," Jo said, "but I—"

"You'd be doing us a favor. I made too much."

"Pork chops, applesauce, green beans, and mashed potatoes," Ursa said. "Gabe grows everything at the homestead. He even makes the applesauce. There are apple trees here, Jo! I climbed them today!"

"Kittens, piglets, apple trees—talk about a kid's fantasy world," Jo said.

"She's been quite happy," he said.

"I see that."

Ursa dragged Jo by the hand up the cabin stairs beneath a wooden sign that said THE NASH FAMILY HOMESTEAD. They passed a row of rocking chairs on the covered porch and entered the house. The cabin interior was an appealing space with log walls, wood floors, a stone fireplace, and furniture made from tree timber. The home was posher than Jo would have imagined, especially considering the neglected driveway and decrepit NO TRESPASSING sign. The cabin had modern kitchen appliances and beautiful granite counters. And unlike Kinney Cottage, which was cooled with aging window air conditioners, the Nash homestead had central air.

A handsome white-haired woman, probably Gabe's grandmother, sat at the kitchen table, a cane with a four-legged bottom placed near her. "I'm Katherine Nash," she said, scrutinizing Jo with sharp azure eyes. She held out a hand that trembled from what might be Parkinson's disease.

Jo grasped her hand. "Nice to meet you. I'm Joanna Teale, but you can call me Jo."

"Ursa's been talking about you all day."

"Sorry about that," Jo said, and Katherine smiled.

Gabe was already dishing warm food from pots and pans on the stove. He set the plate on the table and pulled out a chair.

"Are you sure?" Jo said. "My boots are making a mess of your floor."

"Nonsense," Katherine said. "My husband used to say log cabins don't look authentic without some dirt on the floor."

"A philosophy that worked well for a kid who was always covered in dirt," Gabe said.

Jo wondered if he'd been raised by his grandparents. Earlier he'd said his mother was sick. Maybe she had a long-term illness, something that had incapacitated her since he was a child.

Jo sat down, cut into the tender braised meat, and swallowed a delicious bite of seasoned pork chop. "This cabin is beautiful," she told Katherine. "Was it here when you bought the property?"

"Arthur—my husband—and some of his friends built it," she said. "George Kinney, the man who owns the property you're renting, helped, too. He and my husband were great friends, you know."

"I didn't," Jo said.

"They met as undergraduate roommates at the University of Illinois. After graduate school, they ended up in Illinois again. My husband taught English literature at the University of Chicago, and I'm sure you know George is an entomologist at the University of Illinois."

"Yes," Jo said. She glanced at Gabe, noting he'd been watching her from the kitchen. Now she understood some of his mysteries. The grandfather who'd raised him was a literature professor. That explained his connection to Shakespeare and maybe the reason he'd reacted to Ursa's PhD question. Gabe self-consciously looked away from her gaze and put a plastic container into the refrigerator. "Did Dr. Kinney or your husband buy land down here first?" Jo asked Katherine.

"Arthur and I bought first. We wanted a refuge from the city, and Arthur had dreamed of building a log cabin since he was a boy. George and his wife bought the property next door when it went up for sale a few years later. George loved that he could study his aquatic insects in Turkey Creek, just steps away from his door."

"How old were your kids when you built the cabin?" Jo asked.

"When we finished it, Gabe wasn't born yet and his sister was in high school." She smiled at Jo's confusion. "I suppose you thought I was Gabe's grandmother?"

Jo was too embarrassed to admit it.

"Gabe is what they used to call a 'change-of-life' baby," Katherine said. "I had him when I was forty-six and his father was forty-eight. His sister is nineteen years older than him."

"Is your father still living?" Jo asked Gabe.

Before her son answered, Katherine said, "Arthur died two years ago."

"I'm sorry," Jo said.

"He was fit as could be," Katherine said, "but an aneurysm took him unexpectedly."

Ursa had been listening to the conversation, but she ran into another room when Jo dug into her meal. She returned with a paper in her hands. "I have three names so far," she told Gabe. "Do you want to hear them?"

"Absolutely." He sat in a chair facing her.

"One of the boy kittens has to be Hamlet."

"He may come to a sad fate," Gabe said.

"I know. I read what happened to him," Ursa said, "but Hamlet is an important person."

"He is," Gabe said. "Which one will be Hamlet?"

"The gray one, because gray is kind of a sad color."

"Makes sense," Gabe said.

"The white kitten will be Juliet from *Romeo and Juliet*. I really like that name."

"So do I," Gabe said. "But Juliet had a sad fate, too."

"Stop saying that! These are just names!"

"You're right. After all, Juliet famously asked, 'What's in a name?' What else do you have?"

"Macbeth."

"Okay, and no comments on his fate. Which kitten?"

"The black-and-white one."

"You've been busy. That covers three of Shakespeare's best plays."

"I looked that up—which plays are most important. Next is *Julius Caesar*. But don't you think 'Julius' will be too much like 'Juliet'?"

"You could call him Caesar."

"Maybe. But first I have to read about him so I know which kitten matches the name."

"It's not good . . . fate-wise, I mean."

Ursa pressed her lips in exasperation, and Gabe swiped his hand over a smile.

Jo loved it. They were already like old friends, playing off each other's humor.

"Maybe you should move on to the comedies," Gabe said.

"She should move on home," Katherine said. "Will you take her or will Jo?"

Gabe glanced nervously at Jo. "We hadn't discussed that yet."

"Her parents must be frantic by now," his mother said.

"They aren't," Ursa said. "They're happy I'm here because I'm getting my PhD."

Katherine's sharp blue eyes pinned her son.

"I know, I know," he said. "Let me talk to Jo about it."

"The dinner was delicious. Thank you," Jo said, rising from her chair. Gabe gestured her toward the front door, and when Ursa tried to follow, he said, "Will you do me a favor? Put Jo's dishes in the sink and rinse them."

"You're just saying that so you can talk about me," Ursa said.

"I'm saying it because I hate doing dishes. Go on."

He led Jo out the front door and down the porch steps for further privacy. "She can't stay here. My mother doesn't know she slept here last night."

"How could she not know?"

"I didn't know either. When I went to milk the cow, the dog came barking at me from the barn."

"She slept in the barn?"

"I guess so."

"Poor kid. She's been sleeping in Kinney's shed."

"I have a feeling she's been through worse," he said.

"Thank you for helping her. She looks like a different girl tonight."

"Yeah, but she can't stay. My mother will make me turn her in if she finds out we don't know where she lives."

"I guess we have to figure out how to do that. But I can't take time off tomorrow. I have too many nests that need monitoring."

"Well, don't expect me to do it. I'm not locking her up like an animal."

"I know. It's horrible to imagine, isn't it?"

He looked down at Little Bear, as tame as Jo had seen him, licking at the pork chop scent on her fingers. "What if we wait?" he said.

"Wait for what?"

"Don't you think it's odd that she set this deadline with the five miracles? Why do that?"

"To stall, of course."

"But maybe there's a reason. Maybe she's waiting for someone she trusts to come home or something like that."

"Haven't we established she isn't from around here?"

"She could have moved here in the last week." He glanced at the door to make sure Ursa wasn't listening. "Maybe a grandmother takes care of her and she's in the hospital. Maybe when her grandmother got sick she had to come here to live with an abusive relative and she ran away."

"I think up stories like that, too."

"It fits the situation."

"What if the grandmother never gets better?" Jo said.

"What if she does and we got the poor kid put in foster care?"

"How long would we wait for the theoretical grandmother to reappear?"

"I'm just saying we should think about it for a few days. Maybe she'll learn to trust us and tell us the truth."

Ursa stuck her head out the front door. "Are you done talking about me?"

"Nope. Get back inside," he said.

72

The door shut.

"I think we could get in trouble for waiting," Jo said.

"No one's reported her missing. No one gives a crap about her, not even that cop you talked to. And like he said, she could get stuck in a shitty foster home, and I see no reason to rush that when we might find a better solution."

"If we turn her in, we could make sure where she goes isn't shitty."

"How?"

She had no answer.

"If you want to turn her in, do it," he said.

"I don't."

"Then take her back to Kinney's."

"And leave her alone when I go to work in the morning?"

"Drop her at my road as you drive by. I'll be doing morning animal care."

"That's early."

"I know. I hear you drive by. She'll deal with it."

"How will you explain her to your mother?"

"She's a local kid who likes hanging out at our farm."

"I don't feel right doing this," she said.

"Don't you feel worse about locking her in a closet and calling the cops on her?"

"Damn it, I do."

9

For four days Jo and Gabe surreptitiously exchanged Ursa. Sometimes it felt like she and Gabe were a divorced couple passing a child between their homes. But more often it was like some sort of illegal trade because they handed Ursa off in the dark hours of predawn and twilight. Jo checked missing children websites every night when she got home, expecting to see Ursa's haunting brown eyes with every scroll of her finger. But after more than a week, no one had reported her missing.

On the third day, Gabe took Ursa to a yard sale to buy clothing, which resulted in a wardrobe heavily biased toward the color purple and screen prints of big-eyed animals. By the fourth day—dressed in decent clothing, well fed, and playing outdoors for long hours—Ursa didn't look like a changeling anymore. The dark circles under her eyes disappeared, her skin turned a wholesome pink, and she'd gained a few pounds.

Each night after her shower, Ursa told Jo about the fun things she'd done at the homestead, and sometimes Jo was a little jealous of how much Ursa loved being with Gabriel in Wonderland. That was when it felt like a divorce, though she barely knew Gabe.

The tension between the two "parents" became more real on the fifth night when Ursa said, "Guess what Gabe let me do today?"

"Did you milk the cow?"

"I already do that."

"Ride a baby unicorn?"

"I wish! But shooting his guns was almost that fun."

Jo set down her fork.

"I hit close to the middle of the target three times!"

Jo pushed out her chair. "Wait here. I'll be back in a few minutes." She grabbed her keys and slipped on sandals.

"Where are you going?"

"To talk to Gabe."

"Why are you mad?"

"What gives you that idea?"

"Your eyes get like thunder."

"I'm not mad at you. Stay here."

Jo put Little Bear on the porch so he wouldn't follow. She cursed Egg Man every time her mother's precious Honda scraped bottom on his neglected road.

Gabe opened the door wearing a pink apron, and if she hadn't been angry she might have laughed at the muscular bearded guy in Martha Stewart mode. "You should fix that Grand Canyon you call a road," she said.

"You came over to tell me that?" he said.

"No."

"Is Ursa okay?"

"She's great," Jo said, "and I'd like her to stay that way, so please keep your guns away from her from now on."

"Who is it?" his mother called from inside the cabin.

"It's Jo. She needs to borrow some sugar. Wait here," he said to Jo. He returned in less than a minute, minus the apron, with a baggie of sugar in his hand. "You're one of those gun-control militants?" he asked, grinning through his beard.

"I'm against putting a gun in the hands of a little girl who can't possibly understand the danger of firearms."

"She wore ear and eye protection, and I taught her every safety rule."

"She's a kid, and kids do unexpected things. Sometimes they sneak into their dad's gun cabinet and shoot their baby brother."

"She's smarter than that. And who knows where she'll end up? Some day she may need the skill."

"To take out her pesky foster parents?"

"I believe in being prepared," he said.

"Right, for the apocalypse."

"Maybe."

"You're one of those? You're a survivalist nut? How does a guy who reads Shakespeare dumb down his brain enough for that?"

"So all gun owners are dumb people who don't read Shakespeare? Is that really going to be your position?"

"I'm too tired for this. Just keep the guns locked up and away from Ursa." She started down the stairs but went back and plucked the sugar out of his hand. "I actually need this for my coffee. I'm out."

Every doubt she'd had about letting Ursa stay with them resurfaced during her drive back to the cottage, especially her reservations about Egg Man. She truthfully knew nothing about the man.

Ursa was waiting for her return outside on the walkway. "Did you yell at Gabe?" she asked.

"Of course not," Jo said.

"Will he still let me come over?"

She was more distressed by the discord than expected. Jo crouched in front of her and held her hands. "Everything is okay. I only had a little disagreement with Gabe."

"About shooting the guns?" she asked.

"Yes. My parents raised me different than his did. I never saw guns as *fun*. I was taught that their only purpose is to kill."

"We only shot targets."

"And why do people use those targets? So they can learn how to aim the bullet at a heart or a brain. He was teaching you how to kill somebody."

"I didn't think of it like that."

"Well, that's what it's all about, that or killing a deer, and I don't see you doing that."

"I would never kill a deer!"

"Good. No more guns, okay?"

"Okay."

Jo rewarmed her plate of food in the microwave, but just as she started eating, Little Bear began barking on the porch. "Now what?" She went to the porch and watched Gabe's truck squeak to a halt behind her car. "I don't believe this," she said. "You drove over here to continue the argument?"

"I wasn't arguing," he said.

"You defended what you did."

"That's not exactly arguing."

"I'd like to finish my dinner."

"You should," he said, ambling up the walkway.

"Why are you here?"

"To make peace. Nothing like stars to show us our little arguments are meaningless. I brought my telescope."

"The Pinwheel Galaxy!" Ursa said behind Jo. "He promised! He said one night he would show it to us!"

"And this is a perfect night," Gabe said. "No moon, clear atmosphere, your blacked-out utility light inviting burglars to your gun-less home . . ."

She tried to make a peeved face, but his smile bested it.

"Finish your dinner while I get ready," he said. "Want to learn how to set up a telescope?" he asked Ursa.

"Yes!"

Jo held the screen door open as she shot through it. "This is the only way you're allowed to look down a barrel with Gabe. Do you understand?"

"Yes," Ursa said, and Gabe saluted.

After Jo finished eating and cleaned the dishes, she joined them at the edge of the field and discovered Gabe's telescope was much fancier than she'd expected. It had belonged to his father, an astronomy enthusiast who'd taught his children how to find objects in the night sky. Gabe had also brought binoculars, and he showed Ursa how to locate the Pinwheel Galaxy using the stars of the Big Dipper. Jo listened from a lawn chair, too tired from her long day in the field to work at finding a blurry smear of a galaxy.

Even with the impressive scope, locating the Pinwheel took a while because it had something Gabe called "low surface brightness." This meant nothing to Jo other than that she might fall asleep in her chair before he found it.

"Okay, here it is," he said, "Messier 101, also known as the Pinwheel Galaxy."

Ursa stood on a crate he'd brought and looked into the eyepiece. "I see it!" She fell silent as she studied the galaxy. "Do you know what it looks like, Jo?"

"A pinwheel?"

"It looks like an indigo bunting nest. And the white stars are the eggs."

"I have to see this." Jo got off the chair and looked in the telescope. Ursa was right. The ethereal swirl was a celestial nest filled with white star eggs. "Okay, this is the coolest thing I ever saw. It's like an indigo bunting nest viewed from above. They often have that messy shape around the edges."

Gabe took another turn looking. "I see it. And the nest's center spirals down into infinity. I like that so much better than a pinwheel. The Infinite Nest. From now on, that's how I'll see it."

"That's where I live," Ursa said. "I live in the Infinite Nest."

"Lucky girl," Jo said, ruffling her hair with her fingers.

Ursa bounced manically like she was about to rocket into the stars. "Can I toast marshmallows?"

"Ursa . . . I'm too tired to light a fire."

"I will," Gabe said. "Get the marshmallows, Lady of the Nest."

Ursa ran to the back door.

"Is that okay?" he asked.

"I've been up since four thirty," Jo said. Ursa had, too, but Gabe's unexpected visit had energized her.

"Sit down and rest," Gabe said. "I'll monitor the marshmallow toasting with better judgment than I had earlier today." He started throwing twigs into the fire pit. "That was an apology, by the way."

"Okay." She returned to her lawn chair. "And I apologize for saying you're a dumb Shakespeare reader."

"I'm a Shakespeare reader who sells eggs on the road—which amounts to about the same." He studied her face. "You must wonder why I sell eggs and don't have a regular job."

"That's none of my business," she said, though she had often pondered that very question.

"I sell eggs because my hens produce far more than I can use." He looked away from her and took more sticks out of the woodpile. "But the egg stand is also therapy."

"How is it therapy?"

He looked at her again. "For social anxiety, depression, and a touch of agoraphobia."

She sat up in her chair to see how serious he was.

"Don't worry, I'm okay with Ursa. I wouldn't hurt her or anything."

Ursa ran outside and plopped the bag of marshmallows on a lawn chair.

"Would you please bring a lighter?" Gabe said.

She ran back to the house.

"Why would I think you'd hurt Ursa just because you have depression?" Jo said.

He shrugged. "Lots of people don't understand mental illness."

"Where's the lighter, Jo?" Ursa called from the back door.

"The drawer by the toaster."

"It's not there."

"That means Shaw and company put it in the wrong place. You'll have to look around." She turned back to Gabe. "Does medication help?" she asked.

"I blew off the doctors when they tried to put me on drugs."

"When was that?"

"A few years ago. When I was a sophomore at U of C, I had what my parents quaintly called a 'nervous breakdown.' I haven't gotten my shit together since."

"University of Chicago? Where your father taught?"

"Yeah, major embarrassment, right? And all his dreams for his only son down the outhouse hole." He cracked a branch over his knee and tossed the pieces into the fire pit.

"Gabe, I'm sorry."

"Why? It's not like it's anyone's fault. You can't pick your genetics."

"Tell me about it. My breast cancer was caused by the BRCA1 mutation, if you know what that means."

"Shit, yeah, I do."

Ursa returned with the lighter. "You know where they put it? In your desk drawer."

"Weird," Jo said. "I hope that wasn't a subtle judgment about my research."

Gabe ignited a flame on the lighter and grinned. "I promise I won't go near your data."

"You better not," Jo said.

As he lit the twigs in the fire pit, Ursa went off in search of a marshmallow stick.

"I shouldn't have brought up the cancer," Jo said. "I didn't mean to minimize what you told me."

"Go ahead, minimize it—if only."

"You never seem anxious to me. You're more sociable than lots of people I know."

"Yeah? I guess the egg stand has helped. But take me out of my realm and kaplooey."

"Is that why you hate the grocery store?"

He nodded. "If the line is long, sometimes I have to leave."

"Why?"

"The horrific crush of humanity on my soul. Haven't you ever felt it?"

"I think I have—in Walmart."

"Yes! That place is the worst!"

Ursa returned with a stick and poked it into three marshmallows.

"Nice," Gabe said. "One for me, one for Jo, and another for me."

"All for me!" Ursa said.

Jo fell asleep watching them roast marshmallows, thinking how cute they were together. She woke to Gabe's fingers brushing her cheek. "There was a mosquito on you," he said.

"I've probably fed the whole forest."

"You haven't. I've been keeping watch."

She tried to shake off her drowsiness. "On me?"

"On you." He was looking at her as if he might kiss her, and the rush of adrenaline straight from sleep made her feel strange. Dizzy, almost. Her heart jumped against the bones of her chest, as if it were trying to escape.

She sat up to see if Ursa had seen him touch her. She was asleep in a lawn chair on the other side of the fire, melted marshmallow stuck to her chin.

Jo stood shakily. "Ursa has to go to bed. She gets up early."

"I know," he said, rising next to her. "I wanted to take her but didn't know where. Does she sleep in your bed or on the couch?"

"The couch."

He lifted her out of the chair. "Gabe?" Ursa mumbled.

"Don't wake up," he said. "I'll take you to bed."

After they disappeared into the house, Jo watered down the fire.

"I could have done that," Gabe said from the kitchen door. He came outside, took the hose from her hand, and coiled it over the spigot.

"Where is the telescope?" she asked.

"I put it away."

"How long was I asleep?"

"About fifteen degrees of star movement." He stood close to her, his face lit by the fluorescent stove light inside the house. She saw what he wanted. He wanted to sleep with her.

The stuttering beat in her chest returned. Was it hormonal, something to do with the surgeries? Why did a man coming on to her—a kindhearted, good-looking one, at that—make her body react like she was confronting a pissed-off grizzly?

She tried to remember how she used to respond when a guy she was attracted to came on too strong or too fast. She'd have made a joke to tone things down a little. The humor would have come easily because she'd be confident and relaxed. And probably a little turned on by his interest. But Jo couldn't find her, that self-possessed woman she used to be, and the discovery of her absence made her shudder like a fever had come over her. She had to hug her arms around her body to try to make it stop.

She had no idea what her terror looked like to Gabe. Whatever he saw, he backed away, his eyes alight with fluorescent panic.

"I think . . . you'd better go," she said.

He vanished so fast she might have dreamed he'd been right there in front of her if she didn't hear the rumble of his pickup fading into the distance.

10

Jo waited until five to wake Ursa because she'd been up late. "Can I go with you today?" Ursa asked while they ate bowls of Raisin Bran.

"Why?"

"I want to see what you do."

"You saw."

"I want to see those places way in the forest. Are you going there today?"

"I am."

"Please!"

"It wouldn't be as fun as going to Gabe's farm."

"Yes it would."

"If you hate it, I can't come back. You'll be stuck out there with me."

"I promise I won't hate it."

Jo didn't see any harm in it, and having someone to talk to for a change might be enjoyable. "We have to tell Gabe, because he's expecting you."

"We will," Ursa said.

"I don't have his cell phone number."

"We have to go there to tell him. I don't even know if he has a phone."

Jo made two sandwiches and packed extra water and snacks. She had Ursa change into long pants and a long-sleeved T-shirt Gabe had bought her at the yard sale. After Ursa put on her beloved purple gym shoes, Jo showed her how to tuck her pants into her socks and her shirt into her pants to prevent ticks from crawling inside her clothing.

Before they locked the house, Ursa poured a big bowl of dog food. Jo had given in to buying it when she agreed to "wait awhile" with Ursa. Each morning they fed the dog at the rear door to distract him while they made a quick getaway down Turkey Creek Road.

Jo stopped the Honda at Gabe's potholed lane, nocturnal insects swooping in the beams of the car's headlights. "I hate this road. It tears up my car."

Ursa unbuckled. "Then wait here. You wouldn't know how to find him anyway." She jumped out and disappeared at a run down the dark driveway. Minutes later, she returned breathless and got in the car.

"What did he say?"

"He said okay."

"That's all?"

"He was busy."

"Doing what?"

"Fixing the hog pen gate. But he might be mad," she added, buckling her seat belt.

"Why do you say that?"

"Usually he's happy when he sees me in the morning, but he wasn't. Do you think he wanted me to stay with him instead of go with you?"

"I'm sure he's just busy with the gate."

There was more to it than that. Now rested and thinking clearly, Jo replayed the previous night's events in her mind and decided she'd misinterpreted Gabe's behavior. If he had social anxiety, there was no way he'd wanted to sleep with a woman he hardly knew. He probably hadn't almost kissed her either. Jo had panicked, maybe because she'd felt a connection with him—her first since her surgeries. She'd given the poor guy mixed signals, and even worse, he might think she'd rejected him because of what he'd confessed about his depression. If she'd opened up to a man about her cancer and he suddenly rebuffed her, she'd have been as hurt.

"Shit," Jo said under her breath.

"What's wrong?" Ursa said.

"Nothing."

They began at North Fork Creek, the most distant of her "natural edge" study sites. As always, Ursa was unfazed by the hardships of a new environment. No matter how dense, wet, or prickly the creek-side vegetation, she never complained. Even pesky mosquitoes and ticks crawling up her clothes didn't bother her.

Jo explained their three goals: monitoring the nests she'd already found, finding new nests, and downloading data from nest cameras onto her laptop. She showed Ursa how to search for nests by watching the birds' movements and listening for alarm calls, which might mean they were protecting a nearby nest. Ursa immediately recognized how alarm calls were different from other bird sounds, and she often went off on her own to investigate when she heard one.

After North Fork, they went to the Jessie Branch study site, and after that, to Summers Creek, the prettiest of Jo's study sites. Ursa didn't find a new nest all day, but she saw many eggs and baby birds. She also spotted a doe and her fawn, caught a leopard frog, watched a humming-bird drink nectar from cardinal flowers, and took a swim with minnows in a creek pool to cool off.

The pool was Jo's favorite resting point. While Ursa played in the water, Jo turned on her cell phone and discovered three messages from Tabby. Tabby's first text at nine thirty in the morning said, OMG, the peony and iris house is for rent.

The second text had come at one fifteen. I talked to owner. Lots of interest. Will go fast.

The third text—sent a minute later—said, Answer damn you! And get your ass up here!

Jo and Tabby had been apartment-mates for years, but when Jo returned to graduate school after her cancer treatment, they decided they would look for a rental house, a place with actual trees around it. The peony and iris house was on a jogging route they'd been running in Urbana since their junior year of undergrad. It was a little white clapboard house with a porch, and the first time they saw it, a profusion of peonies and irises colored the front yard. The house was ideally located in the quaint neighborhood just east of campus known as the "state streets."

Can you grab it? Jo sent.

The text went through after about twenty seconds. Tabby was on phone sentry. She responded immediately. She says she needs us both to sign. In hurry to rent. Someone in Maine is sick and she's going up there.

Jo knew that sudden upheaval all too well.

Tabby texted, Please come! I love this house! U have to see inside! And the backyard OMG!

While she had some reception, Jo checked the weather for the next day: 70 percent chance of rain. She would probably have a short field day anyway.

I'll be there around noon tomorrow. Ask her to hold it.

Tabby texted back. Will try. Meet at house. Love U! She sent an emoji of a monkey with its hand on its mouth and a pair of lips, her "monkey-blown" kiss.

Jo put the phone in her backpack and watched Ursa try to catch fish with her hands. "You need a net," she called to her.

"Do you have one?"

"I saw one at Kinney Cottage. Maybe one day we can take it down to Turkey Creek and see what we find."

"I want to! There's a really pretty one in here, but I can't get close enough to see him."

"You'd better come out now. I need you to drip dry before we go back to the car."

Ursa waded out of the chest-deep water and crossed the dry streambed to the big mossy rocks where they'd eaten lunch. She had a smudge of mud across her nose and cheek. Just like Jo at that age, a little mud hen, as her father used to call her.

"Where are we going now?" Ursa asked.

"Sadly, the best part is over. Now we'll monitor and look for nests next to a cornfield until it gets dark."

"That will be fun, too."

"It will be hot. Good thing you cooled off."

"Why don't you?"

"Being wet isn't good for handling data sheets."

Ursa picked up a rock that caught her attention.

"Ursa . . . tomorrow I have to go up to where I live."

She stopped rock hunting and looked at her. "The place called Champaign-Urbana?"

"Yes."

"Can I come with you?"

Taking someone else's kid on a trip was wrong on many levels. But Ursa couldn't stay with Gabe because Jo might get home past the time she was allowed to stay at his farm. Gabe's mother was already asking worrisome questions about Ursa and why she was at their farm every day.

"Can I?"

"Are you sure you want to?" Jo asked.

"Yes!"

"It will be boring. I'm going to look at a house."

"Why?"

"Because I'm probably going to rent it. My friend and I want to move out of our apartment when our lease runs out in August."

"It's a real house?"

"It is, and that's what's so great about it. It even has a porch swing."

Ursa turned away and threw the rocks she'd found into the pool. "I don't want you to go live in that house."

"I know you don't, but I have to leave when I'm done with my fieldwork. That's why you need to tell me why you left your home. We have to figure out what to do before I go."

Ursa faced her. "I told you why I left my home."

"I wish you would trust me."

"I do, but that doesn't change anything."

"What doesn't it change? Tell me."

"I'll probably be gone by the time you leave anyway. I'll have seen five miracles by then."

11

Jo parked the Honda in the oak shade behind Tabby's red VW Bug. Tabby climbed out of the VW dressed in purple Dr. Martens boots, jean cutoffs, and an orange University of Illinois T-shirt that belonged to Jo. Though she wore her amethyst nose stud and her brown hair was streaked with blue and purple, Jo had rarely seen her dressed so conservatively. She met Tabby on the street halfway between their cars and gave her a hug.

"You look great—all tan and shit," Tabby said. "But more importantly, you look conventional. Maybe this lady will want to rent to us when she sees you."

"Is that why you're wearing my T-shirt?"

"I'm showing my school spirit. The lady's father was a professor here."

"It's a fail on you."

"Only because you know I don't do rah-rah." She looked at Jo's windshield. "Were you aware that there's a little girl in your car?"

"I am aware."

Tabby stared at Ursa. "Oh my god . . ." She turned back to Jo. "Is this the girl, the one with bruises who wouldn't go home?"

"Yes. Keep your voice down."

"I thought you said she ran away?" Tabby whispered.

"Obviously, she came back."

"Why the hell is she with you?"

"It's complicated."

"What does that mean?"

"What I said."

Tabby glanced at Ursa again. "So this is what it's like in Banjo Land? You just randomly collect kids?"

"Stop calling it that. Banjo Land is way south of Illinois."

"You have to call the cops!" she whispered.

"I told you I did already! She'll just run again. I'm trying to figure out what to do."

"You have enough on your plate!"

"I know, but I had to do something. Be nice to her." Jo walked around the front of the car to the passenger door. Normally Ursa would have gotten out by then, but she'd been reticent all morning, probably because seeing the house scared her about her future. Jo opened the door. "Ursa, this is Tabby. Tabby, meet my friend Ursa."

"Come out of there, little person with a big name," Tabby said, reaching inside the car and hauling out Ursa. "You're so lucky to be named after a bear!"

"I know," Ursa said. "You're lucky to be named after a cat. Gabe has a tabby kitten I call Caesar."

"How cool, but I'm not named after a cat. My completely insane mother named me after a TV witch."

"Really?"

"For real, and that's why if anyone calls me by my real name"— she leaned down and whispered "Tabitha" in Ursa's ear—"I will punch them in the nose."

Ursa smiled for the first time that day.

"She means that," Jo said. She looked at the house, as enchanting as ever. "How much? You still haven't told me."

"The rent is only a little high," Tabby evaded, "especially considering we don't have to buy furniture. But she wants rent now because she's leaving."

"Now? We'd be paying for two places until August."

Tabby dropped to her knees on the sidewalk and held her hands in a prayer gesture toward Jo. "Please, please, please use some of that wonderful money you inherited to help us get this house. I'm begging you!"

Ursa had probably never seen an adult act so goofy, but she loved it. Her left cheek was dimpled in a big grin.

"Get up, you dope," Jo said.

"Please?"

"Let me look at the house and talk to the lady."

Tabby sprang to her feet. "It's our dream house! How often did we wish we lived here when we jogged past it?"

Jo walked to the front of the little house and looked up the walkway lined with a rainbow of bearded irises. "Imagine us drinking wine and pondering mysteries of the universe on that porch swing," Tabby said.

"Will we be able to afford wine?" Jo said.

"If we correctly prioritize our grocery list."

Frances Ivey, the retired physical therapist who owned the house, greeted them at the door, casting a wary stare on Ursa. "Who is this?" she asked.

"Jo is babysitting her today," Tabby said.

"Good," Ms. Ivey said. "No kids. No dogs. No smoking."

"But cats are okay," Tabby said. "Ms. Ivey has two."

Ursa squatted down to pet the calico weaving between their legs.

"I hope neither of you are allergic?" Ms. Ivey said.

"That would be a bummer for a veterinary student," Tabby said.

"It would," Ms. Ivey said with a hint of a smile. "Of course, I'll take my cats with me to Maine." She closed the front door behind them. "Tabby told me you're doing your PhD research down in the Shawnee Forest," she said to Jo. "And you study birds?"

"Yes, bird ecology and conservation."

"I like birds. I have several feeders out back. If you decide to rent, I'd appreciate it if you kept them filled. The birds have gotten used to me feeding them all these years."

"I'd love to feed them. Having birds to watch would be great after apartment living."

Ms. Ivey took Jo on a tour of the house. Up a wooden stairway with baluster handrails, three bedrooms, one small and two tiny, shared a full bath with antique tile and a claw-foot bathtub. Downstairs, the living room had a working fireplace with a gorgeous old oak mantel. Next to it was a dining room that had been converted to a reading room, and a kitchen with a breakfast nook. The downstairs half bath was as quaint as the bathroom upstairs. The rugs and furniture were simple, giving emphasis to the early nineteenth-century charm of carved woodwork, burnished oak floors, and stained-glass window transoms.

A wooden deck beyond the kitchen french doors overlooked a small backyard, a private garden of cottage-style flower beds, redbud trees, and forsythia and rhododendron bushes. A sizeable river birch shaded the western side of the garden and a bench surrounded by ferns and blooming hostas and astilbes. A house wren sang its burbling song near its nest box and a variety of bird feeders.

"I love the natural look of your garden," Jo said.

"Thank you," Ms. Ivey said. "Do you know how to take care of flowers?"

"I do. My mom had a big garden."

"I didn't grow up with a garden, but I love flowers," Tabby said. "That's why your house was one of the best on our jogging route."

"Let's go inside and look at the lease," Ms. Ivey said.

"You're going to let us rent it?" Tabby said.

"If you agree to the terms."

"We'll agree to anything," Tabby said. "I'll sign over my firstborn."

Ms. Ivey smiled. "I'm glad you love it that much."

Ms. Ivey served iced tea while they talked about the lease in the living room. She gave Ursa milk and cookies at the kitchen table. She also gave her crayons and paper, probably too childish for her, but Ursa obediently drew pictures while they talked business in the other room.

They soon discovered they shared many more interests than flowers, birds, and cats, and Frances, as she insisted they call her, eventually trusted them enough to tell them why she was leaving her beloved house. Her former partner, Nancy, who'd moved away after they split two years earlier, had been in a devastating car wreck and had no one to help her. Nancy had a shattered arm and leg, and the foot on her other leg had been amputated. Frances needed to leave immediately. She would stay in Maine for at least one school year to keep the lease simple.

Though the rent was high and Jo hated to pay for two houses until August, she signed the lease and paid the portion Tabby couldn't afford. As Tabby had said, why not use some of the money she'd inherited? Her mother would have loved the house. Every time Jo sat in the garden, she would feel connected to her.

Tabby wanted to go out for pizza to celebrate after they signed the lease. Jo followed her to the restaurant, and as she pulled into the space next to her, Tabby climbed out of her VW and peeled off her shirt in the busy parking lot.

"A little exhibitionist, don't you think?" Jo said.

"Who cares?" Tabby said. "And no way I'll be seen in public wearing that hideous shirt."

"Gee, thanks."

"Right, like you're so emotionally involved with a T-shirt." She pulled a tee with a Rolling Stones tongue over her black lace bra.

Ursa's dimple marked her grin again. She took the crayons Frances had given her into the restaurant so she could finish a drawing. They ordered slices, and Tabby got a beer. Jo had water, and she let Ursa have a Sprite. When the drinks arrived, Tabby held up her beer for a toast. "To our awesomest house." Jo and Ursa tapped their glasses to hers.

"Don't you think it has to be fate that this happened?" Tabby said. "I mean, how weird that we loved that house so much and now we're going to *live* in it!"

"I made it happen," Ursa said.

"How'd you make it happen?" Tabby said.

"I'm from another planet. My people can make good things happen."

"Really?" Tabby said.

"She likes to pretend," Jo said.

"It's not pretend," Ursa said. "And the proof is that house."

"How do your people make things happen?" Tabby asked.

"It's hard to explain," Ursa said. "When we find Earth people we like, good things all of a sudden start to happen for them. It's how we reward them for being nice to us."

"But that means you made Nancy get in a car wreck," Tabby said.

"I didn't want that," Ursa said, "but sometimes bad things happen to make good things happen."

"You know what I hope happens?" Tabby said. "I hope Nancy realizes she still loves Frances, because Frances is obviously still shitloads in love with her."

"Maybe that will happen—because I like Frances," Ursa said. "Are Frances and Nancy lesbians?"

Tabby grinned. "Yeah, they're lesbians. You cool with that?"

"I support gay rights," Ursa said.

"Wow," Tabby said to Jo, "and from Banjo Land, no less."

"I'm from Hetrayeh," Ursa said.

"Is that your planet?" Tabby asked.

Ursa nodded. "It's in the Infinite Nest Galaxy."

"Whatever that is," Tabby said. "How do you know about gay rights if you're an alien?"

"I saw it on the internet at Gabe's house. I'm supposed to learn about Earth, kind of like getting a PhD."

"Awesome," Tabby said. "Who's this Gabe you keep mentioning?"

"He owns the property next to my rental house," Jo said.

"*This* is Gabe," Ursa said, sliding a paper out from under her drawing of a house.

Tabby studied the crayon drawing of a bearded man with blue eyes. "This is good, Ursa. How old are you?"

"My age wouldn't make sense to Earth people," she said.

Tabby looked at Jo. Jo shrugged.

After they ate, Tabby drank another beer and they discussed their move to the rental house. Ursa worked on her second drawing, a front view of Frances Ivey's house. When she went to the bathroom, Tabby said, "Tell me more about this kid."

"I know about as much as you do."

"Do you have any idea where she lives?"

"I don't." Jo watched Ursa walk into the bathroom on the other side of the restaurant. "And she hasn't been reported missing. I check the internet almost every day."

Tabby leaned across the table, whispering, "You shouldn't have brought her up here. What if something happened to her while she was with you?"

"I didn't want to leave her alone all day."

"You could get in big trouble, Jo!"

"Do you think I can't see what a mess it is? But I don't know what to do other than literally tie her up and drag her to the sheriff. And then she goes back to the people who hurt her."

"Shit."

"I'm hoping it'll work itself out somehow."

Tabby swallowed a swig of beer. "Is she . . . normal, do you think?"

"As normal as she can be under the circumstances."

"But does she actually believe she's an alien?"

"I don't think so."

Tabby picked up Ursa's drawing of the house. "There's something odd about this."

"About what?"

"Look at the way she drew depth and dimension in this picture. And she saw the house from the outside for maybe a few minutes, but she got all these details. She even remembered the design in the stained glass above the front windows."

"She's really bright."

"How does that Gabe guy figure in?"

"She likes to hang out at his farm."

"He's okay with that?"

"It's a village-raises-the-kid kind of thing."

"You know the guy? Are you sure he's not a weirdo?"

"He seems okay."

"Seems?"

"His dad taught literature at the University of Chicago. He went there for a while, too."

"He could still be a creeper."

"Ursa would tell me."

"Since when is Banjo Land inhabited by literature professors?"

"Since before you became a bigot."

"I'm not a bigot!"

"If you believe everyone who lives in rural America is a backward hick, you're a bigot."

"Okay, so maybe they *all* aren't." She picked up the drawing of Gabe. "Maybe this guy isn't, even though he uses his beard to clean grits off his plate."

"He reads Shakespeare."

"No shit?"

"All his barn kittens are named after Shakespearean characters."

Tabby burst into laughter.

"Seriously."

She laughed harder, wiping at tears.

Ursa nearly ran back to the table. "What's so funny?"

"Shakespeare," Tabby said.

"Not usually," Ursa said. "Most of his characters have sad fates."

"Oh my god!" Tabby said. "Even she reads Shakespeare! I take it all back about Banjo Land!"

"What is Banjo Land?" Ursa asked.

"It's where purple shoes are harvested." Tabby pushed her purple boot out from under the table and wedged it next to Ursa's purple gym shoes. "We have the same color taste in footwear."

"Purple is my favorite color," Ursa said.

"I see that," Tabby said, noting her lavender puppy shirt and purple shorts. She looked at Jo. "She has to hear it."

"No," Jo said.

"Hear what?" Ursa said.

"You see that thing over there, little alien?" Tabby said.

"What thing?" Ursa said.

"That machine with the colored lights."

"What about it?" Ursa said.

"It's called a jukebox, and it plays music from all of human history, all the way back to the original version of 'Walk Like an Egyptian.'"

Ursa stared at the jukebox.

"The most awesome song ever written is in there," Tabby said.

"Please don't," Jo said.

"What song?" Ursa said.

"'The Purple People Eater.' Have you ever heard it?"

"No," Ursa said.

"It's about an alien," Tabby said.

"For real?"

"For real," Tabby said, digging in her wallet.

"This is lunch," Jo said.

"What about it?"

"Only drunk people think this is funny."

"Quit being so uptight." Tabby took Ursa's hand and led her to the jukebox. After explaining how it worked, she let Ursa put the money in the machine and select the song. When the absurd song came on, Tabby started singing and dancing in front of everybody. She'd been doing that since she'd discovered the song their sophomore year, but usually she had more than two beers in her. The diners laughed when she took Ursa's hand and showed her how to dance. "Look at the alien go!" Tabby called to Jo. "Jojo, get over here!"

"Come dance with us!" Ursa shouted.

Everyone turned expectant smiles on Jo, which made remaining in her seat more humiliating than dancing. She took Ursa's other hand and tried to look like she was dancing. Ursa had no idea how to dance either, but she didn't care. She laughed and jumped and shimmied, as radiant as Jo had ever seen her, as if starlight shined straight from her Hetrayen soul.

12

At the start of the trip back to Southern Illinois, Ursa used her third and last piece of paper to draw a picture of Tabby. An hour later, she was still working on the portrait.

"How can you draw in a moving car without getting carsick?" Jo asked.

"I'm used to doing things at star speed," Ursa said.

"You mean light speed?"

"We call it star speed. It's different from light speed."

"You love drawing, don't you?"

"Yes."

"Maybe I'll get you colored pencils. Those crayons are too thick to get good detail."

"I know," Ursa said. "I made the purple jewel in her nose too big."

"Art is supposed to represent how you see the world, not exactly copy it."

"I wish I could exactly copy Tabby."

"Why?"

"So I could always have her with me."

"I know the feeling. She's the most free-spirited person I've ever met. Even when I was really sick, she could make me laugh."

"It's done." Ursa handed Jo the drawing over the seat.

Jo glanced at it as she drove. "This is good! It looks like her."

"Tabby is my third miracle."

"Really? Tabby ranks up there with baby birds and kittens?"

"She's kind of like a baby. She didn't know she was supposed to grow up, and that makes her more fun than other grown-up people."

"Good assessment."

Ursa looked at the approaching exit ramp. "Why are you slowing down?"

"To get gas."

She looked around in all directions. "Wait . . . where is this?"

"A city called Effingham. I usually stop here. There's a station that has cheap gas."

"I don't want to stop."

"I'm out of gas. I have to."

"Can't you go somewhere else?"

"Why?"

"I don't like this place."

Jo looked in the rearview mirror. "Have you been here before?"

She didn't answer.

"Have you?" Jo said.

"I said I don't like it because it's ugly."

"Maybe it is, but we'll only be here for ten minutes. You'd better use the bathroom. They have a clean one here."

"I don't have to go."

"You had two Sprites."

Ursa scrunched down in her seat. "I'm going to sleep."

Jo fueled the car and used the restroom. She also bought two Necco rolls, a candy she rarely saw in stores. That was the other, more important, reason she stopped at that particular gas station.

Jo thought Ursa was asleep when she returned to the locked car, but Ursa sat up a few miles down the highway. "Want a Necco?" Jo said.

"What is that?"

"A candy I like." She handed the open roll back to Ursa.

"Can I have a purple one?"

"How far down is it?"

"Only three."

"Go ahead, but purple isn't grape if that's what you're expecting. It's clove, and some people don't like it."

Ursa pried out the purple wafer and laid it on her tongue. "I like it!"

Half a Necco package later, Ursa said she had to go to the bathroom.

"Why didn't you go in Effingham?"

"I didn't have to go when we were there."

Jo stopped in Salem and took her into a bathroom. They made it all the way to Turkey Creek Road without another bathroom break. After they turned onto the road, Ursa asked if they could see the kittens. Earlier that day, they'd stopped to tell Gabe they were going to Urbana, but when they saw a silver SUV parked in front of the cabin, Jo decided they shouldn't disturb him and his mother when they had visitors.

As they approached the Nash property, Ursa begged her to stop. It was 7:10, early enough for a quick visit, and Jo wanted to make sure Gabe didn't have the wrong idea about what had happened the other night. But the silver SUV was still parked at the end of the potholed drive. "Maybe we should leave," Jo said.

"Gabe won't care." Ursa was out the door before Jo could stop her. A woman with a lightly grayed ponytail came through the front door of the cabin. She was in her midforties, her features broad and bullish, and the extra pounds she carried on her tall, powerful frame made her appear more intimidating than overweight. But it was probably the harsh blue of her eyes that made Ursa retreat down the stairs and reach for Jo's hand. The woman seemed angry with them, and Jo couldn't imagine why.

"We came by to see Gabe," Jo said. "I'm Joanna Teale, and this is my friend Ursa. I'm renting the property next door."

"I know who you are," the woman said before Jo finished speaking.

"Where is Gabe?" Ursa asked.

"He's not well," the woman said.

"He's sick?" Ursa asked.

The woman made an irritated face.

"Can I see him?" Ursa said.

"You may not."

"Who are you?" Ursa asked.

Jo was thinking a similar question: *Who the hell do you think you are?*

"I'm Gabriel's sister."

Jo never would have guessed that. She looked nothing like him.

"Can I go see the kittens?" Ursa asked.

"I think it's best if you leave," the woman said.

"Is his illness serious?" Jo asked.

She was already walking into the cabin. "I'll tell him you stopped by." The door closed.

"She's mean," Ursa said when they got in the car.

Or what they'd interpreted as meanness was distress. Maybe Gabe's sister was upset because he was seriously ill.

Jo took Ursa with her to do fieldwork the next day. The heat was brutal and most of the work was on roads, but Ursa never once complained. She found a new nest with two cardinal eggs. Jo told her she might have to pay her field assistant wages.

After they finished monitoring nests on Turkey Creek Road, Jo drove to the Nash property and parked next to the silver SUV. She and Ursa knocked on the front door, rapping louder when no one answered. Gabe's mother slowly opened the wooden door, holding her four-legged cane.

"We came to see how Gabe is doing," Jo said through the screened door.

"Lacey told me you stopped by last night."

Gabe's sister must be Lacey, a frilly name that didn't suit her menacing appearance.

"How is he?" Jo asked.

"Not so well," Katherine said.

"I'm sorry to hear that. Can we visit with him, maybe just for a few minutes?"

"He wouldn't want that," she said.

"Why don't you ask him? We might cheer him up."

"I don't think you will," Katherine said. "I'm sorry."

Jo and Ursa watched her close the door with shaking hands. Lacey had come down the road that led to the outbuildings. She was dressed in dirty work clothes and rubber boots smeared with manure. Probably doing Gabe's usual chores.

"Need something?" she asked.

"We'd hoped to see Gabe," Jo said.

"Did my mother answer the door?"

"Yes, we talked to her."

"Damn it," she muttered.

"I'm sorry. If we'd known you were out back, we'd have—"

"Better if you didn't. I have lots of crap to deal with, and I mean that literally." She walked away toward the barns.

Jo was about to call something to her, but everything she wanted to say would sound too combative. She got in the car with Ursa.

"Why won't they let us see Gabe?" Ursa said.

"I don't know. Something weird is going on." She drove to the Kinney house, unable to keep her creeping thoughts at bay. Maybe Gabe was having another breakdown. Even worse, Jo was afraid her awkward interaction with him the other night might have triggered it.

While she and Ursa were out tending to the nests the next day, Jo decided she would be more forceful with Lacey that evening. They finished the fieldwork a little early and arrived on the Nash property about an hour before sunset. "This time we won't take no for an answer, right?" Jo said.

"Right," Ursa said.

Ursa knocked on the cabin door. Lacey opened the door, wiping her hands on a dish towel. "You really don't give up, do you?"

"He's our friend and we're worried about him," Jo said.

"How long will he be your friend when you leave at the end of the summer?"

Jo was too shocked to respond. But she wished she had when Lacey added, "Do him a favor and forget him now instead of later." Gabe's sister closed the door.

She apparently believed Jo and Gabe were in a relationship. And she had already concluded that Jo was going to dump him. Jo doubted Gabe had given her those ideas, and that had to mean Lacey had far overstepped the bounds of her sibling bond. Jo had heard of controlling sisters—the kind who disliked the women their brothers dated—but this was outrageous. Lacey was trying to sabotage a relationship that hadn't even begun.

Jo didn't notice Ursa was still on the porch until she got to the car. "Ursa, let's go."

Ursa came to the upper edge of the porch stairs. "You said we wouldn't take no for an answer."

"That's just a saying."

"No, it isn't."

"He doesn't want to see us."

"Maybe he does and they won't let him," Ursa said.

"I know, but there's nothing we can do about it."

"Yes, there is."

"What?"

"She didn't lock the door, and I know where his room is."

"Oh my god! Ursa, get down here this instant!" Jo hissed.

"I don't have to listen to you because I'm not from this planet. We have our own rules." She scampered to the door.

"Ursa!"

Ursa pushed the inner door ajar and slid through the gap. Jo contemplated whether to follow and decided she couldn't let a child deal with Lacey alone. She entered just in time to see Ursa disappear behind a log wall. Lacey was at the kitchen sink doing dishes, and Katherine sat at the table talking to her. Both had their backs to the front door, and their conversation, along with the running water, had prevented them from hearing Ursa walk in.

Jo crept across the living room, hunched over to keep a smaller profile. She slipped down the hallway and saw Ursa opening a door at the end of the corridor. "Knock first!" Jo whispered, but too late to stop her from entering unannounced.

Jo and Ursa stood in the doorway and surveyed Gabe. Dressed in gray pajama pants and a light-blue T-shirt, he was curled on his side in a log-frame bed with his back to them. Stacks of books were piled everywhere. The only decoration in the room was a star chart pinned to one of the walls.

"Gabe?" Ursa said. "Are you okay?"

He rolled onto his back, his puffy eyes bewildered. "Ursa?"

"Are you sick?" Ursa asked.

"Who told you that?"

"Your mean sister."

He snorted a soft laugh and sat up, pushing strands of wavy hair off his face. His eyes focused into familiar blue sharpness when he looked at Jo. "She let you in?"

"Actually . . . no," Jo said.

"My mother did?"

"It's more of a search and rescue operation," Jo said.

"You're kidding?"

"I'm not."

"They don't know you're here?"

Jo shook her head. "The alien made me do it."

His grin was short-lived. "Jesus, I must look bad," he said, running his hands over his beard and through his hair.

"You look good," Ursa said. "You don't look sick at all."

"Yeah, well, there are different ways of being sick." He dragged his legs over the edge of the bed, clearly unaccustomed to moving. His eyes settled on Jo's. "What made you think I needed rescue?"

"They wouldn't let us see you."

"Why did you want to?"

"We need eggs."

He smiled.

"You missed your egg morning out on the road. It's caused a county-wide crisis."

"Not a national emergency?"

"Your delusions are a bit far-reaching," she said.

"Maybe they are."

"Can I see the kittens?" Ursa asked.

He stood a little shakily. "Thou shall see the Shakespearean cats, my lady."

"You don't have to get up," Jo said. "We only wanted to make sure you were all right."

"I do have to get up. I have to see Lacey's face when she gets you in her crosshairs."

"I'm a little scared about that," Jo said.

"I'll run interference. But I warn you, she doesn't take her cracked baby brother very seriously."

"Cracked like an egg?" Ursa said.

"Hey, good analogy." He slid his feet into old tan loafers. "Let's go see those kittens."

"Are their eyes open yet?" Ursa asked.

"I don't know. I haven't seen them for a few days." He led the way down the hallway. When they arrived in the open space between the kitchen and living room, he waved at his sister and mother. "Don't mind us," he said, "just passing through."

"Gabe!" Lacey said.

"What?"

"How did they get in?"

"Who?"

"Them!"

"Wait . . . you can see them? I thought they were my hallucination."

Lacey strode over to Jo. "You had the nerve to sneak into our house?"

"I didn't," Jo said. "One hundred percent of the nerve came from another source."

"And no one is going to yell at a little girl—right, Lace?" Gabe said.

"So you're okay now? Just like that?" Lacey said. "Couldn't you have done that before I drove over here to do your work?"

"I never told you to come."

"Who the hell was supposed to take care of Mom?"

"Can we push the play button on this recording later? My friends don't want to hear it. Let's go," he said to Jo and Ursa.

"Where are you going?" Lacey said.

"Ursa wants to see the kittens," he said.

"Yeah, and what about that? I told you no more cats."

"My cats are all spayed. The mother was a stray that showed up pregnant."

"Well, I haven't found them yet, but I'm thinking of taking them to the river."

Gabe charged her with startling intimidation, and she backed away until her butt hit a kitchen chair. "You do anything to those kittens and they'll find *you* in the river! I mean that, Lacey!"

"You're friggin' nuts!" Lacey said.

"I am, so don't mess with me! And don't say things like that in front of this little girl ever again!"

Lacey's sour gaze fell on Ursa. "Who is she? Mom says you feed her every day."

To keep Ursa from hearing more, Gabe lifted her into his arms and hastened to the door. "I'm sorry," he said in Ursa's ear. "Don't worry about any of that."

Jo pushed on his back in her urgency to get out. They scurried down the gravel drive on the west side of the house. Halfway to the barn, Gabe set Ursa on her feet. "My bad," he said. "You're too old to be carried."

"It's okay," Ursa said.

Jo glanced over her shoulder to see if Lacey was following. She wasn't, and the cabin had disappeared behind trees that surrounded it on all sides.

"I'm sorry you two had to see that," Gabe said when they reached the barn. "My sister is . . . she and I have never gotten along. She was in college when I was born, and she's always been more like my mean stepmother than my sister."

"You don't need to apologize," Jo said.

"Can I go see them?" Ursa said.

"Go on," he said.

Ursa ran inside. Gabe and Jo followed her to the stacks of hay at the rear of the building. "The mother cat is surprisingly tame," Gabe said, picking up the orange tabby that had come to greet him with her meows. He held her to his chest, and she rolled her head against his fingers as he scratched behind her ears.

"She obviously wasn't born in the wild," Jo said.

"I know. I think someone dumped her on my property when they saw she was pregnant. People around here know I keep barn cats."

Jo stroked the cat in his arms.

"She gave birth to the first kitten next to my toolshed, but she let me move her to the barn. The kittens are safer from predators in here because I keep the door closed at night."

"Predators like your sister?" Jo said.

"Yeah, worse than a rat snake, right?"

"Should we hide them better?" Ursa asked.

Gabe squatted in front of her. "I won't let her hurt them."

"But she said—"

"I think she'll leave tomorrow. She hates farm chores."

Ursa took Jo's hand and led her to a nest of multicolored kittens tucked between two big bales of hay. "I'm betting there's more than one father," Jo said.

"She's discovered your deepest, darkest secret," Gabe whispered in the mother cat's ear.

Jo smiled at his humor. He'd looked bad when they first saw him, but he'd livened remarkably in the last ten minutes. The alien kid apparently had better instincts than Jo.

"Their eyes are open!" Ursa said, a white kitten in her hands. It mewed softly, its squinted eyes trying to make sense of her human face. "This is Juliet," Ursa said. "Want to hold her?"

Jo cradled the kitten against her chest.

"The gray one is Hamlet," Ursa said, pointing at a kitten. "This brown tabby is Caesar. The black-and-white one is Macbeth, and the orange one is Olivia—"

"Which play is that from?" Jo asked.

"*Twelfth Night*," Gabe said.

"Finally, a comedy."

"And the black one is Othello," Ursa said. "That name was Gabe's idea because Othello is a Moor."

Ursa took Juliet from Jo's hands. "Juliet and Hamlet are my favorites." She scooped Hamlet out of the nest and reclined against a hay bale with the two kittens on her chest.

Balancing the mother cat on one arm, Gabe lifted Olivia and handed her to Jo. "Have a little comedy. We need it."

Jo warmed the tiny orange kitten until it settled down. Gabe was watching her, smiling. "How do you feel?" she asked him. But immediately she regretted asking the question that had dogged her since her diagnosis. "Are you up to having dinner with us?"

He tried to read her motives.

"Ursa and I are making burgers, sweet potato fries, and salad. But I should warn you, they're turkey burgers. I don't eat much red meat."

"I don't mind turkey burgers," he said.

"Have you eaten?"

"No."

"Then come over."

"I'd have to shower first."

"We can start cooking while you do that."

"Are you sure?"

"I'm positive."

"Guess what, you guys?" Ursa said.

"What?" Gabe said.

Ursa sat up, white and gray kitten in each hand. "I'm going to write a play about Juliet and Hamlet."

"Is it a play about cats or people?" he asked.

"People. Juliet and Hamlet meet in a magic forest *before* all the bad things happen, and that changes their fates. It's a comedy, and everyone is happy at the end."

"I like it," Gabe said.

"I really like it," Jo said. "Can we buy tickets in advance?"

13

Ursa explored the prairie edge with a flashlight while Jo stoked the fire for the burgers.

"What are you doing?" Jo asked.

"Picking flowers for the table."

"I thought we'd eat outside like we usually do when we grill."

"No! Gabe coming for dinner is special."

Jo didn't want it to be. Maybe she and Gabe would get awkward again, and eating at the kitchen table in fluorescent light would only make it worse. When Jo went inside to check the potatoes, she saw that their dinner wouldn't be eaten in fluorescence. Ursa had turned out all the lights and placed two half-burned pillar candles on the table on either side of her flower bouquet. It looked way too romantic, but before Jo could do anything about it, Little Bear was barking to announce Gabe's arrival. She hurried outside to quiet him.

"Good watchdog," Gabe said, closing his truck door.

"It's not good. It's annoying."

Gabe patted the dog and came up the walkway. He held out a carton of eggs. "Do you really need them?"

"We do. Thanks." She took the carton from his hand, noticing the warm scent of soap on his skin. "Just to warn you, Ursa has turned this into an haute cuisine affair."

"Did she find caviar in the creek?"

"The menu is the same, but she's trying to create dining ambiance."

"Sounds nice. I hope I'm suitably dressed for a restaurant."

In the yellow glow of the porch light, Jo appraised his clothing—a blue button-down shirt and light-colored pants, much nicer than the T-shirt and frayed jeans he usually wore. He looked like he was dressed for a date. She suppressed a spike of panic. "It's perfect," she said. "A tux would have been overkill."

She led the way into the house, where Ursa was folding paper towels into napkins at the kitchen table. "I was afraid Lacey wouldn't let you come," she said.

"She did her best to prevent me, but I got the chains off," he said.

Maybe that wasn't so far from the truth.

"Need help with dinner?" he asked.

"Thanks, but all that's left is grilling the burgers," Jo said. "Stay in the air-conditioning—if you can call it that." When Ursa insisted on eating inside, Jo turned the living room window unit to its highest setting, but it was old and hadn't done much to lower the temperature yet.

Jo stayed outside while she cooked four turkey burgers and grilled the buns. When she brought the food inside, the living room light was on. Gabe and Ursa were seated on the couch looking at Ursa's crayon drawings of him, Tabby, and Frances Ivey's house.

"Ursa says you drove up to Urbana to rent a house the day before yesterday," Gabe said.

"We did. I'm sorry I didn't get a chance to let you know before we left. But if Tabby and I didn't move fast, the house would've been gone."

"That's okay." He returned her pointed gaze. He knew her apology was meant to cover more. "Tabby must be quite a person if she was Ursa's third miracle."

"Tabby is miraculous in more ways than I can explain," Jo said. "I've known her since our sophomore year in college, and we've roomed together since junior year."

"Ursa said she's going to be a vet."

"And her name is a cat!" Ursa said. "Isn't that funny?"

"It is," he said.

Jo set the bowl of sweet potato fries on the table next to the burgers. "Dinner is served."

Ursa turned off all lights in the living room and kitchen. "Yikes, spooky," Gabe said to discharge some of the tension. Ursa took the seat next to Gabe at the candlelit table, and Jo sat across from him.

"I made the salad," Ursa said.

"Good job," he said.

"The extra burger without cheese is for you," Jo said.

"Not sure if I'll be able to handle it," he said. "I haven't eaten much the last few days."

"Because you were throwing up?" Ursa asked.

"No, I just wasn't hungry."

Jo had expected as much, but she'd put a fourth burger on the grill anyway. Just like the meals she'd brought her dying mother—always too big—as if she could feed her back to wellness. Sometimes she thought about herself in the same way, afraid the cancer had come back if she didn't have an appetite.

Good thing she never had those worries about Ursa. She was famished, her usual chatter silenced by a mouthful of burger.

"I hear Ursa has become quite the ornithologist," Gabe said.

"She has," Jo said. "She's found two nests."

He held up his hand and let Ursa high-five him. He was pretending he felt better than he did. He'd put down his burger before he'd eaten half of it, and while Jo and Ursa finished eating, he picked at his salad to have something to do. "How's the research going?" he asked.

"Better than expected for my first field season."

"How many more will you have?"

"At least one more."

"You'll be living here next summer?"

"That's the plan."

He looked down at the fork he was poking in his salad before he returned his gaze to hers. "Why are you studying buntings?"

"I'm doing a nesting study, and bunting nests are plentiful and easy to find. Historically, they nested in forests that were disturbed by fire and floods. These days, they're attracted to the edges of our roads and crop fields, and those habitats aren't so good for them. Lots of birds that nest in those shrubby kinds of landscapes are declining."

"Interesting," he said.

"So I'm comparing nesting success between habitats created by natural and human disturbances."

He nodded. "What brought you into the world of birds in the first place?"

"I'd have to say my parents," she said. "My dad was a geologist, and my mother was a botanist. When I was a kid, my family camped and hiked all over the United States. That was when I learned my first birds, mostly with my mom."

"Jo's mom and dad are dead," Ursa announced.

Gabe didn't look especially surprised when Jo had used past tense to describe her parents. But unlike most people, he didn't ask what had happened to them.

"My dad did research in the Andes," Jo said. "He was in an airplane that crashed into a mountain when I was fifteen. Two other geologists and the Peruvian pilot died with him."

"Jesus. How old was he?"

"Forty-one."

"Was your mom there, doing research with him?"

"No, she was home with my brother and me. She never finished her botany PhD after my brother was born. My dad went on long research trips, and she didn't want to put my brother in day care while she finished her degree."

"Jo's mom died from breast cancer," Ursa said. "She saved Jo's life."

"As you can see," Jo said, "Ursa has been very curious about my family." Looking at Ursa, she added, "I wish she'd tell me as much as I've told her."

"You wouldn't understand if I told you about my Hetrayeh family," Ursa said.

"I would. You know I would."

"Tell Gabe about how your mom saved your life."

"Changing the subject won't help anything," Jo said.

"You changed it," Ursa said, "because you didn't want to talk about your mom." She pushed out her chair and left the table to go to the bathroom.

"Outsmarted again," Jo said.

He smiled.

She slid away her empty plate. "You're probably wondering what Ursa meant about my mother saving my life."

"I'm guessing her cancer led to the discovery of yours."

Jo nodded.

"How long ago did that happen?"

"About two years ago. She died this past winter."

"And all the while you were dealing with your own cancer. Were you a graduate student yet when you were diagnosed?"

"I was, but I lost two years—between helping my mom and my treatments and surgeries."

"More than one surgery?"

Her lack of breasts was obvious, but she hadn't intended to mention the oophorectomy. Especially to a man her age. But she had to get over all of that.

116

"They found my cancer at an early stage," she said, "but I still had a full mastectomy and my ovaries removed—because I was at high risk for recurring breast cancer and ovarian cancer."

He leaned toward her, his face washed in candlelight.

"You don't have to say anything."

He sat back in his chair. "I won't. As always, words fail when you most want to say the right thing."

"People think they have to say something, and it never makes me feel better."

"I know. I've decided language isn't as advanced as we think it is. We're still apes trying to express our thoughts with grunts while most of what we want to communicate stays locked in our brains."

"*This* from the son of a literature professor?"

"Maybe I didn't get the literary gene from him."

Jo rose to collect plates so he wouldn't feel obligated to eat what he couldn't finish. He helped, stacking his dish on top of Ursa's.

"What is your mother's field of work?" she asked.

"She was an elementary school teacher for a while, but she did what your mom did: she quit when Lacey was born. She's also a poet," he said, following Jo into the kitchen. "She has two books of poetry published."

"Really? Does she still write?"

"She can't. The Parkinson's makes her hands shake too much to write or type."

"She could recite it while you write it down for her."

"I suggested that, but she says that would ruin the creative process."

"I guess I can see that."

"The Parkinson's is probably wiping out the poetry anyway."

"That's sad."

"Yeah."

Ursa already had the marshmallow bag in her hand.

"Don't you ever get tired of marshmallows?" Jo said.

"We don't have anything else for dessert, and the fire is going. Please?"

"Go ahead."

"Do you want some?" Ursa asked Gabe.

He looked at Jo. "Maybe I should get going."

"Stay for a while," Jo said.

"Are you sure?"

"The longer you can avoid the chains, the better, right?"

14

They settled into lawn chairs while Ursa cooked marshmallows. Gabe was quiet, staring moodily into the fire. Ursa didn't say much either, her usual exuberance diminished by his silence.

"Is Lacey leaving tomorrow?" Jo asked.

"Now that I'm up, she probably will," he said, still gazing into the fire.

"Where does she live?"

"Saint Louis."

"That's good."

He looked at her. "Why?"

"Because it's a short drive."

"It would be better if it were longer."

"She visits too much?"

"Not because she wants to. She comes when my mother calls her and tells her to come."

"Does your mother do that often?"

"If I lie down for a long nap, my mother calls Lacey. If I'm in a quiet mood, she calls Lacey. If I skip the morning chores, she calls Lacey."

"Why?"

"Because she thinks I'm going down again." He glanced at Ursa to see if she understood his meaning. "She's terrified I'll stop taking care of her and the animals."

"Has that ever happened?"

He made a wry sound. "I wouldn't know."

"What do you mean?"

"I've never had a chance to see if I would let it get that bad. Lacey always shows up before it does."

"And then you shut down because you can and they expect you to."

His eyes lit up with more than reflected fire. "Exactly!"

"That's messed up. And having Lacey around would make anyone shut down. She almost seemed pissed that you were able to get up."

"She was. She complains about coming here when I get depressed, but in reality I think she enjoys it. It's some power thing with her."

"That's why she wouldn't let us see you. She was threatened by the possibility that you have friends."

"Who might give me a reason to get out of bed . . . which you did, by the way, and thank you for that."

"Thank Ursa. I was too chicken to do it."

"Thanks for sticking to your guns, Ursa. I mean . . . not guns . . ."

Jo and Ursa laughed.

He looked better and maybe felt better, because he toasted two marshmallows and ate them both. But anything he gained would be lost when he returned to the poisonous atmosphere of his home. "What did your sister say when you left to come here?" Jo asked while Ursa ran after a firefly.

"You can imagine." He tossed his marshmallow stick into the fire. "No, you probably can't, because you're a normal person."

"What did she say?"

He glanced at Ursa to make sure she couldn't hear. "First, she ripped into me for buying clothes for Ursa. My mother told her about that while we were in the barn. When I ignored her, she got nastier until I got angry, like she always does. She said I might be accused of being a pedophile if I kept letting Ursa come to the farm. I asked her if that was a threat, and she said maybe. She said it was weird that I was picking her up in my arms."

"That's terrible!"

"Yeah, it was bad. And she mocked me about you—like she thought we were involved or something."

So Jo had guessed right about that. "What a bitch! If she thought you found someone, she should be happy."

"My happiness can only make Lacey miserable and vice versa. She's hated me since I was in the womb."

"You know what she said to me?"

"What?" he asked with alarm. Apparently he didn't trust anything his sister said.

"She told me I should dump you now, rather than later when my research was done."

"God damn her!" he said, looking in the direction of his cabin.

"Don't worry about it. I could see what was going on. But I thought you should know."

He studied Jo's eyes. "Did she say anything else?"

"That was the gist of it."

He kept his eyes on hers, as if searching for the truth beyond her reply.

"What did you think she'd said?"

He looked down at his hands, rubbing his palms between his knees. "She and my mother think you're the reason I went down—because I was last with you before it happened."

She had surmised as much when he first disappeared, but she wouldn't ask if it was true. That question might lead to why she had suddenly turned cold the night they looked at the galaxy. She never talked about how the surgeries had changed her view of her body. She could only visit that desolate place in private.

Gabe turned his face toward her. "She had no right to lay that on you. I'm sorry she involved you in our family bullshit."

"It's okay. I'm sorry I called her a bitch. I shouldn't have done that."

"Why not?" He cupped his hands to his mouth and shouted, "You bitch!" in the direction of his property.

"I doubt she heard."

"You never know. You can hear loud noises between these houses. I'm sure you hear our cow."

"I do."

"I meant Lacey."

"Okay, stop. We should feel sorry for her. People as bitter as her usually have a reason. Is she divorced or something like that?"

"No, but you're right about her being bitter. She was always desperate for our father's approval, and she hated that he bragged about how smart I was when I was little. Mostly to please him, she majored in English and tried to become a writer, but she failed. Around that time, she got really mean. She used to tease me relentlessly until my temper blew. She enjoyed trying to make me look bad in front of our parents, especially our father."

"That's all pretty typical sibling rivalry."

"Is it typical for a woman in her twenties to play games with a little kid so she could crush him and tell him how dumb he was? Or to say her newborn brother looked like a toad and call him Mr. Toad into adulthood? Around her, I felt like the ugliest, stupidest thing on Earth."

"That's awful. I'm really sorry."

"Don't be. I got over it a long time ago," he said in a hostile tone that contradicted his assertion. "I stopped hoping she would like me the day she abandoned me in the woods. I was picking flowers for my mom, and she just walked away. I still remember how terrified I was."

"How old were you?"

"Five. It took my mother an hour to find me. She'd asked Lacey to take me for a walk while she worked on a poem. Lacey lied, said I'd wandered off. And she went on and on about how I'd have found my way home if I was smarter."

"God, I hope she never had kids of her own."

"She has two sons, and she spoiled them rotten. They're both in college now."

"Does she have a job?"

"She kept writing while she did the stay-at-home mom thing, but none of her books ever took off. She felt like she'd disappointed my dad. But she shouldn't have chosen that field just to please him—especially once she realized writing wasn't her talent."

Ursa had returned during their conversation. "Are you talking about Lacey?"

"Yes," Jo said.

"Why did you yell when I was over there?" she asked Gabe.

"I was just fooling around."

"I thought Lacey was here and she came to make you leave."

"She can't make me," he said.

"Will you stay?"

"I'll go soon. I'm sure you two are tired."

"You have to stay!" Ursa said. "If you go back, they'll keep you prisoner again. But this time, they'll lock the door and we won't be able to rescue you."

"It's not as dire as all that," he said.

"Please? Jo wants you to stay. Jo, tell him not to go!"

"Maybe you shouldn't go back," Jo said. "Show your sister you have a life of your own. And your mother needs to learn that, too. Why doesn't she ever stay with Lacey in Saint Louis so you can have a break? Or they could hire someone to help her. Who voted you the forever caregiver? You're way too young for that burden."

Gabe stared at her.

"I'm sorry," she said. "I tend to spew opinions when I'm pissed."

"Don't apologize. Everything you said is true."

"Then teach them a lesson and sleep on the couch. Ursa can sleep with me, if that's okay with her."

"Yes, it's okay!" Ursa said, thrusting her arms in the air. "And tomorrow Gabe can come with us to Summers Creek! It's the best place, Gabe! It's like a magic forest!"

"I've never seen a magic forest," he said.

"It's pretty damn magical," Jo said.

15

"Hey, Jo . . ."

Gabe stood thirty yards away in chest-high vegetation. "What?" she called.

"I think there's a nest over here that lost its tag."

She waded through the brush toward him. "I don't believe this—did you really find a nest your first hour out?"

"It has three white eggs in it."

"That's an indigo bunting nest!"

Ursa heard what was going on and ran over. She and Jo arrived next to Gabe at the same time and looked down at the nest built in cane stalks. "Congratulations on your first nest," Jo said. "But damn it, now I have to pay you field assistant wages, too."

"It probably beats selling eggs," he said.

"We're all ornithologists now!" Ursa said.

Gabe touched one finger to a tiny egg.

"It's kind of a rush, isn't it?" Jo said.

"I've seen nests before, but finding one when you're *looking* for one is way better."

"Watch out, nest searching can become addictive. There's something about it . . . you're uncovering these little secrets of the wild."

He smiled.

"Do I sound like a kook?"

"No. I totally get it."

He watched Ursa record location, date, and status on a new data sheet as Jo dictated. She carefully printed *Gabriel Nash* on the FOUND BY line.

"I've contributed a data point to science. My existence is no longer meaningless," he said.

Jo liked that. "We'd better go," she said. "The parents are going nuts, and we don't want to bring in a predator."

"No predator may touch my nest," Gabe called into the forest as they walked away.

"Maybe saying that will be magic that protects it," Ursa said.

"That could be a new line of research," he said. "*The Use of Magic in Preventing Predation on Bird Nests.*"

"I'm sure you'll get a grant from the National Science Foundation," Jo said.

"Ursa Major will be my coauthor."

"Yeah, you'll definitely get funded," Jo said.

Gabe's beginner's luck didn't continue at the next study site, but he had high hopes for their last study area, Ursa's magic forest. They arrived at Summers Creek in the early afternoon. Gabe was immediately charmed by the wooded ravines, mossy waterfalls, and ferny rocks of the burbling stream. He told Ursa he felt the magic, and every so often he'd claim he saw a nymph or a fairy or a unicorn. Ursa started seeing phantasms, too, and soon the two of them were working harder at inventing fantastical creatures than looking for nests. Jo loved it, even if it was a little distracting.

Midway through their work, they sat at the usual big, clear pool to eat the second half of their lunch. Before Jo perched on her favorite flat rock to eat, Ursa was in the water, barefoot and grabbing at fish. "You should eat your sandwich before you get your clothes all wet," Jo called to her.

"I don't want to," she said, belly flopping into the deepest water.

"So much for my disciplinary skills," Jo said, handing Gabe a turkey-and-cheddar sandwich.

"She's a good kid. She doesn't need discipline."

"Other than the fact that she won't tell me where she's from no matter how much I beg?"

He sat on the rock next to her. "She told you where she's from."

"Right, the big nest in the sky."

"Sometimes I can almost believe it," he said. "She's not like any kid I ever knew."

"I know. And there's still no one looking for her."

"You check the internet?"

"I do, but it gets harder every time. I'm afraid I'll see her on one of those pages, and she'll go back to the idiots who never even reported her missing."

"They won't get her back. She'll go to foster care."

Jo faced him. "How much longer are we going to wait until we involve the sheriff again? It's been almost two weeks."

His hand holding the sandwich slackened as if he'd lost his appetite. "I thought about that a lot the last few days."

"I think about it all the time. We have to figure out a way to get her to the sheriff."

"Yeah."

They finished their sandwiches in gloomy silence, watching Ursa play in the water. Jo handed Gabe a Nalgene bottle filled with water and opened another for herself. "How did your sister and mother react when you went home to change clothes this morning?"

"Lacey went ballistic because she wants to go back to Saint Louis."

"Did your mother say anything?"

"She was too surprised to say much."

"Why would she be surprised?"

"You know why."

"No, I don't. So you had a breakdown when you faced a high-pressure university. Why does that make your life more expendable than Lacey's? Why can't you take a day off with friends? They purposely don't let you recover and move on because they've gotten used to you being the full-time caregiver."

"There's more to it than that."

"I don't think there is."

He looked in her eyes. "I'm sick. I can't just 'recover and move on.'"

"If you believe that, you won't."

"Like most people who've never experienced it, your view of depression is optimistically misguided." He set the water at Jo's feet and walked over to Ursa. She was in ankle-deep water near the creek bank trying to catch something in the convoluted roots of a huge sycamore.

"Did you see that?" she said. "I caught a big frog, but he got away."

"So much for your handsome prince," he said.

"Who wants a stupid handsome prince?"

"What about a smart handsome prince?"

"There are no princes in this magic forest," she said.

"That's modern."

She waded into deeper water. "Are you coming in?"

"I think I will," he said. "I feel all prickly."

"That's from the nettles."

"I know. The word *nettled* has taken on a whole new meaning for me." He took off his boots and long-sleeved University of Chicago T-shirt but left his jeans on. Jo couldn't help staring at his bare torso, lean and strong from working on the farm. When he'd waded deep enough into the pool, he ducked down and disappeared. He came up hooting and flinging water from his hair. "It's surprisingly cold!" he called to Jo. "You should come in."

"Jo doesn't like to get her data sheets wet," Ursa said.

Jo walked to the edge of the pool.

"Are you coming in?" Ursa asked.

"I have to now that you said that."

"Said what?"

"That I don't like to get my data sheets wet. It makes me sound like a dork."

Ursa cheered and jumped on Gabe's back, clinging to him like a baby monkey.

Jo took off her hiking boots and rolled her field pants to her knees. The problem was, she *didn't* want to get her data sheets wet when she went back to work, and the two layers of shirts that kept nettles and mosquitoes away from her skin would never dry.

She unfastened the top buttons and pulled both long-sleeved shirt and tee over her head. Maybe she did it because she'd told Tanner she was happy with what she looked like. Or because her mother had said, *Live passionately for both of us.* Maybe she took off the shirts because she wanted to show Gabe that she knew something about how to "recover and move on." Whatever the reason, the shirts were off and the cold water she was splashing onto her hot chest felt great.

Ursa hardly noticed. She'd seen Jo's chest a few times when they were changing clothes. But Gabe clearly didn't know what to do. First he looked at the scars. Then he looked away. Then he looked at her again, but only at her face.

"I wonder if I'd get arrested for indecent exposure if a forest ranger happened by," Jo said. "Is it indecent when you don't have anything to expose?"

"Good question," he said, visibly relieved by the humor.

She liked that she'd let a man see her chest for the first time in the forest pool. No bedroom. No pressure. In the woods she was relaxed, as whole as she ever felt. She stretched her arms into the water and glided across the pool. She turned around, slipped underwater, and came up in the middle of the pool. Ursa shifted from Gabe's back onto hers, hugging her arms around Jo's collarbones. "Aren't you glad you came in?"

"I'm really glad."

Ursa put her cold, wet lips to Jo's ear. "Let's splash Gabe," she whispered.

"Okay," Jo whispered back. "One, two, three—" Ursa leaped off her back and fell into a frenzy, shoving water at him. Jo helped, but with much less gusto.

"No fair. Two against one!" he said.

"You're bigger," Ursa said.

He sent powerful waves at them with strokes of his arms. Ursa grabbed Jo's shoulders and wildly paddled her legs.

"I surrender! I surrender!" he said.

"Girls win!" Ursa yelled.

"Of course they do. I never stood a chance."

"Hey, did you hear that?" Jo said. They kept still and listened to thunder rumbling from the southwest.

"It's not close yet," Gabe said.

"But we have a long walk back to the car." She left the water. She didn't like how far the distant rumbles carried, and their frequency portended a storm that was ripe with lightning.

"Can I have my sandwich?" Ursa asked.

"Eat it quick while Gabe and I dress," Jo said.

By the time they'd dressed and Ursa had gulped down her sandwich, the woods had darkened and the thunder was much louder.

"That storm is moving fast," Gabe said.

"Those are the worst," Jo said.

They used the rocky creek bed as much as possible to avoid the thick streamside vegetation, but farther upstream, where the creek had more water, they had to walk in the forest. Wind rushed through the treetops, and the temperature dropped at least ten degrees. The sky turned greenish black.

"It's like nighttime!" Ursa said.

"Hunker down or run?" Gabe asked Jo.

"I never know which to do."

"Let's run!" Ursa said. "This is scary!" she shouted as they ran, but Jo sensed her delight in the booming thunder and sudden pelt of rain. The wind and lightning escalated. When branches started cracking, Jo looked for cover but didn't see any.

"Almost there," Gabe shouted over the thunder and wind. "Jo!"

Jo stopped and turned around. Gabe was kneeling on the ground over Ursa. Jo ran to them, her chest throbbing at the sight of Ursa sprawled in the vegetation, face slack, eyes closed. "She tripped?"

He rubbed his hand in Ursa's wet hair and showed Jo the blood. "That branch hit her."

The branch was as thick as Jo's wrist. Jo knelt at Ursa's side and rubbed her cheek. "Ursa? Ursa, do you hear me?"

She opened her eyes, but they looked unfocused.

"We have to get her to a hospital," Gabe said. He pushed his arms under her body and lifted her up. Jo ran ahead and unlocked the car.

He laid Ursa across the back seat. "Stay with her. I know where the nearest hospital is."

"Where?"

"Marion. I've been there with my parents." He took the keys and gave Jo the extra T-shirt from his backpack. "Use this to put pressure on the cut."

Jo cradled Ursa's head in her lap and held the shirt to the wound on her scalp while Gabe drove. The windshield wipers slapped wildly as rain, thunder, and lightning assaulted the car. Everything felt like a sensory translation of her panic.

Ursa tried to sit up. "You're hurt," Jo said. "Don't get up."

"I'm okay. A piece of a tree hit me." She lifted her head and looked at Gabe. "Why is Gabe driving your car?"

"Because I know where the hospital is," he said.

"I don't want to go to the hospital!" Jo couldn't hold her down. "I want to go home! Don't go to the hospital!"

"You were unconscious for at least ten seconds," Gabe said. "You probably have a concussion, and you might need that cut stitched up."

"I was just playing a joke! I wasn't really unconscious!"

"You were," Jo said.

"Everything will be okay," Gabe said.

"It's not okay!"

She was right. Nothing would be okay when they arrived at the hospital. How would they explain why Ursa had been with them in the forest? Even worse, she'd been living at Kinney Cottage for almost two weeks. If the university found out, Jo might be in serious trouble.

"Will police come?" Ursa asked, betraying similar thoughts.

"Yes, the police will probably come," Gabe said.

"They'll take me away from you!" Ursa said through a gush of tears. "I'm not going!"

Jo tried to hug her, but Ursa pushed her away.

"I'm sorry," Gabe said, "but we have to do what's best for you, even if you don't want it."

Ursa fell quiet, tears dripping down her cheeks. The rain and thunder diminished, the only sound in the car the intermittent swish of windshield wipers. On the outskirts of Marion, Gabe slowed behind another car at a stop sign. Before the Honda came to a full stop, Ursa popped open her seat belt, flipped the lock, and slammed the door behind her. Jo scooted across the seat, but Ursa had already sprinted into a thicket at the edge of the woods. By the time Jo pushed through the dense vegetation, Ursa had vanished. "Ursa!" she shouted. "Ursa, come back!"

Gabe emerged from the undergrowth, scanning the trees. "She must be hiding. She can't have gotten far that fast." He jogged a short way into the forest and stopped. "Ursa, I know you can hear me!" he called. "Come out and we'll talk about it, okay?"

"Ursa, please!" Jo shouted. "Please come out!"

They searched behind all the trees that were big enough to hide her.

"She's still running," Jo said. "We'll never find her!"

"Ursa!" Gabe shouted as loud as he could. "If you come out, we won't go to the hospital."

They waited. Rain dripped from the trees. A chickadee scolded.

"She's gone," Jo said.

"Looks like she is." He saw that Jo was about to cry. "We'll find her. Let's drive down the road in the direction she went."

"Was that a promise?" Ursa said behind them.

They turned around. She was standing at the edge of the roadside thicket.

"I'll run again if you don't promise to take me home," she said.

"But . . . where is your home?" Gabe said.

"My home on Earth is with Jo!" she shouted.

"Ursa . . ."

"You aren't my friend if you don't do what you said! You said we wouldn't go to the hospital!"

"We won't," Jo said.

"Do you promise?"

"Yes." Jo walked toward her slowly to keep her calm. "How is your head?"

"It's okay."

When Jo reached her, she lifted her hair to assess the cut. "Look, it's stopped bleeding," she said to Gabe.

"Because she has the hardest goddamn head I ever saw. Where the hell were you?"

"In a metal thing," Ursa said. "It's in here." She led them into the thicket and showed them the opening of a corrugated drainage pipe, rainwater swirling out of it. They would never have found her in there.

"I give up," Gabe said. "This alien is way too smart for me."

"Can we go home?" Ursa said.

"We're going home," Jo said.

16

Jo had hardly stopped the Honda when Ursa jumped out, grabbed a stick, and threw it for Little Bear. All the way home she'd been manic, trying to prove that the blow to her head hadn't done any damage.

Jo unlocked the front door of the house. "Ursa, inside for a bath."

"You mean a shower?" Ursa said.

"No, I don't want you standing up."

"I'm okay."

"At the very least, your head has to hurt. Do what I said. I'll be in the bathroom to help in a minute."

"I don't need help," Ursa said, though she obediently walked inside.

Still cloaked in his bloodstained shirt, Gabe put his backpack in the back of his truck. "She looks good."

"I think a lot of that is fake," Jo said.

He laid the bloody shirt they'd used to put pressure on Ursa's cut next to the backpack.

"Will you come back after you clean up?" she asked.

"Do you want me to?"

"I do. What if I can't wake her up in the middle of the night or something like that?"

"That's the risk we're taking by letting her call the shots."

"Come on . . . I feel bad enough."

He gently touched her arm. "I'll be back soon."

"You're welcome to have dinner with us," she said.

"Are you sure you have enough? Your fridge looked pretty bare when I put things away last night."

"I know. We'll have to do omelets with the eggs you brought."

"I'll bring something over to cook. Let me handle dinner. You look beat."

"You must be about the same."

His weary smile confirmed it. "We'll manage. I'll see you soon."

Jo had Ursa undress and sit in warm water. After she cleaned the wound on Ursa's scalp, she gave her the soapy cloth and let her wash her body. Ursa came out of the bathroom wearing the pink Hello Kitty pajamas she and Gabe had bought at a yard sale. She didn't want to lie down on the couch while Jo showered, but Jo made her.

Jo bathed and dressed in shorts and a T-shirt. When she emerged from the bathroom, Gabe was already in the kitchen cooking. "Hope you don't mind if Ursa let me in," he said. "I wanted to get dinner on as fast as possible." He was seasoning a chicken in a roasting pan, and he'd brought bread stuffing to cook on the stove top.

"This looks great," Jo said.

"I want to make the stuffing, but he won't let me," Ursa said.

"Because you're supposed to be resting," Gabe said. "Go back to the couch."

"I'm not an invalid," she said on her way to the living room.

"*Invalid,*" Gabe said. "My sister doesn't use vocabulary like that, and she's a writer."

"How is Lacey?"

"Spittin' nails, as they sometimes say around here." He poured the stuffing mix into a mixture of water and melted butter. "I think she suspects we've committed a murder."

"The blood! How did you explain it?"

135

"I told her Ursa got hurt. And that led to another lecture on why I shouldn't be going around with someone else's kid. She threatened to call the cops."

"Will she?"

"Never know with Lacey."

"What did she say when you left again?"

"She demanded I stop my *childish fling*—as she called it—and stay home. She says she's leaving in the morning no matter what."

"Do you have to go home tonight?"

He quit stirring and faced her. "You asked me to stay the night, and I'm staying."

"Only if you want to."

"I do. I'm worried about Ursa, too."

"How can I help with dinner? Looks like we need a vegetable."

"I've got it covered. Lacey and my mother had leftover green beans and corn in the refrigerator. They only need to be heated."

An hour later, they sat down to the chicken, stuffing, and vegetables. Gabe had also brought a partial container of fudge ripple ice cream for dessert. Jo was too full to eat it, but Ursa and Gabe each had a bowl. "That knock on the head certainly hasn't affected your appetite," he said to Ursa.

"I told you I didn't need to go to the hospital," she said.

"Well, you gave us quite a scare. So much for your magic forest."

"It's not the forest's fault," Ursa said. "I made it happen."

"You made a branch conk you on the head and nearly kill you?"

"It wouldn't have killed me. But like I told Tabby and Jo, sometimes a bad thing has to happen to make a good thing happen."

"What was the good thing that came of it?" Gabe asked.

"You're staying overnight again."

"You knew I would stay overnight if you got hurt?"

"I didn't exactly *know*. It all just happens. People from Hetrayeh give off these invisible specks, kind of like quarks—except different—and they make good stuff happen around us when we meet earthlings we like."

He laid his spoon in his empty dish. "So I guess these quark things are kind of like giving off good vibes."

"They can change people's fates."

"What's so good about me staying overnight?"

"Jo and I like you." She picked up her bowl and drank the last of her melted ice cream. "You didn't want to be over there with your mean sister anyway, right? That's another way it's good."

"What do you think, science lady?" he asked Jo.

"Why not? We can't see gravity, and it has a strong effect on us."

"True." He stood and nested Ursa's bowl inside his. "Maybe tomorrow I'll find a million dollars under my pillow."

"Probably not," Ursa said.

"Why not?"

"The quark things know what you *really* want."

"I don't want a million dollars?"

"I don't think so."

"Darn it." He went to the sink and washed the bowls.

"Do you have that medicine Earth people call Motrin?" Ursa asked Jo.

"Do you have a headache?"

"Only a little one."

"Don't lie. How bad does it hurt?"

"Kind of bad." She saw Jo and Gabe glance at each other. "I'll be okay. I heard a cold washcloth and Motrin helps a lot."

She must have had that remedy in the past. Who had taken care of her when she was sick, and why hadn't that person reported her missing?

They took Ursa to the couch, gave her a Motrin, and had her lie down with a cold washcloth over her eyes and forehead. They darkened the room and lit Ursa's two candles. She fell into a deep sleep immediately. Jo sat on the edge of the couch watching her breathe.

"You can't sit up like that all night," Gabe said.

"I have to be next to her."

"Let me put her in your bed." He carried her to the first bedroom and rested her on the queen mattress on the wooden floor. He drew Jo's blanket over her, carefully tucking it around her shoulders. He pulled aside the strands of hair that covered her face. He looked up and caught Jo's smile. "Are you going to bed right away?" he asked.

"I'll stay awake as long as I can to keep watch on her."

"Do you mind if I sit here next to the bed?"

"Not at all." She retrieved the two candles and put one on the dresser and the other on the nightstand. She sat on the mattress facing Ursa, and Gabe sat on the floor on Ursa's other side.

"I had a good day," he said. "Before Ursa got hurt, obviously."

"You stood up to the heat, insects, and bushwhacking very well."

"Not to mention the stinging nettle."

"Yeah, don't mention it."

Silence lingered between them. He lifted the book lying next to Ursa. "*Slaughterhouse-Five*," he said, turning the book in his hands. "I've never seen it in hardcover. How old is it?"

"Printed in 1969, the year it came out."

He looked up at her. "With the original cover? It must be worth a fortune."

"It's not in the greatest shape—but it *is* priceless. It was handed down from my grandfather, to my dad, to my brother, to me. My mother read that copy more than once, too." She reached over Ursa and took the book from him, resting it on her crossed legs. "This book often came up in our conversations," she said, stroking her hand over the cover. "It was a favorite for all of us."

"My dad would love that."

"What?"

"How you still connect with your parents through a book."

She did, and not only through that one. She had most of the books that had belonged to her parents, and she read passages from them every night before she fell asleep or when she had insomnia. As she read, her fingers touching the same pages theirs had touched, her father and mother were right there with her.

"Your family sounds interesting if they all liked an unusual book like that."

"We were definitely interesting," she said. "Kind of weird, truthfully, and sometimes that made it hard for my brother and me to relate to other kids."

"How so?"

She thought for a few seconds. "Since I've gone into field biology, I've noticed most scientists who work out in the natural world are a little different from other people. Maybe it has something to do with how they can turn their backs on the comforts of society for long periods of time. But it's not just that they *can* forgo society, it's more like they *need* to. For people like that, the natural world is vital, a spiritual experience."

His candlelit eyes were intent on her.

"That's how my parents were. They rarely took us to do the things other kids did—amusement parks and touristy beaches. On weekends we hiked and kayaked or went in search of salamanders or fossils. Our vacations were usually camping trips, sometimes to far places like Maine to see puffins or Utah to see rock formations. And anywhere we went, we would go rock-hounding to look for minerals and gems."

"Cool," he said.

"It was. You should see our family collection. My dad's excitement about geology was contagious, almost manic. He was always pointing out the geology of the landscapes around us. That probably sounds boring, but it wasn't. The way he described how the forces of nature had shaped the earth was almost poetic."

"Sounds like an interesting guy."

"He was. And my mom—she was a force of nature, too, but in a relaxed, rippled stream kind of way. If I got into some screwed-up situation at school or with my friends, she could always help me see it was no big deal and bring positive light to it. And her garden . . . it was gorgeous, a wilderness of flowers and ponds and trees in the middle of suburbia. My friend Tabby used to say she was pretty sure fairies lived in my mother's garden—it was that magical."

"Where did you live?" he asked.

"Evanston. My dad taught nearby at Northwestern."

"Really! Not far from where my dad taught."

"To Chicagoans it's far," she said. "Did you live in the city when your dad was at U of C?"

"In Brookfield, in the house my dad grew up in. Do you know where that is?"

"I do. I went to the Brookfield Zoo a few times."

"My house was about a half mile from the zoo."

She gazed down at the book in her lap. "It's weird . . ."

"What is?"

"When I first bought eggs from you, I never would have thought our backgrounds were so similar."

"You thought I was just a dumb, gun-totin' redneck?"

"I didn't know what you were."

Neither knew what to say next, but the silence didn't feel awkward. Jo got up and put the book on the bed stand. She grabbed the pillow and blanket off the living room couch and laid them next to Ursa on the bed. "You look tired," she told him. "Why don't you lie down?"

"Are you sure?"

"If we're both here, we have more contact with her. Anytime you wake up, you can check her, and I'll do the same."

"I think she's okay."

"She fell asleep so fast, and all this time we've been talking she hasn't moved."

"Because she's exhausted."

"She is. I'd better let her sleep in."

"Good idea."

Jo set her phone alarm for 7:00 a.m. and blew out the two candles. She stretched out on the mattress and heard him do the same on the other side of Ursa.

"Do you have enough room?" she asked.

"Enough to sleep in."

The air conditioner hummed and rattled in the window. She hoped it didn't bother him. She preferred the sounds of field and forest at night, but she slept poorly when the bedroom was warm and muggy.

"I'm sorry I talked your ear off about my family," she said.

"Don't apologize. I enjoyed it," he said.

"I'd like to hear more about your parents sometime. Growing up with a poet and lit professor who built a cabin in the woods must have been amazing."

After a silence he said, "Yeah, it was amazing, but not in the way you're thinking."

Jo propped on her elbow and tried to see him in the darkness. "What do you mean?"

"Never mind." He rolled over, turning his back to her.

17

The windows rattled. Jo opened her eyes and tried to make sense of what she'd heard until another long rumble of thunder shook the panes. She put her hand on Ursa to make sure she was breathing and picked up her phone. It was 6:03. After a few minutes she got enough signal to check the weather. The remnants of a tropical storm in the Gulf were hitting Southern Illinois, and rain was expected until at least noon. More thunder rolled in the distance.

"Just what we need, another storm," Gabe said.

"It is what we need. I get to stay in bed. And that's good for Ursa." She turned off the alarm on her phone.

"You don't work when it rains?"

"It's not good to pull birds off their nests in rainy weather."

"Makes sense."

"Gabe?" Ursa said. She sat up and stared blearily at him.

"Go back to sleep," Jo said. "It's raining. No fieldwork."

"Good." She curled on her side with her arm around Gabe and fell back asleep.

"Well, guess I can't get up now," he said.

"You can't," Jo said. "Rainy mornings are the best."

They slept for two more hours. Ursa woke first, laying one hand on Jo and the other on Gabe. "This is like a nest. I feel like a baby bird."

"Bet you're as hungry as one, too," Jo said.

"I am, but I never want to leave the nest."

Gabe sat up. "Half your nest is going to the bathroom."

"Gabe!"

"Sorry, birdie. I'll brew some coffee. Stay in bed if you want," he told Jo.

"Nope," Jo said. "I'm aiming in the same direction."

Ursa's nest moved to the kitchen, where her beak was stuffed with fried eggs, half an English muffin, and orange slices. After breakfast cleanup, Gabe worked on the clogged kitchen sink with tools he had in his truck. He ended up taking apart all the pipes. He was putting them back together when Little Bear started barking outside. From the porch, Jo watched Lacey stop her silver SUV next to Gabe's pickup. She marched down the front sidewalk, ignoring the steady rain and Little Bear's attempts at scaring her off. "I need to see Gabe," she announced, striding into the house.

"Come on in," Jo said to her back. Lacey stopped in the kitchen doorway. She looked at Gabe on the floor fastening pipes and Ursa seated at the table drawing an indigo bunting with her new colored pencils. "Isn't this the picture of domestic bliss," she said.

Ursa looked like a cave troll had entered the room, and Gabe scrambled to his feet.

"I guess her broken sink was more important than me leaving," Lacey said.

"I guess it was," he said.

Lacey focused on Ursa. "I hear you got hurt yesterday."

Ursa nodded slightly.

"What happened?"

Ursa glanced nervously at Jo. "There was a storm. A branch fell . . ."

"What did your parents say about that? I bet they were worried."

"Is there a reason you're here?" Gabe asked.

"Several reasons," Lacey said. "Thanks to your raid on our kitchen last night, we need groceries."

"There's plenty of food in the big freezer," he said.

"Well, there isn't toilet paper in the freezer, and we need that, too. And Mom's out of that cream she puts on her eczema. She's upset you haven't gotten it yet."

"I'll go as soon as I'm done here," he said.

"Too late. I'm on my way."

"I thought you were leaving?"

"I thought so, too, but there's a lot that has to be done at the cabin while you're screwing around over here at Kinney's." Nodding at the sink, she said, "George will be grateful to you for fixing it. Maybe you should hire on as his handyman."

Lacey sniffed a soft laugh before she left the room, and Gabe's eyes took on a strange glassiness. He turned away, staring out the window, his hands clenched on the sink edge. Little Bear barked at Lacey's departure, and Gabe turned around, all traces of anger, or whatever it was, gone from his eyes.

"What was with that dig about being George Kinney's handyman?" Jo asked.

"Just Lacey being Lacey." He got on the floor to finish the plumbing.

For the next two hours, Jo entered data from her nest logs into her laptop, and Gabe showed Ursa how to play war and solitaire with an old deck of cards. At twelve thirty, the rain was still pouring down and Jo decided to give up on fieldwork. She needed to make good use of the day off work with a much-needed trip to the Laundromat and grocery store.

She asked Gabe if he would stay with Ursa. She didn't want to risk taking her near the Vienna sheriff's station in case she ran into Deputy Dean. If Ursa was going to be taken into custody by the police, the handover had to go down on Jo's terms. She was well aware, though, that everything that had come to pass so far had transpired wholly on Ursa the Alien's terms.

Jo wedged two dirty kitchen towels into her laundry bag, already overstuffed with the addition of Ursa's clothing. Gabe and Ursa were seated at the kitchen table, waiting for tomato soup to boil. He was teaching her how to play poker, and they were using oyster crackers as betting chips.

"First guns, now gambling," Jo said. "You're a bad influence."

"Not for long," he said. "We can't stop eating our money."

"I'm sorry there's not more to eat around here," she said. "I'll bring back lots of groceries."

"Don't forget macaroni and cheese!" Ursa said. She laid the five cards in her hand on the table. "I have three aces. I beat you."

"Quit cheating with your quarks!" he said.

When she arrived in town, Jo ordered a chef's salad at a café near the Laundromat. She looked out the window at the slow bustle of small town life, relaxing into accustomed solitude. In quiet moments of the past year, she had often dwelled on those who were gone, her mother and father, or her presurgery self. Today she contemplated the living, Ursa and Gabe. She let her relief for Ursa's recovery from the head injury sink in. She wondered what would have happened if they'd taken Ursa to the hospital, if she and Gabe had been questioned by the police. Whatever might have happened, one thing was certain: Ursa would no longer be with Jo. Jo didn't even want to imagine the moment when Ursa was forced to leave her and Gabe. Fortunately, her food arrived before she dwelled on it for long.

She folded the top layer of egg slices into the heart of her salad. A few weeks back, she'd never have believed the enigmatic Egg Man would be a part of her daily life. Something that improbable almost had to be caused by an alien's intervention. She smiled, remembering how Ursa had snuggled up to Gabe that morning, fully trusting in his gentle nature.

She stopped eating to focus on a surprising sensation. The kind of inner warmth she used to feel when she was attracted to a man. She was relieved her body could still feel that way. But maybe it wasn't her body. It was probably the replacement hormones.

The warmth faded with her cold appraisal. Such was life with a double dose of analytical genes. Falling for Gabe would be too inconvenient anyway. Her research was an ambitious project that normally would require at least one assistant. And why risk her emotional recovery when he'd shown no interest beyond friendship? He'd slept over twice and hadn't made even the slightest move.

Not one move. Maybe he was turned off by her body. Or simply by the idea of the cancer. As compassionate as he was, he was unlikely to want a woman who lacked the usual anatomy. She let her fork fall into the last bit of her salad, paid the bill, and left.

The last of the gray rain clouds finally cleared away as she arrived home. The forest around Kinney Cottage was glorious, every leaf and bough sparkling with raindrop jewels of golden sun.

Gabe and Ursa weren't in the house. Gabe's note read,

We're at the creek catching fish with a holey net. Understandably, this may take some time. Come join us if you enjoy frustration.

Ursa left a note next to it that said,

I hope you got pie!!!!

Jo had bought a pie, dutch apple, and vanilla ice cream to go with it. After she put groceries and laundry away, she decided to start a spaghetti dinner rather than go down to the creek. At around seven, Ursa burst in the front door shouting, "Did you get pie? We caught these pretty fish called darters! And Gabe showed me water beetles! They carry a bubble of air under their body to give them oxygen underwater."

"How cool is that?" Jo said.

"And we found these larvae called caddis flies that can build a house that moves! They make a tube of silky stuff and stick sand and little pieces of rocks and wood on it. They use it to keep their soft bodies safe from predators."

"I've seen those," Jo said. "They're amazing."

Gabe arrived in the kitchen and set two sandy jars in the sink, his clothing as wet and muddy as Ursa's. Jo tried not to think about how good forest and stream looked on him. "I didn't know you were an aquatic insect expert," she said.

"I'm not," he said.

"He is," Ursa said. "He knows the names of everything!"

"Are you self-taught, or did someone show you?" Jo asked.

"George Kinney did. It smells great in here. What is it?" He lifted the lid on the skillet.

"Spaghetti sauce with turkey sausage," Jo said.

"Yay, pie!" Ursa said, lifting the pastry off the counter.

"Put it back," Jo said. "It's dessert. But you can only have it if you eat your green stuff."

Outside, Little Bear started going berserk.

"Damn it. It's Lacey again," Gabe said. The three of them went to the front window, and when they saw the sheriff's car rolling down the gravel lane, Ursa vanished. Jo experienced something like déjà vu as the rear screen door creaked open and banged shut.

"Fucking Lacey!" Gabe said. "I knew she was up to something when she came over here."

"What will we say?"

"Tell the truth, as much as possible."

Jo walked outside and tried to call Little Bear off the cop. Gabe stayed on the front walkway. The deputy wasn't K. Dean. He was older, in his midforties, but leaner and fitter than most twenty-year-olds. His dark-brown eyes had an alarming look, sharp with accusation.

"Would you be Joanne Teale?" the deputy asked.

"Yes, *Joanna*," Jo said. "How can I help you?"

The deputy walked toward her, unconcerned by the half-grown mongrel barking at him, his gaze fixed on Gabe.

"Is there a problem?" Jo asked.

"Maybe you can tell me," the deputy drawled. "I was told to look for an injured girl at this property."

"Who said that?"

"Why would you need to know? Is the report true or not?"

"There is a girl who comes around," she said. "I called the sheriff about her a few weeks ago."

He hadn't expected her to say that.

"Deputy Dean came out," she said.

He nodded, his stern demeanor softening. He was clearly familiar with Dean.

"But the girl saw him coming and ran away."

"Why would she do that?"

"Maybe she was afraid he would make her go home. She had bruises on her."

"You told Kyle—Deputy Dean—about that?"

"I did."

"She still comes around?" he asked.

"She does. Has someone reported her missing?"

"Someone's reported her as endangered. Last you saw her, was she hurt?"

"She had a cut on her head yesterday. I cleaned it up for her."

"Did the cut look like it was from abuse?"

"It wasn't. It was from a tree branch that fell during the big storm." Jo's stomach muscles clenched. Maybe she'd said too much. How would she answer if he asked where that had happened?

"Have you met her family?" the deputy asked.

"No. I don't know where she lives, and she won't tell me."

The deputy looked at Gabe.

"That's my friend. He lives next door," Jo said.

"And you own this property?" he asked Jo.

"I rent it. I'm doing research."

"What kind of research?"

"On birds."

"Well, someone's got to do it," he said, smiling to himself. He strode over to Gabe. "Have you seen the little girl?"

"I have," he said. "She comes over to my property, too," he added, knowing Lacey would have given the information.

"What does she want?" the deputy asked.

"She likes the animals."

"Do you know where she is right now?"

"She's probably around somewhere," Gabe said.

"Is that *yes* or *no*?" the deputy asked, looking in his eyes.

"She was here a short time ago, but she left. We don't know where she went."

The deputy nodded. "Do you mind if I look in the house?" he asked Jo.

The request was well beyond what Jo expected. She'd always thought the police needed a search warrant to enter a person's house. But Gabe nodded at her, signaling that she should let him inside. "No problem," she said, opening the porch door.

Jo and Gabe followed the deputy into the house. Fortunately, Jo had put Ursa's clean clothing inside the dresser. But what if he looked in the drawers?

The deputy walked from room to room of the small house, scrutinizing everything. When he got to the kitchen, he pointed to Ursa's drawing of an indigo bunting, attached with a magnet to the outside of the refrigerator. "Who did that?" he asked.

"The girl," Jo said.

"Do you often let her inside the house?"

"I'm rarely here. Most of the day, I'm out doing research."

"I asked if you let her in."

"I do because I feel sorry for her. I think someone isn't taking good care of her."

"Does this girl have a name?"

"She calls herself Ursa Major, but I assume that's a made-up name . . . because that's the name of a constellation."

"I know what it is," the deputy said. He walked out the back door and looked around the edge of the prairie before going over to the derelict shed. Jo and Gabe stood in the front yard under the hickory tree while he searched around the outbuilding, Little Bear following him everywhere he went. "Well, I see no girl," the deputy said. "But there's some concern for this child, so I'd appreciate a call to the sheriff if you see her again." He handed Jo a card with his information. "Have a good night."

"You too," Jo said in unison with Gabe.

They watched the deputy climb into his patrol car and drive away, Little Bear sending him off with a running flurry of barks.

When he was fully out of sight, Gabe said, "I have to go home. I'm going to kick Lacey in the ass back to Saint Louis."

"Don't make her mad! She'll do something worse."

"I won't. But if I go home, she'll leave."

"That's why she did this. I really can't believe you're related to that scheming woman!"

Gabe walked away. "I want to find Ursa before I go."

Jo followed him to the back of the house. "The last time this happened, she didn't go far. But that was at night."

They looked around the grassy field calling Ursa's name, but not too loud in case the deputy had stopped at the Nash cabin on his way out. Following a trail of broken stems, they came to the far edge of the field, a slope that dropped down into forest. They searched for a little while, but the sun was setting and they didn't have a flashlight.

Standing at the back door, Gabe looked out at the darkening field. "She's hunkered down somewhere. She'll come back at night to make sure the sheriff's car is gone."

They cooked the pasta but didn't eat much. And they didn't cut the pie. At ten, they lit a fire in the pit behind the house to signal Ursa to come home. They sat in lawn chairs, waiting, too worried to say much. At ten thirty, Gabe said, "Either she's lost or she's not coming back. Which do you think?"

"She trusted me enough to come back twice before, but she's so smart, it's hard to believe she's lost. She would know to follow Turkey Creek to get back here, and the moon is bright enough to see by."

"I have a theory about that." He stood and faced the prairie. "After she ran out the back door, she probably went straight north through the tall grass to keep the house between her and the sheriff. If she went down that slope back there, she would come to Guthrie Creek." Pointing eastward he said, "Turkey Creek splits off around this hill. If she crossed Guthrie on her way out and came back in the dark, she might not see Turkey Creek split off. She would follow the wrong creek trying to find us."

"You're right. Where they split, Turkey Creek is full of vegetation. It hardly looks like a creek."

"Did she know the lay of the land back there?"

"I don't think she did. She stuck pretty close to the house and shed."

He stared out at the dark field, rubbing his beard.

"I bet this reminds you of the day Lacey left you in the woods," Jo said.

He looked surprised, as if he hadn't expected her to make that connection. "That's exactly what I'm remembering," he said. "Do you have a good flashlight? I want to walk down Guthrie and try to find her."

Jo dug through her supplies and found a headlamp for him and a regular flashlight for herself. They called Little Bear and urged him to follow, hoping he might hear or smell Ursa.

Having spent many childhood days roaming the Kinney property, Gabe knew the easiest way down the hill to Guthrie Creek. They intermittently called for Ursa as they walked. The going was slow in the dark creek bed, and they stumbled often on roots and rocks. Little Bear was enjoying the excursion, often running off into the dark forest to explore but always returning.

"If she walked this long, she would have known she was off course. She would have turned around," Jo said after about forty minutes of searching.

"I know. Should we go back?"

"I'm going a little farther. I can't give up yet."

He nodded and stayed at her side. "Ursa, it's Jo! Come out!" she called. After another fifteen minutes, they decided to turn around. Jo was trying not to cry.

Gabe spontaneously put his arms around her. "It's okay," he said. "She's smart. She'll be okay." His shirt had dried since he'd been at the stream with Ursa, but he still smelled of creek water and wet sand and minnows. Jo closed her eyes and submerged herself in the comfort of his unexpected intimacy. He pressed closer. He seemed to need her, too.

Little Bear ran barking down the creek in the direction of the Kinney property. Jo and Gabe pulled apart and ran after him. The dog's barking abruptly stopped ahead, and as they rounded a bend, their lights fell on Ursa kneeling in the creek bed, hugging Little Bear. "Jo!" she said. She splashed through a shallow pool and fell against Jo's body, a sob bursting from her. "Are the police going to take me?"

"He's gone," Gabe said.

Ursa transferred her arms to his waist.

"Where were you? How did we pass without you hearing us?" he asked.

"I got lost!" she said. "I tried to find that one trail that goes up to the road, but I never saw it. It was dark and everything looked different! I turned around and walked a long time, but I still couldn't find it."

"Then you turned around again," he said.

Ursa nodded, wiping her hands over dirty streaks of tears on her cheeks.

"She was southwest of us when we went northeast looking for her," he said.

"You were smart to follow the creek," Jo told her. "But you followed the wrong creek. This is Guthrie Creek, not Turkey Creek."

"That's why everything looked different," Gabe said.

"I was scared," Ursa said, new tears falling. "I thought I would never see you again."

Gabe crouched. "Get on my back. I'll carry you for a while." Ursa clambered onto his back and wrapped her arms around his neck. He gripped her legs and stood.

"Am I too heavy?" she asked.

"Is that little stone fly on my back saying something, Jo?"

"I thought I heard it squeak," Jo said.

"Gabe and I found a stone fly larva today," Ursa said. "They eat detritus."

"Good word," Jo said.

"I learned that word today. It's gunky stuff that's made of rotten plants and animals."

"Sounds delicious," Jo said.

"Did you eat the pie?"

"Nope. We were waiting for you."

When they arrived at Kinney Cottage, Gabe lowered Ursa to the ground near his truck. "I have to go," he said. He took off the headlamp and handed it to Jo. "I have to make sure Lacey packs her bags tonight."

"I think she called the police," Ursa said.

"I think so, too." He turned to Jo. "Make sure Ursa stays out of sight. Don't take her on the road to look at nests for a while."

"I'm not working Turkey Creek tomorrow."

"Good." He half turned to his truck. "I guess I'll see you . . ."

"When?"

"I don't know. We have to make sure this blows over."

Jo moved toward him. She thought they would embrace again. But he climbed into his truck and drove away.

18

The next day, Jo let Ursa stay in bed a few extra hours to make up for missed sleep. But that put her further behind in nest monitoring after the rain day. They had to work late to catch up as much as possible, arriving at Turkey Creek Road after sunset, too late to catch Gabe at his Monday evening egg sale. "Can we stop at Gabe's?" Ursa asked.

"We can't. Lacey might be there."

"I could sneak in and see if her car is there."

"We aren't doing any more sneaking."

They had a similar conversation the next day, and the day after that one. Three days and no word from Gabe. Jo regretted that she hadn't asked him if he had a cell phone. But mostly she was glad they didn't talk via text. For some reason, she couldn't imagine communicating with him that way.

The next morning, Jo let Ursa sleep until first light. "Is it raining?" she asked when she opened her eyes and saw gray light.

"I let you sleep a little later. We're starting on Turkey Creek Road."

"I like when we do that." She sat at the kitchen table and sleepily ate a waffle.

Usually they left the house in quiet darkness. But when they began on Turkey Creek Road, they were greeted by a full dawn chorus, the riotous song of birds defending territories after a long night. As always, they fed Little Bear behind the house before they drove away. "You missed the first nest," Ursa said, pointing out the window at the orange flag.

"I'm going to park between the nests we have to monitor. We'll walk the road and do some nest searching first."

Early morning was a great time to look for nests. After a long night, nestlings were hungry and their parents visited them often, sometimes leading Jo straight to the nest. She stopped the car about a quarter mile past Gabe's driveway and pulled off the road into the weeds. Ursa put on the cheap spare binoculars Jo let her use and hopped out of the car. She stared longingly in the direction of Gabe's house. "Can we see Gabe today?"

"We may see him very soon," Jo said. "It's Thursday. He sells eggs in the morning."

"Unless he's sick again," Ursa said.

Jo didn't admit that was part of the reason she was working near his house on egg morning. She wanted to make sure he was okay.

Ursa looked up at Jo as they walked. "What makes Gabe get sick?"

"I'm not sure," Jo said.

"I think Lacey makes him sick."

"It's more than that. Human bodies are very complicated. Inside us there are all kinds of genes, hormones, and chemicals that affect our moods, and sometimes people have a certain combination of those things that makes them feel sad."

"All the time?"

"Usually not all the time."

"Gabe wasn't sad until Lacey came."

"Our environment—what's happening around us—affects the chemicals inside our bodies."

"Lacey made my body's chemicals feel bad," Ursa said.

"Mine too," Jo said.

They checked the nest at the far end of the length of road, then headed in the direction of the Nash driveway. They were on their way to monitor a cardinal nest, wading through vegetation powdered with lime-rock dust, when they heard Gabe's truck. "Gabe! Gabe!" Ursa called, waving her arms.

Gabe slowed the truck, smiled, and waved back but kept on driving.

"Why didn't he stop?" Ursa asked.

"I guess he didn't want to bother us when we're working. He has work to do, too."

"But he could have stopped for one minute!"

He could have.

An hour later, they finished the work and drove to the intersection where Gabe was seated beneath his blue canopy and **FRESH EGGS** sign. Jo parked in the ditch behind his truck. Ursa sprang outside and ran to his table. "We missed you!" she said. "Why haven't you come over?"

"I thought it best to let things settle down," he said, his eyes on Jo as she approached.

Jo stood next to Ursa. "Did Lacey leave?"

"She left the day before yesterday."

Which meant she'd stayed at the cabin one more day. "How have you been?"

"Just great," he said brusquely, aware of the question's implication.

"Can I stay at Gabe's farm today, like I used to?" Ursa asked. "Can I? Please?"

"That would be up to Gabe," Jo said.

"That can't happen anymore," he said.

"Why not?" Ursa said.

"You know why. If my mother tells my sister you're spending days at the farm again, Lacey will call the police."

"I could stay in places your mom can't see."

"It's not a good idea," he said, watching a car pull up to his stand.

"Can I see the kittens tonight? When Jo and I get back? Your mom won't see me in the dark."

"How's it going, Jen?" he said to the approaching middle-aged woman in a nurse's uniform.

"I'm beat and ready for bed," the woman said. "I'll take a dozen." She handed Gabe a five.

"Thank you, ma'am," he said, giving her change.

She took a carton off the table. "Have a good one, Gabe."

"You too." As Jen walked away, he lifted a battered copy of *Zen and the Art of Motorcycle Maintenance* out of his lap.

"Can I?" Ursa said.

"Can you *what*?" he said.

"See the kittens tonight."

"I told you why you can't be at my place anymore. If the sheriff comes again, they'll be set on taking you where you belong." Looking at Jo, he added, "They have to do what's right."

Ursa stared at him like she didn't know who he was.

"Come on," Jo said. When Ursa didn't move, Jo took her hand and tugged her toward the car. Gabe kept his eyes fixed on the paperback in his hands.

"Why is Gabe mad at us?" Ursa asked when they were driving again.

"We shouldn't assume he's mad." She wished he were only angry. Because what he was doing was much worse. He was freezing them out, shutting down his emotions.

They worked a typical day, but everything felt strange. Ursa was more subdued than Jo had ever seen her. She barely even reacted when they saw a fox running along the edge of a cornfield. At the end of the day she was still quiet, and Jo thought they might make it past the Nash homestead without reference to Gabe.

That would not be their fate. As the Honda's headlights hit the dark Nash driveway, they shined on Gabe seated on his open pickup gate. He dropped to his feet and waved them down.

"What's up?" Jo said out her window.

"I've been waiting for you. You're getting in late."

"I had to run to the grocery store."

"Are you too hungry to see the kittens?"

"No!" Ursa said.

"Follow me in," he said.

At the barn, Ursa jumped outside as Jo shut down the car. "Can I go in?" she said.

"Hold your horses and wait for Jo," Gabe said.

"I wish I had horses to hold," Ursa said.

The interior of the barn was black, but Gabe turned on a lantern to light their way to the kittens. The mother cat emerged from shadows, mewing at Gabe as he set the lantern on a hay bale near her nest.

"Look how big they got!" Ursa said. "And they can kind of walk!" She petted each kitten as she said its name. She scooped Juliet and Hamlet into her hands and held them against her cheeks. "Did you miss me? I missed you."

"Would you come outside for a minute?" Gabe asked Jo.

Ursa sprawled on her belly, watching Juliet and Hamlet clumsily tussle.

"Jo and I will be right back," Gabe said.

Once outside, he closed the barn door and led Jo out of Ursa's earshot. "I wanted to apologize for how I behaved this morning," he said.

"You should be saying that to Ursa."

"Was she upset?"

"I think she was."

He studied the ground, preparing to say something. He looked at her. "That's more the reason she can't come around."

"I'm not sure what you're saying."

"She's gotten too attached. And I have . . ." He looked away from Jo's eyes for a few seconds. "This can't end well," he said. "Every day you don't turn her in to the police, you're making it worse for all of us."

She bristled at his phrasing—*you* instead of *we*—as if he were abandoning all responsibility for keeping Ursa.

"Do you even think about what you're doing?" he asked. "You're bonding with a kid who'll be heartbroken when you go back to your life up at the university. You're feeding a dog that will starve when you leave, and you've let Ursa get attached to him. No way will that dog be going wherever she ends up."

She didn't need his lecture. She harangued herself on those same points constantly.

"I can't be a part of this anymore," he said. "Everyone's going to get hurt."

"More like it already hurts and you want it to stop before it gets worse."

"Yeah, it already hurts—maybe for her more than us. This thing has gone too far." He waited for her to respond. "Don't you agree?"

"I do. It's gone further than I ever imagined." Jo scraped a line in the gravel with the toe of her boot. "When I knew my mother would be dead in a few months, I had two choices . . ." She looked at him. "I could distance myself from the pain or get closer to it. Maybe because I'd lost my dad without getting a chance to tell him what he meant to me, I decided to get closer. I got so close, her pain and fear became my own. We shared everything and loved each other like we never had when death was some distant thing. In the end, part of me died with her. I'm not recovered from it even now, but I made the conscious choice to enter the darkness with her. Everyone I know who's lost someone they love has voiced regrets—they wish they'd done this or that or loved them more. I have no regrets. None."

He had nothing to say.

"I guess it's impossible for you to understand."

"The dumb farm guy isn't quite that dumb," he said. "I've always thought what's happening with you and Ursa has something to do with what you've been through. But it's not the same as what happened with your mother. In the end, you *will* have regrets. Loving her will only have increased Ursa's pain."

"What if the end is different from what you imagine?"

"How?"

"I might try to become her foster parent." She had never vocalized the tantalizing idea. Finally, it was out there. And she felt good about it.

He just stared at her.

"I know you have to get certified or whatever, but I doubt that's too difficult. And even though I'm single, I have the resources they'll want a foster parent to have. My dad had a big life insurance policy because his work was risky. My mom used some of that money to buy another policy because she was a single parent. I have enough money to hire people who can watch Ursa when I'm in school. And I have a plan for Little Bear, too. I can't have dogs where I live, but Tabby is good at finding homes for strays. I'm hoping one of her vet friends will adopt him and Ursa can visit."

"No matter how much money you have and what you plan for the dog, you can't change the fact that you've lied to the police."

"I haven't broken any laws."

"You have. We both have. Do you know what that deputy told Lacey? He said letting someone else's kid stay in your home—especially when she's hurt—is considered child endangerment. Maybe even kidnapping. Do you really think they'd let you become a foster parent after what you've done?"

"I've only ever been good to her! Ursa would verify that."

"What about when she tells them she went to work with you every day—for twelve hours in extreme heat, no less?"

"She wants to go. And leaving her home alone would be worse."

The hollowness of her last words echoed in his silence.

"Okay, you know what?" she said. "I won't let Lacey shit all over my life like you do."

"This has nothing to do with Lacey!"

"Doesn't it? That last day she stayed here she did a great job of sucking all the joy out of you. Ursa and I saw the change in you this morning. If you keep this up—being afraid to get involved with people—you'll end up as bitter as she is, which is exactly what she wants." She walked to the barn, opened the door, and called, "Ursa, let's go. We need to eat dinner before we're too tired to cook."

Ursa appeared from behind the hay bales. "Can Gabe have dinner with us?"

"I don't think so."

Ursa ran to Gabe, standing halfway between the parked cars and the barn. "Do you want to come over for dinner? We're having chili and cornbread."

"Sounds great, but I'd better get back to my mom." Tousling her hair, he said, "Have a good dinner, kiddo."

Ursa was as quiet as Jo on the drive home. Little Bear danced around the car as she parked in the moonlit driveway. "Are you and Gabe mad at each other?" Ursa asked.

"Not exactly mad," Jo said.

"Then what's wrong?"

"Gabe has decided he doesn't want to hang out with us anymore. He still really likes you—don't ever doubt that—but he's afraid about what could happen."

"What could happen?"

"For one thing, he's afraid he'll get in trouble with the police."

"He wouldn't get in trouble. I'd tell the police my home is in the stars."

"You know they won't believe that." Jo turned around in her seat to face her, a dark shape in slightly brighter darkness. "I hope someday soon you'll tell me the truth. You should trust me enough by now. You know I'll fight for what makes you happiest."

Ursa turned her face to the car window. "What if . . ."

Jo didn't move, almost didn't breathe, to give her a refuge of silence in which to speak. She was certain Ursa was on the brink of telling her something important.

But Ursa only kept staring out at the dark forest.

"What were you going to say?" Jo asked.

She looked at Jo. "What if I really am from another world? Have you ever, even for a second, believed me?"

She'd lost her nerve. Or she'd never intended to say anything. Whichever it was, Jo understood her predicament. Ursa Major was fictional, only the shape of a bear bounded in stars. The girl lived as a parallel constellation. Like a child who obsessively colors within the lines, she had to regulate her every move or she might end up in the terrifying universe that lay beyond the shape she'd drawn to contain herself.

"Why won't you believe me?" Ursa pressed.

"I'm a scientist, Ursa."

"Do you believe in aliens at all?"

"Considering the vastness of the universe, it's probable there are other life-forms out there."

"And I'm one of them."

Sometimes Jo was overwhelmed when she tried to imagine what events could make a child stop wanting to be human. And this was one of those times. Ursa, fortunately, couldn't see her tears in the darkness.

"Will you and Gabe ever talk to each other again?" Ursa asked.

"When we buy eggs we'll talk to him."

"That's all?"

Jo wouldn't lie. "Yes, that's probably all."

19

The next morning Ursa wasn't on the couch when Jo went into the living room to wake her. She wasn't in the bathroom either. Jo opened the door to the screened porch and found Little Bear curled up on the rug, looking dozily at her. Next to him was an empty bowl.

Ursa knew she wasn't allowed to feed the dog on the porch. She must have let him in during the night and given him food to keep him quiet while she crept away. Jo had no doubts about where she'd gone.

She returned to the house and verified that Ursa's purple shoes were missing. The clothes Jo had laid out for the morning also were gone. Jo hurriedly dressed, ate, and made the usual lunch food. She packed enough water for her and Ursa. When she carried her gear outside, she shooed Little Bear off the porch and gave him his bowl of food on the back concrete slab.

She drove onto the Nash property in the predawn darkness. She assumed Gabe would be up early, milking the cow and whatever else he did in the morning. She only hoped she didn't have to go to the cabin door. As the car jounced down the wooded driveway and turned toward the barns, her headlights fell on Gabe, lantern in hand, his jeans covered to the knee in rubber boots. He'd heard her coming. Jo rolled down her window. "Ursa's gone."

"Shit. Let's check the kitten barn."

"That was my first guess."

He waved her on to the barn, following at a jog. They entered the barn and walked toward the back wall. The light from Gabe's lantern fell on Ursa. She was asleep with the six kittens, her curled body forming one boundary of a warm nest, the mother cat's body the other. Jo and Gabe didn't move, neither willing to disturb the beauty of the scene.

The mother cat got up and stepped over her co–den mother, waking her. Ursa shielded her eyes from the light of the lantern. "Gabe?" she said.

"And Jo," he said.

Ursa squinted up at them.

"Why are you here?" Jo asked.

Ursa sat up, hay prickled in her tangled hair. "I don't want to never see the kittens or Gabe again."

"Shouldn't that be Gabe's decision?"

Ursa stood and looked at him.

"I'm sorry," he said, "but Jo and I disagree—about where this is going."

"Where *what* is going?" Ursa said.

"You," he said. "I think you need to find a stable home, wherever that may be."

"I have a stable home in the stars."

"He really doesn't want to hear this again," Jo said. "I have an egg sandwich in the car for you. Are you coming with me?"

"I'd rather stay here."

"Here on Earth we don't always get what we want."

"But you and Gabe don't know what you want."

"I'm in no mood, Ursa." She pulled her out of the barn by the hand and let her go. "You'll walk to the car or stay here and risk Gabe calling the police."

"Would you?" she asked Gabe.

He didn't answer.

"I'm leaving," Jo said.

Ursa followed her to the car and climbed into the back seat. "Bye, Gabe," she said mournfully.

"Have a good day," he said, closing her door.

Again, Ursa didn't say much while Jo monitored and searched for nests, but this time, Jo didn't encourage her to talk. She appreciated the silence. Without the distraction of Ursa's chatter, her thoughts were more linear, the way they used to be before Ursa and Gabe. By the end of the day, she agreed with almost everything Gabe had said. There was no way anyone would let her be a foster parent when she'd kept Ursa with her for so long. And that meant Gabe was right about turning her in immediately to reduce the pain.

That night, while Ursa drew a picture with her colored pencils, Jo scanned the missing children websites she hadn't checked for a few days. Though the prospect was painful, she hoped Ursa would be listed. She would have an unarguable reason to help the police ensnare her. But the remarkable child with a dimple in one cheek still wasn't listed as missing.

Jo put Ursa's drawing of a monarch butterfly on the refrigerator next to the indigo bunting. She reminded Ursa to brush her teeth after she put on her pajamas. They went to bed, Ursa on the couch and Jo in the bedroom. Ursa called her usual "Good night, Jo" after Jo put out the lamp.

Jo's usual nocturnal restlessness was worsened by Gabe's abandonment. Bearing the burden of responsibility for Ursa without him was agonizing. Wide awake at one in the morning, she went in the living room to check on Ursa.

She was gone.

Jo stared at the empty couch, contemplating what to do. If she drove to Gabe's, she was letting Ursa control her. If she didn't and she went to work in the morning, Gabe might call the police when he discovered her on his property.

If he did, Ursa would run. Jo knew that with certainty. Ursa would possibly try to hide at the Kinney property, which would bring down a shit storm on Jo and the Kinneys and maybe on the University of Illinois Biology Department, who paid the rent.

If Ursa didn't hide at Kinney Cottage, she could end up anywhere. She was way too trusting, and there were all kinds of dangerous people who might take advantage of that.

Jo slipped her feet into flats and grabbed her keys and a flashlight. Once again, she found Little Bear closed in the screen room with an empty bowl. She left him there, frustrated and barking at her departure.

She shut off the Honda's headlights and turned on parking lights as she arrived at the Nash entry road. She negotiated the ruts at slow speed to minimize noise, and she killed all headlights when she approached the cabin. The house was dark except for a porch light, and all the doors and windows were closed to keep in the air-conditioning. Gabe and his mother probably wouldn't hear her car if she drove slowly.

Using the utility pole light to guide her, she crept down the road to the livestock buildings. She parked and pushed the car door closed with gentle pressure. She didn't turn on the flashlight until she was inside the barn. She walked around the stacks of hay bales and shined her light in the direction of the kitten nest. The mother cat blinked and mewed at her, but Ursa wasn't there. Jo searched the barn, illuminating every niche and corner. No Ursa.

Outside, she looked at the other buildings: a cow shed with two small pastures, a muddy pig field, a chicken coop with a large enclosed outdoor run, and a small wooden building that probably was Gabe's toolshed. Jo doubted Ursa would go in the chicken coop. That left the cow and toolsheds. But she was afraid to sneak around any more than she had on a gun owner's property. She had to get Gabe.

She walked the barn road to the cabin. She stopped in the shadows near the pole light and looked at the cabin, recalling the night she and Ursa had visited Gabe in his bedroom. They'd turned after the living room, and Gabe's room had been the second small one on the left. Jo walked the left wall of the log cabin past the big living room window and the small window of the first bedroom. She stopped at the next one. Hoping Gabe wasn't trigger-happy at night, she lightly rapped on the window with one knuckle. Nothing happened. She knocked louder, and a light came on. The curtains parted, and Gabe appeared in the rectangle of light.

She reacted to the sight of him. More powerfully than she would have expected.

She stepped closer to the window and waved. He unlocked the window and pushed it up. "Gone again?"

"Yes. And I already checked the kitten barn."

"Figures she wouldn't be there. She's too smart for that. I'll meet you out front."

She walked to the porch and waited at the base of the stairs. He came out minutes later wearing a dark T-shirt, work jeans, and his leather slip-on shoes. He'd brought a flashlight.

"I'm really sorry," she said.

"I hope you see this is getting out of hand," he said.

"I know. Did I wake your mother?"

"No." He walked past her and headed for the barns. Jo followed in silence. They checked the toolshed first, the cow barn next. He looked in the chicken coop, rousing disgruntled clucks. He stood in front of the coop, pondering.

"Maybe she finally ran away," Jo said. "She barely said a word today."

"She knows she's worn out the welcome mat."

"Do you think she's gone?"

"No. It's more of her games."

"Let's not forget she's a scared little kid."

"Yeah." He walked away in a new direction.

"Where are we going?"

"The tree house."

Jo followed him about a hundred yards down a trail until his flashlight hit a decayed sign painted with the faded, childishly printed words **Gabe's Homestead**. Below it, on the same stake, was a broken-off board that read **No Tressp**. He shined his flashlight up a huge oak tree onto an incredible tree house. It was high, three times Gabe's height, and supported by four tall log beams. An enchanting spiral staircase with sinuous branch banisters led to its entrance.

"This is the best tree house I ever saw," she said.

"I loved this place. My dad and I built it when I was seven. We constructed it on timbers so we wouldn't hurt the tree." He walked to the staircase that encircled the trunk and thunked his foot on the first stair. "Still in good shape, too."

"Ursa knew about it?"

"She spent hours up here. This is where she stayed out of my mother's sight when I sold eggs."

"I'm surprised she didn't want to sell eggs with you."

"She did."

"Why didn't you let her?"

He faced her. "Funny you don't think of these things."

"What?"

"I was afraid to have her out there on the road. What if whoever she ran from saw her out there? I'd have to let him take her, and I'd have no idea if I was doing the right thing."

"That makes sense."

"You need a little more of that."

The jab hurt, but she was in no mood to retaliate. "What sense can there be when I'm under an alien's control?"

The scowl he'd worn since he came out of the cabin relaxed into a slight smile.

"You may not believe this," she said, "but before star-girl showed up, I used to be a sensible person, almost to the point of annoyance."

"I know the feeling," he said. "I've been fighting a riptide of quarks since I set eyes on her." He held his hand out. "You go up first. I want to be behind you in case you trip."

She didn't need his help, but she accepted his warm hand and caution as reconciliation. But when he released her fingers, he touched her again, on the waist this time, lightly guiding her up the stairs. Was he being a gentleman, or did he crave physical contact with her the way she did from him? Based on the data she'd so far collected, she supposed the former was more probable.

The handrail was sturdy, and good thing, because the treads spiraled dangerously high. Jo arrived at the top, shining her light into a room divided by two large boughs of the oak. A small rope hammock was strung between a wall and one of the trunks. A child-size chair and desk made of what looked like wood pallets sat on the other side of the space. The room opened to two views of the forest, one balcony facing the incoming trail and the other looking down a beautiful wooded ravine. Jo shined her light into the gorge, imagining little Gabe as king of all he surveyed.

"Weird," Gabe said behind her.

She turned around. His flashlight illuminated the small desk. On its surface were two pencils with erasers, an illustrated book of fairy tales, and several pieces of white printer paper weighed down with rocks. The rocks threw sparks of light from crystals embedded in them, the kind Ursa liked to collect.

Jo looked at Ursa's pencil drawings with Gabe: a cartoonish sketch of a frog, a very realistic rendering of a newborn kitten, and the drawing he had pulled out from beneath them. It was a picture of a rectangular grave colored dark with pencil. A white cross with no lettering stood over the burial dirt. Next to the grave, Ursa had written I love you on one side and I am sorry on the other.

"There's a person in that grave," Jo said.

"I know." He picked up the paper, and they examined the grave. Ursa had drawn a prone woman with closed eyes and shoulder-length hair before she colored the dark dirt over her. "Jesus," Gabe said. "Are you thinking what I am?"

"Someone she cared about died, and that's why she's on her own." He nodded.

Jo took the drawing out of his hand. "I wonder why she wrote *I am sorry.*"

"I know. It's creepy," he said.

"Please don't tell me you think that little girl killed someone."

"Who knows what happened? That's why you should have taken her to the police right away."

Jo returned the drawing to the table. "You know, I'm tired of your sudden virtue. I think you've forgotten *you* were the one who decided we should keep her until we found out more about her."

"You're doing it again," he said.

"What am I doing?"

"You attack me to avoid the problem with Ursa."

"Who avoids the problem of Ursa more than you? You dumped us like we were stray cats you didn't want to deal with anymore—only I know you'd have treated cats better."

He came close, right up in her face. "That was a shitty thing to say!"

"It was a shitty thing to do."

"I had to do something. We're already in big trouble. Don't you get that, Jo? We could be arrested for kidnapping and put in jail."

She kept her eyes on his. "That's not why you dumped us."

He couldn't maintain eye contact. And that revealed much more than he'd tried to hide by looking away. Aware that she was onto him, he turned to leave.

Without thinking, she grabbed his forearm. "Don't," she said.

He faced her, his features carefully sculpted. "Don't *what?*"

"Don't close yourself off from me. We need to talk about what's happening between us."

His detached facade faded into outright fear.

At least he knew what she was talking about. "Can't we be honest with each other?"

He stepped back, pulling his arm free of her hand. "I have been honest. I'm fucked up. You know I can't do this."

"You aren't fucked up."

"No?" He wrapped his arms around his chest. "I've never been with a woman. How fucked up is that?"

"Clever," she said.

He unfolded his arms. "What is?"

"You remind me of Ursa—always fortifying the fortress walls, even against the people who fight on your side."

"What does that have to do with anything?"

"You're hoping I'll be shocked and turned off by a twenty-five-year-old guy who's never been with a woman. You said that to get rid of me—just like you use your illness to keep me at a distance."

His jaw clenched, and he glanced at the stairs.

"Please don't run out on me right now."

"We have to find Ursa," he said.

"Is that really all you have to say?"

"What do you want me to say?"

She looked down at Ursa's drawing of the grave. In the dark rectangle that enclosed the dead woman, she saw the empty crematory box that had held her mother's cindered remains. After she'd fulfilled her mother's last wishes—poured her ashes into a cold roll of whitecaps on Lake Michigan—Jo couldn't discard the box, dusted with the pale powder of her mother's body. She still had it. Its emptiness was always there, hidden inside her, a void where her mother's love had been and, more tangibly, where her female body parts had been.

He was looking at the grave with her.

"I'm as afraid as you are, you know," she said.

He raised his eyes from the drawing to hers.

"Remember that feeling you described—the 'horrific crush of humanity' on your soul—maybe that's another way of saying you're afraid people will hurt you if you let them get close."

He kept silent. But how would he know how to respond if he'd never experienced intimacy?

"When you said you'd never been with a woman, did that include kissing?" she asked.

"I didn't know how to be with girls in high school. I had social anxiety."

"Never kissed?"

"Never."

Where they stood, high in the dark forest, felt like a fulcrum, a pinnacle of honesty they'd finally achieved. Ursa had steered them where she wanted them, but any second their unsteady emotions could tip them off that tiny point of balance. Ursa had to be found, certainly, but Jo knew she was safely hidden and not in any real danger. The only danger of the moment was that Jo—and Gabe—might let those seconds pass away without seeing them as Ursa did, as her own teeny tweak of fate in a vast and miraculous universe, as a wondrous gift she was offering to them.

Jo turned off her flashlight and set it on the desk next to her. She tugged his flashlight out of his hand and flicked it off. He startled, moving backward in the sudden darkness. "What are you doing?" he asked.

"Making it easier for you."

"Making what easier?"

"Your first kiss."

20

She had no trouble finding him in the darkness. His body was radiating heat—and maybe fear. He recoiled a little when she put her palms against his chest. She slid her hands up his neck. His skin was warm and humid, like the summer night around them. She ran her hands through his beard and touched her lips to his. Once he got the hang of it, she pressed closer. He'd showered before he went to bed, but the smell of his fit body, with tinges of forest and farm, overpowered the light fragrance of soap. "I love the way you smell."

"You do?"

"I have a weirdly primitive sense of smell." She slipped her hands under the bottom edge of his T-shirt and pushed it upward. She placed her face against his skin and breathed him in. "Mmm . . ."

"Jo . . ."

She tilted her face up to his. "What?"

He touched his mouth to hers. An exceptional kiss.

After they parted lips, she pressed her body against his. He wanted it, too, holding her tighter. They fit together with ease, as if their bodies had known this outcome and prepared for it since the day they first met out on the road. They melted into one another and into the night. She hadn't believed darkness could ever feel that good again.

"Is this too much crush on your soul?" she asked.

"It's the perfect amount of soul crushing," he said.

But Ursa was there with them. Jo was haunted by the drawing of the grave. "I wish we could do this all night," she said, "but we have to find Ursa."

He pulled back but kept one hand on her waist. "I think I know where she is. It's the only place left to look."

"Then she better be there."

He felt around for a flashlight. Jo found one first and turned it on. A man often looked different to her after the first release of sexual tension—as if he were somehow softer, especially in the eyes—and she wondered if Gabe saw her differently. He was staring intently.

"Where do you think she is?"

"In the little cabin. My dad built it when our family outgrew the big cabin. Lacey's boys loved staying out there alone when they got old enough."

"Ursa knew about it?"

"I showed it to her one day. You always have to keep that girl's brain stimulated."

"That's for sure."

He held her hand on the way to the stairs, letting it go with reluctance as he led the way down. They descended from the giddy atmosphere of the treetops to the soft earth of the forest. "This way," he said.

They passed the **GABE'S HOMESTEAD** sign and turned onto a new trail. After a few minutes, Jo saw the little cabin in Gabe's flashlight beam. The rustic tin-roofed structure reminded her of a summer camp cabin. It was made of unpainted cedar shingles and elevated about three feet from the ground on wooden poles. "This is beautiful," she said. "Who'd ever think a literature professor would be so good at building things?"

"Arthur Nash was what you'd call a Renaissance man. He could do anything."

She followed him up the wooden stairs and onto a screened porch with two rocking chairs that faced the woods. He slowly opened a wooden door, its rusted hinges whining from lack of use. The door led to a small open area with a table and chairs, behind it two sleeping rooms. Gabe shined his light into the left bedroom, while Jo looked in the right. "Here," Gabe said. Jo went to him and saw Ursa curled on her side on the lower bunk of a two-tiered bed. She still had on the blue flower-print pajamas she'd worn to bed, and she'd brought the afghan from the porch couch to use as a pillow. Her eyelids quivered in a dream state.

"Don't say anything about the grave drawing," Jo whispered. "Not tonight."

He nodded.

She turned off her light and sat on the edge of the lower bunk. She stroked Ursa's hair. "Come on, Big Bear, wake up," she said.

Ursa's soulful brown eyes opened, and her first sleepy words confirmed the strategy behind her elopement. "Is Gabe here?"

"I am," Gabe said. He walked over, keeping his flashlight out of her eyes. "Jo and I have decided you have to sleep in a locked dog crate from now on."

Ursa sat up. "No I don't."

"You'll get used to it."

She smiled drowsily.

He crouched in front of her like he had the night she got lost on the creek. "Get on my back and I'll carry you home."

"That's too far to carry her," Jo said.

"Then I'll take her to your car and ride home with you."

"You will?" Ursa said.

"Yep. Climb aboard. The Gabriel Express is leaving."

Ursa scrambled up onto his back.

"Look who's enabling her now," Jo muttered. "How did that happen?"

He carried Ursa out the door, a covert smile peeking from under his beard. Jo bundled the afghan into her arms and followed. When they arrived at the car, Gabe deposited Ursa into the back seat and sat next to her.

"Are you sure you can leave your mom?" Jo said. "What if she has to go to the bathroom?"

"She still manages that herself, thank god. But her balance is getting worse, and she refuses to use the walker Lacey bought."

Jo looked at him in the rearview mirror as she began to drive. Ursa was snuggled against his chest, and he had his arms around her. She hated to take her eyes off them but had to confront the rutted road ahead. "Damn it," she said when the chassis scraped bottom. "Your road is ruining my mom's car."

"This was hers?" he said.

"Yes." Jo turned left on Turkey Creek Road and drove to the Kinney property, where Little Bear, locked on the screened porch, barked rowdily.

Gabe carried Ursa into the house. He tried to lay her on the couch, but she sat up. "You have to sleep," he said.

"Don't leave," she said.

"I'll stay right here. Go to sleep." He covered her with a blanket as she put her head on the pillow. Jo kept the house dark, turning only the stove light on.

"Why are you nice again?" Ursa asked him.

"I'm always nice," he said.

"Not sometimes."

"Close your eyes." He sat on the edge of the couch, his arm resting across her as she fell asleep. Jo sat in the chair next to them. When Ursa's breathing became deep and regular, Gabe motioned to the front door. They stepped out of the cooled cottage into the sultry forest.

"I'll drive you home," Jo said.

"I'd rather walk," he said.

"Need to expend the first-kiss energy?"

"Is that what this is? To expend it all, I'd have to walk thirty miles."

"Same here. Maybe a good-night peck will help." She wrapped her arms around him and gave him more than a peck.

"I think that made it worse." He held her, looking at the house over her shoulder. "It's so strange that I love coming here now. I used to hate this house. I hadn't looked at it for years until that day you asked me to bring over the eggs."

Jo pulled out of his arms. "Why would you hate it? I thought you were close with the Kinneys?"

"Not really."

"You said George Kinney taught you about aquatic insects."

"He did."

"Well, your mom obviously likes him, so it must be your dad who didn't."

"Arthur and George had a weird love-hate relationship."

"Why?"

"Arthur had the kind of confident intelligence that was always on display. He had to be the smartest guy in the room, the one who had the last brilliant word on any topic. George is as smart and confident as him, but in a quiet way. I don't know what he's like now, but when I was a kid, George Kinney was . . . it was like he knew actual mysteries of the universe, but he was too laid-back to care about sharing them."

"Silent waters run deep?"

"Definitely, and George's quiet confidence bothered Arthur. Arthur would try to undermine him with these underhanded jabs that he disguised as jokes. Like, he often pointed out that George was a 'bug picker' at the University of Illinois while he was a lit scholar at the University of Chicago."

"Geez, poor George."

"You don't have to feel sorry for him. It rolled off George like water off a duck. He'd laugh along, and Arthur would end up looking like a jerk. Somehow, George always got the upper hand. Arthur dominated social situations with funny stories and intellectual discussions, and then there would be George, quietly collecting the smartest people in the room with his few carefully selected words."

"He didn't have to work at it."

"Right."

"That's why your dad and George stopped being friends?"

"They were friends until the day Arthur died."

"Then why did you hate this house?"

He gazed pensively into the forest. "Have you seen the old graveyard between these two properties?"

"What, did you think the graveyard was haunted when you were little?"

His lips twisted into a wry smile. "Yeah, I'd have to say it's haunted."

"Really? What's the ghost's name?"

His smile vanished. "Get your flashlight and I'll show you."

21

Jo needed sleep, but she had to find out what had caused Gabe's cryptic mood change. She checked Ursa in the living room and grabbed a flashlight, turning it on as she met Gabe on the walkway. "This way," he said, leading her toward the forest. Little Bear followed, his tail wagging, game for a stroll even at that late hour.

Gabe shined his light on the western side of the gravel driveway. "It's been a while, but I think we go in here." They pushed through thick vegetation at the edge of the driveway. But once they were deeper in, the woods opened up and were easier to navigate.

"My parents and I came down here at least one weekend of every month during the school year, and we stayed most of the summer," Gabe said as they walked. "George and Lynne—his wife—didn't visit their property as often, but they were around a lot when I was a kid."

After a short pause, he said, "When I was eleven, I noticed my mom and George had this strange inside joke. My mom almost always started it. She'd use the words *hope* or *love it* when she was talking to him."

"I'm not sure I get what you mean."

"She would say *One can only hope* in response to something George said, or *Look at that sunset—you have to love it.*"

"Weird," Jo said.

"Yeah, it intrigued me." He and Jo stepped over a log together. "It made me pay more attention to them. Most adults don't realize kids are listening or how much they understand."

"That's for sure."

He stopped walking and shined his light back and forth to orient himself. He steered toward a rock outcrop to the left. "So the more I eavesdropped on them, the more I saw that bothered me."

"Uh-oh."

"Yeah, uh-oh. By the time I was twelve, I was convinced they were having an affair. That summer I was down at the creek looking at insects with George, and he mentioned that he was tired because he'd had insomnia the night before."

"So what?"

"My mother often had insomnia, and she said the only thing that cured it was going for a long walk."

"That's hardly proof."

"I know. But just a few weeks later, I explored a new patch of woods between the Nash and Kinney properties. I always took the road, usually on my bike, when I went over to the Kinneys'."

"You were here, in these woods?"

"I was, and this was what I stumbled on." He aimed his light left, illuminating a cluster of tombstones. "In the eighteen hundreds there was a small church here, and some people were buried in its graveyard before it burned down in 1911."

They walked to the graves, Gabe shining his light on the tallest marker. It was a cross made of worn white stone that immediately brought Ursa's drawing to mind. It was scoured by time but still readable. The etched lettering in the middle of the cross read HOPE LOVETT, AUG. 11, 1881 – DEC. 26, 1899.

"*Hope Lovett*," Jo said.

"Do you see the connection?"

"I do, but are you sure it's a connection? Maybe it's a coincidence."

"I considered that, but I decided it had to be linked to my mother's inside joke with George."

"Was this . . ." She hated to say it.

"Where they met?"

"Was it?"

"I was determined to find out," he said. "George and Lynne arrived a week and half after I found this place, and as usual, they came over to the cabin for drinks and dinner. I kept George and my mother within earshot the whole night, but I didn't hear what I was waiting for until George and his wife were leaving. My mother and George walked outside before my dad and Lynne. I slipped outside and sat on the porch rocker to listen. George said something about how hot it was, and my mother said, *I hope it rains tonight and cools things off.* George smiled but didn't say anything. *Don't you love it when it storms at night?* my mother said, and George answered, *Yes.*"

"So you thought that was the code to meet at this grave marker?"

"Of course."

"It all sounds too childish. Are you sure their affair wasn't concocted by your overactive twelve-year-old mind?"

"I staked them out."

"How?"

"I set up my tent in the woods down in the ravine. By then, the cabin and tree house were too tame for me."

"You snuck out of the tent and came here?"

"I didn't have to sneak. My parents let me roam these properties as much as I wanted." He shined his light on a pile of boulders nearby. "Those rocks were probably dug from the foundation when they built the church. That's where I staked them out." He walked over to the boulders, and Jo followed. "You see what a good view I had?"

"I see. Tell me what happened. The suspense is killing me."

"I arrived here shortly after sunset and waited. I'd brought water and snacks and a book of crossword puzzles because I knew I'd have trouble staying awake."

"Crossword puzzles while you were staking out your mother's affair?"

"My dad and I loved crosswords. I was a major nerd."

"Tell me what happened!"

"At five minutes to midnight, I saw a flashlight coming from the direction of my cabin. It was my mother. She was carrying a blanket and wearing a flowered dress I'd always liked."

"Oh god."

"She spread the blanket on Hope's grave and looked toward the Kinney property. About five minutes later, another light approached from the Kinney side of the forest. My mother put her light on the ground so it reflected off the white cross. George Kinney came into view holding an old kerosene lantern. He put down his lantern and they kissed."

"Gabe, I'm so sorry."

He didn't hear. He stared at the white cross. "My mother said, *Hope's ghost has missed us* as she opened his pants, and old George showed about as much emotion as I'd ever seen in him."

"What did you do?"

"What could I do? I was stuck. One move and they'd hear me crunching leaves and twigs. All I could do was watch." He looked at the cross again. "I learned a lot about sex that night. They did pretty much everything you can do."

Jo held his hand. "Let's go."

"You haven't heard the best part," he said in a sarcastic tone that didn't sound like him. "Afterward they talked. At first they didn't say anything that interesting. But then George said, *Did you know Gabe and I sampled the creek again? His appetite for the natural world is insatiable.*

My mother said, *The apple doesn't fall far, does it? I'm so happy you can spend time with your son.*"

Jo tried to hold him, but his body was wooden. He wouldn't take his eyes off the cross. She tried to turn his face away with her hand. He wouldn't move. "Turns out everyone knew," he said. "I have his face. That's why I grew the beard, so I wouldn't have to see him in the fucking mirror every day. I haven't seen my face since I could grow a full beard—since I was sixteen."

"Your father knew?"

"He had to. Their affair was obvious. I'd figured it out at age twelve even though I knew nothing about things like that. And like I said, I'm a replica of George. The only person who probably didn't know was Lynne, George's wife. She wasn't the brightest person, and I think that's part of the reason George went for my mother. Katherine is smart but very devious. Lacey is a lot like her."

"Lacey knows?"

Finally, he looked at her. "Of course. That's why she hates me. She has our father's face—the heavy chin and nose—and I got George's even features. That night I figured out why she'd tortured me since I was a baby."

"I'm sure it's about more than looks."

"It is. I'm evidence of Katherine and Arthur's failures. Lacey revered her father, and she hated that he remained friends with George, even when he was screwing his wife. It was painful to see what a pitiful creature Arthur was."

"Have you ever talked to her about any of this?"

"Tonight is the first time I've told anyone."

"You didn't tell your psychologist when you had your breakdown?"

"Why would I?"

"To help you come to terms with it. Before you knew George was your father, you liked him. He and your mother never meant for you to see what you did."

"But I did see! Do you know when it was finally over I vomited? I didn't get out of bed for two full days. They couldn't figure out why I didn't have a fever."

"So that's when it started."

"What?"

"Using your bed to shut out the world when something upset you."

He stared at her, his eyes "like thunder," as Ursa said.

"Maybe it all has to do with that night," she said.

"Right, and you never had cancer. You cut off your breasts just to make yourself miserable."

"Gabe!"

"You see how it feels?" He walked away.

"I'm not saying you don't have depression," she said to his back. "I was talking about the cause. Depression can come from genetics, environment, or both."

He kept walking.

"I don't believe this! You're doing it again. Is that why you brought me here and told me this story—so you'd have another reason to push me away?"

His body disappeared into the trees, the glow of his flashlight fading with him. She walked to Hope Lovett's grave and shined her light on the cross. Hope had died at age eighteen—the day after Christmas, just before the start of a new century. It couldn't get much sadder than that. The grave was a strange place to meet a lover.

But maybe not. Katherine was a poet. She might have seen it as a metaphor—a renewal of hope and youth—after she'd given up many dreams for her marriage and children.

Jo swept her flashlight over more faded grave markers, astounded by how many of the dead were babies and children, often buried next to the parents who'd watched them die. Maybe Katherine had been paying tribute to them. Gabe may have been conceived right there, with Hope's ghost watching.

Jo walked back to George Kinney's house, Little Bear following. It was 3:40 when she arrived, and Ursa was in a deep sleep. No way Jo could get up in an hour. She didn't set her alarm.

When she tried to sleep, her thoughts manically cycled through everything that had happened in the last few hours. By four thirty, she was delirious. She desperately needed sleep and relief from her thoughts. Thoughts of the graves and Ursa's buried woman overshadowed her intimacy with Gabe in the tree house. Everything was wrong. She shouldn't have kissed Gabe. She shouldn't have let Ursa stay. Why had she let such a mess interfere with her research?

22

"Jo?"

Ursa stood over her, still wearing her pajamas. Jo picked up her phone and looked at the time. 9:16 a.m.!

"Are you sick?" Ursa asked.

"No," Jo said. "Did you just get up?"

"Yes."

"You must have been as tired as I was."

"Where's Gabe?"

"At home."

"He said he would stay."

"He can't. He has to take care of everything at his house. You know his mother is sick."

"Will we see him today?"

"I don't know." Jo got up and made coffee and breakfast. They didn't get out the door until 10:20. She slowed the Honda when she saw Gabe standing in the middle of Turkey Creek Road. He had a metal rake in his gloved hands, and his clothes were soaked with sweat. He looked up, surprised when he saw them. Jo stopped the car, her eyes drawn to his shockingly white driveway, its dirt and ruts covered with a thick layer of new white gravel. She opened her window.

"You're getting a late start," he said breathlessly, dragging a sleeve over his dripping brow. "I assumed you were out."

"I needed a little extra sleep."

"I know the feeling." He gestured his chin toward his road. "What do you think?"

"You did all of that this morning?"

"The delivery guy did some of it. I raked it and trimmed back the trees."

"You need a new No Trespassing sign to keep up with the improvements."

"Or a Welcome sign," he said, a quick glance at her eyes. He looked at Ursa in the back seat. "Hey, runaway bunny, how are you?"

"Good," Ursa said. "I like your road."

"You'll have to try it out sometime."

"Can we have dinner with Gabe tonight?" Ursa asked Jo.

Jo and Gabe's eyes met. "I'm sorry I ran off," he said, leaning closer.

"Me too—for what I said."

"Don't be." He stepped back and set gloved hands atop his rake handle. "So, dinner?"

"We'll get back late because I have to catch up."

"I can eat light with my mother." When Jo didn't answer right away, he backed up farther. "Let me know if you want to. You'd better get going."

Jo nodded and put the car in drive. They worked the riparian edges of North Fork and Jessie Branch. Summers Creek was next, but a late-afternoon storm had darkened the western sky by the time they arrived. "It's like the day we came here with Gabe," Ursa said.

"I know. They say lightning doesn't strike twice in the same place, but I'm not going to risk it." Jo pulled the Honda out of the ditch.

"Where are we going?"

"Home. That storm looks ominous."

The storm hit while they drove back to Kinney's. Jo had to pull over because she couldn't see the road through the downpour. Ursa loved it. While they waited, Jo taught her how to count seconds between lightning and thunder to estimate how far away the storm's center was.

They arrived at Turkey Creek Road at quarter to five, just as the severe weather cleared. As expected, their approach to the Nash property elicited Ursa's pleadings. "Are we having dinner with Gabe? He said we should let him know."

Jo stopped the car and contemplated the bright-white welcome of gravel in his driveway. He was sending a clear message. But the status of their relationship was far from transparent. And if she was to go further, she had to see her path at least a little better. She turned the Honda down the lane.

"Yay!" Ursa said.

The drive to the cabin took less than half the time it had with all the ruts. "Scrunch down," Jo said before she stopped next to Gabe's truck.

"Why?" Ursa said.

"You know why. I don't want Katherine to see you. She might mention it to Lacey."

Ursa slouched below the window.

"I'll be back in five minutes," Jo said.

"That long?"

"Stay down."

She walked up the porch stairs and knocked on the door. Gabe answered, releasing a redolence of roasting beef from the house. He was wearing the pink apron again. "Can I kiss the cook?" she said. He smiled but glanced anxiously backward before he let her peck his lips.

"I guess the storm brought you home early," he said.

Jo nodded. "We were at Summers Creek when we first saw it."

"No wonder you came back."

"Have you eaten?" she asked.

"I was just making dinner, but I can come over after."

"That sounds good. Do you like grilled mahi? I'm making it for Ursa to try tonight."

"I love grilled mahi."

"Is your mom in the kitchen?"

"Yeah, why?"

"I want to say hello."

"You don't have to," he said, blocking the door with his body.

She pushed past him and walked into the house. His mother was seated at the kitchen table, and she smiled when she saw Jo. "How are you, Katherine?" Jo said.

"Just fine," she said. She studied Jo's field clothes and messy hair. "How is your bird research coming along?"

"Good. Did Gabe tell you he came out with me one day? He even found a nest."

"Really!" she said, looking at Gabe.

Gabe made an evasive move when Jo reached for him, but she captured him around the waist before he got away.

Katherine's bright-blue eyes sharpened.

"Can I borrow your son this evening?" Jo asked. "I've invited him over for dinner."

"Oh . . . yes . . . that would be all right," she said.

Jo kissed Gabe's bearded cheek. "Can you be there around six?"

"Sure," he said tensely, very aware that his mother was scrutinizing Jo's intimate gestures. When Jo let him go, he bolted to the stove and busied himself with a simmering pot.

"I have another request," Jo said, "and I hope it doesn't sound too pushy."

Gabe turned around, his expression panicked.

"Gabe told me you write poetry . . ."

"Now, why would you go and do that?" she said to Gabe.

"I'd love to read it," Jo said. "Do you have copies of your two books I could borrow?"

The tremble in Katherine's hands worsened, as if by her agitation. "I think he's made it sound better than it is."

"As a biologist, I'll be completely nonjudgmental. I just like the idea of reading poetry that has its roots in this place. Did you ever write about the nature of Southern Illinois?"

"I did," she said. "There are even a few birds in my poems. One is about a nest I found."

"What kind?"

"It was a yellow-breasted chat."

"I love chats. I found a nest last month."

"Well, that's something, isn't it?" She said to Gabe, "You know where the extras are. Get her one of each."

After he left the room, Katherine asked, "Whatever happened to that little girl who used to come around?"

"She still comes and goes," Jo said.

Gabe returned and handed Jo two softcover books, one titled *Creature Hush*, the other *Hope's Ghost*. He watched Jo to see how she reacted to the second title. "Thanks," she said.

"You can keep them," Katherine said. "No one wants them, least of all me."

"Well, we're always our own worst critic, I guess. I'd better let you get back to dinner before something burns. Have a nice night, Katherine."

"You too," she said.

Gabe walked her to the door. "I know what you're doing, you sneak," he said once they got outside.

"What?"

"You're bringing her to your corner."

"If it's a boxing ring, who are the two fighters?"

He pondered. "You know, I'm not sure—because you're as devious as she is."

"Why do men often call smart women *devious*?"

"Okay, you're as *smart* as her."

She kissed him. "Save that sexy talk for later."

191

23

Gabe brought leftover cauliflower in cheese sauce for dinner.

"Not yuckyflower!" Ursa said. "Jo made me eat it last night!"

"This has gooey cheese on it," he said, "and gooey cheese makes anything, even dirt, taste delicious."

"Can I eat dirt instead?"

"I love women with razor-sharp wit," he said. "Though I'm badly outnumbered by them lately." He put the bowl of cauliflower on the kitchen table. "How can I help?"

"You've already cooked a whole dinner," Jo said. "You'll go outside into the roaring heat—greatly increased by the fire—and enjoy a cold beer and hors d'oeuvre with Ursa. Except Ursa can't have a beer." She handed a plate of crackers topped with cheddar cheese to Ursa.

"I made these," Ursa said.

"They look great," he said.

Jo took a beer out of the refrigerator, opened it, and placed it in his hand. "Go outside. I'll start grilling in a few minutes."

"Jo is making me eat something called *mahi-mahi*," Ursa said as they went out the back door.

"I've heard of that—I think it's giant caterpillars," he said, closing the door behind them.

Jo seasoned melted butter and brought it outside with the fish and vegetable skewers. She laid the skewers over the fire first. When they were nearly done cooking, she put on the mahi fillets, basting them with butter as they grilled. Despite the heat, they ate outside, sitting in the frayed lawn chairs that probably dated back to the Kinneys' occupation of the house.

"I read a few of your mother's poems after I showered," Jo said as they finished eating.

"Which book?"

"*Creature Hush*. I want to read them chronologically."

"That's the only one I've read," he said. "It came out two years before I was born."

"You've never read any of the poems in *Hope's Ghost*?"

"No. It was published when I was thirteen—just a year after . . ."

"After what?" Ursa said.

"After I discovered the meaning of life," he said.

Ursa studied him, trying to understand what he'd meant. She was like Gabe had been as a child, highly attuned to every nuance of adult behavior. Trying to keep their budding romance secret would be pointless. Certainly she already sensed the difference between them.

"Wow, a clean plate," Jo said to her. "Even the cauliflower is gone."

"The cheese made it okay," she said. "You should do that when you make yuckyflower."

"Thanks," Jo told Gabe. "You've set the bar way too high for my simplistic cooking skills."

"You're welcome. But I'll vouch for your simple cooking. The fish was delicious."

"Can I get the marshmallows?" Ursa asked.

"Let's wait a little," Jo said.

Ursa slouched in her chair.

"I wanted to ask you about something," Jo said to her.

"What?"

"Last night when Gabe and I were looking for you, we checked the tree house and found some of your drawings."

Ursa remained slumped, her expression impassive.

"In the picture of the grave, who was buried under the dirt?"

"A dead person," Ursa said.

"Yes, but who?"

She sat up. "It was me."

"You?" Gabe said.

"This body, I mean. I took a dead girl's body, remember?" Jo and Gabe waited for further explanation. "I felt bad about taking it. I knew people on this planet are supposed to be buried, so I did that. I drew her and then I buried her and put one of those cross things over her like you see in cemeteries."

"Why did the picture say 'I love you' and 'I am sorry'?" Jo asked.

"Because I love her. It's because of her I have a body. And I said I'm sorry because she never got to be buried."

Gabe looked at Jo and lifted his brows.

"Who did you think it was?" Ursa asked.

"Someone from your past," Jo said.

"I have no past on this planet." She climbed off her chair. "Can I have more milk?"

"Sure," Jo said.

"She gave a plausible answer," Gabe said when Ursa went inside.

"I thought she looked nervous when I asked."

"Face it," he said, "she's too smart to be tripped up even when she trips up."

"Well, I need her to talk before I leave."

"When is that?"

"About a month, early August."

"Shit," he said.

"I know. Starting this thing was masochism, right?"

"Speaking of *this thing* . . ." He leaned over and kissed her. "I've been dying to do that. You looked quite fetching while you slaved over the fire."

"You're a real cave guy."

"No doubt."

They kissed again. "You'll never get that fish smell out of your beard," she said.

"As a cave woman, you shouldn't mind."

"I'm not a cave woman."

"You don't like beards?"

"Truthfully, no. I love a clean-shaven face."

He rubbed his hand over the beard. "I could trim it."

"You could shave it."

"Nope."

"Sit down," she said.

"Why?"

"Sit down."

He sat just as Ursa came out with her milk.

"If you won't shave it, I will," Jo said. And before he could get up, she sat sideways in his lap.

"Jo, what are you doing?" Ursa said.

"I'm holding Gabe hostage. Bring me scissors and a razor from the bathroom."

"Why?"

"You and I are going to shave off his beard."

"Really?" Ursa said.

"No," Gabe said.

"Don't you think he'd look handsome?" Jo said.

"I don't know . . . ," Ursa said.

"You see?" he said.

"But I want to!" Ursa said. "It will be fun!"

"Ursa! You're supposed to be on my side," he said.

"I'm getting the stuff." She scooted to the door, milk sloshing over her hand.

"I'll need that can of shaving cream someone left under the sink," Jo called to her. "And a bowl of warm water."

"Jo, come on . . . ," Gabe said.

"You come on. You said you haven't seen your face since you could grow a beard."

"You know why."

"Don't you think it's time to stop hiding from who you are?"

"I don't want to see his face every day!"

"You aren't him. Anyway, your face has a lot of your mother in it. Your eyes are like hers."

"I know. I tried to grow the beard over them, but it wouldn't take."

She stroked her fingers on the hair below his eye. "It nearly has." She kissed him softly. "Please let me. If you hate it, you can grow it back." She kissed him again. "Don't you want to be irresistible to me?"

"Like George?"

"I've seen George. He's not really my type."

"Where have you seen him?"

"In the biology office. He's an emeritus professor—retired, but still doing research."

"Figures. He'll do research till the day he dies."

"My advisor said that about him. He's a legend among entomologists."

"Yeah, around here, too."

Jo grabbed the bottom of his T-shirt and lifted it.

"Are you going to shave my chest, too?"

"No, I like chest hair. But you have to take this off or it'll get wet."

He let her pull the shirt over his head. She tossed it on the chair and placed her hands on his pectoral muscles. "Nice," she said. "You have more up here than I do."

"Your body is beautiful," he said.

She got off his lap.

"It is, you know."

"Yeah, the scars show how brave I am and blah, blah, blah."

"I wouldn't have said that."

"No matter what you say, I won't believe it. You might as well not say anything."

"That's not fair."

"Tell me about it."

Ursa came out, shaving cream can pressed to her chest while she held a bowl of water in one hand and a razor and scissors in her other. Jo went over to help. They put the supplies on a little plastic table next to Gabe. "We should have a towel," Jo said.

"I'll get it," Ursa said, "but don't start without me!" She ran for the door again.

"At least someone will enjoy this," Gabe said.

"I'll make it as enjoyable as possible," Jo said.

Ursa returned with the towel, and Jo wrapped it around Gabe's neck. She pulled a lawn chair in front of him and sat with her legs straddled around his. He looked quite captivated by her open legs and short cutoff jeans, but they knew they had to keep things G-rated in Ursa's presence. Jo picked up the scissors to draw his eyes to a more decent level. "Ready?"

"No," Gabe said, but Ursa shouted, "Yes!"

Jo snipped at the dark hair, burnished gold by the setting sun. She had to be careful not to pinch his skin as she cropped closer to his face. After she'd pared the beard, Jo wet the hair and let Ursa shake the shaving cream. She sprayed a big puff of it into her hand. "Smear it all over the hair," Jo said.

"This is fun," Ursa said, piling it on with abandon.

"I need to breathe, ladies," he said.

Jo used the towel to clear shaving cream out of his nostrils and off his lips. She picked up the razor. "Here we go . . ."

"Can I do it?" Ursa said.

"No way!" he said.

"Razors should be handled by adults," Jo said.

Ursa leaned close to watch the first strokes of the blade. "His skin looks regular under there," she said.

"Did you think it would be green alien skin?" he asked.

"I'm an alien, so that wouldn't have surprised me."

"Do your people have green skin?" he asked.

"We look like starlight on the outside."

Jo enjoyed uncovering Gabe's face. It was reminiscent of George Kinney's, but much more handsome. The high forehead, strong, subtly hooked nose, and square chin were all George. But the slight slant of his deeply blue eyes came from Katherine, as did the well-defined bow of his upper lip and the contour of his smile. Jo rubbed her finger over a half-inch line on his left cheekbone, barely resisting her urge to kiss him there. "How did you get this scar?"

"You'll never believe it," he said.

"How?"

"Running with scissors."

"So it's true."

"Yep, nearly put my eye out when I was six years old."

Ursa dumped the water clotted with shaving cream and hair and brought out more warm water. After Jo gently scraped finishing touches, she wet one end of the towel and cleaned off his face. He gazed into her eyes as she wiped. "Well?" he said.

"You should be fined for covering this face all these years."

"Who would I pay?"

"Me." She sat in his lap, wrapped her arms behind his neck, and kissed his lips.

"I did it! I did it! I did it!" Ursa sang, pumping her fists and dancing around them.

"What did you do?" Gabe said.

"I made you and Jo fall in love. My quark things did it. I knew it! I knew it!"

Jo and Gabe kissed again while Ursa continued her quark dance and Little Bear barked and frisked at her capering. "If this is how a crushed soul feels, it's not so bad," Gabe whispered in her ear.

"This is for sure my fourth miracle!" Ursa said.

"That means you only have one left," Gabe said.

"I know. I'll save it for something really good."

After they cleaned the dinner dishes, Gabe and Ursa roasted marshmallows. Jo watched, enjoying his new face and their playful banter.

Gabe sat next to Jo, holding her hand. "Look, you guys," Ursa said. "I'm making stars." She poked her stick again and again into the fire, and they watched cascades of sparks vanish into the starry black sky. Jo wanted to live as she did, in each sweet moment. But every second she spent with Ursa was overshadowed by the uncertainty of her future. And now Gabe was part of that onrushing fate, summer already on the wane.

When Ursa was in pajamas and ready for bed, Gabe went out to his truck and brought in a beat-up copy of *The Runaway Bunny*. "I remember that book," Jo said.

"Every kid remembers this book. Do Hetrayens know it?" he asked Ursa.

"No," she said.

"I thought of it when I called you 'runaway bunny' this morning."

"It's a baby book," Ursa said.

"But great literature, all the same. My father was a literature professor, and he loved this book."

"Seriously?" Jo said.

"He liked how it encapsulated the conflicting urges of parental protection versus a child's desire for independence. He often read it to me at night, even when I got older."

"My mom read it to me," Jo said.

"Get in bed, alien," Gabe said. "It can teach Hetrayens something important about humans."

Ursa climbed onto the couch and pulled up the blanket. Gabe read about the little bunny who told his mother the many places he would hide from her when he ran away, while his mother countered his every plan with inspired ways of finding him. Jo had always loved how patient the mother bunny was, how she loved her baby unconditionally.

When he finished, Ursa said, "Now I see why you called me 'runaway bunny.'"

"It's a good name for you, isn't it? But stay in bed tonight. Jo and I are too tired to run after you again."

"Are you staying?"

"Maybe for a while."

"I'll stay in bed so you and Jo can kiss."

"Sounds like a decent plan," he said.

24

Gabe came over for dinner the next night—and the night after. When Ursa fell asleep, they would cuddle on the porch in the light of the two candles Ursa had found for their first dinner together. So far, resolving their attraction hadn't helped the situation with Ursa. If anything, their indecision worsened. The word *sheriff* wasn't part of their vocabulary anymore. They never talked about Ursa's future or what they would do when Jo moved away. Savoring his first relationship, Gabe started to live as Ursa did, in an infinite present disconnected from the past or future.

Jo let him have his fantasy. And she let Ursa have hers. Working twelve-hour days left her with little time or mental capacity to think about losing them both. She came home tired, content to curl up with Gabe and Ursa in their iridescent bubble.

The third night Gabe came over, Jo brought Katherine's second book, *Hope's Ghost*, out to the porch after Ursa went to bed. She'd finished reading the poems earlier that day. Gabe grimaced when he saw the book in her hand.

"I thought we might read a few of these poems," she said. "You said you've never read this book."

"For good reason."

"Some of the poetry is about you. I think you should see it."

He tossed the book to the floor. "We're not going to waste our precious time talking about my screwed-up family." He pulled her down to the couch and kissed her.

"Lots of families are screwed up," she said. "What matters is how much love there is." She lifted the book off the floor. "Your mother was brave enough to expose her love in these poems. If you won't read them, I will. Just a few."

He reclined against the cushions like he was about to hear a time-share sales pitch. Two of the poems were about Gabe when he was little. Katherine's references to the child of her lover were metaphorical but easy to interpret now that Jo knew the story. They revealed an intensity to Katherine's maternal love that made Jo cry. The third poem referenced George and how deeply she loved him. The book's title poem, "Hope's Ghost," expressed some of Katherine's regrets about her divided family.

Gabe had dropped his aloof front by the time Jo finished the fourth poem. He was barely able to keep himself from crying.

"I think she wrote that one after you found out about her and George," Jo said. "She knew she'd screwed things up and driven you away from your father."

"He's not my father."

"He's your biological father, and you're his son. They *all* loved you, Gabe. From everything you've told me about your childhood, I'm positive Arthur, Katherine, and George all loved you. Each of them encouraged your interests and talents to the greatest extent possible, and only very good parents do that."

"They did encourage me," he said. "But then I turned into a little shit when I was twelve—after I found out. They thought it was puberty, and none of them had any idea what to do with me."

Jo put down the book and rubbed his arm.

"Of course, later, they decided my problem was mental illness."

"You say that like you don't believe it anymore."

"I feel so much better with you. Is that temporary, do you think?"

"I can't say."

"Lacey called today."

"Why?"

"She was worried because she hadn't heard from my mother. I think my mother didn't want her to know what's been going on with us. She's afraid Lacey will come and ruin it. My mom nearly pushes me out the door to come over here every night."

"I knew a woman who made love in a graveyard had to be an incredible romantic."

He aimed a piercing stare at her.

"Love isn't a crime, Gabe."

"She said vows to Arthur Nash. She should have let him out instead of turning him into a cuckold—with his best friend, no less."

"What about that? His best friend. Have you ever considered that Arthur was okay with it?"

"You can't be serious."

"Polygamy is common in the animal world and more common among humans than we realize."

"So are things like infanticide and rape. Do you want to glorify those, too?"

Jo looked down at the book of poems in her hands. *Hope's Ghost.* Hope Lovett, dead at age eighteen on a cold winter night in 1899. Had she ever been in love? Made love? In those days, if she was unmarried, probably not. Unlike many male poets of the past, Jo found nothing romantic in the death of a virginal young woman. Or man.

She put the book aside and picked up the two candles. "Come on," she said.

"Where are we going?"

She led him into the house. They passed Ursa and entered Jo's bedroom. Jo set one candle on the floor, the other on the bed stand. She locked the door behind Gabe.

He stayed near the door. "What are we doing? I don't know if I'm—"

"Relax," she said. "We're only going to lie down." She slid off her shorts and sat cross-legged in pink panties and a white camisole, looking up at him. He'd never seen her in her underpants before. But he just stood there.

She stretched out on her side. "Come on, I don't bite. Unless you want me to."

He smiled, taking in the length of her body. She patted her hand on the mattress where she wanted him.

He slid off his shoes.

"Pants too," she said.

"I'm pretty sure I'm being seduced," he said.

"You know how tired I am after a day in the field. I may fall asleep."

"Oh no you don't." The jeans came off in a hurry. As he reclined on his back, she wrapped around him. "Still mad at me?"

"I never was."

She leaned over him. "Prove it."

He tenderly kissed her lips, then her neck. Jo loved his way of loving. His inexperience made him curious, attendant to little details. A pattern of freckles on her shoulder intrigued him. He looked at them closely in the candlelight, connecting the marks with his finger. "These look like the stars of the Big Dipper."

She had never wanted a man more. The surgeries hadn't changed anything. Except in one way. She was deeply mindful of the passion she felt for him, a miracle of body and mind she used to take for granted.

She slid off his T-shirt and briefs and lay over the length of his warm body.

He wrapped his arms around her. "I know what you're doing."

She kissed his cheek. "What am I doing?"

"You think showing me how great sex is will make me forgive my mother and George."

She sat up, straddled across his belly, and looked down at him. "Any chance we can continue without your mother and George in the room?" Before he could answer, she stood up, removed her panties, and sat down again. "What do you think?"

"They're gone . . . totally gone." He sat up and nestled her in his lap. "Any chance you'll take off that shirt?"

"I'm sure you'd rather I leave it on."

He held her face in his hands. "I want you exactly the way you are. Do you understand?"

She let him raise the camisole over her head.

"There's nothing wanting," he said. "You're the most whole person I've ever known." He tenderly placed his hands, warm and rough, on the scars on her chest. "Is it too sensitive here? Should I not touch them?"

"I don't mind, if you don't."

He lifted his hands and traced his index finger over the scar near her heart. She saw no signs of pity or grief in his eyes. He drew the line as he had connected the stars on her shoulder, with loving wonder. As if he wanted to know and explore every secret of her body.

He moved his hand to the right scar, skimming his warm fingers over it.

"In a way, those scars brought us together," she said.

He looked in her eyes. "Mine did, too. And what could be more beautiful than that?"

"Nothing." She gently pressed him down to the mattress. "Except maybe this . . ."

25

As the first week of July passed, Jo fully entered the fantasy. She gave in to Ursa's vortex, the timeless whirl of stars Gabe had named the Infinite Nest. Nothing could touch the three of them in that boundless spin of love. Not their pasts. Not their futures. Jo stopped checking the missing children's websites, and she suspected Gabe did as well.

But even galaxies don't last forever. The first wobble in their universe started with a phone call from Tabby. A friend of hers was dating a British man, and he'd come over to the States to be with her. The couple wanted to crash at Jo and Tabby's apartment, and they were willing to pay the last month of rent. That was great news, but Jo's belongings were still in the apartment. Tabby had started living in the rental house a few weeks earlier. Jo had planned to move after her field season was over, but now she'd have to take a day off.

She quit work early to catch Gabe at his Monday evening egg sale. He smiled from beneath his blue canopy when she pulled in behind his pickup. "You're done early," he said. "Sudden urge for an omelet?"

"Sudden urge for you," she said, leaning over the egg cartons to kiss him.

"Guess what?" Ursa said. "We're going to Champaign-Urbana tomorrow, and you're coming with us!"

"Slow down," Jo said. "I said we would ask him."

The spark in his eyes dimmed. "Why are you going up there?"

"I have to get my stuff out of the old apartment. We found renters for it."

"They're moving in right away?"

"They're already in, and I'm not keen on them messing with my belongings."

"How can you miss fieldwork?"

"One day can't hurt. I don't have as many active nests as I did a few weeks ago."

"But going all the way up there to move a few things? Can't Tabby do it for you?"

"I can't ask her to do that. It's more than a few things. Any chance you'd like to help?"

He rubbed his cheek as if the beard were still there.

"I'd love to show you around up there."

"You can meet Tabby and see the pretty house," Ursa said, bouncing on her toes.

Jo couldn't interpret what she saw in his eyes, but it wasn't good.

"Can we talk about this later?" he said.

"Sure. When will you come over?"

"Maybe around eight."

Jo wasn't surprised when he didn't arrive at eight. He didn't show up until nine. While Ursa fell asleep, they sat on the porch couch to talk as usual. "Have you thought about coming with us tomorrow?" Jo said.

"I have," he said.

"Is that a *yes*?"

"I can't leave my mother all day."

"That was why I tried to talk about it earlier in the day—so you'd have time to call Lacey."

"I thought we agreed Lacey shouldn't come here?"

"We won't let her see Ursa."

"It's too late to call her."

"You never even considered it, did you?"

He looked out the screen at the dark forest.

"We have to figure out how to make you part of my life up there."

"I knew it," he said. "This isn't about moving a few boxes."

"What is it about?"

"You want me to move up there."

"I know you can't do that. I'm not asking you to leave your mother and your farm. I'm just asking you to imagine a way we can be together."

He turned his body toward her. "Do you really want that?"

"What we have doesn't happen every day. I'm afraid it will never happen again in my life."

"I know. I'm afraid of that, too."

"Then do something to keep it." She clasped his hands. "Please try."

"If you think it will help, I'll go."

"It will help. I can't always come to you at the farm. You have to be willing to face the world."

He nodded, but tensely.

"Who will take care of your mother tomorrow?" she asked.

"I'll go call Lacey right now."

"It's nine thirty."

"That doesn't matter—she comes when my mother says she has to."

"Is that what you'll do, have your mother call?"

"I don't know." He rose off the couch. "Let me go home and talk to my mother. But I already know she'll want me to go up there with you."

Jo stood next to him. "Because she loves you."

"Yeah." He kissed her cheek and walked out the screen door.

"How will I know if you're going?" Jo called to him.

"I'm going. Lacey will come."

26

Gabe watched the town of Mount Vernon slip by. He'd said little since they left, and Jo thought it best to let him have his quiet. He'd probably had a less than pleasant interaction with Lacey. She'd driven over from Saint Louis at six in the morning.

Jo looked in the rearview mirror. Ursa was still coloring a picture for Tabby, a drawing of the tabby kitten she'd named Caesar. It would take a long time to draw all the stripes, Ursa had said. Jo didn't doubt she'd do it well.

Gabe wiped his palms on his jeans.

"You okay?" Jo said.

"Yeah," he said.

"Interstate 57 must bring back memories."

"Sure does."

"Mostly good?"

"I guess so."

She left him alone.

They passed Salem, Farina, and Watson, and the farther they drove in silence, the guiltier Jo felt about prying him out of his comfort zone. But she had to know how bad it was with him. She was deeply invested. And if the trip proved he couldn't handle the outside world, she'd have to start the painful process of cutting ties.

When they arrived at the edge of Effingham, where Jo often stopped for cheap gas and Necco candy, Gabe perked up. "We used to eat at a good pizza place here."

"Is it near the highway?"

"No, not that close."

"How did you find it?"

"My dad hated chain restaurants. He was a connoisseur of local eateries, especially in small towns. He actually did research to find places with a homegrown atmosphere. I've eaten at quirky pie shops and old-time diners all over this state."

"Your dad was an interesting guy."

"You'd have liked him."

She waited for more, but he lapsed into silence again. She looked in the rearview mirror at Ursa. She'd fallen asleep, rare for her busy brain. "This boring scenery even puts Ursa to sleep," she said. "If you can call corn and soybean fields *scenery*."

"It is if you haven't seen it for a while," he said. "Now that I live in the forest, I'm not used to seeing so much sky. It was kind of shocking at first."

He'd once said he had a touch of agoraphobia. Maybe that was why he'd been so quiet. She tried a few more times to open conversation but got little response and gave up.

They arrived in Urbana on schedule, around noon. The plan was to meet Tabby at the old apartment and load Jo's belongings into her VW and the Honda. Jo hoped they would need only one trip, because going up and down the stairs to the third-floor apartment would make the move slow enough.

When Jo saw the building she and Tabby had lived in since senior year, she was relieved they were moving. Other than being a convenient distance to campus, the ugly building and congested location were far from the kind of relaxing home Jo had craved since her surgeries.

"Look, there's Tabby's car," Ursa said.

"She'll be upstairs," Jo said. She wrapped her arm around Gabe's waist and kissed his cheek as they walked toward the stairs. "Are you hungry?"

"Not yet," he said.

"I am," Ursa said.

"We're having sandwiches at the house with Tabby."

Ursa skipped the rest of the way to the stairs. They climbed to the third floor and walked the outer balcony to apartment 307. Jo knocked rather than use her key in case the new renters were inside. Tabby opened the door wearing a midriff-baring blue lace tank, rolled-up green army pants, and ripped red Converse shoes. "Jojo! You're gorgeous!" she said, throwing her arms around Jo.

"Thanks. So are you. I like the new color," she said of Tabby's pale denim-colored hair.

Tabby could hardly drag her eyes away from Gabe to greet Ursa. Jo hadn't told her she was bringing Gabe and Ursa, or even that she was in a relationship. Everything had been too complicated to explain, especially the situation with Ursa. No one in the outer world, not even Jo's closest friend, could possibly understand. And explaining her life in the forest cottage—being forced to defend it—would certainly ruin its fragile beauty.

"Ursa, my favorite alien," Tabby said, leaning down to hug her. "How's it going, girlfriend?"

"Good," Ursa said. "I have a picture for you in the car."

"Awesome! And you wore our color." She gave Ursa a high five for her purple T-shirt.

"Tabby, this is Gabe Nash," Jo said. "Gabe, this is Tabby Roberti."

Gabe smiled tensely and shook Tabby's hand.

"Wait . . . *Gabe*?" Tabby said. "The guy in Ursa's picture?"

"Yes, minus the beard," Jo said.

"We shaved it!" Ursa said.

"Who did?" Tabby said.

"Jo and me. But I only helped. I wasn't allowed to use the razor."

Tabby couldn't hide her shock. Or her injury. If Jo was intimate enough with a guy to shave him, Tabby expected to know. And it had to sound very weird that Ursa had helped with the beard removal.

"Let's get going," Jo said. "It's already crazy hot out here."

"I guess I could let you into the air-conditioning," Tabby said. She stepped back and ushered them inside. "Anyone want water? I can't offer anything else because the stuff in the fridge belongs to the new renters."

"Are they here?" Jo asked.

"They cleared out to give us some space."

"Are you sure they won't trash the place? We'll be responsible if they do."

"I trust her. I don't know him, but he seems quite the well-mannered Brit." She said the last in a stuffy British accent that made Ursa laugh.

"Have they paid?" Jo said.

"Cash in hand," Tabby said. "Need the bathroom?" she asked Gabe. "I want to talk about you behind your back to Jo."

He smiled, his first all day. "Where is it?"

"First door on the left in that hallway."

As soon as the bathroom door clicked closed, Tabby said, "Bitch! You always get these really hot guys. Why didn't you tell me?"

"I wasn't sure where it was going."

She arched her eyebrows, nudging for more. "Where has it gone so far?"

"They're in love," Ursa said. "I made it happen."

"With her alien powers," Jo said, winking.

"I did!" Ursa said.

"I don't care who made it happen. Is it true?" Tabby whispered.

Jo looked in the direction of the bathroom. "You know I can't talk about this right now."

"Yeah," Tabby said. She clutched Jo's shirt under her neck. "But I'm gonna beat it out of you later. You hear?"

"I hear."

Tabby released Jo's shirt and folded her into her arms. "I'm happy for you, Jo."

The bathroom door opened.

"Does he play the banjo?" Tabby whispered in her ear.

"Shut up." Jo walked past her and brought Gabe into her bedroom. She loaded his arms with clothes from the closet and sent him down to the car. Jo grabbed an armload and followed him before Tabby could corner her and ask more questions.

With all four of them working, Jo's belongings were packed into the two cars in less than an hour. They drove to the new house, and Jo gave Gabe a tour while Tabby and Ursa made sandwiches and lemonade. She showed him the backyard last.

He cupped his hand on a red lily flower. "This place suits you."

"Someday I'd rather live in the woods like you do. But if I have to live in town, it's not bad."

"You'd rather live in the woods?" he said.

"Of course. Or the mountains or on a lake. I want nature out my front door."

"That's how humans should live." Looking at a nearby house, he said, "We're not meant to live on top of each other."

She pressed against him, wrapping her arms around his neck. "I thought you liked it when we were on top of each other."

He glanced nervously at the back door.

"Tabby knows," she said. "Anyway, what's to hide?"

"I don't know. I'm trying to get used to all of this."

She kept her hands on the nape of his neck. "You're trying to get used to trusting us."

"Maybe."

She kissed him. "I have to trust everything. I want no regrets if . . .". She couldn't say it aloud. She never had.

"If what?"

"If the cancer comes back."

His body tensed against her. "Could it?"

"It's always a possibility, but the prognosis is good. They caught it early."

He held her so tight it hurt. But it was an excellent kind of ache.

"Yo, barnacles!" Tabby called from the deck. "Lunch awaits."

Gabe went in the half bath to wash his hands, and Jo pulled Tabby into the living room. "Don't ask him a lot of questions," she whispered. "There are some things he won't want to talk about."

"Like what? That ax murder he committed last month?"

"He's had some bad times. Just keep it light."

"More bad times than you?"

"It's a different kind of bad stuff."

"My god. You two are some match."

"Yeah—weird that we found each other, isn't it?"

Tabby hugged her. "I'll stick to weather and politics. But, wait . . . is he liberal or conservative?"

"You know, I'm not sure."

"What? That's the first thing I have to know!"

"It hasn't come up," Jo said.

"Holy shit. Is the sex really that good?"

"Shh!" Jo returned to the house, relieved when she found Gabe in the kitchen with Ursa. Ursa's drawing of the tabby kitten—exceptional as always—was already stuck to the refrigerator with a veterinary magnet that read PLEASE DON'T LITTER. SPAY AND NEUTER YOUR CRITTER!

During lunch Tabby only asked Gabe a few neutral questions such as, *How long have you lived in Southern Illinois?* She steered the conversation onto politics, and they discovered Gabe leaned toward libertarian views. Jo could work with that.

They finished unloading the cars by around three. Jo didn't have time to unpack because she had to run a few errands on campus. She had to leave everything stacked on the floor and the bed Frances Ivey had left behind. Tabby had cleared her day for the move, and she insisted Jo take Gabe to campus without Ursa. "Alien and I are gonna do human girl stuff," she said.

"Tabby is going to paint my nails," Ursa said. "We're doing purple."

"Are you sure you want to stay here?" Jo asked Ursa.

"I do!"

Jo wished she and Gabe could walk to campus through the state-street neighborhood, but she had to get to the biology office and her bank on Green Street before they closed. On the drive out, Gabe said, "I was last here when I was a kid, but these streets look familiar. I think George Kinney lives in this neighborhood."

"He may," Jo said. "Some students call the state streets the Professor Ghetto."

"I remember that. My father joked about it both times we came here."

"More jabs at George?"

"Definitely."

She parked near Morrill Hall, where the Animal Biology office was located. She had to submit paperwork for her fall classes, but first she wanted to show Gabe the quad. She held his hand as they walked into the large rectangular space surrounded by old buildings. "Pretty campus," he said.

"That's Illini Union, the student center," she said, pointing to the north. "And the big domed building on the south end is Foellinger Auditorium."

They walked one of the diagonal paths. The quad was mostly empty, typical of midsummer. A few students lounged in the grass, and in the south end, a shirtless guy threw a Frisbee for his dog.

"This reminds me of the quad at the University of Chicago."

"I've never seen it."

"It's beautiful."

"Do you ever think about going back to school?"

"No."

"That was a fast answer."

"Why wouldn't it be?"

"Because keeping your gifted brain hidden in the woods is as criminal as hiding your face behind the beard."

He stopped walking and faced her. "I knew this was why you brought me here."

"This is my world, Gabe. If you could find a way to be in it, everything would be much simpler."

"You said you wanted to live in the woods."

"I have years to go before I get my degree and find a job at a university."

He sat on a bench and put his head in his hands. "This is impossible. Why did we ever start this?"

"I don't recall having much control over it."

He looked up at her. "Me either. Do you know I was attracted to you from the first time you bought eggs at my stand?"

"You sure didn't act like it."

"You couldn't see me checking you out when you walked away."

"You mean my ass?"

He only smiled.

She tugged him to his feet by his hand. "Good thing you're an ass man and not a breast guy."

"I'm an ass man?"

"Yeah, like the guy in *Midsummer Night's Dream*."

"Nick Bottom."

She pulled him down the sidewalk. "Come on, Nick. I have stuff to do."

They entered Morrill Hall and took the stairs to the fifth-floor biology office. Jo left Gabe out in the hall so he wouldn't have to chitchat with the secretary while she did her paperwork. "Now, the bank," she said when she left the office.

Gabe started for the stairway they'd used on the way up. "No, this way," Jo said, gesturing toward the eastern stairwell. "We'll come out closer to my car." They walked a long corridor past office doors. The majority of biology professors and graduate students were away from campus working on their summer research.

"After the bank, are we getting on the road?" Gabe asked.

"Only with a fight."

"Why?"

"Ursa is set on having dinner with Tabby at a restaurant she likes. Would that be okay?"

"I guess so."

Jo wrapped her hand around his. "It's a pizza place—really casual."

"Gabe?" a man said behind them.

They turned around, hands parting. Dr. George Kinney stood in front of an open office. He walked toward them, clearly confused but smiling, his gaze fixed on Gabe. "I thought I was imagining it when I saw you walk by." He stopped in front of Gabe. It was like a strange mirror of time, the elder reliving the face of his youth, the young man confronting his future.

27

They looked more alike than Jo had realized. They were about the same height. Dr. Kinney also had blue eyes, but a lighter shade. His hair was white and he wore it on the long side like Gabe, his part on the right, while Gabe parted left. Dr. Kinney was slimmer than Gabe, but robust, as fit as a man could be at the age of seventy-three.

"I almost didn't recognize you without the beard," Dr. Kinney said.

The irony of the comment wasn't lost on Gabe. But he said nothing.

To ease the awkward silence, Dr. Kinney turned to Jo. "Good to see you, Jo. How's your research going?"

"Very well," she said.

"Glad to hear it. I hope that living room air conditioner isn't giving you too much trouble. Do I need to replace it?"

"It's fine. I don't use it much."

"I see you've met the neighbors," he said, glancing at Gabe.

"Yes," Jo said.

"We should go," Gabe said to Jo as if Kinney weren't there. His contempt was palpable, shocking even Dr. Kinney, who must have been accustomed to it. But rather than back down and retreat to his office, Kinney said, "Gabe . . ."

Gabe reluctantly looked at him.

"I'd like to talk to you"—he directed his arm toward the open door down the hall—"in my office." Relaxing his tone, he added, "If you can call it that. When you're emeritus, they give you a closet. Sometimes the janitor accidentally puts his mop in there."

Jo smiled. Gabe didn't.

Dr. Kinney kept his eyes on Gabe's. "Lynne is very sick. She has a month at most."

"I'm sorry," Gabe said at last.

Dr. Kinney nodded. "Please come into my office. I need to talk with you."

"Sounds like you two need privacy," Jo said. "I'll run over to the bank while you talk. Meet me on the benches out front when you're done," she said to Gabe.

"Sounds good," Dr. Kinney said.

She walked away before Gabe could refuse. "Take as long as you want," she said over her shoulder.

She expected Gabe to be at her side any second, but she made it outside alone. Somehow she found her car and made it to the bank, though every bit of her brain was focused on Gabe and Dr. Kinney.

She drove back to Morrill Hall. Gabe wasn't on the benches. Either he'd run off in a panic and forgotten the meeting place, or he was still talking to Dr. Kinney. She sat on a bench and waited. After fifteen minutes, she started browsing on her phone.

When forty minutes passed, her worries intensified. Maybe Gabe had snapped and run off. She considered going inside to see if he was still in Kinney's office, but interrupting them would be weird and intrusive. She also contemplated calling Tabby to see if he'd gone home, but she couldn't possibly explain a call like that.

Ten minutes later, Gabe came out of Morrill Hall, his body limp.

Jo approached, but he kept walking. "Are you okay?"

"Yes," he said.

"What happened?"

"We talked. About everything." He kept walking, no apparent thought to his direction.

She had to let him come back to reality on his own. She remained silent as they walked. When they arrived at the large expanse of the quad, he stopped and stared, seeming to register where he was. He started walking again, fast, as if hurrying to some known destination. He stopped at the closest tree and flopped to the ground in its long shade. He lay on his back in the grass, the bottoms of his palms pressed into his eyes. Jo sat next to him, caressing his chest.

"You were right," he said, hands still pressed on his eyes. "My father—Arthur—knew and let it all happen."

Jo considered saying *I'm sorry*, but it made no sense.

He took his hands off his eyes and looked at her. "He was *glad* George gave Katherine a son. Arthur was glad to have a son, too. He was impotent. Lacey happened one of the rare times when he could do it."

He put his palms over his eyes again. "Lynne's liver is shot. I never knew it, but all those years she was an alcoholic. When I was a kid, I thought her stony face and silence were signs of how dumb and uninteresting she was. But I guess she was drunk."

"He keeps that private," Jo said. "I'd only heard rumors that his wife was sick."

His hands were still on his eyes. "Guess what he asked me?"

"What?"

"He wants to marry my mother when Lynne dies. He asked my permission."

Jo hadn't expected that. She supposed that was why Kinney had been so forceful about making Gabe talk. "What did you say?"

He took his hands off his eyes and looked at her. "Did you take me past his office hoping this would happen?"

"No! I didn't even know that was his office. I've only talked to him twice—both times in the main office."

220

"He said he moved into the smaller space two years ago. He had to retire earlier than he wanted to take care of Lynne."

"Two years ago I was getting cancer treatment. When I left, his office was still in the entomology department."

Gabe nodded, conceding that Jo hadn't steered the meeting.

"Does he know your mother has Parkinson's?" she asked.

"He does, and he still wants to marry her." He sat up and looked at her. "Are you crying?"

"I'm trying not to."

"Why?"

"I think this story is beautiful. But really sad, too. Maybe Lynne knew George didn't love her. Maybe that was why she started to drink."

"That's why there's nothing beautiful about it. Their selfishness wrecked people's lives."

Their *love* had changed lives. That mattered to Jo.

"He told me how it all happened," Gabe said. "He'd been going down to the Shawnee Forest with his biology classes, and he turned my dad on to the area. One weekend in their senior year, George and Lynne and Arthur and Katherine did a couples campout. Bet you can't guess what happened . . ."

"George and Katherine fell for each other."

"Yeah, but they didn't do anything about it. George and Arthur stayed close while they were in different graduate programs—best man in each other's weddings and all that. And even after their families started hanging out, George and Katherine still hadn't touched each other—or so George says."

"Why would he lie when it eventually happened?"

"True."

"When did they get together?"

"After my dad bought the property in Southern Illinois. He was still working on the cabin when the property next door went up for sale. He considered buying it, but my mother suggested they ask George and

Lynne if they were interested. That way they could get together when they were vacationing down there."

"I sense an ulterior motive."

"Do you?" he said sarcastically.

"When did Arthur find out about their affair?"

"When my mother got pregnant. He knew it wasn't his because they hadn't had sex for years. When my mother was four months pregnant with me, she made Arthur and George sit down with her and talk about what they were going to do."

"Okay, I like Katherine even more now. That was a cool thing to do."

"They decided against a divorce. And agreed Lynne couldn't know because her alcoholism made her fragile. To this day George has never told his wife or two daughters."

"They didn't notice how much you two look alike?"

"I guess Lynne was too wrapped up in her own misery, and the Kinney girls rarely saw me. They were Lacey's age when I was born."

"Apparently, they decided not to tell you either."

"That was one of Arthur's two stipulations: I would be raised as his son, and George and Katherine weren't allowed to make love on his property."

"Which is why they met in the woods."

"Right. The graveyard is on Kinney's property—just a few feet from the Nash boundary. No doubt that was part of the joke of meeting there."

"Do you really think it was a joke?" she said. "Your mother is a compassionate person—I can tell from her poetry. She had to know how much Arthur was hurting."

"Yeah, no doubt she knew," he said bitterly, "but, hey, he got the consolation prize, right? He got me."

Jo caressed his arm. "Yes, he got you."

He ripped out a divot of grass and threw it on the ground. "You know what George said? He said he wants to be a real father to me."

"What did you say?"

"Nothing, because it's bullshit. He says his daughters can never know. How *real* would that be?"

"Why do you hate him so much now that you know the whole story? George and your mother obviously stayed with people they didn't love to make their partners happy. Maybe they realized they shouldn't have done that, but by then, they had children who would be hurt by a divorce. When they finally got together, they tried to do it in a way that hurt as few people as possible. Can't you see the beauty in their sacrifices? And in a power of love that withstands so many years?"

"If it was your parents, you'd understand," he said.

"I would. If I could have my parents back, I'd let them love anyone they wanted to love."

He plucked more grass and rolled it in his palms.

"We have to go soon," she said. "We've left Ursa with Tabby too long."

He was too absorbed in his thoughts to hear her. "When I was leaving, George said it was like some strange providence that I walked past his door today. He said right before we went by, he was thinking about me." He brushed the grass out of his hands and looked at her. "You know what I was thinking? I was thinking of Ursa's quarks. There's something really odd about what's been happening since that girl showed up."

28

Gabe was in a hurry to go home. Ursa wanted to get pizza at the restaurant with the "Purple People Eater" song, but Gabe was in no mood for dinner or conversation. He wouldn't even leave the car when they went back to the house. Jo told Ursa and Tabby that he wasn't feeling well, and she made Ursa get in the back seat despite her protests and tears. "We'll stop for food on the way home," Jo said. "Maybe McDonald's and you can have ice cream."

"I want pizza with Tabby!" Ursa said.

"I'm sorry."

"Can I talk to you inside for a minute?" Tabby said before Jo got in the car.

Jo followed her into the house, dreading what she had to say. Whether she wanted to discuss Gabe or Ursa, Tabby would be intense, and Jo had little energy left.

"I was surprised you had Ursa with you today," Tabby said, closing the front door.

"Were you?"

"Don't pretend it isn't weird. What the hell is going on? She said she lives with you."

"I guess she does."

The whites of Tabby's green eyes doubled in size. "You have to take her to the police!"

"You know she runs."

"So you put her in the car and don't tell her where you're taking her."

"She's too smart. She jumped out of the car when we tried that."

"She did?"

"We almost didn't find her."

"What is this *we*? She told me Gabe sleeps over."

"What about it?"

"You can't play house with someone else's kid! You could get in big trouble. And what will you do when your field season is over?"

"I haven't told Ursa yet—don't freak out . . ."

"What?"

"I might try to become her foster parent."

Tabby slapped her hand to her forehead. "Holy fucking shit. You're serious."

"I am."

"Frances Ivey said no kids."

"Do you think that's going to stop me? I love this kid."

They both went silent, Jo as shocked as Tabby.

"Jo . . ."

"What?"

"I think you should call that doctor you saw up in Chicago."

"I had lots of doctors."

"You know what I mean," Tabby said.

"The psychologist—the one you used to call Dr. Death?"

"Yeah, her."

"You know what she told me? She said survivors can live and love more fully than people who haven't stared death in the face."

"Seriously . . . what are you doing?"

"I guess I'm being a survivor." She opened the door and strode down the walkway.

"I love you, Jojo!" Tabby called from the porch.

"Love you, too, Tabs."

Suffering wounds large and small, the three of them kept silent during the drive to Interstate 57. Not a word was spoken all the way to the town of Mattoon.

"My dad liked a barbeque place here," Gabe said.

Jo hit the brake pedal. "Should I stop? We need gas, and Ursa is hungry."

"I wanted pizza!" Ursa said.

Gabe turned around to look at her. "There's a good pizza place coming up down the road. It's one of those old-fashioned places that has a jukebox."

"I want Tabby!"

"I don't think they serve that," he said.

"Shut up!"

"Hey, that's not nice," Jo said.

Gabe turned back to face the windshield. The car fell silent again. Jo drove past Mattoon.

"I'm sorry, Gabe," Ursa said a few minutes later.

"Apology accepted. And I'm sorry I messed up your plans." He twisted around to look at her again. "Do you want to try the pizza place up ahead? I used to go there when I was your age. I liked to play the jukebox, too."

"I bet they don't have 'Purple People Eater.'"

"We'll find something good."

"You better make sure this place is still in business," Jo said.

"It will be. It was huge with the locals and always crowded."

He used his cell phone to find the restaurant. Jo glanced in the rearview mirror at Ursa. She was drawing again. The colored pencils and art pad had been great purchases. "What are you drawing?" Jo asked.

"A purple people eater."

Art was a form of self-soothing for Ursa. When she wanted something or missed someone, she would often draw whatever it was to satisfy her need.

They arrived in Effingham at dusk. At that late hour, Jo would rather have gotten fast food than stop for a sit-down dinner. But if Gabe was up for seeing a childhood haunt, she was, too. Connecting with his dad might be just what he needed.

While Gabe navigated to the restaurant, Ursa hunched over her art pad, wholly focused on her drawing despite the failing light. "Bring your art stuff inside," Gabe said as Jo parked. "The pizza takes a while to cook, and it'll give you something to do."

Jo surveyed the long row of motorcycles parked beneath the multicolored bulbs strung along the eaves of the restaurant. "Are you sure this is the right place?"

"This is it," Gabe said. He opened Ursa's door. "Thank god they haven't changed it. The parking lot is still all gravel. And look how many cars are here."

"Look how many Harleys are here," Jo said.

"I know. Isn't it great? It's straight out of the sixties."

"I wouldn't know how authentic it is."

"Arthur did. Too bad he isn't here. He loved this place at night."

"It looks a little rough."

"You see, that's the problem with people now. They glimpse a little color in their gray fast-food world and they panic. Places like this are too real for them. But this is the kind of place where the really interesting stories of humanity play out."

"I think I'm getting one of Dr. Nash's lit lectures."

"You are, and I completely agree with him. Imagine this place described in a book you're reading and try to put McDonald's in its place."

"I think those two restaurants would be used for very different purposes in a book."

"Exactly. No comparison. One would be a metaphor for all that's dreary in our lives and the other for what little unpredictability still exists."

"As long as the unpredictability doesn't include a biker knife fight, I'm up for it."

"A biker knife fight—now that would be excellent!"

"You know, the Arthur side of you is a little scary," she said.

"Ursa, are you planning to come out of the car anytime this century?" he said.

"I don't want to eat here," she said.

"Not you, too!"

"I'm not hungry," she said. "I want to go home."

"This place is perfectly safe."

"It's not that. I'm just not hungry."

"What's with her tonight?" he asked Jo.

"She's in Tabby withdrawal—it can be rough. Go inside and get a table and let me talk to her."

"Should I give you the tire iron for protection first?"

She swatted his shoulder. "Go. Make sure there's a table before I expend a lot of energy out here."

Jo leaned into the open door and said, "Gabe really wants to do this. Can you cooperate, please, just for him? Even if you're not hungry?"

"This place looks stupid," she said.

"Bring your pencils and paper and don't look at it."

She didn't move.

"You heard what Gabe said—his dad loved this place. His father died two years ago, and this is a way for Gabe to connect with him. Do you understand how that would be?"

"Yes," she said.

"Then come on. Do it for Gabe. He's in there waiting at a table."

Ursa reluctantly slid out of the car. Jo reached in and got her box of colored pencils and pad of paper. She looked at the purple people eater on the top of the pad. "That's great," she said. "I love how you did his mouth."

"It has to be that big because he can eat people whole."

"The teeth are pretty scary."

"He doesn't actually eat people anymore. He went to the magic forest where Juliet and Hamlet live, and they taught him to be nice."

"He'll be in your play about Juliet and Hamlet?"

"I don't know. I only pretended he was in the magic forest while I drew him."

They mounted a worn plank porch lit with colored bulbs. Jo pulled back the heavy wooden door, and as soon as she stepped inside, she understood Arthur's fascination with the place. The interior was mostly made of timber—plank floors, paneled walls, and wooden booths and tables—and the scoured wood seemed imbued with the smell of time, of people's stories, as Gabe had said. The place was redolent of pine and pizza grease, and of sweat, whiskey, and tobacco, the mingled smells aging like wine in an old oak barrel. Nancy Sinatra's sixties hit "These Boots Are Made for Walkin'" was playing on the flashing jukebox. It perfectly suited the vibe, but the song was nearly drowned out by laughter and voices. The atmosphere was dark, mostly lit with colored lights, except for billiard lamps over three pool tables at the rear of the room. Around the tables, a group of tattooed men and women drank beers and gabbed as they watched the pool balls roll.

Many eyes followed Jo and Ursa to Gabe, seated at a table in the middle of the room. The patrons—mostly locals from what Jo could tell—probably knew she and Gabe were tourists. Their jeans and T-shirts blended in, but Jo's AMERICAN ORNITHOLOGICAL SOCIETY shirt certainly outed her.

Jo sat opposite Gabe, and Ursa took the chair between them at the little square table. "Great, isn't it?" Gabe said.

"I have to admit, I feel like I've gone back to another era. But I think they all know we're time travelers."

"They don't care. We're supporting the local economy." He picked up Ursa's hand and looked at her lavender fingernails. "That's a nice color. Did Tabby do your toenails, too?"

Ursa nodded. "They're dark purple." Pencil in hand, she bent over her purple people eater again, her face hovering close to the paper so she could see in the dim light.

Gabe opened the menu. "What do you want on your pizza, Ursa?"

She didn't lift her head. "Whatever you want."

Because Jo ate little red meat, especially cured meat, they ordered a large pizza that was half vegetarian and half sausage and pepperoni.

"What to drink, darlin'?" asked a fortyish waitress with heavy makeup and burgundy pigtails.

Ursa kept drawing.

"How about a kiddie cocktail?" Gabe asked. "I used to get those here."

"Okay," Ursa said without looking up.

Jo looked at what had her thoroughly focused. She was drawing plants and trees around the purple people eater. "Is that the magic forest?" Jo asked.

"Yes."

"It's like a jungle."

"It's magic. It keeps him safe."

"Can't he use all those teeth to keep himself safe?"

"Not when there's bad stuff around."

Gabe raised his eyebrows at Jo, noting her odd mood. "Want to play the jukebox?" he asked. "No one's using it."

"You can if you want to," Ursa said.

"I'll see if your song is on it." He left the table and stood over the jukebox.

"Is something wrong, Ursa?" Jo asked.

"I didn't want to come here," she said.

"I'm sorry. Thanks for sticking it out for Gabe."

Gabe's first song, "Smells Like Teen Spirit," came on before he returned to the table.

"Are you a Nirvana fan?" she asked him as he sat down.

"Not in any dedicated kind of way. But I like this song."

Jo's water, Gabe's beer, and Ursa's kiddie cocktail arrived. Raising his glass, Gabe said, "I want to propose a toast."

Jo picked up her water. "To what?"

"To Katherine and George's marriage. May it be long."

"Really?"

"It's a great idea. At least someone in my family will get closure on this thing."

He held out his glass.

"Ursa, we're doing a toast," Jo said.

"I don't get it. Katherine is your mother," Ursa said, proof that she'd been listening.

"She sure is," he said.

"She's getting married?" Ursa asked.

"Maybe," Jo said.

"Who's George?"

"George Kinney," Jo said.

"The man who owns our house?"

"It's not ours," Jo said. "But yes. Pick up your glass and toast."

Ursa tapped her glass on theirs and drank. After her first sip of the sweet drink, most of it went down quickly. "Isn't George married?"

"He is," Gabe said, "but soon he won't be."

"They're getting a divorce?"

"Something like that."

"Your mom is kind of old to get married," Ursa said.

"People can be in love at any age," Jo said.

Ursa wasn't listening anymore. She sat motionless, staring across the room. Jo followed her line of sight. She was looking at the bar. A scruffy young man with a phone pressed to his ear glanced in their direction. When he saw Jo and Ursa looking his way, he swiveled his stool around to face the bar. Ursa kept looking at something, but Jo couldn't figure out what it was.

"What has you two so mesmerized? Is there a hot guy over there or what?" Gabe asked.

Ursa picked up a green pencil and made another leaf in her magic forest.

"You're the hottest guy in the room," Jo said.

"Only because I'm up against aging bikers."

He was wrong. The crowd was fairly young, especially the people seated at the bar. The guy Ursa seemed to have been looking at got off the barstool and walked past their table, staring as he passed. Ursa watched him leave the restaurant.

"Do you know that man?" Jo asked.

"What man?" she said.

"The one you were just looking at."

"I was looking at that thing over the door."

"The horseshoe?"

"Why's it there?" Ursa asked.

"To give good luck to people who come through the door. It's a superstition."

Ursa stared at the horseshoe for a few more seconds before going back to her drawing.

Now that he'd embraced Katherine and George's future, Gabe was in a good mood. The restaurant probably contributed, too. He and Jo talked about music and other things until the pizza came, but Ursa kept scrawling away, the protective forest around her purple alien growing more and more elaborate.

Gabe raved about the pizza. Jo liked it well enough, but she had a feeling Arthur's enthusiasm about the restaurant had added more flavor to the pizza than Gabe realized. He insisted on paying the bill and left a big tip for the waitress.

On their way out of town, Jo stopped for gas and made Ursa use the bathroom because she'd refused to go at the restaurant. She was still acting oddly withdrawn. Jo thought fatigue might be the root of her moodiness and hoped she would sleep most of the way back to the cottage.

Jo and Gabe wandered through several topics during the ride but steered clear of what had happened with George because Ursa was still awake. She was restless, shifting from window to window, and more than once Jo had to tell her to put her seat belt back on.

When Jo pulled onto the county highway, she saw lights in her mirrors. The car behind turned off with them and followed the six miles to Turkey Creek Road. "Don't tell me they're turning here, too," she said.

"Who?" Gabe said.

Ursa looked out the rear window.

"That car behind us," Jo said. "I swear it's been with us for a long time."

As Jo rounded the corner onto Turkey Creek Road, the car suddenly sped up and disappeared.

"They're lost," Gabe said. "They saw the No Outlet sign and realized this isn't the road they're looking for."

Jo drove to Gabe's newly graveled driveway but stopped in the road to make sure Lacey didn't see Ursa. She got out of the car to say goodbye. "Was it a good trip, despite seeing George?"

"It was interesting—that's for sure. I doubt I'll sleep much."

She smiled. "Is that a hint? Should I leave the front door unlocked?"

He kissed her. "Put a key in the usual place. You should keep your doors locked at night."

29

Ursa wanted to sleep in Jo's bed, but Jo couldn't let her. She'd slept in Jo's room only twice: the first night Gabe stayed over and when she injured her head. Jo had to be careful about keeping their beds separate, especially now that she might apply to become her foster parent. People might spin it wrong if she slept with Ursa. As it was, they would probably ask Ursa uncomfortable questions about her relationship with Jo.

After Ursa put on her Hello Kitty pajamas and brushed her teeth, Jo turned out all the lights except the one on the stove and tucked Ursa into the couch. She kissed Ursa's cheek. "Sweet dreams, Big Bear."

"Is Gabe coming over?"

"Probably not. He's more tired than he realizes. We all are."

"I wish he was here."

Jo rose from the couch. "Go to sleep. We'll get up later than usual because it's so late."

When Jo walked away, Ursa said, "Leave your door open."

"Okay."

"Can I please sleep with you?"

"You know the rules. Go to sleep." Jo wished she could give in. She'd never seen Ursa afraid at bedtime, not even when she first arrived. Maybe it had something to do with the drawing of the alien with big teeth. Her mood had changed after she drew it.

The loud drone of the air conditioner put Jo to sleep quickly. But after only a few hours, Little Bear woke her. She looked at her cell phone. It was 2:10, too late for the dog to be greeting Gabe. He was probably barking at a raccoon or a deer. The air conditioner was in its off cycle, and Jo wished it would turn on to mask the noise.

Little Bear suddenly went berserk, his barks generated so fast he hardly took a breath between. He would wake Ursa, if he hadn't already. Jo had to get up and quiet him.

She stopped cold in the entry to the living room. Ursa was standing next to the couch staring at her, her body unnaturally frozen. Her face appeared a ghostly blue cast by the fluorescent stove light, and her eyes looked like two black holes. She had become a changeling again.

"Jo . . . ," she said.

Jo ignored the irrational pounding of her heart. "Get back in bed," she said. "Maybe there's a coyote out there. I'd better put him on the porch."

When Jo moved toward the front door, Ursa ran to the door and threw her back against it with her arms spread open. "Don't go out!"

"Why not?"

A sob caught in her throat. "The bad men! The bad men are here!"

Jo's body went cold. "What bad men?"

She began crying. "I'm sorry! I should have told you! They'll kill you, too! I'm sorry! I'm sorry!"

Little Bear had stopped barking for about ten seconds, but he started again, this time much closer to the house. Jo grabbed Ursa's shoulders. "Stop crying and tell me what's happening. Was it that man in the restaurant?"

"Yes! But it's not him!"

"That makes no sense!" Jo gave her body a little jolt by the shoulders, trying to shake something clearer out of her. "Tell me what's going on! I have to know!"

Two gunshots rang out, and Little Bear wailed a horrific sound.

"Little Bear!" Ursa screamed. "Little—"

Jo clamped her hand over her mouth. "Quiet!" she hissed.

Little Bear's wailing yelps didn't stop. Another shot fired and he went silent. Ursa nearly collapsed in gasping sobs. Jo put her hands on her cheeks to focus her attention. "How many men are there? Do you know?"

"I . . . think two. In that car. I don't know for sure! They killed Little Bear!"

"That car followed us from Effingham?"

Ursa nodded, her body shuddering with heaving sobs.

"You have to stop crying! Please! If they hear you, they'll know where we are!"

Ursa swallowed her crying in gulps, and the silence gave Jo a chance to concentrate. In the part of her brain that could function outside survival instinct, she comprehended that the men must have something to do with Ursa's past. But she couldn't think beyond that or her urge to keep Ursa safe. The men could shoot into the house any second. Connecting to 911 and describing their remote location would waste too much time. She hoped Gabe had heard the gunshots and called the police, but she had no guarantee that he had.

To get in, the men would have to use the front or rear wooden doors. The old house was raised up on cinder blocks, and the windows were located halfway up the wall, too high for easy access from the outside. Jo dragged Ursa away from the door, afraid a bullet might pierce through. She stood at the entrance to her bedroom, trying to think. The men would know their shots had awakened them. Little Bear had thwarted a surprise attack. Now the men were on the defensive. They would assume Gabe was still with them because they hadn't seen Jo drop him off at his cabin. They would be afraid Gabe and Jo owned a gun.

But they would get bolder the longer there was silence in the house. They would know they had their quarry trapped and would kick in the doors. Jo and Ursa would have to go out through a window, but that would force them to run into the open area around the house before they could hide in the woods. The two bug bulbs on the porches would give the men plenty of light to see them and take aim.

A line from the Nirvana song Gabe had played on the jukebox ran through Jo's mind. Darkness would be less dangerous. "Get down and stay here," she whispered to Ursa. Ursa obeyed, crumpling to the floor in the doorway. Jo crept into the kitchen and quickly pushed the stove light button off. She crouched in the darkness, waiting to see if anything happened. Maybe they would worry when they saw the light go out. They would imagine someone lying in wait with a gun.

She crawled on the floor to the back door, shot up to flick off the bug bulb, and dropped down again. Now the rear of the house was dark. Only the dim bug bulb at the front screen door remained on, but she couldn't turn it off because its switch was on the porch. From the floor, she opened the knife drawer and took out the biggest blade.

She crawled back to Ursa with the knife clutched in her hand. "Get up and be quiet," Jo whispered, pulling her cold, clammy hand. Ursa stood, her body trembling. Though being near a window was risky, Jo had to ready an exit. The lower part of the window in her bedroom was blocked by the air conditioner. The one in the other bedroom was a better choice anyway, because it was on the dark rear side of the house. When the men came in the doors, Jo and Ursa would climb out the window and run for the woods.

It was a good plan. It would work. Unless more than two men had surrounded the house. But if there were that many, surely they would have attacked by now.

Jo pulled Ursa into the empty bedroom and pushed up on the window. It was stuck. The summer humidity must have made it swell. She shoved with all her strength, and the wooden frame finally budged. The air conditioner was on again, and she hoped it had masked the sound.

Jo used the knife to cut away the screen. "If they come in, jump out the window and run for Gabe's house through the woods," Jo whispered close to Ursa's ear. "Don't use the road. Stay in the woods. Hide if you think someone is following you. They'll never find you out there in the darkness." When Jo started to leave, Ursa clutched her arm. "I'm going to get my phone and your shoes," she explained, but she had to pry Ursa's hand away.

She crept to her bedroom and felt around for her phone on the floor. When she found it, she set the door lock and closed the door. After she got Ursa's shoes from the living room, she returned to the spare bedroom, closed the door, and set the knob lock. Now the men had two more locked doors to break down. That would give Jo and Ursa time to make it to the woods without being seen.

Jo slipped Ursa's purple gym shoes on each of her cold bare feet and tied them with shaking hands. She realized she'd forgotten to get her own shoes, but she didn't risk going to get them.

She pressed Ursa to the wall next to the open window. Only minutes had passed since the shots were fired, but it felt like an hour. Even if he'd heard, Gabe couldn't have driven over that fast. She pressed 911 in her phone. The call didn't connect. She moved to a different place in the room and entered the numbers again. She watched as the phone tried to connect, her every nerve more electrified with each squandered second.

A foot kicked the front door hard. Jo jumped and nearly dropped the phone.

"Jo!" Ursa said.

Jo put the phone on the floor and held her close. "It'll be okay. Do what I said. Stay in the woods until you get to Gabe's. If you can't find his cabin, run far and hide. We'll find you when it's safe." The man continued kicking the front door. The terrifying sound was amplified by more kicking on the rear door. Now Jo knew where both men were, but she couldn't send Ursa yet. The man at the back door might see her running. Jo lifted Ursa and placed her rear on the windowsill. The doors were breaking. Jo and Ursa pressed together, sharing the same wild heartbeat. One of the men would get through any second. Jo hoped it would be the one at the back door.

A shot cracked and then another. The man at the front door was using his gun to take out the bolt lock. He fired again. Almost simultaneously, the kitchen door's lock gave way with a crash of breaking wood. Jo lowered Ursa to the ground, but she stood petrified, staring up at Jo. "Run!" Jo whispered. "Hurry! I'll follow!"

Ursa took off for the woods to the west. As Jo crawled out the window, she heard the rev of an engine on Turkey Creek Road. She dropped to the ground and ran for the woods just as Gabe's truck careened around the corner spraying gravel. He fired a shot into the air, trying to draw the gunmen away from the house.

His timing couldn't have been worse for Jo. She was out in the open. But at least Ursa had made it to the woods.

Gabe skidded the truck to a halt near Jo's Honda, jumped out, and crouched down, using the cab for cover.

"Gabe! Watch out!" Ursa screamed.

"No! Get back!" Jo shouted when Ursa burst out of the tree line.

Still running, Jo heard feet thudding behind her. Shots fired. The man from the back door was shooting at Ursa. Or maybe at Jo. Gabe was trying to cover Ursa as she ran, but the man at the front door was firing on him.

Jo was running through a battlefield. Guns cracked all around her. She collapsed, the back of her left thigh burning. She couldn't move, in shock from the bullet wound. The man who'd shot her pounded past.

He was heading for Ursa. Jo got up, feeling no pain, but her damaged leg prevented her from running as fast as she needed to. In the pale celestial light, she saw Ursa running toward Gabe's truck. She had almost reached it when the man fired. Ursa went down. Jo stopped and pressed her hand to her mouth to cover her scream. But the man knew she was there. He turned around, his gun aimed straight at her.

Gabe bellowed a primal sound of rage and fired his gun. He was in the open, charging the man to divert his attention from Jo. The man turned away from Jo to return fire, but he stumbled backward and slouched to the ground before firing more than two shots.

Gabe was still standing. "Get down!" he shouted.

Jo flattened on the ground and watched him run to the man. He took the man's gun away and patted his body. He found another weapon and took it.

"How many are there?" he called to Jo.

"I think two. Ursa is hurt!"

"I know, but stay down!" He scuttled over to Ursa, his gun ready.

Jo was relieved when she heard him speak to Ursa. She must be okay. Gabe left Ursa and ran to Jo. "Are you hurt?"

"Just a little. What about Ursa?"

He didn't answer.

"Tell me!"

"It's bad."

"Oh my god!" She got up and ran for Ursa, dragging her left leg. "You have to stay down!" he said, running with her. "I've killed two, but there could be more."

Jo sank to the ground next to Ursa and Gabe crouched over her, peering around for more assailants. Ursa was on her back. Jo didn't need a light to see where she was hurt. In the dim glow of stars, she saw the dark stain soaked into the fabric of her pink Hello Kitty pajamas. She'd been shot once, on the right side of her stomach. She was breathing, but she was in shock. Her body trembled and her eyes stared at Jo, but she didn't seem to see her. "Is an ambulance coming?"

"Lacey called 911 when we heard the first shots."

"They might not bring an ambulance!"

"She heard all the gunfire. They'll bring an ambulance," he said, but he looked worried. He laid down his gun to call Lacey. "Are the police coming?" he said. "What about an ambulance? Not me. Ursa is hurt bad." After a pause, he said, "Yes, the girl." He listened for a few more seconds before ending the call.

"Lacey has called twice," he said. "First she said we needed police. When she heard the gunfight, she called back and said they needed to send lots of police and ambulances."

"What if they don't get here in time?" Jo wept.

"They will."

"No one finds this road!"

"The sheriff knows where it is. And Lacey said she'd call back to tell them Ursa is hurt." He pulled off his T-shirt. "Use this to put pressure on the wound. Press firmly, but not so much that you hurt her." He grabbed his gun again.

Jo held the shirt on the awful wound, uncertain of how hard to press. "What if there's an exit wound?"

"There probably is," he said. "He shot at close range."

Keeping pressure on the front wound, Jo slid her hand under Ursa's right side. She felt blood oozing out of her back. The bullet could have entered from either side. She stripped off her T-shirt and pushed it under Ursa's body, keeping pressure on both wounds. "You're going to be okay, love bug," she said, touching her lips to Ursa's cheek. "Stay with Gabe and me, okay? Try hard to stay with us."

Ursa was awake, her eyes focused on Jo. "D-don't cry," she said through chattering teeth. "Jo . . . stop crying!"

"I can't," Jo said. "I'm sorry, but I can't."

Ursa stared into her eyes. "Are you c-crying because you love me?"

"Yes! I love you so much!"

Ursa smiled. "That's it . . . the fifth miracle. That was what I want . . . wanted m-most, and I m-made it happen."

Jo cried harder, and tears spilled from the corners of Ursa's eyes.

"Jo . . ."

"What?"

"If I die, don't be sad. It's n-not me," she said.

"You aren't going to die!"

"I know. I can g-go back now. I saw five miracles. Don't be sad if it happens."

"You're staying here! I want to be your foster parent and maybe adopt you. I was going to tell you . . ."

"You were?" Her eyes brightened. She looked like familiar happy Ursa.

"You'll come live with Tabby and me in the pretty house. Would you like that?"

"Yes . . . but I feel bad. I might . . . I might have to go back in the stars."

"Here they come!" Gabe said.

Jo heard a convoy of distant sirens. But the sound was too distant. Ursa had closed her eyes.

"Ursa?" Jo said. "Ursa, stay with me!"

"Stars . . . ," Ursa murmured. "Jo . . . I see stars."

"Ursa, no! Stay with us!" She tried to keep pressure on Ursa's wounds, but her arms had no strength. Her legs buckled. She collapsed on her side and fell onto her back. She saw stars, too. Where was the bear? Where was Ursa Major? Which stars were those?

Gabe's hands lifted her. "Jo! You're losing a lot of blood! Your pants are soaked!"

He was right. She'd been fighting the fog in her mind since the man had shot her. She closed her eyes and let the darkness come. She would find Ursa. She would find her, even if she had to climb into the sky and pull her down from the stars herself.

30

Ursa. Ursa. Ursa. It was the mantra that drew her out of anesthesia. When she opened her eyes, she wasn't surprised to see a hospital room. She wasn't afraid either. The environment was all too familiar.

A middle-aged nurse who'd been fiddling with her IV bag looked at her. "Awake already? I didn't expect that for another hour at least."

"Do you know if the little girl who came in with me is okay?"

"You're asking the wrong person."

"Meaning, they told you not to say."

"How do you feel?" the nurse asked, lifting Jo's wrist to find her pulse.

"Well enough to be told what happened."

"Do you know what happened to you?" She probably had to establish that Jo could handle the news.

"I was shot in the back of the leg."

"Do you know where you are?"

"In Marion?"

"You're in Saint Louis."

"Saint Louis?"

"Don't you remember? You came to this hospital by medevac."

Now that she knew, she did remember. She'd thought the loud whir of the helicopter had been part of her delirium. "What's going on with my leg?"

"You received several units of blood, and the surgery involved vascular and tissue repair. The surgeon will explain when he comes by."

"Is a man named Gabriel Nash here?"

"Are you feeling up to seeing visitors?"

"Yes, I want to see him."

"Are you sure you're well enough?"

"Yes!"

The nurse left the room. A few minutes later, the door opened. It wasn't Gabe. A uniformed officer and a man dressed in a white shirt and khaki pants entered. Each of the men wore a gun, which meant the one in plain clothes must be a detective. They were both in their midforties but opposite in looks. The deputy was about six feet tall with dark eyes and short black hair, and the detective was five inches shorter with light eyes and blondish hair worn in a stubby ponytail. Their solemn faces made Jo wish she hadn't awakened.

"Joanna Teale?" the detective asked.

"Yes," she said.

"I'm Detective Kellen out of Effingham, and this is Chief Deputy McNabb from Vienna."

"I need to know about Ursa. Did she die? Just tell me."

"How did you know her name is Ursa?" he asked.

"She told me."

"Did she tell you her whole name?"

"Are you really going to do this to me? You're going to ask me a hundred questions without answering the only one that matters?"

"We can't answer because she's still in surgery or post-op. We don't know if she'll pull through."

She put her hands over her face, the only privacy available. She thought Ursa had died on the Kinney property. "Is she here—in this hospital?"

After a pause, the detective said, "Yes."

The other cop, McNabb, shot Kellen a disapproving glance. For some reason he hadn't wanted the detective to relay Ursa's whereabouts.

"Do you know why those men shot Ursa?" Jo asked.

"Please let us ask the questions, Ms. Teale," Deputy McNabb said.

"Are you feeling well enough?" Kellen asked.

She consented, and for the next twenty minutes, she answered their many questions. McNabb, who'd been at the crime scene, mostly asked about the shooting, while Kellen focused more on Jo's history with Ursa. Though they didn't say it, many of their questions were clearly aimed at corroborating statements Gabe had made. Jo tried to keep him out of her story as much as possible, but the two cops brought him up frequently. "Was Gabriel Nash there when that happened?" the detective often asked.

When Jo talked about Ursa and how she'd come to live with her, it all sounded wrong. She saw the judgment in the men's eyes and heard it in their questions. As the interrogation continued, Jo began to think she might be in serious trouble with the law. The anxiety, combined with the many other stresses on her mind and body, wore her out quickly. The police saw she was losing coherence and decided to quit for the time being.

"Is Gabe here?" Jo asked before they left.

"He was an hour ago," Kellen said. "Get some rest." He and the deputy walked out the door.

Jo pushed her call button. "Is there some way you can see if a visitor is in the waiting room and bring him here?" Jo asked the nurse when she arrived.

"Is it a family member?"

"No."

"For now, only family is allowed in."

"Wouldn't that be up to me?"

"You'll have to speak with your doctor."

"Okay, let me speak to him."

"I can't say when he'll be here. He'll see you when he makes rounds."

The hospital runaround. Jo knew it well. But she was too tired to wrangle. She quit fighting the drugs and succumbed to sleep.

When she woke hours later, she discovered she'd missed the doctor. She was desperate for news about Ursa, but she had a new nurse who was even less communicative than the last one. The pain medication the nurse gave her put her under again.

Jo thought she was dreaming when she felt lips touch her cheek. She won a battle with her heavy eyelids and looked into familiar green eyes. "Tabby!"

"This hospital thing is getting old, Jojo," Tabby said. She looked toward a dark window and said, "Go on, kiss her. She needs it." She stepped aside, and there was Gabe, his face haggard and shadowed with a beard. At first he and Jo could only stare at one another.

"Come on, Nash, just kiss her," Tabby said.

He leaned over and held her. They embraced for a long time before they obeyed Tabby with a short kiss. "How did you get in?" Jo asked. "They've been withholding visitors since I woke up this morning."

"Tabby did it," Gabe said. "In all of two minutes, she got the gate-keepers to open the door, and I've been trying all day."

"How did you do it?" she asked Tabby.

"I said you're an orphan and cancer survivor who has no one to lean on but us."

"She was persuasive," Gabe said. "The nurse at the desk was nearly teary."

"I'm experienced with hospital ogres," Tabby said, "because Jo comes to these places often. She must like the food."

"How did you find out I was here?"

"Gabe."

"I knew you would want her here," he said, "and she was listed in the university's directory service."

"I'm always listed," Tabby said. "You never know when some hot guy needs your number." She winked at Gabe.

"No one could find your brother's number," Gabe said.

"Good," Jo said. "Better if he doesn't know."

"You have to call him," Tabby said.

"You know he just started his residency up in Washington. My health issues have caused enough disruption in his life."

"Jo . . . ," Gabe said.

"Okay, I'll call him. Have they told you anything about Ursa?"

"They won't tell me anything," Gabe said. "And the local news didn't help either. It was reported as an attempted burglary. All they said was two men were shot dead and a child and woman were airlifted to a hospital for gunshot wounds."

"That does say something," Jo said. "Ursa must have survived the surgery! If a little girl died in a robbery, that news would travel fast."

"You're right," Tabby said. "The media never misses an opportunity to exploit a kid tragedy. That news probably would make it up to Chicago."

"Gabe . . . ," Jo said.

"What?"

"I just realized . . . you killed two people. Are you okay?"

"Yeah."

"Why the grim phizogs?" Tabby said. Patting Gabe's back, she said, "This guy is a hero. He saved your life and Ursa's."

"She's wrong, isn't she?" he said. "I nearly got both of you killed. If I hadn't shown up when I did, Ursa wouldn't have gotten shot."

"You can't feel guilty about that. There's no way you could have known," Jo said.

"I do. I feel like shit. Ursa came out of hiding to warn me. I didn't even know where you were when she screamed and ran out of the woods. I tried to cover for her, but I was taking fire from the guy by the front door when the other one came out the back door. I couldn't cover them both."

"It was an impossible situation," Jo said.

"Not for you," he said. "When I went in the house with the police, we pieced together what you did. You waited until they broke in before you sent Ursa out the window. She for sure would have been safe, and you probably would have been, too. They hadn't broken in the door to the room you were hiding in. We found your phone in there. It was still connected to 911 and they'd heard all the gunfire. That was when they dispatched the helicopters."

"When I think of you locked in that room with Ursa . . . ," Tabby said. She hugged Jo and kissed her again. "Will your leg be okay? The bone must not be broken or you'd have a cast."

"It was mostly vascular. The nurses say I'll be fine, but I haven't had a chance to talk to the doctor. I've hardly been able to keep my eyes open."

"You lost a lot of blood," Gabe said. "Last night when you passed out . . . I was afraid both you and Ursa were going to die."

"I wish we could visit her," Jo said. "Imagine how upset she is."

"Check this out," Tabby said. She pulled her phone from her purse, moved her finger over it, and held the screen up for Jo to see. It was a school photo of Ursa smiling, and over the picture were the words MISSING, Ursa Ann Dupree.

"I checked that website almost every day!" Jo said.

"She must have been reported recently," Gabe said.

"I shouldn't have stopped looking," Jo said.

"I stopped, too," he said.

Jo took the phone out of Tabby's hand and read the information below Ursa's photo. She went missing on June 6 from Effingham, Illinois. She was eight years old. Her ninth birthday would be on August 30.

"I can't believe she's only eight!" Jo said.

"I know," Tabby said, taking the phone back. "That's only third grade."

"It doesn't seem possible," Gabe said.

"The first night I talked to her, she used the word *salutation*," Jo said.

"Maybe she really is a smart alien in a kid's body," Tabby said.

A nurse came in to record Jo's vitals. "When can I get out of bed?" Jo asked him.

"Tomorrow morning you'll have physical therapy," he said.

After the nurse left, Gabe sat on the edge of the bed and held her hand. "They said we can only stay for a few minutes, and I need to tell you something."

"This can't be good."

"It's not. We're in trouble. But it's worse for you because Ursa slept at your rental house and went to work with you."

"Did the cops tell you that?"

"They've implied it, even though I told them I was as responsible as you were for letting Ursa stay." He squeezed her hand. "I hate to say this when you've barely recovered, but I have to. Call your lawyer if you have one. I think you're going to be charged with a child endangerment felony."

Child endangerment. Not possible. Not when all she'd done was give food, shelter, and love to an abandoned little girl.

But then she saw Ursa running under the stars. A gun fired again and again, and Ursa stumbled and slumped to the ground. All because Jo hadn't turned her over to the sheriff.

She dropped her arm over her eyes and cried.

31

The next morning someone knocked on her door. "Come in," she said, pulling her hospital gown over her bandaged leg. She was expecting Gabe and Tabby. They'd spent the night at a nearby hotel. Instead, her research advisor walked in. "So . . . when were you going to tell me you were shot and nearly died?" Shaw asked.

"Never, if possible. I figured you were tired of my endless doom and gloom."

"I'm not, and if I'd known, I'd have been here in a heartbeat." He folded his long body into the chair in front of hers. "Is your brother here?"

"I talked to him last night. He wanted to come, but I told him I was perfectly fine and I'd be pissed if he came."

"Perfectly fine?" Shaw said, looking at her propped leg.

"I am. How did you find out?"

"From George Kinney. The police had to contact him because it happened on his property."

"That must have been surprising news—a shoot-out and two guys dead on his property."

"The timing was bad. His wife died earlier the same night."

"Lynne died?"

Shaw's white brows arched in confusion. "You knew Lynne?"

"No . . . not really."

He studied her for a few seconds. "George told me you brought someone he knows to campus that same day—Gabriel Nash?"

Jo nodded. "He helped me move my stuff into the new house."

"George said he lives on the property next to his. His family and George's go way back." He waited for Jo to explain how she knew Gabe, but she stayed silent. "George told me Gabe may have saved your life."

"I had a gun pointing straight at me, and he took out the guy before he fired."

"My god!" Shaw said, thrusting his fingers into his silky white hair. "I have to meet this guy and thank him."

"You may get your wish. He's supposed to be here any minute."

"Should I leave?"

"No, visitors are all that make a hospital bearable."

"I thought good drugs did that?"

"I've had it with the drugs. I'm already weaning off."

"Why am I not surprised to hear that?" He relaxed against the back of his chair. "I hear the little girl is doing well."

"Is she?"

"They didn't tell you?"

"No. They won't tell me anything."

"She's in intensive care, but she's out of danger. They expect her to make it."

If her advisor weren't sitting in front of her, she'd have blubbered in relief. "Did the police tell Dr. Kinney why those men were after her?"

Shaw sat erect. "She didn't get hit by accident?"

"I'm pretty sure they came there to kill her."

"Have you told the police?"

"I've told them everything."

"They told George it was probably a robbery."

"I think they're saying that because it's a criminal investigation and they can't leak anything. It's all linked to something that happened in Effingham. A detective from there asked me a lot of questions."

Shaw's blue gaze was penetrating. "George said the police asked him if he'd been aware that the little girl was living on his property."

Jo couldn't think of anything to say.

"Was she?"

"Yes."

He rumpled his hair again.

"I think I'm in pretty big trouble."

"What the hell were you doing?"

"I felt sorry for her. One night she showed up hungry and wearing dirty pajamas. She didn't even have shoes."

"I remember—you'd given her your sandals."

"I called the sheriff the next day, but she ran into the woods when he got there."

"But that was . . . what, more than a month ago?"

"I know."

He waited for more explanation.

"I hated for her to go to foster parents. You hear all those bad stories . . ."

"Were you sure her parents weren't looking for her?"

"If they were, they never told the police. I checked the internet every day for the first few weeks. And by then . . . I know this will sound crazy, but I really cared about her. I was even thinking of trying to be her foster parent."

"My god, Jo, your heart is just too big for this mean world."

"If I'm charged with something, will it cause trouble at the university?"

"It might."

"Could I get kicked out of grad school?"

"You never know with our current butt-brain of a department head." He saw how devastated she was. "You know I'll fight for you. And I know what you've been through—how it could have . . . influenced what you did."

Why did everyone think that? She kept her mouth shut, but she wanted to say that she wouldn't have done anything different if she still had her mother and her breasts and her ovaries. She would love Ursa just as much.

Shaw saw he'd perturbed her and changed the subject. "Do you need help wrapping up your research?"

"To tell the truth, I can't stop worrying about my nest logs and computer and everything sitting in that house."

"I'd be the same way. If my head was blown off my body, my brain would still be worrying about my data."

"No doubt about that."

"I'll go straight to Kinney's when I leave Saint Louis. I have a key to get in."

"I don't think there's much door left to unlock."

"Jesus, I need to get over there."

"Isn't it a crime scene? Do you think you can go in?"

"I might have to get the sheriff's help. Will your nest logs be obvious?"

"They're on the desk in a folder marked *Nest Logs*."

"I guess that's obvious."

"My laptop and binoculars are on the desk, too. Would you bring them back to campus and put them somewhere safe?"

"I will. And I wanted to ask—do you mind if we finish monitoring your active nests?"

"Mind? I'd be thrilled! But you don't have the time for that."

"I don't." He rubbed the arthritic left elbow he'd once broken, usually a sign that he was about to say something he didn't want to say.

"Tanner and Carly said they'd come down and monitor your nests while you're in the hospital."

"They can't stay at the house. Like I said, the doors are broken, and I'm sure it's considered a crime scene."

"They were going to camp at some nearby place."

Probably where Jo and Tanner had made love in the stream, Tanner's favorite campground since a group of graduate students had brought him there. "Are you sure they can take the time off?"

"Are you kidding? When students finish their research, they'll do anything possible to avoid writing their thesis. They said they'd planned to go camping anyway."

"If they want to take a working vacation, I'm happy for the help."

"And Carly knows your study sites—she worked in many of those same areas."

"The nest cameras can be removed if they don't want to deal with them. And I have everything clearly marked on maps in the folders."

"Of course you do," he said. "We'll make copies of—"

Someone knocked on the door.

"Come in," Jo said.

Gabe walked in. "I'm sorry," he said when he saw Shaw. "I'll come back later."

"No, stay. Gabe, this is my advisor, Dr. Shaw Daniels. Shaw, this is Gabriel Nash."

Shaw sprang from his chair and shook Gabe's hand. "Good to meet you!" he said. "Thank you for helping Jo! You saved her life! And the little girl!"

Gabe didn't deny it, but his eyes betrayed his feelings of guilt. Jo studied Shaw, looking for signs that he saw George Kinney in Gabe's face. If he noticed the resemblance, his reaction wasn't obvious.

"I was expecting you a long time ago," Jo said. "Where's Tabby?"

Gabe glanced at Shaw. "She's . . . in the gift shop."

"What? She better not buy me any of that overpriced crap!"

Shaw wiped his brow in a mock gesture of relief. "Thank god I didn't buy that Get Well balloon!"

"I was about to say: unless it's a balloon."

"Damn it!" He leaned down and hugged her lightly. "I'd better go. I want to get over to Kinney's and make sure your data are safe."

"I put her nest logs in the desk's file drawer to make them less obvious," Gabe said. "And the police let me lock her laptop and binoculars in the lower drawer that has a key lock. I hid the key inside a paper-clip box in the top drawer."

"I like this guy," Shaw said to Jo. "He thinks data safety like a scientist."

"Rubbed off, I guess," Jo said, smiling at Gabe.

"I hope to see you again," Shaw said, clasping Gabe's hand once more. "Let's have a beer sometime, and I'm buying."

"Sounds great," Gabe said. He was more relaxed with a stranger than Jo had ever seen him. Spending time with Tabby had that effect on people.

"He seems like a great guy," Gabe said after Shaw left.

"He is. He's why I stayed at U of I rather than apply for another PhD program. I only wanted to work with him." She reached her arms up toward him. "Get down here and give me a kiss."

"You're only saying that because I'm clean shaven and irresistible again."

"You know it." They kissed over her propped-up leg.

"I'm glad to see you're out of bed."

"So am I. What's going on with Tabby? Why did you look nervous when you said she's in the gift shop?"

"You don't miss anything, do you? Just like Ursa. I never could make a move around you two."

"What move were you going to make?"

"I don't know, because I never tried." He sat in the chair. "So . . . about Tabby . . ."

"Uh-oh."

"Yeah."

"Oh god, what is she up to now?"

"I had a feeling she does things like this often."

"What is she doing?"

"She stole a maid's shirt from a staff room at our hotel—"

"What!"

"She wanted it to look official . . ."

"She wanted *what* to look official?"

"She's buying a gift for Ursa in the shop, and she's going to pretend she's a delivery person from a florist shop. She's going to try to see Ursa."

"Ursa is in the ICU. The door will be locked."

"I tried to stop her," he said.

"There's no stopping Tabby when she gets one of her ideas. Did she tell you she once snuck a lamb into the hospital?"

"Wait—did you just say *a lamb*?"

"Yep. Her vet specialty is large animals. One of the lambs from the research herd lost its mother, and she was helping bottle-feed it. She knows I love the baby farm animals she works with, so she packs the lamb in her car with its milk, drives up to Chicago, and sneaks it into my room two days after my breasts were removed. She takes this tiny lamb out of a shoulder bag, lays it on my bed, and hands me the bottle. *There,* she says, *who needs tits anyway? There are other ways to give milk.*"

Gabe looked away and blinked.

"I know. I cried like a baby. At first she thought it was because I was upset. But I loved it. It was one of the best crazy things she's ever done."

"She made me go out with her when we left the hospital last night," he said. "She wanted to explore, and we ended up—"

"In some weird place."

"Yes!"

"Let me guess—a hippie massage parlor? A Japanese karaoke bar?"

"She's taken you to those places?"

"In Chicago. She made me do lots of weird things when my mother was dying. She said I had to remember there was a big amazing world beyond the borders of my sad little country—she used those exact words. I've always thought Tabby should be a novelist."

"I know. Veterinarian doesn't seem right for her."

"It makes more sense if you know she grew up in a city apartment. She's hardly touched her foot to a blade of grass, and she's going to work with cows, horses, and sheep. Her dad owns an automotive shop, and he thinks it's the funniest thing."

"He's angry about it?"

"No, I meant *funny* funny. He's a great guy, quirky, like she is. He raised Tabby and her sister alone when their mother split."

"Tabby is the kind of character Arthur would like."

"Tell me where she took you last night."

"First we went to a Welsh restaurant called a 'public house,' where we ate and drank at a communal table."

"Wow, how'd that go for you?"

"It was fun, believe it or not. We met two really nice guys—and that was how we ended up at the gay bar."

"That is so Tabby!"

"What is so Tabby?" Tabby said, sticking her head in the door. She came in, still wearing the blue maid's shirt.

"Did you see Ursa?" Gabe asked.

She sat on the bed. "I almost did."

"You got past the ICU doors?" Jo asked.

She nodded. "I bought a balloon and stuffed animal and wrote a note that said *Ursa, We love you! Get better fast!* I signed it *Hugs and kisses, Jo, Gabe, and Tabby.* The stuffed animal was a tabby cat, by the way—isn't that awesome?"

"Tell the story!" Jo said.

"I went to the hospital directory lady, but she didn't have Ursa listed. She looked at my toy and asked if the patient was a child. When I said she was, the lady said Ursa was probably at their children's hospital a few blocks away. She checked for me, but they didn't have her listed either."

"That's weird."

"That's what I thought. I went to the ICU in this hospital to look around, but the doors were locked. I waited until a nurse came out with a guy in a wheelchair—"

"You didn't."

"I did. I ran in. Before anyone realized I wasn't supposed to be in there, I went looking for Ursa. That was when I saw her room."

"How do you know?" Gabe said.

"There was a cop guarding her door."

"A cop!" Jo said.

"Are you sure it was her room?" Gabe said.

"Before I got to the door, a nurse stopped me and asked who I was. I said I had a gift for Ursa Dupree. I told her I was supposed to deliver the toy and balloon and sing her a song. I assumed the cop was guarding Ursa, so I started walking fast toward him. The nurse yelled *Stop her!* and guess what happened?"

"Oh my god," Jo said.

"Yeah, the cop drew his gun on me. I got hauled to some security office, and they asked me a bunch of questions about how I knew what room to go to—which means that really is Ursa's room. She's probably not in the children's hospital because the police know that's too obvious."

"How did you lie your way out of security?" Jo asked.

"I didn't. Lying was too dangerous. I told them I knew Ursa through you, and I was upset because the hospital wouldn't let me see her. I admitted I hatched the plan to sneak in."

"What did they do?"

"They took my name and address, but they were only trying to scare me. And they said I'd be arrested if I tried it again."

"I can't believe this," Jo said. "Ursa is under police guard."

"I believe it," Gabe said.

"So do I," Tabby said. She lowered her voice and leaned forward. "I bet the government knows she's an alien in Ursa Dupree's body!"

32

Jo had looked through every magazine in the ICU waiting room, even *Guns and Gardens*, which would have amused her pacifist-gardener mother. Her favorite seat was the one next to an adjacent table on which she could support her bandaged leg. She exercised every hour, walking in circles on her crutches around the room. She used the handicapped stall in the waiting-room bathroom to bathe and brush her teeth, and she slept on the couch. She ate when Gabe brought her food. He was still at the nearby hotel, and he washed and dried her clothing in his room every night.

Tabby had wanted to join Jo in her sit-in, but she couldn't be away from her job any longer. Gabe wanted Jo to leave. He said the police would never let her see Ursa, but Jo couldn't accept that. She needed to see Ursa again. She knew without the slightest doubt that Ursa wanted to see her, too.

Word of her sit-in had spread through the hospital. Jo's surgeon came to talk to her on the third day. He said she was risking infection from stress and maybe a blood clot from sitting too much. Hospital security also came the third day. They told her to leave, but Jo said she wouldn't until she saw Ursa. They said they'd have the police physically remove her, but that hadn't happened yet.

Jo watched everyone who went down Ursa's ICU corridor. She took note of police and official-looking people who went through the doors. A woman with a white-streaked Afro visited frequently, and Jo began to suspect she was Ursa's court-designated counselor. The woman often looked at Jo while she waited for the ICU doors to open. At first she assessed Jo with apparent coldness. But by the third day, there seemed to be some grudging admiration in her stare.

Gabe came in with lunch on the fourth day of her sit-in. He had dark circles under his eyes, and his cheekbones seemed more prominent. He was in contact with Lacey and his mother, but he didn't tell them the truth, that Jo had been discharged from the hospital after three days.

Gabe took off his backpack and sat next to her. "Turkey, provolone, avocado, and lettuce on wheat," he said, handing her a white paper bag.

"Aren't you going to eat?"

"I'm not hungry."

"I wish you'd go home."

"I wish you would stop this insanity," he said.

"I can't."

"She's probably not here anymore. I'm sure they've moved her."

"She must still be in there. That woman with the Afro went in about an hour ago."

"You don't even know if that woman is connected to Ursa!"

"I think she is. She always stares at me."

"Everyone does—because what you're doing is crazy. You need to get out of here and find a lawyer."

"I don't need a lawyer."

Rather than argue about that again, he shook his head and looked away.

"Did you bring me clean clothes?"

"Yes, but they're still damp."

As she finished the sandwich, he closed his eyes and leaned back in his chair. Jo kissed his cheek. "Don't you want to get back to your birds?" he said, eyes still closed.

"I can't on crutches, and Tanner and Carly are finishing my work."

He opened his eyes and looked at her. "I'd think you want to make sure they're doing everything right."

"Tanner has to get it right."

"Why?"

"He's using my nests to get back in Shaw's good graces. Shaw was pissed when he dropped me like I was Typhoid Mary after my diagnosis."

"I still can't believe he did that."

"I can. Tanner is—"

The ICU doors opened. Jo looked into the sharp eyes of the woman with the Afro. She was wearing a light-gray skirt with a peach shirt that nicely complemented her brown skin. Her shape was like Lacey's, full-bodied and strong, but not quite as tall.

She walked straight toward Jo and Gabe. "Joanna Teale, right?" she said.

"Yes," Jo said.

"And you must be Gabriel Nash," the woman said, stopping in front of them.

"Yes," he said with tense vocal cords.

She crossed her arms and looked down at Jo. "So . . . how long have you been out here?"

"This is the fourth day," Jo said.

"After surgery, no less. You're as stubborn as her."

"Ursa?" Jo said.

"Who else? I never met a more stubborn child in all my days."

"I know how you feel," Jo said. "She mule-kicked me for a long time before I decided to back off."

"You know, when I first heard this story, I couldn't imagine why you did what you did. How could you not bring her to the police for a whole month? How could you not know that was wrong?"

"I knew it was wrong."

"But the alien got in your head—with her powers—right?"

"She still says she's an alien?"

"Oh yeah, I know all about her planet. Hetrayeh is its name, and her people's skin looks like starlight."

"Did she tell you about the five miracles?"

"She sure did. You know why she didn't go back to her planet after the fifth miracle?"

"How did she explain it?"

"She said she decided to stay when she found out you loved her. The fifth miracle made her stay instead of go."

Jo had to look away.

The woman waited for her to recover. "Want to know a little secret? Say Hetrayeh backwards."

Jo and Gabe looked at each other, trying to work it out.

"It's not easy, right?" the woman said. "People with regular brains do it slow."

"Eyarteh?" Gabe said.

"A *th* sound can't be reversed unless you put a vowel in. Try that at the end."

"Earth!" Jo said.

The woman nodded.

Jo tried reversing Ursa's name. "Ursa Ann Dupree is Earpood Na Asru. She said that was her alien name."

"You got it," the woman said. "But she does it fast. Give her a book and she can read the words backward as fast as she can read them forward." The woman smiled at Jo and Gabe's confusion. "No, she's not an alien. But in a way she is—at least to the rest of us. She's a genius. In first grade, her IQ measured over 160."

"This explains so much!" Jo said.

"Doesn't it, though?" She extended her hand toward Jo. "I'm Lenora Rhodes from Children and Family Services." Jo and Gabe shook her hand. "I've been assigned the impossible task of getting Ursa to tell me what happened the night she ran away."

"She won't tell you anything?" Jo asked.

Lenora pulled a chair out and set it in front of them. "She says she'll only tell you, Jo. For five days we've tried, and she says it has to be you."

"Smart," Gabe said.

"I'm about to tear my hair out, she's so smart," Lenora said. "I'm going to tell you what I know in exchange for your help."

"Does she have family?" Jo asked.

"Her only known living relatives are a drug-addicted grandmother who lives in a trailer and a grandfather with Alzheimer's who's living in a senior home. She also has an uncle whose whereabouts are unknown because he's wanted by the police."

"If she has nowhere to go, I'd like to apply to be her foster parent."

"Slow down. Let's take it a step at a time. Will you agree to talk to her?"

"Of course. Do you know what happened to her parents?"

Lenora looked around to make sure no one was listening. She leaned forward in her chair. "We know all about her parents. They both grew up in Paducah, Kentucky. Ursa probably got her smarts from her father, Dylan Dupree. He was on a great trajectory, one of those kids who succeeds at everything—until he fell for Portia Wilkins his sophomore year. Somehow, one of the smartest students at that high school got involved with one of the most troubled. Portia was a real looker—maybe that's how it happened."

"Or she was as smart as he was, and that attracted him," Jo said. "Lots of smart kids get into trouble."

"True," Lenora said. "Whatever the reason, everything went downhill for Dylan when he started seeing Portia. He got into drugs and alcohol, his grades dropped, and he was often in trouble. The summer between junior and senior year, Portia got pregnant. When both families refused to support their decision to keep the baby, Dylan and Portia ran away. They hitchhiked their way out of Kentucky and ended up in Effingham, Illinois."

"Did they get married?" Jo asked.

"They did, but not until after Ursa was born. Portia was waitressing, and Dylan worked with a contractor. By the time Ursa was two, their combined income was high enough to move into a decent apartment. There are no arrest records during that time, but we believe Dylan and Portia were using drugs and alcohol regularly."

"Why do you think that?" Jo asked.

"Because Dylan drowned, and they found heavy drugs in his system. That was when Ursa was five."

"Poor Ursa," Gabe said.

"Friends who were at the lake verified he was high when he went in to swim. Ursa was on shore with her mother, who also was intoxicated."

Lenora stopped talking when a couple stepped out of the elevator. She waited until they went through the ICU doors before continuing. "Dylan was the glue in the family, and when he died, everything came unstuck. During the next three years, Portia was constantly in trouble. She was fired from several waitressing jobs, arrested on a drug misdemeanor, and investigated for writing bad checks. She also lost her driver's license after getting a DUI. When Ursa was in second grade, her school had Portia investigated for child neglect. Ursa was showing up to school in dirty clothing, and more than once she was found wandering the grounds long after school was over. Her behavior became increasingly odd—"

"Smart kids are often considered odd," Jo said.

"They took that into account. But she disrupted class often. She would read things backward obsessively and raise her hand to tell wild stories to the teacher."

"She was bored," Gabe said. "Can you imagine what a second-grade curriculum would be like for a person with an IQ like that?"

Lenora smiled. "I love how you two defend her. But when a child is acting out like that, it's usually a sign of a stressful home situation. During the home investigation, the social workers got the impression that Ursa basically took care of herself. She knew how to cook easy things like macaroni and cheese, and she did her homework, got ready for school, and went to the bus stop without any help. Her clothes were dirty because she couldn't get to the Laundromat by herself. After Dylan died, Portia had to move to a dirt-cheap apartment that had no washer or dryer."

"Did the social workers consider taking her away from her mother?" Jo asked.

"It has to be really bad for that to happen. They decided what was going on wasn't that atypical for a child with a single mother. What they didn't know was that Ursa lied when they asked if her mother used drugs and alcohol. Portia's drug habit had gotten so bad that she was prostituting herself to get money to pay for it. She was a waitress at a bar-restaurant—"

"What was it called—the restaurant?" Jo asked.

"It's not the place you stopped the night of the shooting."

"You know about that?"

"I know about everything," Lenora said. "We think Ursa had been to that restaurant before, but not because her mother had worked there. The last place Portia worked was a rough spot where she found men who would help her support her drug habit. Because she didn't have a driver's license, a friend who waitressed with her often drove her to and from work. One day in June, she went to pick up Portia at her apartment and got no answer. When Portia didn't show up to work for two days, the friend convinced Portia's landlord to let her look in the apartment. Inside they found a note on the refrigerator that said she and a friend had taken Ursa to Wisconsin for a vacation."

"That was after school had ended?" Jo asked.

"Yes, Ursa was out of school. But Portia's friend knew of no friend who would drive them to Wisconsin. She also knew Portia and Ursa wouldn't leave behind their clothing. For a week she pestered the police, but when they finally started asking her questions, she suddenly backed off. She got scared because she also was a drug user and prostitute. The police pretty much dropped it after that."

"When a little girl's life was at stake?" Jo said.

"They had no leads, and the mother left a note. And by the second week, they had no evidence to search because Portia's landlord dumped all her belongings and cleaned the apartment for new renters. Portia hadn't paid rent for two months."

"The police shouldn't have let the landlord do that," Jo said.

"They realized that two weeks ago when Portia's body was found in a borrow pit."

"Jesus," Gabe said.

"Do they know how she died?" Jo said.

"The body was decomposed, but there's evidence of trauma on the right side of the skull. Decomposition matched the date she went missing. She probably died the night of June sixth."

"And Ursa showed up in my front yard on June seventh," Jo said.

Lenora nodded. "And a week ago you stopped in Effingham for dinner and noticed Ursa seemed afraid of a man. Possibly that man called two men who followed you home. You told the police Ursa said *They'll kill you, too* just before the men started shooting."

"Those men murdered Portia," Gabe said.

"Probably," Lenora said, "and we think Ursa saw it happen."

"Why is Ursa being guarded if the presumed murderers are dead?" Jo asked.

"Who knows if only those two were involved? Maybe the man on the phone at the restaurant took part in the murder. We think Ursa knows who that man is and what happened the night her mother died." Lenora leaned toward Jo. "To get that story, we need your help."

"When?"

"Today. Her safety is up to you, Joanna. You have to make her talk."

33

The ICU gatekeepers opened their doors to the two rogues in their waiting room. But there were rules. They couldn't discuss what happened the night Ursa's mother died until Detective Kellen and Deputy McNabb arrived. Ursa's statement had to be witnessed by law enforcement to make sure she wasn't coerced. And Jo and Gabe couldn't tell Ursa they knew anything about her background. Most importantly, they couldn't reveal that her mother's body had been found. Lenora said knowing that might alter how Ursa told her story.

As Jo approached the ICU central desk on her crutches, a silvery balloon caught her eye. It was tied to a stuffed tabby kitten. Jo veered away from Lenora Rhodes and Gabe.

"Jo, what are you doing?" Gabe said.

She had to go behind the desk to reach the gifts.

"You aren't allowed back here," a man said. "Ma'am . . ."

Jo rested one crutch on her body, grabbed the tabby kitten, and faced the indignant staff. "Why wasn't this given to Ursa?"

No one answered.

"Do you see this note? It clearly says her name. This would have meant a lot to her, and it's been sitting out here for a week." Jo looked around at them. "Why would you keep this from a sick little girl who needs it?"

"We wanted to give it to her . . . ," a nurse said.

"They weren't allowed," Lenora said.

"Why not?"

"I think you know why."

"You were trying to erase us—Gabe, Tabby, and me. You wanted her to forget us."

"We thought it would be more painful than helpful to remind her," Lenora said.

"That's just wrong. And *I'm* the one in trouble!" Jo held the kitten against her crutch handle and walked from behind the desk, the balloon fluttering against her head.

Lenora clucked her tongue and shook her head. "Aren't you a match for Miss Ursa, though?"

They continued down the corridor, past rooms mostly occupied by elderly people attached to machines. Jo's stomach fluttered with anticipation when she saw the policeman seated next to Ursa's room. The policeman stood, his hand on his holster.

"It's all right," Lenora said. "I'm letting them in."

The officer gave her a questioning gaze.

"My girl ain't gonna talk if we don't," she said. "I think we've established that well enough."

The officer stepped aside for Jo. Ursa was seated in her hospital bed, remnants of her lunch spread on a rolling table in front of her. She was intently studying the IV in her arm.

"Oh no you don't, young lady!" Lenora said. "Don't even think about pulling that out again."

Ursa looked up guiltily. But when she saw Jo and Gabe, her expression turned to pure joy. "Jo! Gabe!" she said.

Jo moved toward her as fast as the crutches would allow. She put the kitten on the bed and leaned into Ursa's outstretched arms. They cried and held each other for a few minutes. Then Gabe did the same as Lenora and a nurse watched from the doorway.

When Gabe let Ursa go, Jo showed her the kitten and balloon. "This is from Tabby."

Ursa pressed the kitten to her cheek. "I love him! He's like Caesar! Is Tabby here?"

"She was here for a long time, but she had to go back to work," Jo said.

"You and Gabe were here, too?"

"Ever since what happened," Jo said.

Ursa glowered at Lenora. "I knew it! I knew they were here!"

"You got me cold, little lady," Lenora said. "But I only ever wanted you to get better."

"Are you going to let me live with Jo and Tabby?"

"Let's just enjoy the moment," Lenora said. She sat in a chair in the corner.

"Are you going to finish your lunch?" the nurse asked Ursa.

"I don't like it."

"You asked for macaroni and cheese."

"You have to make it from the blue box," Ursa said, "and the shapes make it taste better."

"Try *Star Wars* shapes next time," Jo told the nurse.

"Don't think our kitchen has that," the nurse said, picking up the tray.

"Now that Jo is here, she can bring some," Ursa said.

Jo rolled the table away and sat on the edge of the bed. Gabe pulled over a chair. Jo held Ursa's hand. "Do you feel okay?"

Her brown eyes melted into gloom. "Is Little Bear dead?"

Jo took Ursa's hand in both of hers and held tight. "He is. I'm very sorry."

A sob burst from her chest, and tears dripped down her cheeks.

"I'm so proud of him," Jo said. "He saved both of us. You know that, right?"

Ursa nodded, crying.

"When you get better, we'll have a nice funeral for him."

"With a cross?"

"I can make one," Gabe said.

"Where is he?" she asked Gabe.

"He's buried in the woods near the Kinney house," he said.

Ursa cried harder, and Jo held her again.

"What's wrong with your leg?" Ursa asked when her tears subsided.

"One of the men shot the back of my thigh."

More tears. "I'm sorry, Jo! It's my fault! It's my fault you got hurt and Little Bear is dead!"

"No, it isn't! None of what happened was your fault. Don't ever think that."

"I should have told you! I was pretty sure they were following us . . ."

"You were scared. It's okay."

Ursa looked at Gabe. "The police said you killed them."

"Yes," he said.

"Are you in trouble?"

"No."

Jo drew tissues from the box on the table and wiped Ursa's runny nose. She used another to dab her tears.

"I love you, Jo," Ursa said.

"I love you, too, love bug."

She smiled. "You called me that the night I got shot. That was when I figured out that you love me."

"My mom used to call me love bug—even when I grew up."

"I wish I had my pencils. I just got an idea for something to draw."

"What?"

"A love bug. It will be pink with purple spots. Its eyes will be big, and it will have long antennas."

"It sounds cute."

"I'll draw pink and red hearts all around it."

"There's an office store near my hotel," Gabe said. "How about I get you colored pencils and paper?"

"Not now! You have to stay!" She turned to Jo. "I forgot! I forgot to tell you why I stayed after the fifth miracle."

"Why did you?"

"Because I decided to stay with you. When you said you loved me and maybe would adopt me, I wanted that more than anything. Even more than my own planet. I was in the stars when I decided to come back."

"Were you?"

"Yes! It was all glittery and black and really pretty. But I only wanted you, and I tried hard to get back to you."

Jo kissed her cheek. "I'm glad you came back."

Ursa glanced at Lenora. "I'm not staying if they don't let me be with you."

"Let's not worry about that yet, okay?" Jo said.

"I do worry about it—all the time. When they lied and said you weren't here, I tried to run away and find you."

"Twice, as a matter of fact," Lenora said.

"That reminds me," Gabe said. He rummaged in his backpack and pulled out his battered copy of *The Runaway Bunny*. "I brought this for you."

"Will you read it?" Ursa said.

"I sure will."

Jo changed places with him so he could show her the pictures as he read.

"Read it again? Please?" Ursa pleaded when he finished.

He started over. The story had the same lulling effect it had when he'd read it to her at Kinney Cottage. She was nearly asleep when he finished. He and Jo gently stroked her arm until she fell into a deep sleep.

Lenora walked to the bed. "Her pain medication has been reduced, but it still makes her sleepy. Her emotions tend to wear her out, too."

She looked at the door. "Well, I need to eat some lunch before the others get here, and I'm sorry to say you have to go back to the waiting room. She's not allowed unattended visitors."

"That went well," Lenora said on their walk back through the ICU. "She's very comfortable with you two. I think you'll get her to say what Josh Kellen needs to know." A nurse opened the outer doors for them. "There's nothing Kellen hates more than kid killers," Lenora said. "He has to settle this." She directed her hand at Jo's usual chair in the waiting room. "Have a seat, and please don't go anywhere. As soon as everyone gets here, we'll all go in and talk to Ursa. Good thing she'll be well rested."

Jo and Gabe sat side by side in the waiting room. "Why do I feel like I'm about to do something shitty?" Jo said.

"Because it will be shitty," he said. "We're going to make her talk about her mother's murder."

"That's not what I meant. I feel like we're being forced to trick her. She's terrified she'll be separated from us, and they're going to use that to their advantage."

"They're trying to solve a murder, Jo."

"I know, but that's a little girl in there. She's not just a tool to unlock their case."

34

Two hours later, Lenora Rhodes nearly ran from the elevator to the ICU doors.

"What's going on?" Jo said.

"She woke up and saw you weren't there. She's making a fuss again."

"I can help," Jo said.

"No, it's better if she learns her tantrums don't work." She hurried through the doors.

"What the hell?" Jo said.

"Yeah," Gabe said. "Why not give a sick kid what makes her feel better—especially before she's got to talk about her dead mother?"

"Because they have their heads up their asses!"

They sat and waited again. A half hour later, Detective Kellen, Deputy McNabb, and a woman with shoulder-length bleached hair stepped out of the elevator. Jo and Gabe stood. "This is Dr. Shaley," Kellen said, gesturing toward the blonde woman. "She's Ursa's state-appointed psychologist."

Jo and Gabe shook the woman's hand.

"I heard about your vigil," Shaley told Jo. "I'm impressed by your dedication. Four days in a hospital waiting room! I hear you bathe in the bathroom."

"People who have no voice need others to speak for them," Jo said.

"Ursa, you mean?"

"Yes, Ursa."

"Why do you assume she has no voice?"

"Because she's been asking for me for a week, and she wasn't allowed to see me."

"We're trying to do what's best for her, not just for now, but in the future."

"You know, she's very aware that her future is hanging in the balance, and she's smart enough to know what's best for her. When she ran away in June, I think she was searching for a new home. She wanted to choose it rather than have it chosen for her."

Shaley and the two officers were incredulous.

"And you believe you are that home?" Shaley asked.

"I would love to be. But it's her choice."

"She's not even nine years old," McNabb said.

"And what choice does she have when you were the first person she encountered?" Shaley said. "There are many wonderful foster parents who would love to give her an excellent home."

"I hope you're right," Jo said. "She'll leave if she doesn't like it, and she may not run into good people the second time around."

"We know what we're doing, Joanna. Have faith in us," Shaley said. She and the two men walked away.

"We'll send for you once we've established Ursa is well enough to give a statement," Kellen said before he followed the others into the ICU.

Jo wanted to throw a crutch at them. "*We'll send for you!* You see how we're being used?"

"Calm down," Gabe said. "Saying these things to them can only hurt you."

"Why? Everything I said was the truth. Ursa *was* looking for her new home. That was the purpose of the five miracles—to give her time to decide and to give us time to bond with her."

"Jo . . . you aren't the only person in this world who can love her."

"I know! But why look further if it's what she and I both want?"

"You're single, for one thing. They'll try to place her with a mother and father."

"Yeah, what bullshit is that anyway? Why is that better? What about a gay couple? Will they consider that?"

"Jo . . ."

"What?"

"You're falling apart. You've been in this room too long. You need to get out of here and get some rest."

"Not until we make her talk. Will they let us see her after they solve their murder? Maybe they're tricking us, too."

"They never said we could see her after."

"I know." She fell back in a chair. "God damn it!"

Gabe sat next to her and held her hand.

A few minutes later, Lenora came out and saw Jo crumpled in the chair. "Are you all right? Are you up to this?"

Jo had no choice. If she didn't coerce Ursa into telling the story, she'd never see her again. If she did, she at least had a chance.

"Yes, I'm up to it."

Lenora led them into the ICU. Detective Kellen, Deputy McNabb, and the sentry police officer were conversing quietly out of Ursa's sight. Dr. Shaley was inside the room talking to her. "Jo!" Ursa screamed when she saw her. She bounced up on her knees, stretching her IV line taut.

"Careful!" a nurse said. "You won't like it if I have to put it in again!" She pulled Ursa back to the pillows.

Jo set her crutches down and held her.

"Why did you leave?" Ursa said into her chest.

"They said we had to. We didn't want to."

Ursa withdrew from her arms and turned a bitter stare on the nurse. "You lied! You said you didn't know why they went away!"

The nurse left the room muttering, "This girl is gonna be the death of me."

Ursa's eyes were red. She'd been crying very hard.

"Did you pull out your IV?" Jo asked.

She nodded. "I wanted to find you and Gabe."

"We were out in the waiting room. You have to stop pulling out your IV. It hurts when they put it back, doesn't it?"

"Yes! They're mean here! They held me down!"

"They had to because we couldn't sedate her," Lenora explained.

Because they had to keep her awake for their statement.

"I want to leave!" Ursa said. "I hate it here! I want to go with you and Gabe!"

"You aren't well enough yet," Jo said.

"Can I go with you when I am? Please?"

Jo wouldn't lie. "I wish you could, but it's not up to me."

Dr. Shaley pressed her red lips tight, clearly unhappy with Jo's answer.

"Who is it up to?" Ursa asked.

"You have visitors, Ursa," Lenora said to distract her. "Do you mind if they come in?"

Ursa turned a suspicious stare at the door. "Who?"

"Do you remember Josh Kellen?"

"The man with the gun?"

"He wears it because he's a police officer," Dr. Shaley said. "He's one of the good guys."

She'd said it in a voice one used to speak to a toddler. And Ursa was smarter than all of them.

Lenora stepped outside and told Kellen and McNabb to come in. Jo looked at Gabe. He seemed as dismayed as she was. Two cops, a counselor, and a shrink would stare at Ursa while she talked about how her mother had died.

Ursa's eyes flooded with fear. She knew why they were there.

Lenora approached the bed. "Ursa . . . Jo and Gabe want you to tell them what happened the night you ran away."

Ursa turned a stunned look on Jo, as if she suddenly saw her as the enemy. Jo nodded at Gabe, gesturing him to one side of Ursa's bed while she sat on the other. He saw what she had in mind. He sat close to Ursa, his body and Jo's obstructing her view of the other four people in the room.

Jo held Ursa's hand. "Everyone wants to keep you safe," she said. "And to do that, the police have to know what happened the night you ran away from home."

"You know why I left Hetrayeh. I left my home to get my PhD."

"Ursa . . . I know *Hetrayeh* is *Earth* spelled backwards."

"I had to do that! People on Earth can't say what my planet is called. We don't use words."

"You told me your name backwards, too."

"Don't you get it? I do everything Ursa used to do. Her brain is my brain."

"Joanna . . . ," Dr. Shaley said.

Jo looked at her.

"We don't need to talk about this right now. I'm helping her with it."

Jo turned back to Ursa. "They need to know what happened because they're afraid to let you out of here. They're worried there are other men who might be after you."

She looked at Gabe. "You killed them."

"Did I kill them all?" he asked.

She nodded.

"What about the man we saw at the restaurant?" Jo said.

Ursa didn't answer.

"The police worry he might be dangerous. They're afraid for you— and so are Gabe and I."

"Gabe killed the really bad ones," Ursa said.

"But why did the man in the restaurant call them and tell them you were there?"

"He was their friend."

Detective Kellen stepped closer, unfortunately drawing Ursa's attention away from Jo. "Do you know the man's name?" Kellen asked.

"Tell him," Jo said. "It's okay."

"If I tell him, will he leave?"

"No. The police have to know what happened to your mother."

"I don't have a mother," Ursa said in a quiet voice.

Jo squeezed her hand. "Please get this thing out. It's hurting you to keep it inside. Don't do it for them or for me and Gabe. Do it for yourself."

"I told them I would only tell them if they let me live with you and Tabby in Urbana."

"We're working on that," Lenora said.

Jo bit back an urge to call her a liar.

"I'll run away if you don't let me," Ursa told Lenora.

"I know. You told me a few times," Lenora said.

Jo put her hand on Ursa's cheek. "Tell us so we can get you out of this hospital without being afraid for you. Forget they're all here and just say it to Gabe and me. Why did you run away that night? Did something happen to your mother?"

"She wasn't my mother."

"Portia wasn't your mother?"

Ursa reacted to the name, apparently surprised that Jo knew it. But Jo couldn't worry about breaking one of their rules. She had to follow her instincts. "Why do you say Portia wasn't your mother?"

"Because she was Ursa's mother. I wasn't in Ursa's body yet. I didn't take it over until after the men killed her."

"You mean they killed your mother?"

"I meant Ursa."

"What about Portia?"

"They killed her first."

"Did you see that happen?"

"Ursa saw it happen. And when I went in her body, I saw it because it was still in her brain."

Jo somehow kept going without crying. "Tell me what you saw in her brain. Tell me everything that happened that night."

Ursa looked away from Jo. She grabbed the stuffed cat Tabby had given her, the only distraction at hand, and she tilted her head backward as she spread the plush animal's body over her face.

"Ursa . . . ," Jo said.

Ursa pressed the kitten to her face with both hands and closed her eyes. "I'm going to call him Caesar," she said. "I like the way he smells, like Tabby's perfume."

Jo gently took the toy off her face and laid it on the bedcovers. "Ursa, you can do this. Tell Gabe and me what happened that night."

She kept staring at the kitten.

"How about you pretend you're writing a play?" Gabe said.

Ursa looked up at him with bright eyes, apparently intrigued by his suggestion.

"What is the first thing that happens?" he asked.

"It's at night and I come down from the stars," she said. "I'm looking for a body to use."

"Then what?" he asked.

"I see a little girl jump out of the window of a building." She saw Jo's shock. "It wasn't that high," she explained. She turned back to Gabe. "The girl falls in bushes. That's how she gets some of the bruises. She's scared because two men are chasing her. They come outside and choke her. I see them kill her."

Looking at Jo, she abruptly switched from the play to reality—to the fantasy that had become her reality. "That was when I went in Ursa's body, because I hated that she had to die. I wanted her body to be alive even if she wasn't."

"What happened after you went in her body?" Jo asked.

"First I had to make her breathe again—with my powers. I made her better and I got up. I knew the men would think I was Ursa, so I ran. I got ahead of them because they were kind of scared that Ursa was still alive. There was a gas station by Ursa's house, and I ran there. I saw a truck—like the kind Gabe has but bigger—"

"An open-bed pickup truck?" Gabe said.

She nodded. "It was parked by the side of the store in the gas station, and I climbed into the back of it. There was stuff in there I could hide under. I was afraid to move, and all of a sudden the guy who owned the truck got in and started driving. I guess he went onto that road you take to Champaign-Urbana, the one called 57. I was really scared because the truck was going so fast, and I was in a new body and everything."

Jo and Gabe looked at each other.

"That was how I found you," Ursa said. "My quark things did it for sure. They make good things like that happen."

"How, exactly, did you find me?" Jo asked.

"The truck drove for a really long time. Before it stopped, it went down a bumpy road. Later I found out that was Turkey Creek Road."

"What color was the truck?" Gabe asked.

"It was red."

"Was it beat up—kind of like my truck?"

She nodded.

"That's probably Dave Hildebrandt's truck. His property is across the road from mine."

Detective Kellen had a notebook in his hand. "Dave Hildebrandt?" he said as he wrote.

"Yes," Gabe said. "He travels around looking for auto parts. He rebuilds cars."

"Did Dave see you?" Gabe asked Ursa.

She shook her head. "He scared me. When he got home, right away he started yelling at someone. They had a big fight."

"That would be Theresa, his wife," Gabe said.

Kellen scribbled in his notebook again.

"When did you get out of the truck?" Jo asked.

"I waited until he stopped yelling. But when I climbed out, a big dog was barking at me. I ran because I was afraid it would bite me. I kept falling down because it was dark and I was in a forest. I stopped when I came to water."

"Turkey Creek?" Gabe asked.

"Yes, but I didn't know its name yet. I followed it and came out at that place where the road ends at the hill—right next to Jo's house . . . I mean Kinney's. I was too afraid to go by the house, so I went in the shed. There was a bed in there—just the mattress part—and I laid down on it. I fell asleep and didn't wake up for a long time. When I did, it was daytime and I saw a puppy—that was Little Bear." Her eyes filled with tears. "He was my first friend. Little Bear was my first friend after I came down from the stars. And now he's dead."

35

Now they knew how Ursa had traveled from Effingham to Jo's rental house. But there was still a big hole in her story—the worst part. Why had she jumped out the window of her apartment? Jo hated to put her through more, but the police would never leave her alone until they stamped CLOSED on the Portia Dupree murder case.

Gabe dabbed Ursa's teary face with the edge of the bedsheet, and Jo held her hand. "Let's get this over with. Tell Gabe and me why you had to jump out the window."

"*Ursa* did that. She was still in her body when that happened."

"Okay, tell me why Ursa had to do something so dangerous."

"I told you. Those two men were going to kill her."

"Which two?"

"The ones Gabe killed."

"Tell me their names."

Ursa turned to Kellen, aware that the names mostly mattered to him. "The kind of little one was Jimmie Acer—people called him Ace. The more strong one was called Cory. Ursa didn't know his last name because she never saw him before."

"She never saw him before that night?" Jo said.

"No."

"Why were Jimmie Acer and Cory at Ursa's apartment?"

"Because . . ." She looked away from Jo, her fingers twisting the corner of the sheet.

"Were they doing things Ursa's mother told her not to talk about?"

Ursa nodded, her head down.

"You're not Ursa, so you can tell us."

She looked up. "I guess you're right."

"What was going on with Ace and Cory?"

"Ace was there because he was always there. And he . . . you know . . ."

"What?"

"He went in Ursa's mother's room with her. Her mother said they were partying when they did that." The glint of shame in her eyes revealed that she knew very well what they were doing in the bedroom.

"Why was Cory there?"

Ursa looked down again. "He came with Ace. To party."

"Was he using drugs?"

"He acted like that, and he was drinking beer. He was waiting . . ." She leaned over and again picked up the stuffed tabby kitten to give her fingers something to fiddle with.

"Was Cory waiting to go in the bedroom with Ursa's mother?"

"Yes," Ursa said.

"What was Ursa doing?"

"She was watching TV in the living room. There was a movie on—that one where the twins meet at camp."

"*Parent Trap*."

"Ursa liked that movie."

"Was Cory in the same room with Ursa?"

"Yes," Ursa said, looking down at the tabby kitten.

"Tell me what Cory was doing," Jo said.

"He kept laughing at the movie and saying how stupid it was. It made Ursa mad."

"Then what?"

Ursa finally looked at Jo, begging with her eyes not to say more.

"Please tell me. It will be okay."

Tears dripped from her eyes. "He put his hand on Ursa where he wasn't supposed to. She told him to stop it and pushed him away. He said he would give her five dollars if she let him do it. He said she was going to be like her mother anyway, and if she was going to be a whore, she should start when she was little . . . because girls were prettier when they were little . . ."

Gabe pressed his hand to his mouth.

"What did Ursa do?" Jo said.

"She said her mother wasn't a whore. But Cory laughed. Ursa got mad and turned off the TV. She tried to go in her room, but Cory grabbed her arm. He pushed her onto the couch and he—" Her tears became sobs. "He tried to take off her pajamas. She was screaming and hitting him . . ."

Jo was too choked up to ask, but Kellen did. "What happened? Tell us."

"Ursa's mother ran out of the bedroom," she cried. "She screamed for him to get off Ursa, and she picked up a chair and hit Cory on the back with it. Ace grabbed the chair away from her, but Cory took it from him. He smashed it on the side of Ursa's mother's head." Ursa covered her face. "He hit her really hard! She fell on the floor, and something was coming out of her head. It was her brains, I think . . . they were coming out . . ."

Jo pulled Ursa against her chest and held her.

That wasn't enough for Kellen. "Why did you run?" he asked. "Did they threaten you?"

"It wasn't me!" Ursa screamed.

"Why did Ursa run?"

"Ace was cussing at Cory and saying Ursa saw and she would tell the police. Cory said she wouldn't tell, and he grabbed Ursa. He put his hand on her neck and pressed hard. Ursa knew he was going to kill her. She kicked him and bit him and got away. She ran in her room and jumped out the open window."

"Wasn't there a screen?" Kellen said.

Ursa shook her head, wiping her palms down her cheeks. "The landlord wouldn't put screens in even though Ursa's mother wanted them. They used to get in fights about it."

"What was the name of the man in the restaurant?" Kellen asked. "You said he was Ace and Cory's friend."

"I don't know if he was Cory's. He was Ace's friend. He used to party with Ace and Ursa's mother."

"What's his name?"

"I'm not sure. Sometimes they called him 'Nate' and sometimes they called him 'Todd.'"

"Nathan Todd!" The detective slapped the back of his hand against his notebook. "Now I've got him!"

"Do you know him?" Gabe said.

"Oh yeah, I know him. And the phone we found on Ace's body shows he received a call from Todd around the time you were in the restaurant. With Ursa's ID, I can pick him up."

"On what charge?" Gabe asked.

"He's an accessory to attempted murder."

"Won't that be difficult to prove?" Gabe said.

"We have our ways." He put the notebook in his pants pocket and walked over to Gabe. "I have to thank you, Mr. Nash," he said, shaking his hand. "We're rid of two major scumbags. You've made my job a lot easier." Jo found it unsettling that he was congratulating him for killing two human beings. But she saw the world differently than most, having been raised by pacifist parents.

Jo had absorbed many of her parents' philosophies, and one of them was the belief that children deserved to be told the truth as much as possible. She often pondered how Gabe's life might have been different if he'd been raised with the truth, knowing he had two fathers who cherished him.

Jo climbed off the bed. "Before you all leave, I'd like to say something."

Everyone in the room—detective, deputy, psychologist, and social worker—faced her. Gabe looked nervous, maybe for good reason. Jo was too exhausted to know if what she was about to do was best for Ursa.

"I have a feeling this will be the only time I have so many people who are deciding Ursa's future in one room." Facing the two law officers, she said, "I know you won't decide where Ursa goes, but whether or not I'm charged with a felony will affect her future."

"Let's have this conversation in the waiting room," Lenora said.

"Why? Ursa wants to know what's going on, and you know she can handle it." Jo turned back to the policemen. "If I'm charged, I may be expelled from the university and graduate school."

"Are you sure?" Gabe said.

"My advisor confirmed it. Before you decide my fate," she said, turning to the men, "I want you to know what could happen if you charge me. I admit I made bad decisions with Ursa, but everything I did came from a place of compassion. Please make sure the punishment fits the crime before you completely wreck my life—and Ursa's—because I'll have no hope of becoming her foster parent if I'm charged."

"I want you to be my foster parent!" Ursa said.

"I know, love bug. Let me finish, okay?" She faced Lenora and Dr. Shaley. "I have a lot more to say to you two. I have to be certain Ursa won't be haunted with doubts about me if someone lies to her in the future." Jo stepped back so Ursa could clearly see her face. "Right here, in front of Ursa, I'm asking you to please let me be Ursa's foster parent. I would also like to apply for adoption rights. Let me tell you my qualifications—"

"Joanna," Lenora said, "this isn't the time or—"

"Please, hear me out. My number one qualification is that I love her—and I know no other applicant can say that. Number two, she and I are bonded by this tragedy. My understanding of what she's been through will be healing for her. Number three—my parents left me significant inheritances when they passed away, so I have the financial resources to raise a child as a single parent. Number four, I don't drink or use drugs, and I've never been in trouble with the law—not even for a traffic ticket. Number five—"

"I think we've heard enough," Dr. Shaley said.

"This one is important," Jo said. "Number five, my parents were scientists who taught me to value nature and be curious about the world. Ursa thrives in natural and scientific realms because they satisfy her need for intellectual stimulation. My goal is to be a professor at a top university, and I can't imagine a better environment than academia for a child with Ursa's abilities."

"Are we done?" Dr. Shaley asked.

"Not yet. I'd like to talk about something you may see as a problem. I'm a cancer survivor. But my cancer was caught at an early stage, and my prognosis is good."

Jo looked at Ursa. "Do you understand everything I said? No matter what happens, never doubt that I love you and I tried to keep us together. Beyond this, I have no control over what happens." Jo sat on the bed next to her. "Seems our fates are as topsy-turvy as the characters in Shakespeare's plays."

"But this will end like *Twelfth Night*!" Ursa said. "Everyone will be happy!"

"Good lord, she knows Shakespeare?" Lenora said.

Detective Kellen grinned. "Our wills and fates do so contrary run," he said.

"*Hamlet*, great line," Gabe said.

"My favorite since high school," Kellen said.

A nurse entered with liquid medication in a cup for Ursa.

"Looks like Ursa is fated to get some rest," Lenora said. "Let's take this conversation to the waiting room."

"I don't want to rest!" Ursa said. "Jo and Gabe have to stay!"

Jo and Gabe kissed her goodbye and let the nurse handle the imminent clash of will and fate.

36

Gabe's hotel room was unaccustomed luxury and privacy after Jo's sit-in at the ICU. The warm shower felt especially extravagant. "Sorry about this," Jo told Gabe, "but I didn't bring clothes in the bathroom." She couldn't hold the towel around herself while using the crutches.

Gabe looked up from his phone and appraised her naked body. "You're apologizing?"

"Will you help me rebandage my leg?"

"Sure, I'm up for playing doctor."

She put the bag of medical supplies on the bed and lay on her stomach.

"Especially when I get to look at your ass while doing it," he said.

"Does it look okay?"

He stroked her cheeks. "It looks great."

"What about the wound, Mr. Bottom? How does it look?"

"It looks like someone put a bullet in you."

"Not infected?"

"Nope, it's good."

"First put on the antibiotic ointment—then a gauze pad before you wrap it."

He touched her gently as he worked. He wrapped her leg, his fingers brushing her inner thighs. "I was badly distracted, but I think that will hold," he said, taping down the edge of the bandage.

She rolled over. "Take off your clothes."

He stood over her, staring into her eyes as he pulled off his clothing. He stretched his warm body over hers. "Am I too heavy on your leg? I don't want to hurt you."

"I'm not exactly feeling my leg at the moment."

Afterward, they held each other in a private little galaxy created by blackout curtains and the air-conditioning set on high. Only the loudest sounds of the city reached them.

"Tomorrow I have to go home and take over my mother's care," he said. "I was texting with Lacey when you came out. She has to come back to Saint Louis because her sons will be home the day after tomorrow. She wants to spend time with them before they go back to college."

"That's nice they'll all be together."

"Want to come home with me—just to pick up your car?"

"I can rent a car when I leave. I have to be here for Ursa."

"You do." He cuddled her closer. "It was good that you spoke your mind today. At first I wasn't sure, but I think what you said is part of the reason they'll let you keep visiting."

"Or they're using me to keep her under control."

"Maybe a little of both."

"I got the idea to speak out from your mother."

"Really?"

"I knew what I wanted to say while they were all there, but I almost lost my nerve. Then I thought of Katherine having the guts to bring Arthur and George together."

"You two are badass ladies." He was drifting into sleep.

"Gabe . . . ?"

"What?"

"Does it worry you that Ursa refers to herself in third person?"

"It does. But I guess it's how she's handling it."

"I'm afraid making her talk before she was ready split her in two."

"That's what the psychologist is for."

"I don't like that woman."

"I think it's mutual. Go to sleep."

Jo's first rest in a regular bed since Kinney Cottage was more like a coma. The soap-scented steam of Gabe's shower woke her. "You were exhausted," he said.

"I was. I like this room. I'm going to keep it."

"Should I check out?"

"No. I wanted to pay the bill anyway."

"You don't have to do that."

"I know, but I want to."

"All right, moneybags. Let's have breakfast before I get on the road—your treat."

After breakfast they bought Ursa colored pencils and art paper and Jo purchased a new cell phone. Jo walked Gabe to the parking garage. He gave Jo his two room keys. And for the first time since they'd been together, they exchanged phone numbers. "I guess we're a normal couple now," Jo said.

"I wouldn't go that far," he said.

"Can I go so far as to say, I love you? I know it's not the most romantic place to say it the first time—in front of a parking garage and all . . ."

"I love you, too, Jo." They pressed their bodies together, Jo's crutches clattering to the ground. People stared as they walked by.

Jo acutely felt his absence as she walked to the hospital. Ursa missed him, too.

The sentry policeman was gone. Later that day, Jo heard Nathan Todd had been arrested. Ursa was moved to a regular room in the children's hospital the next day. Jo was allowed to visit as much as she wanted except during her counseling sessions. Those hours gave Jo time out to have a meal or to buy something for Ursa to keep her mind occupied.

Keeping Ursa engaged wasn't easy. After several days, she was bored with books, drawing, and TV. Jo brought her an adult puzzle—a picture of a doe and fawn standing in a wooded scene that looked like Ursa's beloved magic forest. They were working on putting the outer edge together when someone knocked on the half-open door. Lacey entered, two stuffed kittens in her hands. "Am I intruding?" she asked.

"Not at all," Jo said.

Lacey held up the beanbag kittens, one white and one gray. "I know they aren't as good as the real thing, but these are supposed to be Juliet and Hamlet."

"Gabe told you their names?" Ursa said.

"He told me all their names," Lacey said. "You did a great job naming them." When she held out the kittens, Ursa looked at Jo, apparently suspicious of Lacey's intentions.

"Go on, and you know what to say," Jo said.

Ursa took the kittens. "Thank you," she said. She lifted the tabby cat, Caesar, off her pillow and laid the three kittens together. "I only need Olivia, Macbeth, and Othello now."

"You look like you're feeling well," Lacey said.

"I am," Ursa said. "Tomorrow or the next day they'll let me go to Urbana with Jo. I'm going to live with her and Tabby."

"That sounds nice," Lacey said.

"But that's more wishful thinking than reality," Jo said.

"It's not!" Ursa said.

"If it's not, no one told me, love bug."

"Maybe they didn't tell you yet, but I know it's going to happen."

Jo got off the bed. "Have a seat," she told Lacey, pulling out a chair.

"I can't stay," Lacey said. "I wanted to see how Ursa is doing and talk with you for a few minutes. Would you mind a quick chat out in the waiting room?"

"Of course not." She told Ursa, "Find more edge pieces while I'm gone."

"Will you come back and help?" she asked.

"I will, but I have to leave soon. Dr. Shaley will be here in thirty minutes."

"I don't want to talk to her!"

"Can we please not have this discussion every time?" Jo said.

"She talks about stupid things!"

"She's trying to help you. I'll be back in a few minutes."

Jo was curious about what had caused Lacey's transformation. Even her face looked different, calm and radiant, and her torn jeans and bright peasant blouse matched her mysteriously relaxed mood. They sat in a colorful room decorated to cheer sick children. "How are things going?" Lacey asked.

"Depends on which things you mean."

"I hope you won't be angry, but Gabe told me you might be charged with a child endangerment felony. He said the police told you not to travel outside of Illinois when you return home."

Jo *was* peeved, and a little surprised, he would talk about her situation with his sister.

"He also said you're unlikely to become Ursa's foster parent, even though you're obviously the one who should get her."

Maybe Lacey had an identical twin sister Gabe didn't know about. Another family secret.

"The social workers haven't said anything to you?" Lacey asked.

"They haven't, and I take that to be a bad sign. But you saw how Ursa is counting on it." She looked out the window at slices of blue sky enclosed in buildings. "Sometimes I think I'm doing the wrong thing sticking around here. Maybe I'm making everything worse for her."

"Then why do you?"

"Because I care about what happens to her. I think I have a stabilizing effect on her, and she's been to hell and back."

"I guess you two have that in common."

Jo wasn't sure if she meant the cancer and her mother dying, the shooting, or both. If she meant the cancer, she had to have found out from Gabe.

"So the reason I'm here . . . Gabe doesn't know, by the way."

"What doesn't he know?"

"That I'm here. He also doesn't know I talked to my husband about your situation. Troy is a family law attorney. He mostly handles divorces, but he occasionally does child custody and adoption cases. If you'll let him, he wants to help you, and he'll do it free of cost."

"I have money."

"We wouldn't feel right about taking money from Gabe's girlfriend."

"I'm his girlfriend now?" Jo said.

Lacey knew the comment was sarcasm, but she smiled. "Didn't you know?"

"I guess I didn't get the Nash family memo."

"Well, the rest of us have."

An apology. Subtle, but Jo still welcomed it. "I appreciate the thumbs-up."

"It was Gabe," she said.

"What was?"

"Before I left for Saint Louis, he called a family meeting. When the time came, George Kinney knocked on the door. He'd been over at his property fixing the broken doors. He was as clueless as me about what was going on. Gabe just told him to be there."

Jo smiled. Wonder of wonders, Gabe had pulled a Katherine.

Lacey studied her face. "You knew what he was going to do?"

"I didn't, but I can guess what he did when he got you together."

"He told us the whole thing! About how George and my mom's affair began and how they and my father had agreed that Gabe should never know he was George's son. Obviously, my mom and George knew all that. But they were shocked when he told them he'd seen them make love in the forest and found out he wasn't Arthur's son. He said that was why he'd started hating them. And then he said the most amazing thing."

"What?"

"He told them he forgave them. He said now that he was in love with you, he understood everything they'd done. He said he would rather have died the night the guy pointed the gun at you than watch you die. He said love like that can't be stopped by anything, and he was happy he was born of that kind of passion."

Jo didn't care if Lacey saw her cry.

"I know! All four of us were bawling our eyes out. It was the best fucking thing that ever happened in my family." She opened her shoulder bag and took out two tissues, handing one to Jo. "George has felt little more than responsibility for his wife since she wrecked her body with booze," she said, dabbing the remaining tissue under her eyes. "He and my mom are getting married. George asked Gabe and me if that was okay."

"Are you okay with it?"

"I'm thrilled! We even had an engagement party. I stayed one more night, and we had the best time, grilling ribs and drinking beers. Gabe and I were up late talking, and we vented all the bullshit that's been between us for years."

Jo found it difficult to believe they could get over that much so fast.

"I'm sure he told you how I treated him when he was little," she added, as if she'd read Jo's thoughts.

Jo wouldn't betray anything Gabe had told her in confidence.

Lacey understood her silence. "I guess he did," she said. "I know it's no excuse, but I got bad depression around the time Gabe was born. I felt fat and ugly, and I knew my writing was shit. And there was Gabe, this perfect, beautiful little boy. So damn smart, too. I was so fucking jealous of him."

"Did you know he was George's baby?"

"I'd suspected my mother was having an affair with George. And one night before Gabe was born, my father got really drunk and told me. He was crying—" She choked up and wiped new tears. "I blamed that poor kid for everything. For my mother not loving my father. For how crushed my father was. Even for my depression. And when my father couldn't help adoring that perfect little kid, I totally lost it. I felt abandoned at a time when I really needed my father, when I gave up on writing."

Jo put her hand on Lacey's hand. "I'm sorry. It was a worse situation than I imagined. Do you still suffer from depression?"

She nodded. "But thank god for my husband. He's always been there for me. Even when he should have dumped me." Fresh tears arose.

"It's good that you and Gabe finally talked about all of this."

She nodded again, wiping her eyes with the soaked tissue.

"Gabe never said anything. The other day when I asked how things were going, he texted back one word: *Good*."

"He has been good," she said. "I haven't seen him so happy since he was a young kid. Because of you. You made all of this happen."

"Technically, we have to say Ursa did."

"With her quarks?"

"Gabe told you about that?"

"He told me all about her. Please forgive me for calling the sheriff on that poor little girl."

"You were right to do it. I should have, but I was mired in irrational behavior."

"Because you love her. Let my husband help you."

"I guess I can use any help that's offered. What should I do?"

She pulled a phone from her purse and texted someone. When she finished, she said, "He's out in the car. He's coming up."

"Your husband?"

"Yes, Troy Greenfield, your kickass lawyer."

37

Troy, a genial, stocky man, had Jo tell the whole story right there in the hospital visitors' lounge. He asked lots of questions and took copious notes.

When she went back to her hotel, Jo wasn't necessarily more hopeful about her chances of getting Ursa, but she felt better because she would have fewer regrets. She would know she'd done as much as she could.

Lenora Rhodes and Dr. Shaley disappeared for several days. Now that Ursa was well enough to leave the hospital, they would decide where she would live. Three days after Lacey's visit, Troy called Jo just before she left her hotel room. "I have good news and not-so-good news," he said.

Jo's heart pounded wildly.

"You aren't going to be charged," he said.

"Are you sure?"

"It took a while to make them say it definitively, but I pestered them into giving an answer. I told them we needed to know because we were going to hire John Davidson—a talented defense lawyer—if you were charged."

"Is that why they didn't charge me? They were afraid of Davidson?"

"In all honesty, I doubt that had much to do with it. I had a long talk with Detective Kellen last night, and it mostly boils down to his admiration for Gabe. If you were charged, Gabe was in the crosshairs as well—because Ursa had spent many days on his property. Both McNabb and Kellen hated to see Gabe punished."

"Am I imagining this sounds really chauvinistic?"

"You aren't, and I argued that point. That was when Kellen made it clear he's always been on your side. He respects your drive to help a child you didn't even know. And your case was strengthened by what that first deputy told you the night you called the sheriff. I asked them to question him—"

"Kyle Dean?"

"Yes, and he admitted he'd given you opinions about foster care, very personal opinions, that might have confused you. McNabb had been leaning toward charging you, but when he saw that the questionable behavior of one of his deputies would be a key factor in the trial, he backed off."

"Wow. Lacey is right—you are a kickass lawyer."

"Thank you," he said, chuckling.

Jo was relieved, but she couldn't much appreciate Troy's good news when his not-so-good news was about to slam her.

"As for Ursa," Troy said, "I've made no headway with the social workers, and I can't apply law to their decision about her future. I'm sorry to tell you, I think they've chosen a foster family for her."

"I think they have, too."

"I'll stay on it, Jo. Let's not give up yet."

"Can you get me visiting rights or something like that?"

"As a nonrelative, you have no legal right to visit her. You'd have to work that out with the social workers and the foster family. But I'll look into it, okay?"

"Okay. Thank you for everything you've done." She could hardly see the end button on the phone through her tears.

Lenora was in Ursa's room when Jo got there. She took Jo into the hallway and broke the news. Ursa's prospective foster parents would visit Ursa after lunch. She requested that Jo not be there when they met, and she also asked her to help Ursa accept that she soon would go home with them.

"Did you even consider me?" Jo asked.

"Joanna . . . how could we?"

"Why not?"

"We try to place children in two-parent homes—"

"That's bullshit and you know it. Ursa has clearly stated what she wants, and it's not a mother and a father who are complete strangers. And you know, I have as many resources and qualifications as a married couple."

"It's not only that you're single. It's everything else in addition to that."

"What?"

"You're in school. Your health status is uncertain. And we can't ignore the child endangerment situation."

"They aren't charging me."

"Charged or not, you displayed poor judgment."

"Now that you know what Ursa is like, do you think I could have done better? She was going to run if I got the police involved, and I knew she was safer with me than on the run."

"You know there was more to what you did than that."

"Like what?"

"You were mothering her."

"And that eliminates me as a candidate to be foster parent?"

"It's *why* you did that worries us. You'd just lost your mother and had your reproductive organs removed."

"How did you know that?"

"Ursa told us."

"You pumped a little kid for information about me? Did you ever think to ask me?"

"We didn't *pump* her. She told Dr. Shaley during their sessions."

"That's worse! She used psychotherapy to obtain information that would eliminate me!"

"Please help Ursa accept this. It's the best way to love her."

"I disagree, but I'll try to convince her. I'm afraid she's going to run and something awful will happen to her."

"Don't worry, these kids settle down."

"These kids?" Jo didn't trust her temper enough to stay in Lenora's presence a second longer. She walked into Ursa's room.

"Why are you mad?" Ursa said.

"I'm not."

Ursa stared at her. "What did Lenora say?"

Jo sat on the bed and told her. Ursa cried and protested. She was still crying when her doctor came in an hour later. Jo left the room so he could examine Ursa's wound. When he came out, he said in a quiet voice, "Jo . . . I'm very sorry about what they decided. Most of us here believe they've made a mistake. We've seen how you are with her—the bond between you two."

Jo nodded.

"I don't even know if she would have recovered without you. When we were prepping her for surgery, she woke up. Despite incredible blood loss, she returned to consciousness to ask for you. I told her we had to fix her belly, and she said that was good because she'd come back from the stars to be with Jo, and Jo would be sad if she died."

He saw that he'd made her cry. "God, I'm sorry. Did I make it worse telling you that?"

"No. Thank you. I appreciate your support."

An hour and a half later, Jo cleared out for the new foster parents as Ursa cried bitterly. Jo went to her hotel and called Gabe. He wanted to come to Saint Louis to support her, but he couldn't leave his mother.

Lacey was with her family, and George was in Urbana with his daughters. George had decided to tell them that Gabe was his son. He didn't want any more secrets in his family.

Jo didn't return to the hospital that night. Maybe the foster parents would be there. She hoped they were. Spending lots of quality time with Ursa before the move was the only way to reduce her risk of running.

When Jo arrived at the children's hospital the next morning, Lenora was waiting for her, clearly angry. "Did you even try to help her accept it?" Lenora asked.

"I did! Ask the nurses. I tried to reason with her for hours."

Lenora searched Jo's eyes and saw she was telling the truth.

"What happened?"

"A grand failure is what happened. You know what Ursa said to them?"

"What?"

"First she went on about being an alien. My foster parents were prepared for that because I'd warned them. But when smart little Ursa saw that wouldn't scare them off, she told them she came from a planet of people eaters."

The purple people eater.

"You know what that rascal told her new foster parents? She said when they went to sleep she would stab and kill them—and she would eat them. They have another foster child who's only one, and Ursa said she would be the most delicious and she would kill her first."

"Obviously she was saying the most extreme thing she could think of to scare them off. Ursa doesn't have a violent bone in her body."

"How could those people know that and take the risk? Especially when they have a baby in their house?"

"Do you want me to talk to them?"

"They're done! They left in a hot hurry, and they want nothing to do with her."

"Now what?"

"Door number two—the couple we'd chosen as second best."

"You'd better warn them. I'll talk to them, if you want."

Lenora rubbed her hand up and down the back of her short hair. "Maybe you'd better."

The next day, Jo gave the runner-up couple a crash course on Ursa Alien Dupree. They were nice people. The husband ran an engineering consulting firm, and his wife was a former gym teacher who now stayed home with their six-year-old son. They weren't able to have any more biological children.

Jo talked to Ursa before the couple came in, begging her to cooperate. Ursa refused, insisting that she only wanted to live with Jo. Once again, Jo left the hospital with Ursa's plaintive sobs haunting her.

When Jo returned to the hospital the next day, the foster couple was in Ursa's room for their second visit. Jo was going to leave, but they asked her to stay. "Let's talk," the wife said. "I want us all to be friends."

Jo tried to get Ursa to open up, but she was sullen and only answered direct questions with curt replies. When Jo tried to show the foster parents Ursa's drawings, she said, "I don't want them to see those! They're private!"

When Jo told Ursa it would be nice to have a little brother, she said, "I don't want any stupid little brother!"

"You'll have a swimming pool, Ursa," Jo said. "Won't that be fun?"

"It won't be!" Ursa said. "I only want to swim with you and Gabe in Summers Creek!"

"Please try to be the nice girl I know you are," Jo said.

"I won't be nice to them!" Ursa said. "I only want to live with you! You said you wanted that, too! Why are you trying to make me like them?"

"I'd better go," Jo said.

"Yes," Lenora said. "Thanks for trying."

Jo hugged Ursa, but Ursa wouldn't let her go. "Don't leave!" she wept. "I'll be nice! Don't go!" Two nurses and Lenora had to pry her arms away. Ursa screamed, "Take me with you! I love you, Jo! I only want to be with you!" Jo hurried down the corridor, avoiding the somber gazes of the doctors and nurses.

At seven that night, Jo ate a cup of yogurt and a few grapes in her hotel room. She had to force herself to eat even that. She'd been nauseated and listless since her tearful phone call with Gabe that afternoon. In the morning she would say goodbye to Ursa for the last time. Staying was hurting her too much.

At eight, the first in a series of thunderstorms hit Saint Louis. The city would be under a tornado watch most of the night. Jo went to bed, blackout curtains drawn and air-conditioning turned high. She hardly heard the pounding of thunder and rain on her windows. She closed her eyes and went fetal beneath the covers, arms folded against her bony chest. At 9:52 she was awakened by an unexpected call. "Lenora?" Jo answered.

"She's gone," Lenora said.

Jo threw her legs over the side of the bed. "What do you mean? She went home with them?"

"She ran. We can't find her."

"How could she possibly get out of a hospital as secure as that?"

"You know how—she's damn smart! They think she's still hiding somewhere in the hospital, but they haven't found her."

"How long has she been missing?"

"It's been about an hour since a nurse reported her missing."

"Did the cameras catch anything?"

"They're checking now. At first they thought finding her would be easy."

"They don't know Ursa."

"But you do. You warned us. What if she got out? What if she's out in the city?"

Ursa could have pulled that off, and getting out of the hospital would be her aim. But Jo didn't say that out loud.

"She's probably hiding in a patient room or something like that. I'm sure they'll find her."

"Will you come? I thought maybe if you called for her . . . if she heard your voice . . ."

"Of course. I'm on my way."

"Meet me at the main door and I'll get you in. They have everything locked down."

A half hour later, Jo had been searching hospital rooms with Lenora for only ten minutes when a security guard stopped them. "She's not in the hospital," he said.

"Are you sure?" Lenora said.

"We were looking for a little girl in a hospital gown, but she's wearing regular clothes. This is from a surveillance camera." He held up a picture of Ursa walking down a hospital corridor.

Jo took the photo. Ursa was wearing Jo's navy-blue University of Illinois T-shirt and her black yoga pants rolled up to look like capris. "Those are my clothes," Jo said. "They're the spare set I kept in my backpack in case I had to spend the night with Ursa. I noticed them missing a few days ago and thought they'd fallen out." She scrutinized the photo more closely. Ursa had on her purple gym shoes. Jo had last seen them on Ursa the night of the shooting. "How did she get her shoes?"

"Those were all that could be salvaged of her bloody clothing the night she came in," Lenora said. "Usually personal belongings are put in a bag and stored in the patient's closet."

"Does the video show how she got out of the hospital?" Jo asked.

The security guard nodded, his expression bleak. "She walked out the main lobby doors holding a man's hand. That's why it took so long to identify her on the footage. She had on regular clothes, and she appeared to be with the man."

Jo had to hold on to the wall to stop from swaying.

"Do you think the man abducted her?" Lenora said.

"Considering the girl's history, we're afraid that's a possibility," the guard said.

"Have the police been notified?" Lenora asked.

"Every city cop is on it. They've put out an AMBER Alert, too."

Jo had a flash of insight. "She wasn't abducted. She held the man's hand to look like she was with him."

"You don't know that!" Lenora said.

"I don't," Jo said. "But Ursa knew she couldn't walk out those doors alone."

"How would she get a complete stranger to hold her hand?"

"Believe me, Ursa has her ways." Again, Jo studied the photograph. One of her hands was clenched tight around something. Maybe she'd taken more than clothing from Jo's bag. Jo unzipped the front pocket of her backpack and found her hotel card key. She dug around for Gabe's key, the spare she kept in the paper envelope. It was empty. "I may know where she's going," Jo said.

"Where?" Lenora said.

"Come with me," Jo said, shrugging on her backpack.

"We have to tell the police," Lenora said.

"The police can't be involved until we find her. If she sees them, she'll run."

"Good point."

Lenora grabbed her raincoat on their way out into another downpour. Jo still had on the oversize sweatshirt Gabe had left behind, now soaked through to her shirt from her walk to the hospital. Out in the city, police officers were everywhere, their squad car lights mirrored in pools of rain at all intersections.

"Poor girl," Lenora said. "She must be terrified in this storm."

"I doubt it," Jo said. "Ursa loves thunderstorms."

Lenora saw where they were headed. "Did she know the name of your hotel?"

"Last week she asked me a lot of questions about where I was staying. I just thought she was bored. She even asked if I used a metal key to get in my room, and I told her about the card keys."

"That means she's been plotting this for a while."

"She was waiting to see how things turned out. She ran today because she's desperate. She knows no one will help her—not even me."

"Then maybe she won't go to your room."

"I know. That's what worries me."

"What if she decided to trust that man like she trusted you?" Lenora said. "If he hasn't brought her to the police yet, he must have bad intentions."

"I didn't bring her to the police, and I didn't have bad intentions."

"But how long until that luck runs out?"

"I've been trying to tell you that."

They entered the hotel and rushed to the elevator, Jo limping on her sore leg. The elevator stopped on several floors before they finally arrived at the sixth floor. At room 612, Jo put her key in the slot and pushed the door open.

Ursa wasn't there. Lenora watched her check under the rumpled comforter and beneath the bed. She looked in the closet. There was only one place left to look. She flicked on the bathroom light and opened the shower curtain. Ursa was curled in a ball in the tub, her clothing and hair soaked with rain. She looked up at Jo with mournful brown eyes. "Jo . . . I ran away," she said.

"I see that." Jo lifted her out of the tub and held her.

Ursa clung to her, crying. "Don't you love me anymore? Why do you want me to go live with those people?"

"I don't. But there's nothing else I can do."

Ursa wept miserably as Jo carried her to the bed. She was wet to the skin and shaking with chills. "We need to get these clothes off, love bug." Jo sat her on the bed.

"Why is she here?" Ursa said when she saw Lenora.

"I was afraid for you," Lenora said.

"No matter where you make me go, I'll find Jo!" Ursa said, new tears falling. "Jo and I know how to be happy without you!"

Jo took off her shoes and stripped away her wet pants and T-shirt. She pulled a clean shirt over Ursa's quaking body and lifted her into the bed, tucking the blanket and comforter around her. After she turned off the air conditioner, she went into the bathroom to change out of her wet clothes. When she came out, Lenora was pushing numbers on her phone.

"Please don't have police come here right now," Jo said.

"I have to tell them to stop looking," Lenora said.

"I know, but can we just have a moment?"

Lenora nodded. When she connected with hospital security, she said she had found Ursa and asked them to tell all law agencies that she was safe. She took off her raincoat and slumped in a chair with a weary exhalation.

Jo crawled into bed with Ursa. The rule about separate beds didn't matter anymore. She would give Ursa what she needed. She spooned the small girl against her body and kissed her cheek. "Warm enough?" she asked.

"I want to stay here forever," Ursa said.

"Me too," Jo said. "Please never doubt that I love you. No one can take that away from us."

Thunder growled. Rain clawed at the window. Jo held Ursa in her safe nest, and all the while fate sat watching.

38

A month later, on a rare cool day in late August, Ursa stood between Gabe and Jo, her hands clasped in theirs. Beyond the white marble cross, the minister turned his car onto the cemetery path and drove away. Lenora Rhodes started her car and followed behind him. No one else had come to watch Portia Wilkins Dupree laid to rest, not even her mother. Portia was twenty-six when she died trying to protect her daughter, the same age as Jo.

Ursa let go of Jo's and Gabe's hands and spent a minute rearranging the flowers into a new constellation around the grave. "Bye, Mama. I love you," she said when she finished.

She took hold of their hands again. "I want to see Daddy now."

They walked to the grave of Dylan Joseph Dupree. He was buried next to his mother, and the empty plot next to her was for her husband. Dylan's father lived in a nearby nursing home, his mind too impaired by Alzheimer's disease to understand who his granddaughter was. Because there hadn't been room to bury Portia next to Dylan and his parents, Jo had purchased a plot as close to Dylan's as possible. According to Ursa's wishes, Portia's cross was the same as the one over Dylan's grave.

Ursa let go of Jo's and Gabe's hands as they arrived at Dylan's grave. She took a folded picture from her pocket and laid it against the bottom of the cross. It was an image of the Pinwheel Galaxy, located in Ursa Major.

Dylan had loved anything to do with stars. Before his life fell apart, he'd wanted to be an astrophysicist. He'd named his daughter Ursa for the Big Bear in the sky, and he'd taught her the names of stars and constellations. When Ursa was afraid of the dark, he would open her window a crack and tell her good magic that fell out of the stars was coming in her window. He said the magic would always keep her safe. After he died, Ursa opened her window wide every night, trying to let in lots of good magic. That was how she escaped the grasp of the men who nearly killed her.

Ursa walked to the cross and kissed the top of it. "I love you, Daddy." She pointed behind her. "This is Jo and Gabe. You would like them. Gabe likes stars like you do." She straightened the picture of the galaxy and turned around.

"Ready to go?" Jo said.

"Ready," she said.

They had one more grave to visit. They got in Jo's car and drove from Paducah, Kentucky, to Vienna, Illinois. As they approached Turkey Creek Road, Ursa leaned between the seats as far as her seat belt allowed. She hadn't been back since the night she was airlifted from that very intersection and taken to Saint Louis for surgery.

"What is this?" Jo said when the road came into sight. "Have I traveled forward in time?"

"I thought you said we don't look that much alike?" Gabe said.

"Only because of the age difference."

The older version of Gabe smiled and waved from his chair under the blue canopy and FRESH EGGS sign.

"You didn't tell me he's the new Egg Man."

"I didn't know," Gabe said.

"He never did this before?"

"I'm as surprised as you are."

Jo parked her Honda next to Gabe's white pickup. "He even uses your truck."

"I told him to use it for farm stuff," Gabe said. "His car is nice and gets beat up by the gravel."

"Tell me about it."

Ursa shot out the back door and ran to the egg stand. George Kinney stood and shook her hand. "You must be Ursa."

"I am," Ursa said.

"I'm George and very happy to meet you."

"Why do you look like Gabe?" Ursa asked.

"Because Gabe had two dads, and I'm one of them," he said.

Gabe embraced him.

"How'd it go?" George said.

"No hitches," Gabe said.

"Kat and I worried they'd change their minds."

"Is that why you're out here—to watch for us?"

"I'm out here because the damn eggs are piling up to the roof." He opened his arms to Jo. "Get over here, Wonder Woman."

"I have significantly less in the chest than her," Jo said.

"The better to hug you," George said, squeezing her in his arms.

"We're having a funeral for Little Bear," Ursa said.

"Well, that's really nice," George said. "I hear he was a good dog."

"He was the best dog," Ursa said.

"We'd better go," Gabe said. "Jo has to get on the road right after lunch."

"I'll pack up and see you at the house," George said.

"Need help?" Jo asked.

"Come on, I'm not that old."

Jo, Gabe, and Ursa drove the familiar rough wind of Turkey Creek Road. Ursa stretched high in her seat to see out the window. "It looks different," she said.

"The plants grew and the colors are beginning to change," Jo said.

"Where are the nest flags?"

"I took them down when my study ended. The indigo buntings are getting ready to migrate."

"They're leaving?"

"They'll go in a few weeks, but just for the winter. They'll be back in the spring."

They drove onto the Kinney property, steering for the inviting yellow cottage on the hill. Before Jo turned off the motor, she looked at the hickory tree.

Ursa sprang from the back seat and ran toward the prairie behind the house.

"Ursa, it's this way!" Gabe called after her.

"I'm getting flowers for him!" she said.

Jo watched her vanish into the tall grass. Gabe took her hands and pulled her close to his body. "Do you still sell eggs?" she asked.

"I haven't since the shooting."

"Will you again?"

"I don't know." He stared in the direction of the road, but his eyes were distant. "The egg stand was a thread that kept me connected to the outer world."

"You have something more substantial connecting you now?"

He smiled down at her. "More like the thread was cut and I fell into the real world."

"How's that going?" Jo asked.

"Good. But sometimes I'm afraid to trust how good it is. What if it all starts again?"

"The people who love you will help you."

He kissed her. Before any time seemed to pass, Ursa had enveloped them, one arm around Jo and the other on Gabe. She rested her head against them.

When Ursa was ready, Gabe led them to Little Bear's grave. On a cross made of burnished cedar wood, he had etched LITTLE BEAR, and below the name, HE GAVE HIS LIFE FOR THE PEOPLE HE LOVED.

Ursa sniffled and wiped her cheeks.

"Do you like the cross?" Gabe asked.

"It's exactly perfect," she said. She laid her bouquet of goldenrod, ironweed, and asters on the mound of dirt that was already giving life to new flora.

"Would you like someone to say something?" Jo asked.

"I want to sing him my favorite song. Ursa's dad—I mean, *my* dad—used to sing it when I went to sleep."

"That would be nice," Gabe said.

Looking at the soil that blanketed her dog, Ursa sang, "Twinkle, twinkle, little star, how I wonder what you are. Up above the world so high, like a diamond in the sky, twinkle, twinkle little star, how I wonder what you are."

Gabe squeezed Jo's hand.

When she finished singing, Ursa crouched down and patted the dirt. "I love you, Little Bear."

They returned to the car and drove to the Nash family homestead.

"Whose cars are those?" Ursa asked when they pulled up. "Who's here, Gabe?"

"Maybe you should go inside and see," he said.

Ursa jumped out of the car and ran up the porch steps. Jo and Gabe followed close behind. They wanted to see her reaction.

"Can I go in?" Ursa asked.

"Since when do you ask?" Lacey said from behind the screen door.

Ursa grinned. "Do you remember that, Gabe? Remember when we rescued you?"

"I remember it very well," he said.

"Come in," Lacey said, pushing back the screen door.

Ursa stepped inside, her expression transforming from shock to joy as a chorus of voices sang "Happy Birthday." Dark-purple and pale-lavender balloons floated all over the living room, and the log walls and ceiling were festooned with crepe ribbons in the same colors. Signs that read WELCOME BACK, URSA and HAPPY 9TH BIRTHDAY hovered over a table laden with lunch food and a cake sprinkled with silver stars. Adding yet more liveliness to the festive room, kittens sporting colorful bows were underfoot everywhere.

"I didn't know it was my birthday!" Ursa said.

Jo hadn't wanted her mother's burial to fall on her birthday, but it was the only day she and Lenora could travel to Paducah. Jo and Gabe had planned the party to brighten the day.

Gabe introduced Ursa to George's younger daughter, her husband, and their high school–age son. Gabe and George's daughter were already good friends, but George's other daughter hadn't yet come around to the idea that she had a love-child brother.

Lacey's husband introduced himself to Ursa. When Troy shook her hand, a necklace with a crystal star pendant appeared in her palm. "Where did that come from?" he said.

"I don't know!" Ursa said.

"Do you like it?"

"Yes!"

"Then I guess it's yours."

That was how Jo found out Troy Greenfield, Esq., was an amateur magician.

Jo took Ursa aside to break the news that Tabby had really, really wanted to be at the party but couldn't because her sister was visiting from California. Tabby had to drive her to the airport at the exact time of the party.

"That's okay," Ursa said.

Jo handed her a large box wrapped in cat-print paper. "This is from her."

"Can I open it?"

"You sure can," Jo said.

Ursa sat on the floor, ripped away the paper, and lifted the top of the box. Beaming, she withdrew a big, soft purple creature with a wide toothy grin and dangly arms and legs. Like the alien in the song, it had one central eye, a long horn, and two wings. She squashed the weird thing in her arms. "A purple people eater! He's soft like a pillow!"

She opened her other presents: small binoculars and a bird field guide from Jo, a middle-grade book about stream life from George, a watercolor set from Lacey, a lavender sweater with a white kitten face from George's daughter, and a hardbound copy of *A Midsummer Night's Dream* with gorgeous colored illustrations from Katherine.

"Shoot, I forgot to get you a gift," Gabe said.

Ursa smiled, aware that he was joking.

"Well, I guess I'll have to give you something." He looked around, rubbing his chin. He walked across the room and scooped Juliet and Hamlet into his hands. "How about these guys? I hear your new foster parents will let you have cats."

Ursa looked up at Jo. "Really? Can I?"

"I guess those foster parents aren't so bad after all," Jo said.

Ursa took the kittens and buried her face in their fur.

"Seems you've positively influenced Juliet and Hamlet's fates," Gabe said.

"It was my quark things," Ursa said.

"Wait," he said, "I thought we were done with quark things?"

"How can we be? I'm still making good things happen."

"You are?"

"Jo said I shouldn't talk about Ursa like I'm not her, but just because I pretend I'm Ursa doesn't mean I'm not an alien."

Jo and Gabe exchanged a glance, and Ursa, as usual, perceived their unease. "It's okay," she told Jo. "I'm still doing what you said."

"What did Jo say?" Gabe asked.

"She said the alien could be kind of like Ursa's soul, so Ursa and the alien could be a whole person."

"That's beautiful," Katherine said.

"It is," Ursa said. "But it's more like the other way around: Ursa is the soul of me, the one who came from the stars."

Everyone was quiet, caught in the spell of Ursa's strange magic.

"Would an alien with a human soul have any interest in birthday cake?" George asked.

"Yes!" Ursa said.

"Thank god," he said. "I thought I would have to eat it all myself."

They lit nine candles and sang "Happy Birthday" to Ursa again. Jo hated to leave right after lunch, but she wanted Ursa to arrive at her new home before dark. She and Gabe packed her presents and put the two kittens in a cat carrier Lacey had bought for them.

When they walked outside with the carrier, Ursa cried when she saw the kittens' mother. "She doesn't want me to take her babies!"

"They don't drink her milk anymore," Gabe said.

The orange tabby rubbed her body on Ursa's shins.

"You see?" he said. "She's telling you to take them."

After everyone hugged Ursa and Jo goodbye on the porch, they went inside to give Gabe time alone with them.

"Did George and your mother tell you the wedding date?" Jo said.

He put the cat carrier in the back seat of the Honda. "Romantics that they are, they said they're going to wait until the leaves turn color, and they don't know exactly when that will be."

"I'll need some advance warning," Jo said.

"I told them that."

"Can I go to George and Katherine's wedding?" Ursa asked.

"I don't know," Gabe said. "It depends on whether your foster parents will let you."

"They will," Ursa said.

"Are you sure?" Jo said. "I hear they're the kind of people who'll make you eat green stuff."

"If they do, I might run away."

"Nope, we're done with that for good," Gabe said. He buckled her into the back seat and hugged her. "I'll miss you, bunny."

"Not for very long," Ursa said.

"Why not?"

"The quark things."

He stood back from the car and looked at Jo. "Seems our fates are still tossing on a sea of quarks."

"It's been quite a ride," Jo said. They kissed and held each other. They didn't know when they'd next be together. Gabe had to harvest and put up the farm's fall crops, and Jo would be teaching and taking classes during the fall semester. But she would drive down for Katherine and George's wedding no matter how busy she was. She whispered in Gabe's ear, "I don't think I can wait until the leaves turn color."

"I know. Maybe I'll steal Ursa's paint set and get to work on these damn leaves."

Jo started the car and drove away, watching him recede in the mirrors.

"Don't worry, you'll see him before the wedding," Ursa said.

"You seem much more confident about your quarks these days."

"I'm better at it now."

During the long drive, Ursa read her birthday books, cuddled with her purple people eater, and played with the kittens through the carrier door. When they left the interstate, Ursa peered out the car windows, taking in her new hometown. Jo turned the car onto her pretty tree-lined street, burnished gold with late-afternoon sun. Before she turned into the driveway, she paused to appreciate the white clapboard house, wreathed in a late-summer bloom of flowers.

Tabby stepped onto the porch, smiling and waving.

Ursa climbed out of the car, trying to balance the kittens in her arms.

"You'd better put them back in the cage," Jo said. "If they jump down, they may get lost." Jo looked to Tabby for help with the kittens, but she was talking seriously to someone on her phone.

"They won't get lost," Ursa said. She tucked the squirming kittens against her chest. "I wish Frances Ivey's cats were here. They could be Juliet and Hamlet's foster moms."

"It's a good thing Frances isn't here. She said no kids, and we haven't told her about you yet."

"Something is going to happen to fix that," Ursa said.

"What?"

"You'll see."

As they arrived at the walkway, Tabby ran down the steps. "You'll never guess what just happened!"

"Tabby! How about you say hello to my foster daughter?"

"Right . . ." She pocketed her phone and pressed a kiss on Ursa's cheek. "Happy birthday, awesomest girl in the universe."

"I like the purple people eater you gave me," Ursa said.

"He's from Purpletonia, a faraway planet," Tabby said. "Wow, how cute are those kittens?"

"Gabe gave them to me."

"So what happened?" Jo said.

"Frances Ivey called—I just hung up with her. You won't believe it. She's going to marry Nancy and stay in Maine! She wants to know if we're interested in buying the house."

Jo looked at Ursa. "Okay, this is too weird . . ."

"What is?" Tabby said.

"Ursa just said something would happen to change the no-kids rule."

Tabby grinned. "Did you do this, little alien?"

Ursa squealed. The kittens were clambering up her hair to escape her arms. They jumped to the ground and ran straight up the porch steps, as if following an invisible trail of quarks. Juliet sprawled on the welcome rug and Hamlet flopped onto his back beside her, one paw softly batting her chin.

Ursa clasped Jo's hand in her left hand and Tabby's in her right. She pulled them in tight against her body like a little bird snuggling into its nest. She smiled at the kittens playing on the porch of her new home. "I did make this happen." She turned her face upward. "Didn't I, Jo?"

"You sure did, Big Bear."

ACKNOWLEDGMENTS

This book would not have blossomed without Carly Watters of P.S. Literary Agency. I thank her for her commitment to getting it published, and also for her early pruning of my convoluted backstories. Her deftness with the hedge clippers greatly improved the story.

I am deeply grateful to Alicia Clancy, who supported this book from sea to shining sea. Her unwavering enthusiasm has been a guiding light.

Another talented editor, Laura Chasen, sharpened and polished my writing beyond my imagining. I much appreciated her competent and compassionate style of editing.

I also would like to thank the first people who read this manuscript. Scott, my ever-willing alpha reader, provided thoughtful commentary, as always. Nikki Mentges, editor and beta reader of NAM Editorial, helped me improve the manuscript for the query process. I thank them both for encouraging me to seek publication.

I owe more thanks to the many people at Lake Union Publishing who supported and worked on this book.

I would like to thank the following people who provided insight into the emotional and physical aftereffects of being diagnosed with BRCA-related cancers. My friend Dr. Lisa Davenport offered advice and connected me with Dr. Victoria Seewaldt of City of Hope and Dr. Sue Friedman, executive director and founder of FORCE (Facing

Our Risk of Cancer Empowered). Their guidance was critical to writing Joanna with realism. Dr. Ernestine Lee, kind friend that she is, offered much-needed support when I sought more advice on Joanna's medical history. She talked to numerous oncologists whose advice helped me sort out my concerns.

My brother Dirk Vanderah, a talented paramedic, provided information about gunshot wounds and emergency medical support. I am so very sorry that he did not live to see this book.

I would like to acknowledge Andrew V. Suarez, Karin S. Pfennig, and Scott K. Robinson whose study of indigo buntings in edge habitats provided the scientific basis of Joanna's research.

Infinite thanks and love to Cailley, William, and Grant for their patience while I wrote and for inspiring Ursa's big heart, brilliance, and imagination.

Finally, more gratitude and love to Scott. His encouragement has been steadfast from the start, when the bird biologist he'd known for many years unexpectedly became obsessed with writing fiction. Thank you, Scott, for your extraordinary and often exasperating optimism.

ABOUT THE AUTHOR

Glendy Vanderah worked as an endangered bird specialist in Illinois before she became a writer. Originally from Chicago, she now lives in rural Florida with her husband and as many birds, butterflies, and wildflowers as she can lure to her land. *Where the Forest Meets the Stars* is her debut novel.